T. Allen Winn's

The Detective Trudy Wagner Series

Road Rage
North of the Border

More Fiction by T Allen Winn

Dark Thirty
The Perfect Spook House
Lou Who?

Memoirs

The Caregiver's Son, Outside the Window Looking In
Cornbread and Buttermilk, Good Ole Fashion Home
Cooked Nostalgic Nonsense

Short Stories

'For Your Amusement' featured in Beach Author
Network's **Shorts**
'Ciled Me a Bar' featured in **Mountain Mysts,**
December 2015

Lou Who?

T. Allen Winn

Published by ProsePress
75 Red Maple Drive,
Pawleys Island, South Carolina 29585
www.Prosepress.biz
proseNcons@live.com

Dedication

Mothers
Fathers
Grandfathers
Grandmothers
Uncles
Aunts
Spouses
Friends
Caregivers-Heroes

*With something like cancer, there is a feeling
that you can fight it in some way or control your
response to it, but with dementia there is the fear
of losing control of your mind and your life.*
- Kevin Whately

*"Alzheimer's is the cleverest thief, because she not
only steals from you, but she steals the very thing
you need to remember
what's been stolen."*
- Jarod Kintz

The rope had been tossed over a sturdy limb from the ancient oak. The noose drawn taunt, hands tied behind her back and legs bound at her ankles. Martin made eye contact with those gathered, making certain none were about to betray him and back out of this necessary execution. Each man nodded, assuring him they would abide by his wishes. A mere nod didn't satisfy Martin. He called each by their name and asked them to verbally commit. Hang her…hang her…each and everyone repeated those words without the slightest bit of hesitation.

Still, Martin needed more; he trusted no one and would not be blackmailed later. He pulled the parchment paper, a sharp pen knife and a quill from his coat. He spelled out his instructions. Each of his accomplices, executioners in this particular case, would prick their fingers, using the quill and their blood, would then sign the agreement, binding them to this decision.

Each man did as instructed, no questions asked, none opposing his request. Fear can be a powerful motivator. Martin read the names aloud: *A.B. Abram, Abe Bergmann, Joseph Herzberg, Horatio Thomas, Zachariah Hanson.* Satisfied, he signed his name last, *Martin Kravis.* He folded the paper and placed it back inside his coat. He then ordered every man to grab hold of the hangman's rope.

"On this day, May 17, 1890, I curse the soul of Margarett Levine Reznik. May she burn in hell for eternity for what she has done. She has betrayed each man, now her executioner. You will be laid to rest in an unmarked grave in a secluded location and shall share the maggot infested earth with those not worthy of recognition or descent burials. Gentlemen, hang the witch."

Margarett Levine Reznik vaguely gained consciousness to eye the six bastards one last time. She etched their memory in her mind and silently cursed them one last time. Death came quickly; the rope around her neck had hanged her dead, twenty one years old this very day.

"Happy birthday, Margarett. Now bury the bitch," spoke Martin. "Bury her deep. May your rotting flesh never see the light of day, you worthless whore." He then spat on her corpse and kicked dirt in her bluish discolored face. Justice had been served. Let no man question the verdict.

"The witch knew who had killed her and she snatched pieces of time, here and there, from the business of dying, to make her revenge."

Kelly Link, Magic for Beginners

1

The first signs of spring in the Emerald City prompted Lou to venture out into her vegetable garden and commence doing a little digging and weeding, preparing for planting just a few weeks away. She would wait it out until Good Friday, her preferred time to plant her crop, and hopefully the last frost would be history by then. The auburn haired Emma 'Lou' Stetson, forty five, of medium height, build and weight, could blend into most any crowd, if not for her bubbly personality. No denying it, when she graced any landscape with her presence, it made for a better place for all who occupied the same turf. Her friends said she reminded them of the more mature version of Sally Fields.

Lou possessed natural beauty, rarely ever wearing any serious makeup. Plus, it was too expensive and time consuming, said she. Like me or not, I am who I am, you can't pretty up perfection, she would often quote in jest. Her great love, other than her husband, Wade, was the great outdoors. Greenwood, South Carolina had been their home since their introduction into this world. Both grew up knowing one another, living in the same neighborhood, same street, and just four houses apart.

Friends forever, it made eventual matrimony a piece of cake. They hadn't known they were in love until after both had graduated college; Lou from Clemson and Wade from the University of South Carolina, a house divided when it came to college choices in the Palmetto state. Lou and

Wade always made a friendly wager when the two football programs clashed at season's end. There were no losers.

While most of their high school classmates had vacated Greenwood upon reaching adulthood, Lou and Wade couldn't have fathomed living anywhere else. With the county totaling a population of around seventy thousand, too many considered the town too small, seeking larger venues like Charlotte, North Carolina, Atlanta, Georgia or even the state capitol, Columbia. Not Lou, she could not bear leaving. As history paints it, the county had eventually been named Greenwood around 1824 by John McGehee, Jr.'s wife, Charlotte, after having named their six hundred acre plantation, Green Wood. The green landscape cherished by the local community eventually evolved into the nick name, Emerald City.

Lou breathed in the morning's sunshine. Honeysuckle blooms already accented the air. The fragrance was simply marvelous, all so invigorating, intertwined with the smell of loblolly pine, the yellow pollen already dusting the world around her. Lou's senses were in tune to every smell drifting on the light breeze. Sounds invaded the airwaves, birds chirping and insects buzzing, sure signs spring was alive and well. The backyard was dotted with red Robins, bob, bob, bobbing, cocking their heads in search of fresh wigglers, another sure indication of the arrival of spring.

Lou, on her hands and knees, plucked the fragile greenery, weeds showing their faces in between her spring onions. She reached for the, *now what did they call that thing*? She had forgotten, but it was a hand held three pronged contraption for digging in the soil. She located it and then mistakenly raked the device through the row, dislodging a dozen or so onion bulbs before finally stopping and holding it up to her face. It must be broken, she figured, and she laid it aside and picked up the tiny version of a handheld shovel. Lou turned it in her hand, not sure what use it might be, and finally placed it back on the ground. She stood, looked about, but she didn't know what she expected to see. Having apparently lost interest in her gardening blissfulness, she rubbed the back of her neck as she surveyed her surroundings. A nuzzling of her right leg forced her to shift her attention downward.

"Kramer, what are you doing boy?" The sooner, a mixture of Collie and Sheppard and who knows what else, was wagging his tail. The dog holding his favorite beanbag toy, Kermit the Frog, had dropped it at her feet. Kramer had been rescued from the city pound almost seven years ago and was the most lovable pooch around. Lou reached down and retrieved the ole Kermit, turning the green critter in her hands as if examining it for injuries.

Kramer let out a friendly series of barks, twirling around after each, before repeating his ritual. Lou smiled and gave the ragged frog a toss. Game on, Kramer retrieved it and quickly returned it to Lou's feet, encouraging the next toss with more frantic barks. Lou obliged. After half dozen tosses Lou lost interest and walked towards the cedar swing suspended under a massive oak in the backyard. Kramer kept pace, Kermit in his mouth.

Lou pushed the swing with her hand once, then a second time, until it pitched and slammed into her thigh. She rubbed the throbbing contact point and then slapped her hand at the returning swing, an almost childlike reaction. "Kramer, I don't know what's up with me today. I just don't feel much like usual self. I hope I'm not coming down with something. I don't really feel sick. I might have overdone it in the garden, I suppose. What you say let's you and me go back in the house and have some breakfast."

Inside, Lou fished a carton of eggs from the refrigerator along with a sealed pack of country ham. She rambled in the cupboard until she located a cast iron skillet. She opened the ham and dumped it in the skillet and cracked three eggs alongside it. The eggs formed a moat around the ham and soon both were sizzling and popping. Kramer sat just a couple of feet away, licking his muzzle with his tongue. Lou poured herself a fresh cup of coffee and waited.

Wade stepped up behind her and wrapped his arms around her waist. "I do appreciate this darling, but I told you earlier I didn't want breakfast this morning. I have an 8:30 appointment, meeting with Jim Rogers for breakfast at the Huddle House, then I have a full boat of appointments afterwards; not the way I wanted to spend Saturday, for sure."

"Well then, I guess I'll just have to eat it," replied Lou, smiling and then kissing Wade on the cheek.

"Since when did you eat ham and eggs for breakfast? You hate ham and those eggs are a little too runny for you. Besides, I saw you with your bagel earlier. Tell you what, Tupperware it and I'll have it in the morning."

Lou returned a confused stare before saying, "Yes, sweetie, I'll do just that. Tell Jim hey for me."

"I didn't know you knew Jim Rogers."

"Well, I don't have to know him for you to say hey, do I? I was just messing with you, making sure you were listening to me. Sometime you don't you know."

"Sorry, my brain disengages sometimes causing selective hearing. See you tonight."

"See you tonight," Lou repeated, Wade, giving her a friendly peck on the lips this time, saying he loved her before he dashed out the door.

Just where do we keep that pesky Tupperware, wondered Lou, rambling through a series of kitchen cabinets until she located it. She dumped the contents of the skillet into a bowl and sealed it before placing the container back in the kitchen cabinet. She placed the skillet back on the stove, residue smoldering and smoking up the kitchen. She fanned it about and then raised a window before heading out to the sun porch.

Emma Lou Stinson, a professor at a college in neighboring Newberry County, would be returning from spring break Monday, less than a weekend remaining before classes reconvened. Her contribution in academics anchored her in the Department of Theatre, Visual Arts and Communications. Specifically she taught classes in art and theatre, and cherished every minute spent with her students. The Newberry Opera House offered many opportunities for students to co-op and learn the profession. Lou performed in plays during the summer when on break from teaching. She simply loved the old opera house and its rich history.

Built in 1881 at a cost of $30,000 the Newberry Opera House had served as the City Centerpiece for 118 years. This grand old Victorian edifice with a clock tower stands in the middle of downtown Newberry and has a 400-plus seating auditorium. The building was constructed with brick from three local brickyards. The granite used in the construction came from a quarry approximately two miles outside of the city limits. Local craftsmen's and artisans' talents in woodworking and masonry were used throughout the construction of the original building. The Opera House quickly became know as "the entertainment center of the Midlands". On its stage appeared touring companies of New York plays, minstrel and variety shows, famed vocalists and lecturers, magicians and mind readers, novelty acts and boxing exhibitions.

She never dreaded the drive form Greenwood to Newberry. Emma Lou embraced life in general, always upbeat, smiling and energetic. No better role model existed for young impressionable minds. Her students literally worshipped her and her style of teaching. She reciprocated the sentiment. Her ringing phone jolted Lou from a dream state. She located her cell phone and answered, "This is Lou."

"Lou, where are you," asked Anna Stetson, her sister-in-law, married to Wade's brother, Wyatt.

"I'm home, where are you?"

"I'm at Capri's. Did you forget we were meeting for lunch at noon?" Greenwood's Capri's was a local Italian restaurant, one of Lou's favorites. It had lasagna to kill for.

"Noon, I have plenty of time. What's your hurry? Wade just left for his 9 AM appointment at the Huddle House."

"Lou, stop jerking my chain. Just admit you forgot."

Lou glanced at the clock on the microwave; almost 12:30. Where had the morning gone? Scrambling she said, "Okay, shoot me, Anna. Summer break; guess I've geared it down too much. I'll be there in fifteen, okay."

"What do you a want? I'll order for you."

Lou thought about for a second, and then replied, "Just get me my usual."

"Lasagna and pasta salad, right?"

"Uh, right and I'll be there by the time it graces the table."

Lou looked at the digital display and then checked it by the clock in the den. Both matched. Even her cell phone time confirmed she was late for her lunch with Anna. This just didn't happen to her, always prompt. Most of the time she was early. She was very structured and didn't believe in being fashionably late. This entire morning had been a little bizarre come to think of it but not worth fretting over.

Rounding the corner, heading towards the bedroom, she almost busted her fanny. Honey, darting between her legs, had almost tripped her up. That cat could ambush her from almost any direction. Honey, named such because of her sweet temperament, had been a household pet for nearly eleven years. Declawed and neutered, she was an exclusive house cat, an orangey-white mix, and yet another critter rescued from the shelter.

In record time, Lou made it to Capri's, her pasta salad and a glass of Chardonnay awaiting her arrival. She and her sister-in-law were more like sisters than in-laws. Lou had two brothers, so Anna ended up being the sister she had always hoped to have. They had teaching in common, Anna teaching at a local Christen academy, a private school.

"It's about time you got here, girl," said Anna. "I was beginning to think I had said something wrong that ruffled your feathers."

"You know me better than that. My feathers aren't that easily ruffled, especially by you. How's Wyatt?"

"Down with back woes again I'm afraid. He's been to the chiropractor twice so far this week. I think Doctor Shirley has him almost as good as new, or as new as he'll ever be again."

"What about, Wade, what's up with him today?"

"Full day at it; he had a business breakfast and is off and running as always. I tried to prepare him breakfast but he prefers store bought, I suppose."

"You make a wonderful breakfast. I'm sure it was just all business like you said. Spring break is over for you, back to the grind. I envy you. The Christian Academy doesn't give us but a week off; not governed by the federal regulations, and able to do as they please."

"It will be good to be back with my students. I have such a grand crop this year, so creative and promising. I am indeed a fortunate person, blessed, totally enjoying what I do."

"You don't have to deal with the little snotty, uppity ones I deal with, or you would be singing a different tune. Private school is mostly for those already spoiled rotten and it doesn't matter if we try to twist it by saying it's a Christian based school."

"Anna, don't be so cynical. I know you love teaching."

"I love sex too, but that doesn't mean it's always

satisfying, right?"

"You're terrible," laughed Lou.

"It's true and you know it, Lou. Every time isn't necessarily sky rockets in flight. You have to try new things, mix it up, must be willing to go where no woman has gone before."

"Cut the Star Trek analogies. I'm not going to discuss my sex life with you."

"We can't compare brothers over a friendly lunch? Just how often do you and Wade do it?"

"Anna that is none of your business," blushed Lou.

"Wyatt and I do it at least three times a week, if you count other stuff."

"Spare me the details on the other stuff, please; but three times, really?"

"Honey, tell me you still do it routinely."

"We do have conflicting schedules, long hours and Wade is working most weekends."

"Girl, you have to make time for one of life's little pleasures. Plan date nights or just be spontaneous. Dance naked in front of him or better still, show up at work with a little surprise delivery."

"You're crazy, at work; people get fired for that sort of thing."

"Wade is the boss. No one can fire him, Sugar."

"You're not telling me you have done it in Wyatt's office?"

"I thought you didn't want to know the dirty little details."

"I don't," said Lou, covering her face with her hands. "I don't need visuals."

"Loosen up, sweetheart. You might enjoy life more if you do."

"My life is just fine as it is and quite fulfilling. I don't need any of these perverted covert antics to improve it."

"Don't knock it if you haven't tried it. Let me know when you're ready to spread those wings and I'll toss in a few pointers."

"Thanks but I won't be requiring sex tips from you anytime soon. Can we change the subject, please?"

"Have it your way," winked Anna. "How many kids do you have this year?"

"I have eighteen students, fifteen girls and three boys, all embracing the arts, I am proud to say."

"I have twenty eight in my class, most of them embracing nothing of any value, there to just fill space. I'm just a glorified babysitter without the leeway to discipline them. I miss the old days, spare the rod and spoil the child. Sometimes a good old fashioned butt spanking is what the worst need to adjust their unruly attitude. Sorry, I'm a throwback, a Neanderthal in today's educational system. I struggle with this fact daily."

"Best you curb those feelings or face the right hand of the law and parents chomping at the bits to file a lawsuit."

"You just said a mouthful. There was a time when what the teachers said meant something. It was the gospel. Now I think we're guilty until proven innocent, especially when the parents tend to think their brats are perfect. It's our word against theirs, even ground. God forbid if we lay a hand on them."

"This has been fun, but I have things to do. Monday will be here before you know it."

Anna retrieved the bill. "I've got this. It's the least I can do after traumatizing you over your pitiful sex life and bitching about my job."

"I've got it next time, then. Take care and please try to restrain yourself."

"In bed, no way," laughed Anna.

"I meant in school."

Lou exited Capri's and stood there, puzzled, unsure

what to do next. Anna pulled up to the curbing in her car, seeing her just standing there. "Are you okay?"

"Silly me, this is so embarrassing. I forgot where I parked my car."

Anna looked about and there were no more than a dozen cars still in the parking lot. Lou's was in plain sight, three parking places from where she stood. Before Anna could point it out Lou pressed her remote and the horn sounded and lights blinked. She smiled and waved to Anna as she strolled, unfazed, towards the vehicle. Bewildered, Anna watched for a second, then shrugged it off and bided her sister-in-law farewell, chalking it up to her being unnerved about talking about sex.

Lou sat there, both hands in a death grip on the wheel. I'm here, now what, she thought. She strained to remember her next destination but drew blanks. What was happening to her? She finally started the car, but sat there, motor running and with the radio blaring. Lou eased the stick into reverse and then pressed the accelerator. The car lurched backwards, metal rubbing metal. Lou slammed on the brakes and viewed through her side mirror the red convertible parked in a space directly behind her.

Uncharacteristically, Lou left the scene, deciding not to report her little accident. She wasn't up to explaining how it happened; wasn't sure why she hadn't seen the car parked across the way from her. Obviously she had enough room to back out, so how could she have possibly nailed it? Admission equated quilt and would only open a line of questioning she wasn't prepared to answer. It was nothing, really; could happen to anyone. She had been concealing little things for awhile, finding no harm in doing so. She was fine. Things just happen. She was just having her fair share of them lately. It will get better. It had to.

2

The radio playing loudly signaled Monday morning had arrived early, 5 AM displaying on the digital clock. Wade nudged Lou. This was her alarm setting. It was highly unusual for her feet not to already be hitting the floor at the first indication of a tune playing. She grunted and Wade nudged her a second time. "Duty calls," he whispered.

She mumbled something and stumbled from bed and to the bathroom. Wade slipped out of bed and turned off the radio, something he had never had to do before. He snuggled back under the covers, soon snoring and all forgotten. Lou had to rise and shine at an early hour to ready herself and make the commute to Newberry, a ritual she had been performing since the beginning of time, it seemed. She had done it in her sleep, literally and never minded it. It gave her time to think.

Coffee mug and her briefcase in hand, she was off, but not before she eyed the ugly dent in the left fender. She hadn't noticed that before and would mention it to Wade. It appeared someone had backed into her recently. She tuned the radio to a local talk radio station. Some doctor was on, talking about old people and their health issues. The subject matter varied from arthritis to knee and hip replacements, the elderly taking spills and breaking limbs, and eventually drifted to the subject of Alzheimer's. Lou switched off the radio, not willing to listen. All of it was too depressing and just a little bit scary for this early in the morning.

Lou arrived at the college on schedule, much earlier than most professors, but then again, that was just her. She had a meticulous preparation routine that she staunchly followed. She wasn't compulsive, but close to being obsessive when it came to her academic behavioral patterns. Most considered her a perfectionist. She neither denied nor disputed the claim. In the big scheme it didn't really matter what others thought of her. She couldn't change who she was, that was just a fact of life.

Lou sipped on a cup of hot herbal tea while munching on her blueberry bagel, dwelling on of all things, her sex life, or lack thereof lately. That Anna had planted this seed intentionally, she mumbled. Their intimacy level was just fine, normal. Everyone marched to their own drummer. She certainly didn't feel deprived. Wade seemed satisfied, so why think about it? They were, after all, both in their mid forties, no longer kids with primal desires. Love was the most important factor, not some sexual marathon. Besides, Anna was probably just over exaggerating with that three times a week crap, Wyatt with that bad back and all. She caught herself laughing, thinking the ailing back was from too much acrobatics in bed; bad visuals.

Class would begin in thirty minutes. Lou had just enough time to take a quick potty break, grab another cup of tea and prepare to greet her returning students. On the way down the hallway she met Professor Kato. Auburn Kato, in his mid thirties, was a psychologist, teaching Business, Behavioral and Social Sciences. Kato had grown up on the west coast and dearly missed his life of surfing along the California Coast. Spring break offered him the opportunity to seek out the big waves. Single, he could afford the airfare to travel wherever that might be. This break he had opted for Hawaii, and had returned tanned and toned from the experience.

"Aloha," Lou greeted him. "Did you hang many tens

this break?"

"Waves weren't as large as I hoped but I did achieve a fix for a while, at least until summer. And what did Mrs. Stetson accomplish during her reprieve from scholarly duty?"

"My life is quite boring by comparison. I spent time with the hubby, the pets, and caught up with a bit of gardening. We did visit the kids."

"Ah yes, how are young Heath and Leanne doing?"

"Heath is doing well. He and a colleague have opened an animal hospital in Greenville. You know how he loves dealing with animals. Leanne is engaged to an Attorney in Greensboro. Her dance studio is flourishing."

"You indeed have two gems. How's Wade?"

"Busy as a bee as always; are you ready to dive back into the world of molding impressionable young minds?"

"Probably not as willing and ready as you, but I will do my part to mold them in my own image and prepare them for what waits out there. By the way, I noticed your passenger side door open when I pulled in this morning. I closed it and locked your car. I hope you have your keys with you."

"My door was open?"

"First day jitters, I suppose."

"I had my mug and briefcase and all, must have been preoccupied for sure. Thanks for watching my back."

"Kids will be kids, no need leaving them an open invitation for unwelcome mischief, I always say."

"My students would never do anything like that."

"Mine would. Take care and have a wonderful day. It is Monday all day long."

"Likewise, Auburn," replied Lou, wondering how in the world she had left the door open. She hadn't remembered going around to the passenger side door. Where had she been headed before seeing Auburn? Her bladder reminded her, bathroom silly; then she remembered she needed a refill on her herbal tea.

When Lou returned to her classroom, a student greeted her at the door. It took her a second to grasp his name. "Fabian Pressley…how was your spring break?"

"It was okay I guess. To be honest I'm happy to be back. My dad was in town and he and mom were at it. I know my sister and I are their common thread, but I wish they would stop using us as both a crutch and excuse for their arguments. It gets old after awhile. They're divorced. They need to get over it. They'll never like one another or agree, so what's the point in all the bickering. He hates paying alimony and child support, and she thinks he's not paying enough and never paying it in a timely manner."

"I'm sorry things didn't go so well."

"Yeah, me too, and I'm sorry to be dumping on you like this. You can't do anything to help."

"I can lend a shoulder. Sometimes it just helps to get it off your chest, Fabian."

"Isn't that going above and beyond your role as a professor? It might get you in trouble, getting too involved in our social lives."

"Not if we keep it our little secret, it won't. Besides, I'm not offering advice, so technically I'm not involved."

"It's like this stupid name I have. I'm surprised my parents didn't name me Elvis. I guess mom was more enamored by Fabian instead."

"I think you have a wonderful name, one of character, destined for great things."

"Thanks Professor, you always have a way of cheering me up when I'm down. I don't have to battle self esteem issues when I'm here in your class. You make me feel important."

"You are important and don't you forget it"

The other students soon arrived and Lou whizzed

through the day, mostly uneventful and without any hitches, none that she noticed. She now gathered up her belongings, ready for the commute back to Greenwood. She walked to the parking lot with a couple of the other faculty members. She even located her car without using the remote's alarm. This had been a wonderful day. Everyday spending time with her students was a most rewarding experience. This particular crop brought such creativity and imagination to the table. She couldn't wait to introduce them to the opera house downtown.

Driving along, she hummed a little tune, oblivious to the scenes all around her. She pulled to a stop at the traffic light and to her dismay realized by the road signs she was traveling in the wrong direction, heading towards Greenville, instead of Greenwood. How in the world had she made such an error? She couldn't blame it on any medication because she wasn't on any. Lou didn't do drugs or abuse alcohol.

This incident was quite disturbing. She couldn't explain it. She pulled over and turned around at the first opportunity, righting her wrong, and heading towards the Emerald City. Glancing at the clock on the dashboard, she braked in the middle of the road, almost causing a car behind her to rear end her vehicle. The driver let down on the horn to express his displeasure for her little maneuver.

Lou sped back up. The time must be wrong. It couldn't possibly be almost eight o'clock. She had left the college shortly after five. How could she have been driving for almost three hours? The commute home was less than one hour; that is unless you go in the wrong direction. But still, she could drive back and forth to Greenville a couple of times in that time span. She pulled over a second time, into a convenience store, and she retrieved her cell phone. She called Wade, saying she had lost track of time her first day back, but was now on the way. It wasn't really that much of a fib. She had lost track of time, but where had she been for the past three hours?

This was really troubling and terrifying. What was happening to her? She should probably discuss these incidences with Wade, but why worry him until she could identify the cause. She would conduct a little research on the Net and then hopefully diagnose the cause and discover a remedy for her forgetfulness and memory lapses. One root cause came to mind, but she wasn't willing to face it, not before investigating all the possibilities first. *I'm a professor after all, no dummy, and should be able to determine my little problem logically, using the deduction and analytical skills. This is no more complicated that cause and affect.*

Lou completed the remainder of her journey in record time, luckily avoiding any confrontations with state troopers. She normally didn't possess a lead foot, but whatever she was suffering from, was anything but normal. She had thrown caution to the wind, another unfamiliar trait. Her usual optimistic outlook on life was fading fast. There was a sense of urgency in nipping this as quickly as possible, but the uncertainty and dread won out over rational thinking. She flip flopped more than once and ultimately decided to keep quiet, at least for the time being. She did small talk, chitchatting with Wade over a late meal before retiring. Tomorrow would be a new day and she would assess the situation accordingly,

3

Lou had survived her first week of classes with no major incidences, or at least none she could recall. Today she had actually arrived home before Wade. He had been tied up in some sort of meeting with a client. A freelance telecommunications engineer, Wade was always in high demand, often his job requiring long hours and travel away from home. No one on the east coast was better at designing and overseeing the installation of telecommunications equipment and facilities.

Wade Stetson had made it an art form with his understanding of complex electronic switching systems, copper telephone facilities and fiber optics. It didn't hurt that he could also bring in a wealth of experience with broadcast engineering. Wade Stetson was the ultimate gunslinger for hire. It was trying at times, both being professionals, but they had made it work, so far.

Lou curled up on the couch with a glass of wine, with Honey purring alongside her and Kramer snoring loudly on the floor beside the loveseat. Life was how she remembered it, filled with clarity, no murkiness clouding the water. Wade had said he would pick up Chinese on the way home, so she didn't have to slave in the kitchen tonight. Actually she didn't mind cooking. She had taken some culinary classes and was quite the amateur chef. Wade claimed he was her guinea pig, always test driving new cuisine at his expense. He never complained and said everything was good, and said it sincerely, so she never doubted him.

One mystery still haunted her though; how did that sealed bowl of Tupperware containing ham and eggs get in the kitchen cabinet? She was glad she had discovered it instead of Wade. It would have been most embarrassing for him, if he had to admit putting it there. He was probably in a hurry for a meeting and mistakenly placed it in the cabinet instead of the refrigerator. He often had a one track mind when working on a big project. She'd grant him a pass.

Out of the blue, an odd restlessness overcame her. She began ringing her hands nervously, but wasn't sure why. Lou got up to pour another glass of wine but became distracted by the darkness staring back at her from the kitchen window. She quickly closed the blinds, and then looked about as if expecting someone to be lurking in the dining room shadows. Frantically she began switching on lights in various rooms, and didn't stop until she had completed the tour of the entire house.

Honey and Kramer had followed her, as if providing protection. Even with the lights on, she remained distraught. She began pacing the floor, traveling from the kitchen to the full length of the den and back. She repeated each trip quicker than the last. Perspiration beaded on her brow and above her upper lip. Lou's silk lounging pajamas became saturated from her exertion, her heart pounding, but still she paced with a vengeance, why, she didn't know.

The pets followed her for the first couple of passes, but now they just sat and watched her, Kramer letting out an occasional whimper. Wild eyed, she stopped momentarily, looked about as if expecting the boogey man to jump her. She heard the sound of keys in the door and turned to see the door knob turning and the door opening. She ceased her intake of air, locked on the invader entering the house.

"Are you okay in here, Lou? The house is lit up like a

hotel resort. Why do you have every light in the place on?"

"I thought I heard someone outside, an intruder."

"Why didn't you just call 911 or me?"

"Silly, what if it would have been just my imagination? Wouldn't I have looked foolish? It must have worked. I didn't see or hear anything once I switched on the lights. Besides, you're home now. How safe can a girl be?"

"I'll help you switch them back off, then let's eat. I'm famished. What about you?"

"I could eat, I suppose. What would you like me to cook?"

"No need, I have Chinese, remember?"

"Sorry, I guess I'm still a little shaken."

Lou set the placemats on the bar, while Wade opened the various containers. While eating, Wade explained he had a new contract that would require him leaving Sunday afternoon, and he would be in Richmond, Virginia for at least two weeks, maybe longer. Lou nodded, understanding duty called. After they finished the meal, Wade popped another cork and they settled on the loveseat, sipping wine.

She recognized the routine. Wade would never drink a couple of glasses this late, unless he was easing into the mood. What did Anna call it, a date night lay ahead. With him heading out of town, she welcomed the interlude. After all, it had probably been a couple of weeks since their last encounter but who's counting, she reminded herself.

An hour later, as predicted, mission accomplished. Wade had turned over, already snoring loudly. Sleep evaded Lou. Not one prone to insomnia, but still, she stared at the ceiling, really thinking nothing in particular. Her eyes were burning and tired but her brain just refused to shut down. Honey curled on her pillow blissfully purring. Kramer curled at the foot of the bed, thankfully on Wade's side, the king sized dog sharing their king sized bed.

Unable to drift off, Lou finally decided to raid the

kitchen. Maybe some comfort food would do the trick. She opened a box of dark chocolates, knowing chocolate was the worst food to eat before going to bed, but that's what she craved, so she decided to live a little. She poured a glass of milk and gorged herself with the little dark delights. Now she was bloated like a sun baked beached whale and still wide awake.

Kramer stood at the door whimpering. Lou opened the door and followed the canine outside. She had learned by experience you never let him go outside alone at this hour of the night. Keeping close tabs on him would ensure he returned once he finished his business. The motion sensory flood lights activated when they reached the corner of the porch. Lou, chuckled, thinking why isn't the dark bothering me now. Maybe it's just hormonal changes or something, curse of being a female, that and having to deal with one's menstrual cycle. Men are so lucky, she thought.

Kramer finished his business and she coaxed him back to the door. Still, she wasn't sleepy. It dawned on her. She could do that research on the internet; decipher the changes intruding upon her life. Lou sat down at the desktop computer in the study, but not before closing the door. Bad mistake, both animals vocally alerted her that they wanted in too. She quickly allowed them entry, and then sat down, booted up and logged in. She stared at the screen as if expecting something magical to happen. Dread overwhelmed her. She had an idea where to Google first but her fingers hovered over the keyboard, fearful of what she might learn.

Taking a deep breath, she typed the dreaded word *Alzheimer's* and pressed the Enter key. No shortage of websites on the subject populated the screen. Lou perused them and settled on a website entitled *Seven Stages of Alzheimer's – Concerned about the Symptoms*. Clicking access, she immediately saw the seven stages, gloom and doom spelled out on the screen.

She wasn't sure if she was prepared to go any further. Did she really want to know the specifics of each stage? Maybe this was just a *witch hunt* and she had nothing to fear. Maybe she was just over reacting. That argument wouldn't stand. Something was happening to her, she wasn't stupid. So there they were the seven stages, with all but the first spelling out some decline in life.

> Stage 1: No Impairment
> Stage 2: Very Mild Decline
> Stage 3: Mild Decline
> Stage 4: Moderate Decline
> Stage 5: Moderately Severe Decline
> Stage 6: Severe Decline
> Stage 7: Very Severe Decline

Lou opened stage one first.

No impairment (normal function)
The person does not experience any memory problems. An interview with a medical professional does not show any evidence of symptoms of dementia.

If I'm infected, I'm not at stage one, because I am suffering some memory lapses. She rolled the dice and selected stage two.

Very mild cognitive decline (may be normal age-related changes or earliest signs of Alzheimer's disease)
The person may feel as if he or she is having memory lapses — forgetting familiar words or the location of everyday objects. But no symptoms of dementia can be detected during a medical examination or by friends, family or co-workers.

Maybe, it sort of fits, with the memory lapses, but not

specifically. I'm not forgetting words and I don't think I've forgotten where things are. I'm feeling better about this. Let's see what's behind door number three.

Mild cognitive decline (early-stage Alzheimer's can be diagnosed in some, but not all, individuals with these symptoms). Friends, family or co-workers begin to notice difficulties. During a detailed medical interview, doctors may be able to detect problems in memory or concentration. Common stage 3 difficulties include:

Noticeable problems coming up with the right word or name

Trouble remembering names when introduced to new people

Having noticeably greater difficulty performing tasks in social or work settings Forgetting material that one has just read

Losing or misplacing a valuable object

Increasing trouble with planning or organizing

Nope, none of these are me, not that I can remember. Lou chuckled about that thought. Moving on, she clicked the next stage, number four.

**Moderate cognitive decline
(Mild or early-stage Alzheimer's disease)**
At this point, a careful medical interview should be able to detect clear-cut symptoms in several areas:

Forgetfulness of recent events
Impaired ability to perform challenging mental arithmetic — for example, counting backward from 100 by 7s

Greater difficulty performing complex tasks, such as planning dinner for guests, paying bills or managing finances

Forgetfulness about one's own personal history
Becoming moody or withdrawn, especially in socially

or mentally challenging situations

I think I'm clearing most of the hurdles and am barking up the wrong tree but I may as well finish this out, open stage five.

**Moderately severe cognitive decline
(Moderate or mid-stage Alzheimer's disease)
Gaps in memory and thinking are noticeable, and individuals begin to need help with day-to-day activities. At this stage, those with Alzheimer's may:**

Be unable to recall their own address or telephone number or the high school or college from which they graduated

Become confused about where they are or what day it is

Have trouble with less challenging mental arithmetic; such as counting backward from 40 by subtracting 4s or from 20 by 2s

Need help choosing proper clothing for the season or the occasion

Still remember significant details about themselves and their family

Still require no assistance with eating or using the toilet

No issues, I'm clean on all counts. Number six…

**Severe cognitive decline
(Moderately severe or mid-stage Alzheimer's disease)
Memory continues to worsen, personality changes may take place and individuals need extensive help with daily activities. At this stage, individuals may:**

Lose awareness of recent experiences as well as of their surroundings

Distinguish familiar and unfamiliar faces but have trouble remembering the name of a spouse or caregiver

Need help dressing properly and may, without supervision, make mistakes such as putting pajamas over daytime clothes or shoes on the wrong feet

Experience major changes in sleep patterns — sleeping during the day and becoming restless at night

Need help handling details of toileting (for example, flushing the toilet, wiping or disposing of tissue properly)

Have increasingly frequent trouble controlling their bladder or bowels

Experience major personality and behavioral changes, including suspiciousness and delusions (such as believing that their caregiver is an impostor)or compulsive, repetitive behavior like hand-wringing or tissue shredding

Tend to wander or become lost

Remember: It is difficult to place a person with Alzheimer's in a specific stage as stages may overlap.

Stages may overlap, just wonderful, and on to the grand finally…stage seven

Very severe cognitive decline (Severe or late-stage Alzheimer's disease)

In the final stage of this disease, individuals lose the ability to respond to their environment, to carry on a conversation and, eventually, to control movement. They may still say words or phrases.

At this stage, individuals need help with much of their daily personal care, including eating or using the toilet. They may also lose the ability to smile, to sit without support and to hold their heads up. Reflexes become abnormal. Muscles grow rigid. Swallowing impaired.

Okay, I'm not suffering from this disease, end of story; unless, I can't remember some of these symptoms. It's a catch twenty two. How can I honestly diagnose myself if part of the problem might just be that I don't remember doing the very symptoms mentioned? This is ludicrous Why am I even venturing down this path? Forgetfulness doesn't equate to illness. So, I forgot a lunch appointment and was preoccupied and turned in the wrong direction on the way home. That means absolutely nothing. Everyone forgets stuff. I'm as normal as the next person. I'm done. I'm going to bed.

Lou didn't shut down the computer, something she always did. She exited the study into the kitchen and abruptly stopped. Confused, she momentarily attempted to remember which way was her bedroom. She was frozen in time, afraid to take a step. Her surroundings were vaguely familiar. It was almost like being in someone else's home. Lou began hyperventilating. Kramer whimpered at her side and she reacted, reached down and patted him on the head. That simple touch reactivated her sensory system and she strolled though the den towards her bedroom, unaware of what had just happened. If she could have recalled the incident, she could have related it to her last thoughts. *How can I honestly diagnose myself if part of the problem might just be that I don't remember doing the very symptoms mentioned?*

Perhaps she should have tried counting backwards from one hundred in sevens or counting backward from forty by subtracting fours or even from twenty by twos. That would have also required her identifying the signs, suspecting there was a need to validate her consequences. Lou was spiraling downward, indeed; just how rapidly was yet to be determined. No one could help her if she continued to hide her errors, or until they became evident to family, friends or coworkers.

Her insomnia would not let up. She lay in bed listening to Wade saw very large logs. Oddly, her mind didn't really drift from one subject or the other as one would expect when sleep is evasive. She existed in a sea of nothingness, almost not aware of her surroundings, and yet worrying, but fretful about what? She was there but wasn't.

Lou lay on her back staring into the darkness, a continuum of meaningless existence. She was not capable of fathoming the extent of her illness, nor the progressiveness of the disease. The signs were there, but only if you were looking. As stated, **Remember:** *It is difficult to place a person with Alzheimer's in a specific stage as stages may overlap.* She was further along and an eyelash from the inevitable.

4

Wade had awoken to the alarm. Lou didn't stir, sleeping soundly. Wade tipped around, trying to be as quiet as possible, hesitant to wake her, even though he wanted to say goodbye before heading out. He didn't require her taking him to the airport, opting to drive to Richmond instead, so why not allow her to sleep in Sunday morning. He could phone her later. Before leaving the bedroom he did give her a little peck on the cheek. She remained in an almost comatose state, unresponsive. Wade whispered *I love you* and was on his way. He had seen to the pets before leaving and had left Lou a note on the kitchen counter.

Daylight bright in her face, bleeding in through the blinds, Lou stretched, rubbed her eyes, and then sat up in bed, yawned and stretched again. She felt as if she had been run over by a train. Her eyes were caked with crust, her mouth as dry as cotton and her bladder in maximum overdrive, prompting a quick sprint to the bathroom. After almost zombie like washing her face, brushing her teeth and running a brush through her hair, she focused on a clock resting on a shelf over the tub.

Something must be impossibly wrong. The clock displayed quarter pass three. It was too daylight to be three in the morning. Maybe it had stopped, the batteries dead. No, the second hand was moving. Lou re-entered the bedroom checking the digital readout on the radio clock, 3:17, and a lighted dot adjacent to the time indicated PM, not AM. There could be no way she had remained in bed until mid afternoon. She never slept pass seven in the morning at the latest, on her days off. She required caffeine and was off to the kitchen to make coffee instead of her usual herbal tea. Upon arriving, she found the note by the canisters where her tea and the coffee were stored. .

Good morning, Lou. You were sleeping like a log so I decided not to disturb you. I have already seen to Honey and Kramer. Enjoy your Sunday afternoon without me. I will call you later.

Love you,

Wade

"Sleeping like a log, I don't think so," muttered Lou. "Heck, I don't think I closed my eyes all night." *Really, who are you kidding, Emma Lou Stetson? How can you explain not getting up until after three in the afternoon, if you weren't out like a light?*

Lou stood in front of her Breville One-Touch Tea Maker, having already forgotten about the coffee. Obviously it wasn't going to operate itself. She had to initiate the process. She eventually pressed a button and the beverage maker awoke from its slumber, water trickling into a glass container. She located a mug and stood there waiting for it to stop. Once it spouted its last little noisy sounds she poured a cupful and blew on it before taking her first sip. It tasted like plain old hot water to her. She had forgotten to load a new filter with tea. She poured the pot into the sink, added more fresh water, and then added a new filter with two scoops of the brown granular substance. Allowing it to do its thing, she poured a second cup. Her taste buds told her she had made another grave error. She had loaded it with coffee instead of tea. Lou remembered she preferred tea over coffee. Why weren't the canisters marked appropriately, she wondered. Third try, the charm, she had hot herbal tea.

Lou sat in the sunroom overlooking the backyard and her little garden spot. It looked sadly unattended, weeds overtaking it, but it was after all, early spring. She had plenty of time to whip it into shape and plant her normal crops. Funny, she didn't recall what she usually planted. Straining to remember, she whispered, "Okra, yes okra, and tomato plants, lots of tomato plants, and what else? Let me see, some pepper plants, yes but what kind? It's a large garden spot. I can plant a little of everything. It's too late today though. It will be dark before you know it."

Dark soon, those words echoed in her head and along with them came the dread, the fear and the uncertainty. Uneasiness overwhelmed Lou, but she had no recollection of why she had developed such a late afternoon phobia. Still in her lounging pajamas and almost 4:30 in the afternoon, laziness has its limitations, she finally decided. Lou sprang from her resting place almost too vigorously in contrast to her previous lethargic state. She ascertained that a shower would reinvigorate her, clear the cobwebs and help her salvage what was left of Sunday. Tomorrow would begin another work week; not something she dreaded, quality time with her students.

The shower had indeed improved her disposition and her appetite. Kramer and Honey shadowed her every move, either hungry, or sensing something was not right with their master. The note had read Wade had taken care of the pets before leaving, but what Lou had failed to note, that had been nearly eleven hours ago. Kramer rushed to the back door, sat there and whimpered. While Honey had access to a litter box, Kramer had no such options. If Lou didn't grant him access to the outdoors soon, the canine would have to take nature in to his own paws.

Lou took the hint and opened the door. Kramer needed

no formal invitation. He shot through the door, happy to find relief. Lou eyed Honey, tapping her foot and finally said, "What's the matter? You don't need to go outside?" Honey was a house cat and had no concept of the great outdoors. She simply crossed between Lou's legs, purring up a storm, and then eased into the kitchen. The feline had different priorities. Underfoot at Lou's every step, almost tripping her several times, she had reached her limit. She stomped her foot and yelled, "Scat cat." Honey unaccustomed to this sort of behavior, hissed, and then leapt several feet high before disappearing through the den.

Kramer had quickly finished his business and stood patiently at the back door, ready to come back inside. Honey sat on the opposite side of the full glass door waiting for reinforcements. Lou busied herself with preparing a meal, oblivious to her animals' needs. Open containers and cans speckled the counter space, three types of beans, corn, and array of spices, canned roast beef and tuna were open, and some of the contents already occupied bowls, pots or skillets. Lou wasn't sure what she was cooking, inventing the recipe as she went along. Two back burners were red hot, empty of any pots. The two front stove eyes were occupied by a skillet and a huge stew pot. All the vegetables had been dumped into the pot, and the skillet contained a mixture of roast beef and tuna. Both were sizzling loudly, the skillet beginning to smolder, and the pot not far behind, because no water had been added.

Bread was in the oven, eight slices if counting. Luckily the oven had not been turned on. Soon the smoke alarm was screaming bloody murder. Lou, now in panic mode, snatched up the skillet and tossed it into sink, spraying it with cold water creating a cloud of steam. She attempted to remove the pot without the use of potholders. Jerking her hands back, she scrambled for something to use to pick it up. Unable to focus, she used a set of tongs and long fork used for grilling to shove the pot from the burner and onto the countertop, contents spilling over the side and onto the red hot eyes. Black smoke plumed from that spot now.

In the middle of a full blown crisis now, Lou pulled at her hair with her hands, wild eyed and in awe of the escalating situation. Finally, something, some semblance of her former self kicked in, and she switched off the burners. The fires and steam eventually dissipated, but the stench of burned goods remained in the air. The kitchen was a disaster zone. Lou collapsed in a chair and cried. Her life was crumbling before her very eyes and she didn't know how to stop unraveling. She considered maybe she should conduct a more in depth research on the Web, and just maybe, she could identify this and administer a cure. After all, she was a professor, and in the prime of her life. She was healthy and strong, not sickly in any way. It was just a matter of figuring things out before they became worse.

Foregoing cleaning the kitchen or even eating, she sat back in front of the computer, staring at the screen. The Alzheimer's website stared back, still open from her last usage yesterday. Lou revisited the stages. This time various symptoms appeared to leap at her from the screen, and not all came from the same stage. One haunting statement reared its ugly head.

Remember: It is difficult to place a person with Alzheimer's in a specific stage as stages may overlap.

Lou for whatever reason quickly closed the website. She scanned the page until she spotted another one, The 10 Signs of Alzheimer's – Concerned about Symptoms? She moved the mouse to the site, but hesitated, not sure she was prepared for these revelations. I'm too young, she thought; this only happens to people much older than me. There must be another cause for this, something logical, something that can be tweaked, there has to be. She sighed and clicked the mouse. A similar table appeared, numbered, with a description and examples.

1. Memory loss that disrupts daily life
One of the items listed, forgetting important dates jumped out at Lou. She had forgotten the lunch appointment with Anna.

2. Challenges in planning or solving problems
Perusing the example statements, she noted the one stating may have trouble following a familiar recipe or keeping track of monthly bills. She glanced towards the kitchen aftermath.

3. Difficulty completing familiar tasks at home, at work or at leisure
Bingo, there was another one; people having trouble driving to familiar locations.

4. Confusion with time or place
Her time management skills had suffered terribly lately. The one that really frightened her; sometimes they may forget where they are or how they got there. She turned away from the screen, tears freely flowing now. "My heavens, this can't be happening."

5. Trouble understanding visual images and spatial relationships
So far she didn't remember having any difficulty reading, judging distance and determining color or contrast, and she certainly hadn't passed a mirror thinking someone else was in the room. "Just because I don't remember, doesn't mean t it hasn't already happened," she whispered. It was almost too frightening to imagine the day might come when she didn't recognize her reflection in a mirror.

6. New problems with words in speaking or writing
This one rattled her cage, possibly worse than the others. It would drastically impact her ability to teach if it did indeed happen. People with Alzheimer's may

have trouble following or joining a conversation, may stop in the middle of a conversation and have no idea how to continue, or they repeat themselves, struggle with vocabulary, have problems finding the right word or call things by the wrong name. "This is a cruel disease. It can't be happening to me. I must be suffering from something else."

Lou sat back in her chair. "How can I face this? What will my family think or do? What about my students? Leaning forward, she read on.

7. Misplacing things or losing the ability to retrace steps

A person may put items in unusual places. They may accuse others of stealing. "The Tupperware, the ham and eggs in the kitchen cabinet, that was me, not Wade."

8. Decreased or poor judgment

Examples: using poor judgment when dealing with money, giving large amounts to telemarketers, may pay less attention to grooming or keeping themselves clean. "I did take a shower thank goodness."

9. Withdrawal from work or social activities

It stated this could impact things like hobbies, social activities, work projects or ability to participate or even understand sports. Lou just sighed loudly, wiping tears from her cheeks.

10. Changes in mood and personality

Topping the list were confusion, being suspicious, depressed, fearful or anxious; becoming easily upset at home, at work, with friends or in places out of one's comfort zone. She had already experienced some of these. She read the last notation at the bottom of the list.

If you have questions about any of these warning signs, the Alzheimer's Association recommends consulting a physician. Early diagnosis provides the best opportunities for treatment, support and future planning.

She hung on those last two words, *future planning.*

"What possible future can I have? If I have this, there is no future." Now the real question, where should I go with this information? She should probably tell Wade about her suspicions, but what if I'm wrong, she reasoned. It says consult a doctor. Am I really ready for that? Early diagnosis provides the best opportunities. There is no cure; how can this be viewed as an opportunity?

Darkness invaded her space, twilight approaching. There was nowhere to run, no place to hide. Lou simply tried to remain clear headed and in control. Nowhere did it say you could will this to go away. Barking off in the distance perked her interest. She passed back through the disaster zone, heading to the den. Kramer sat, barking and pawing at the door. How had he gotten outside, wondered Lou. "You let him out stupid, remember?"

She opened the door and he ran past her and to his food dish. The dish was still empty. Kramer nudged it with his nose, and then grabbed it in his mouth and took it to Lou, dropping it at her feet. She received the message loud and clear; shameful she had neglected her pets. She replenished Honey's bowl too. Two animals, side by side, gulped down their vittles as if this might be their last meal, and with their master's current condition, it very well could be. Lou never noticed, She was caught in her web of terror, uncertain what lay ahead.

The phone rang, prompting Lou to pull herself together, as best she could. Wade's name and number was on the display. Should she alert him or not, she weighed her options while listening to the phone ring. She opted to not say anything, especially while he was out of town, thinking what could he really do from Richmond, and why screw up his current contract. She finally mustered up the strength to answer.

"Hey," she said.

"Hey, what you been up to today?"

"Ah, just the usual stuff, you know me. How was your drive?"

"It was a bear as always commuting up 85, but I made it in one piece and with most of my sanity intact. This traffic can make you a little crazy."

You don't have a clue what crazy is, thought Lou. "I'm glad you survived. Have you had supper yet?"

"Heading across the street later to the Cracker Barrel, and what have you whipped up? "

"Just a little of this and that, I'm trying not to prepare too much, and avoid leftovers." She stared at the mess in the kitchen.

"How's next week stacking up for you and your students?"

"Thrills and spills, and all sorts of surprises, I'm sure."

"Rest well with me not by your side and I'll try to catch up with you tomorrow if I don't get tied up too late."

"Not to worry, you take care of business and I'll hold down the fort."

"All right, I love you, goodnight."

"I love you too."

That went well. I sounded sane and made perfectly good sense, didn't I? Maybe things aren't as bad as they seem. Everyone is entitled to a little hiccup occasionally. I'm probably just overreacting, too paranoid, that's all. I need to clean up the kitchen. I'll feel much better after I restore order around here. Cleanliness is the next to...to...to not being dirty.

5

Monday morning came crashing in, catching Lou by surprise. She scrambled to prepare for her drive to Newberry, already dreadfully thirty minutes behind her normal schedule. Rising and shining had come with challenges. She had to cut precious corners to rectify and still she struggled to recapture a routine that had seldom suffered a glitch. Lou had never been so flustered. Nothing seemed to be going her way. Everything offered challenges. Eventually she was on her way, at least heading in the correct direction to hopefully arrive at her final destination, but even this didn't come easy; requiring absolute concentration.

Later than usual, but not actually late for class, Lou wheeled into the faculty parking lot. Before exiting her vehicle, she sat there a moment and took several deep breathes. Without looking, she reached over to the passenger seat to gather up her materials and came away empty handed. Lou pounded the steering wheel with both hands, having failed to bring them. She loudly unleashed a torrent of unladylike phrases. Her rage was muffled by the engine still running and all the windows closed. Griping the steering wheel, Lou sat rigidly, gazing through the windshield insanely.

"Composure," she whispered. "I can do this."

Lou relinquished her death grip, bringing her breathing under control, opened the door. The dinging alarm alerted her she had left the keys in the ignition. She plucked them free and dropping them in her purse, locked the door and headed towards the building where her classroom was located; so far, so good. With each stride, she felt more like her old self, drawing confidence from her familiar surroundings. Convinced she had only suffered a minor panic attack, Lou mustered a smile and marched onward.

Without her materials to load her down, Lou opted to drop by the faculty lounge first and prepare her morning herbal tea. A few short minutes later, she sat at her desk, twenty minutes to spare before her first class would begin. Always the first to arrive, Fabian Pressley entered the room hailing a warm greeting. They exchanged pleasantries, Fabian being in a particularly good mood, having had a wonderful weekend. He shared with Lou, how he had met a girl over the weekend, a Newberry local, working at the Flying Pie, a unique family friendly restaurant. Eventually the classroom began filling with the remainder of students. Lou managed to wing her lessons and she survived the day with not so much as a hiccup, not any that she detected.

Arriving back in Greenwood, Lou was famished. She decided to forego cooking and stopped by Montague's Restaurant instead, opting to treat herself for a job well done. A glass of wine sounded simply marvelous too. She was seated at a small table in the bar, seeing no need to go into the dining room. Waiting for the waitress to return with her wine, she became increasingly agitated. The bar area was hopping noisily with happy hour patrons. The volume of the conversations and laughter derailed Lou's preconceived notion of enjoying a tranquil moment. She could not deal with it, overcome by anxiety and becoming more irate by the moment. Why couldn't these people keep their conversations to themselves, she wondered, placing her hands over her ears and squinting her eyes.

Reaching a breaking point, Lou dashed for the door, just as her waitress arrived with her wine. She shouldered her way past, knocking the drink from the young lady's hand, the glass shattering on the floor. Eyes were upon her and this prompted Lou to curse several of the onlookers quite graphically. Arriving at her car, she heard someone yelling at her from behind. Lou wheeled around, spotting the waitress approaching her. Surely she wasn't going to demand she pay for that wine.

"Sorry Miss, you forgot your purse. I hope it wasn't something I did to make you leave."

Lou snatched her purse from the young girl's hands, scrambling to locate her keys. She never murmured so much as a thank you nor even gave the waitress a second glance, firing up her vehicle and exiting the parking lot, tires screaming on the parking lot pavement. The girl stood there for a moment, dumbfounded, before giving Lou the bird. Lou never saw the parting gesture, too focused on her escape. A mile down the road, it dawned on Lou, where am I going?

"Home," she whispered. "I'm going home. Which way is home?"

Lou never saw the stop sign. By the grace of God, the oncoming SUV somehow swerved and missed her, but lost control and crashed into a power pole. Oblivious to the close call or the accident, Lou motored on, searching for a pathway home. Eventually she obtained her bearings and made it. Entering the house, she rushed off to her bedroom, no longer hungry or in need of that drink. Even though she was home alone, she slammed the bedroom door closed behind her. There she remained until her alarm clock notified her Tuesday morning had arrived. Disoriented, and soaked from perspiration, Lou sat up in bed, still wearing the clothes she had worn Monday.

Unable to turn off the noisy radio, she instead yanked the cord, dislodging it from the receptacle, the plug end whipping across her cheek, leaving a nasty laceration.

Furious, she tossed the alarm clock radio into the tiny trashcan, the battery back-up doing what it was supposed to do, the alarm still blaring. Now standing there rubbing her face and neck, she attempted to gain control. Managing to trek to the kitchen, she made a cup of tea and rummaged through the refrigerator. Nothing there stirred her taste buds so she passed on eating anything, figuring she could grab something later. She did spot her satchel and lesson books, deciding to prop them against the exit door, to ensure she didn't forget them.

The light on the answering machine was flashing, indicating she had messages. Pressing the button, the mechanical voice alerted her she had one message, left Monday at 8 PM. She played it. Wade had called, wondering where she might be. He briefed her on his day and said he would catch up with her Tuesday, possibly around lunch time. He ended it with *I love you*. Lou wondered how she had missed the call. Shrugging, maybe she had been in the bathroom are something.

Ahead of schedule, she was on her way to Newberry. Observing her gas hand rested just below a quarter of a tank, she stopped for gas. After several attempts, she finally keyed in the correct password for her debit card and successfully pumped a full tank. Lou arrived at the college, nearly forty five minutes ahead of her usual arrival time. This time she stopped by her class to drop off her items before heading to the lounge for her morning tea. The lounge was empty, too early for most. Tea in hand, Lou returned to class and spread out her lessons plans in front of her. Thirty minutes were gone before she realized it.

Fabian arrived in a somber mood. He took notice that the professor appeared to be wearing the exact same clothes she had worn to class yesterday, only more wrinkled. She wore little makeup but that wasn't so odd because she didn't wear much anyway, but her hair was bed-head in appearance; pressed tight on one side, standing up on the other. Fabian wasn't accustomed to seeing her like this.

"Fabian, why so gloom," inquired Lou.

"Mrs. Stetson, you know the girl I told you about yesterday? I found out last night she has a steady. The boyfriend wasn't too happy with me cozying up to her when he arrived at the Flying Pie. He threatened to kick my butt, but she talked him down. I'm such a loser."

"You're not a loser, Fabian. It's her loss. I say screw the slut and her sonofabitch boy friend," blurted out Lou. "You can do better than that, Fabian. You don't have to settle for these assholes in Newberry, just because you attend college here."

Fabian, red faced, had never heard his professor use such explicit language before. She proceeded in firing off several f-bombs, bashing the couple that had humiliated her student, the nerve of them. Other students arriving caught the tail end of the irate cursing. Lou dragged them into the conversation, recapping Fabian's altercation and polling them for their opinions. Fabian, now completely humiliated by his professor airing his personal life in front of his classmates, stormed out of the room.

Lou tossed her hands in the air, claiming, "Ungrateful little bastard." Fabian had caught wind of her last comment too. Lou spent another ten minutes lecturing her students on sexual matters before finally settling into the curriculum. Whispers continued, all reeling in shock from the uncharacteristic behavior. Many thought this was some sort of theatrical lesson and waited for the explanation. It never came. The students filed out of class at the end, still conversing about their professor's odd behavior and spicy language.

Lou sat in her sunroom, sipping a cup of tea, still reeling from the meeting with her superiors. How dare they treat her in this manner? She had been placed on administrative leave, pending a psychological examination. They had cited inappropriate language and hygiene concerns. Just who the hell did they think they were treating her like this? She treated her students with the utmost respect and she would never use the profanity they had accused her of using in class this morning. This had to be a joke, or a disgruntled student had fabricated the incident. This could forever tarnish her record. Just being accused of something like this with no facts to support it could ruin a person; guilty until proven innocence. She would sue them, that's it; sue them for degrading her.

Honey rubbed along her leg, purring up a storm. Kramer gave Lou wide birth. She had been kicking at the furniture and throwing items since arriving home. He wanted no part of it, afraid he had done something wrong to prompt her moodiness. Animals can sense when things aren't quite right and this was far from right. The phone rang. Lou answered it on the forth ring.

"Hey Lou, its Wade, where have you been? I've been worried. I called your cell phone several times this morning. Is everything all right?"

Lou, still holding the landline, picked up her cell phone on the counter. No battery bars displayed on the screen. "I forgot to recharge it. I'm sorry. It's dead."

"I phoned you last night."

"Yeah, I got your message, late. I must have been in the bathroom, missed it. It was too late for me to call you once I discovered it. How's the job going?"

"Better than I expected, but we have run into a few snags that might require me staying here a third week. I hope that's okay."

"I wish you were here but I do understand." Tears were running down Lou's cheeks.

"How was your day?

"Fine, "Lou lied.

"I'll let you go. Sleep tight and don't let the bed bugs bite. I love you, Lou."

"I love you too Wyatt."

"I hope this doesn't mean you're messing around with my brother," laughed Wade.

"Why would I do something as terrible as that?

"It was just a joke because you called me Wyatt instead of Wade."

"I'm sorry, tough day."

"Do you want to talk about it? I have a few minutes before I meet with clients for supper."

"I'll be fine. You see to your clients, Wade."

"Love you and we'll talk tomorrow."

"Love you too," Lou replied, too embarrassed to reveal what those bastards at the college had done to her.

The darkness on the other side of the window panes made Lou uneasy, a typical reaction to the night lately. The sheer blackness would have consumed her if she hadn't been preoccupied with the day's events. The sudden uncertainty in her teaching career traumatized her, temporarily winning the battle against the intrusive illness wreaking havoc on her mental health. That war was far from over; Alzheimer's being a foe that could not be defeated, only thwarted at best. In Lou's case it would be relentless and far worse than she could ever imagine.

Wade wouldn't return for maybe three weeks, an eternity in the life of one in her shoes. Rationalizing going forward would not be so simple. Unknown to Lou, those thought processes were already deteriorating. Hindsight, she should have consulted a physician. Remembering to do so now would be easier said than done.

Lou sat in front of the computer reading from a link she had stumbled into, a quote that had profound meaning, one she hoped she would never forget. When the time was right, she would share it with Wade.

"*She is leaving him, not all at once, which would be painful enough, but in a wrenching succession of separations. One moment she is here, and then she is gone again, and each journey takes her a little farther from his reach. He cannot follow her, and he wonders where she goes when she leaves.*"

Debra Dean, *The Madonnas of Leningrad*

6

Wade Stetson was on the home trek, less than fifteen minutes from their house. It had been almost three and half weeks since he had departed for his contract in Richmond, Virginia, and many of those telephone conversations with Lou had bordered on bizarre. At times she would babble incoherent dialogue, and then during other phone calls she sounded like the old Lou. Wade had asked Anna, his sister-in-law to check in on her. Up until recently Lou had met her in the yard or the front porch. Lately she only addressed Anna though a partially open door or didn't answer the door at all.

Anna had struggled through similar phone conversations with Lou. When asked if anything was wrong, Lou became extremely defensive, at times resorting to extremely salty language, very un-Lou like. Wade wasn't sure what he should expect upon arrival but was glad to be home, regardless to the circumstances. He just wanted to make sure Lou was all right. He sensed she was hiding something from them. In less than ten minutes he would have answers. Wade had stopped on the way to purchase some roses and chocolate, both Lou's favorites.

It was nearly midnight by the time he pulled into the drive. Every light in the house appeared to be on. This had only happened that one time when Lou thought she had heard an intruder. Wade didn't bother bringing in his luggage, would go back later for it later. With flowers in one hand, candy tucked under his arm, he used his keys to unlock the door instead of knocking so late. He called out to her as he edged through the door. The stench filled his nostrils, almost taking his breath. His nose sensed a mixture of feces, urine and decaying garbage and two steps inside, his senses were confirmed.

Wade stepped on what appeared to be fresh dog crap, slipping and sliding. The kitchen, he couldn't even begin to describe it. He had never seen anything like it, ever. The sink and counters were stacked with dirty dishes. Open cans and containers were discarded on the floor, shoved in piles. Odder still, he noted that Kramer had not greeted him at the door. Covering his mouth with his shirt sleeve he ventured through the kitchen into the den. It wasn't much better. Feces and urine spots dotted the carpet. Newspapers and paper plates adorned the end tables and coffee table.

Wade called out to Lou again, no answer. Neither of the pets responded to his calls either. Wade made it to the hallway. The floor plan was typical for when they had originally built years ago. A long hall way let to a main bathroom the master bedroom and two guess bedrooms. Glancing into the bathroom almost caused Wade to puke. The toilet had obviously overflowed at some point, towels, wash clothes and dirty clothing scattered on the floor and inside the tub. Various toiletries and medicines were spilled on the vanity.

Wade yelled for Lou again, no response. He was reaching panic mode now. Wadding through more clutter in the hallway, he entered the master bedroom. He removed his arm from his face momentarily to take a breath and was hit with a foul odor and stared at a room hell upside down. All the drawers and closets were open, clothes discarded everywhere. The bed was unrecognizable, piled high with dirty clothes. There was no shortage of feces and urine either. He quickly poked and rummaged through the mess but found no trace of Lou. Some horde of derelicts must have invaded their home. That could be the only explanation. The question, what had they done to Lou and the pets. Before continuing his search, Wade grabbed the landline phone and keyed 911.

"This is 911, how can I assist you?"

"This is Wade Stetson. Something has happened at my house. I've been out of town for several weeks and something dreadful has happened."

"Sir, can you be more specific, please?"

"Someone has trashed our house and my wife is missing; so is our dog and cat. It's indescribable what I have found."

"Sir, are you in the home now?"

"Yes."

"Please exit the premises until officers arrive, Mister Stetson. I am dispatching them to the address listed in your name."

"Okay, I will."

"Mister Stetson, is the phone portable?"

"Yes, it is wireless."

"Then please take the phone with you and remain on the line until they arrive. Do you expect foul play?"

"I don't know what I expect. I've never seen anything like this. If you're asking me if I have seen any blood; the answer is, I don't think so, but it is hard to really tell."

Wade, against the dispatcher's instructions, couldn't leave without checking the other two bedrooms. Guess bedroom number one was not so badly trashed, but the bed covers were in the floor, the bed stripped clean. Several of the drawers were open but only linen and towels were stored in them. The closet was open but for the most part intact. It appeared more rummaged through and ransacked, but there were no valuables stored there to be taken. The door to the last bedroom was closed. This raised a red flag for Wade, wondering if the intruders were still here and hiding inside.

Quick thinking, Wade backtracked and checked his hiding place for his pistol. It was where it should be, had not been found. He loaded the clip and disengaged the safety. He wasn't sure if he could actually pull the trigger on a person, but then again, thieves weren't actually people, were they? If the time came he would find out if he could and if they were. He stood face to face with the closed bedroom door again, his free hand hovering near the doorknob, contemplating how he should make his entrance.

Breathing heavily and perspiring even more, he twisted the knob. The door wasn't locked. Wade pushed it open and stepped aside, figuring it not too smart to stand directly in front of it, making himself an easy target. He clutched the pistol in both hands as he cautiously peeped around the door. He had watched too many police shows, mimicking an officer's moves. The lights were on so he could clearly see the entire room, all except the wall on his blindside and behind the wardrobe cabinet, near the closet on the opposite of the room. This room was in disarray too, but like the other guest room, not as bad as the kitchen and den.

Wade shifted so he could view the blind wall. It was clear. There was nowhere else for anyone to hide, except under the bed or in the closet. He knelt down, still holding his position in the hallway and could see under the bed. It was filled with flat storage boxes. Taking his first step into the room, he thought he heard something. His heart pounded so loudly it almost drowned out the silence. He closed his eyes momentarily, trying to focus on the sound he thought he had just heard.

It happened again. This time he had zoomed in on it, the closet, a slight rustling. Wade wanted to call out, just in case it might be Lou, but feared it might not be. The closet had two double louver style doors. Opening them would be tricky. Worse still, because of the slats in the doors, anyone inside would clearly see his approach. The perpetrator would have the advantage. This would be no fair gunfight if it came down to it. He had to even the playing field. Wade switched off the bedroom overhead light. The room went black. Whoever was inside would know he was here.

Wade waited until his eyes adjusted. He had one more trick up his sleeve. The closet was equipped with a light and the light switch was on the outside wall. He would yank the door open while flipping the switch on at the same time. It would offer him a view of the inside and possibly startle and temporarily blind anyone waiting to ambush him. It wasn't foolproof but the best he could come with, given the circumstances. Hindsight, he should have done what the dispatcher had instructed him to do; go outside and wait for the officers. Too late, he had committed to this plan. It was now or never. Wade would have to live with the consequences of his actions.

Snatching on the door nearest to him, he switched on the closet light, more blinded himself than he had expected. The scream caught him off guard, but somehow he managed not to pull the trigger. Honey had landed on his chest and in his face. Wade's screams had scared the cat, as well as him. After his screaming stopped, he sucked in some air and quickly perused the inside of the closet; empty, except for normal closet stuff. Honey was forever going inside of open closets. Wade couldn't count the number of times she had become trapped inside when either he or Lou closed the doors, not knowing she was inside. This wasn't the first time that cat had ambushed him. Mission accomplished, he decided he should go outside, just in case the officers mistook him for an intruder.

That's when he heard a low whimpering sound. The adjoining bathroom, how stupid; he hadn't checked inside the bathroom. The sound emitting from behind the closed door sounded like a distressed animal. They only owned one other animal, Kramer. It made no sense that he would be shut off in the bathroom. With less caution, he opened the door, but aimed the gun, finger on the trigger, just in case. Unlike his previous experience, nothing leapt out at him this time. He peeked around the corner and saw nothing, but he still heard the sound coming from the shower, the glass door closed. The door gave way to a tiled alcove, blocking the view near the shower head.

Wade rubbed his sweaty chin and neck before reaching for the door handle. He snatched it open but nothing pounced on him. Swallowing what felt like a lemon, his back to the wall, he edged closer so he could peer into the dead spot. Curled into the corner in an almost upright fetal position was Lou. She never looked up. Wade laid the gun on the sink and stepped inside the shower. His wife was completely nude. He spotted what he thought was bruises on her bottom torso, fearing the worst; she had been brutally attacked and raped.

"Lou, it's me, Wade." She let out an odd primal guttural response.

Wade knelt down in front of her. The bruises weren't bruises, they were dried feces. He couldn't image who had done this too her or how long she had been in the shower in this condition. He held her in his arms and cried until the officers arrived and called an ambulance. She never emerged from her induced shock during the ride to the hospital. The two officers conducting the investigation struggled to put words to their report to describe what they had found throughout the home. It defied exclamation.

7

Wade mustered up the courage to phone his kids, Leanne and Heath. They were on their way. He phoned Wyatt and Anna, and Lou's immediate family members to fill them in on the sad state of affairs. He told them he really had no further details other than what he had found upon returning from his trip. Wade added they would lick this situation and she would eventually be brand spanking new. He wasn't sure if he was trying to convince them or himself.

Wade also took time to call the college and report that Lou would be taking a medical leave of absence, without explaining the details. He was shocked to find out she had been placed on administrative leave almost a month ago. He was further shocked when he discovered the reason. His Lou never used profanity and would have never addressed her students in the manner described. Face it; this was no longer his Lou. Something major was going on; he just couldn't fathom what. The doctors were attempting to identify the cause. Police had ruled out any foul play.

It had been almost three days since Lou had been admitted to the hospital. Wade had been there most of the time with the exception of when Anna or Wyatt had subbed and encouraged him to go home and get some shut eye. He had only left long enough to shower, change clothes and grab a quick bite before returning. Doctors had said Lou was severely dehydrated and undernourished when admitted, stating they had detected no signs of any attacks or mistreatment. Other test results were pending to determine the cause for her trauma and deterioration.

Wade sat beside her bed patiently waiting for his Lou to come around. Her facial features were drawn, almost not looking like his beloved wife, at least not the woman he had left less than four weeks ago. How had she gotten in this bad shape in such a short period of time? Thinking back now, some of the phone conversations had been strange. Lou always had an excuse when he pressed her. He should have pressed harder or come home. He hadn't and couldn't undo what was done. Wade held her hand, wishing she would at least open her eyes. The doctor kept her mildly sedated until he could identify the cause for her trauma. Other than the dehydration, she was physically in good shape. The door opened. Wade turned to see the doctor entering with a clipboard.

Doctor Manfred Peavy, dark chocolate complexion, jet black hair, five ten with an average build, an immigrant from New Deli, India, stood at the foot of her bed, smiling a pearly white smile. In his thick Indian accent he said, "Hello Mister Stetson. Has she responded to your presence today?"

"Not a peep. What's wrong with her Doctor, have you figured it out yet?"

"Indeed, I think we have. Your wife displays all the symptoms of Alzheimer's, quite advanced, I must say."

"How is that possible? How could she have been perfectly all right just weeks ago and now like this?"

"I concur; this didn't just happen over a three week span. It has been progressing for a while, I assure you. Possibly the signs were there but, if you were not looking for them, you may have missed them. It is not uncommon for someone stricken with this disease to hide it for as long as possible, fearing ridicule or rejection or even feeling they are broken."

"I thought old people got Alzheimer's. Lou is only forty five."

"It is more common in the elderly, but age is no barrier or protection against this dreadful disease. Nearly two-thirds of Americans with Alzheimer's disease are women, and now some scientists are questioning the long-held assumption that it's just because they tend to live longer than men"

"How did she go downhill so fast? She was fine when I left for Richmond. I mean even if she was hiding it, how could this have happened?"

"She may have appeared fine, but she was in troubled waters long before you departed for your trip. Something triggered her fall over the edge. I'm guessing she suffered episodes of confusion, anxious or even depressed for being at home alone. This most likely reached a feverish pitch, paranoia setting in."

"What can you tell me about this? Help me understand, please."

"It's hard to say what happened in your wife's situation or what often puts women at extra risk. It could be her genetic makeup or maybe biological differences in how women age. It might even be her lifestyle. Discovering these factors could lead to effective treatments or even preventive care. One worrisome hint is that research shows a notorious Alzheimer's-related gene that has a bigger impact on women than men. There are enough biological questions pointing to increased risk in women that we need to delve into that and find out why. A recent Alzheimer's Association report estimates that at age 65, women have about a 1 in 6 chance of developing Alzheimer's during the rest of their lives, compared with a 1 in 11 chance for men."

"She's far from that age. Why her? Why now?"

"On average, women live four or five years longer than men, and we know that Alzheimer's is a disease that starts

20 years before the diagnosis. That's how early cellular damage can quietly begin, It places your wife in this timeframe. There's some evidence that once Alzheimer's is diagnosed, women may worsen faster; scans show more rapid shrinkage of certain brain areas. We have had a tough time understanding whether or not women really are more affected by the disease, or it's just that they live longer."

"This is hard to swallow. Could her having been forced to take administrative leave from the college have triggered this?"

"For sure, it could have contributed, but before you begin casting blame, the college is not the cause for your wife's medical issues, I assure you."

"I didn't say they were and I would never do anything against the college. She loved her job and her students. Please tell me more about why you think she has Alzheimer's."

"First let me say that based on the conditional descriptions of the interior of the home, lack of food or inability to provide, may have accelerated the process. She had become incapacitated and unable to provide for herself, something as simple as drinking water or any beverage. The fact that she wore no clothes is not uncommon. Patients in assisted living facilities have been found roaming the halls totally disrobed. Hygiene takes a big hit. Your wife was speckled with her own feces and that supports this premise. Without going into great detail, there are certain tests and signs that that have directed me to my diagnosis."

"Will she get better?"

"I would say there is a better than average chance she will snap out of this stupor, but I would not count on her returning to her former self. I would place her in the moderately severe category or mid-stage of Alzheimer's. The disease accelerates at different speeds in individuals, some battling it for years, others succumbing much quicker. Unfortunately I think Mrs. Stetson is one of those rare instances that will not battle the disease for a long period."

"What is that supposed to mean?"

"This is a cruel disease, Mister Stetson, and I regret to say, a death sentence."

"She can't die. She's too young. You must be wrong."

"I wish I could say that I am, but I am not. I encourage you to seek a second opinion."

"I don't mistrust you Doctor. I'm not saying that. What can I do, we do?"

"There is a specialist that I would like to recommend. Doctor Kelly Garner is more familiar with these cases. She is better equipped to assist you in the long haul. Other than that, we wait, and pray she snaps out of her present state. Miracles are always possible. My profession doesn't always have all the answers. Take care, Mister Stetson. I will be checking back in on her tonight."

Nurse Monica Sanchez entered the room just as Doctor Peavy exited. She requested Wade to step out of the room while she saw to Lou's needs. Wade leaned over and kissed Lou on the cheek, whispering, "I love you Lou. Hang in there. We're not down for the count yet. Fight like I know you can."

Wade returned to the waiting room and broke the news to Leanne and Heath and then to the rest of the immediate family gathered there, including Lou's. The room remained deathly quiet, each struggling to react. Wade had fluffed it up as much as possible, refusing to use the term death sentence or refer to this as terminal. Again, maybe he was just fooling himself, but he could not give up hope. Miracles are possible, so said the doctor. The family members visited Lou briefly. They returned more traumatized. Wade could see it in their faces. Most had given up on her.

Another couple of days had passed, filled with long hours in the hospital for Wade. Lou had at least opened her eyes and had been capable of ingesting food and drink;

all good signs said Doctor Peavy and Nurse Sanchez. She hadn't uttered a coherent word yet, but appeared alert and taking in her surroundings, maintaining eye contact with visitors as they communicated to her. Wade had already met with Doctor Kelly Garner. She had wonderful bedside manners and was very personable. She had further painted the picture ahead, attempting to keep a positive spin on it, but making sure Wade understood the potential perilous road yet to be traveled and life as a primary caregiver.

Day six, Doctor Garner saw no reason to keep Lou in the hospital. She agreed to release her, but spelled out the care she would have to be provided at home. Lou, simply stated, was not able to see to her needs and would require full time care. Wade told her the Lord made the world in six days and rested on the seventh; just possibly the miracle was a day shy yet. She smiled, acknowledging his optimism, but still encouraged him to secure some assistance. She even offered him a reference name, if he chose to hire a person, rather than handle it among family members. Doctor Garner stressed that caregiving was no easy task and statistics verified it took a toll on family members, even if their intentions were sincere.

The kids lived too far away to assist and Wade didn't want to burden Anna and Wyatt. A victim of self employment, Wade couldn't afford to stay home long term, so he opted to bit the bullet and seek assistance. He phoned the number the doctor had given him and secured an appointment to meet Liz Donley next week. In the interim, he would make do over the weekend, with the kids around to help. All the explaining in the world could have never prepared them for the responsibilities that would turn their world upside down.

Anna had supervised cleaning the house and for the most part it now appeared unscathed. Lou still maintained motor skills and with some assistance could walk, providing someone guided her in the correct direction. She had managed an occasional one or two word phrase, mostly having to do with food or items in the room. Wade welcomed any progress. She lacked the ability to control her bladder or bowels, prompting them to fit her with adult diapers. Doing the needful for an adult was not the same as seeing to an infant's needs. Wade and Leanne shared this duty. Heath couldn't handle it, not even for his mother.

Those stares penetrated Wade's very soul. Lou would look long and hard at him, as if reaching deeply, wanting to communicate with him, but incapable. He hurt so that he could not read those eyes. Her facial expression rarely changed. Five weeks ago she had been his wife, Lou. Now he wasn't sure if she even recognized him as her husband. It just didn't seem possible a person could make a transformation like this in such a short time. Doctors said it happened, varied from case to case, and he was looking at the living proof. Heath was taking it really hard, always having been close to her. That wasn't to say Leanne hadn't been equally impacted, but like her father, she had sucked it up and had done what needed to be done.

By the grace of the good Man above they survived the weekend but with that bitter ending signaled Heath and Leanne's return to their jobs, their lives. Leanne had offered to stay longer. Wade encouraged her to go home, saying he would be okay. Would he? Heath, on the other hand, couldn't depart quickly enough. He made no such offer, but Wade understood his son's agony. Anna would be there for him until he secured assistance. Lou didn't have any immediate family that lived close by. Liz Donley was scheduled to arrive this afternoon for an interview. Doctor Garner had sung her praises, saying Wade would have a difficult time finding anyone more dependable.

Lou was perfectly capable of eating solid foods but she

required assistance, unable to feed herself. Quickly Wade figured out that she didn't appreciate loud conversation, and became especially irritated at particular television programming. Wade had thought the TV would provide therapy but it didn't serve the role of a babysitter as it often did for small children. Lou wasn't a child and she wasn't supposed to be hard of hearing, but Wade often caught himself speaking baby talk or louder than normal. It was tough to carry a one way conversation.

Liz Donley showed up fifteen minutes ahead of schedule. Wade had wished his kids could have met her to see if she met their approval. Instead, he had asked Anna to sit in on the interview. He trusted his sister-in-law's opinion and she was much better at reading people than he. Wade wasn't good at gauging a person's age and he certainly wasn't about to ask her. He guessed she was maybe in her late fifties to sixty. She could be older, considering she had retired from nursing; but then again, he wasn't sure how old one had to be to retire from that profession. She was what Wade would call a big boned, plain Jane, standing about five, seven or eight. Like Lou, she wore minimal makeup. She, as described, was very personable and attentive to Lou, squatting right down beside her, holding her hand and talking to her in a normal tone.

"Mister Stetson, you are a fortunate man and have a beautiful wife, but you know that already don't you." Lou appeared to smile just a bit.

"Yes, I am blessed with one of the rare gems, indeed. So how long have you been doing this, Mrs. Donley?"

"Miss and please, call me Liz. Seven years since retiring, but as a nurse, it was my life. I understand you are concerned about Mrs. Stetson's welfare, and so am I. I don't take this lightly. We must consider the day may come when the shoe is on the other foot. I treat people with that premise in mind."

"I appreciate that. If we proceed, how soon could you start?"

"I'm here. We can get started today. I emphasize WE, Mister Stetson. This is a journey we do not take alone. I will not be here 24/7 so it is imperative that you, as well as any other who might grace Mrs. Stetson's presence, be attuned to her needs. Consider me a tutor as well."

"How do you deal with this," blurted out Anna.

"Rule number one, Mrs. Stetson, everyone in this room has the ability to understand your conversation. Refrain from talking as if the person is in the other room, and do not say anything hurtful, unless you mean what you say. Your sister-in-law will be treated with the utmost respect, no exceptions."

"I didn't mean it that way."

"I know you didn't, dear. Few people ever do."

"Please call me, Anna, too many Mrs. Stetsons are in the room, isn't that right, Lou?"

"I agree. Let's dismiss the formalities. We're just Lou and Wade."

"As for you as your salary and hours go…"

"You'll find it there," said Liz, handing him a sheet of paper. "If these aren't satisfactory, then we can adjust to meet your needs. My calling goes far beyond monetary values, I assure you, and I don't manage a clock. I'm here when needed."

"Just curious," asked Anna. "Is there a reason you are presently unemployed?"

Liz smiled. "Mister Vickers has joined the Lord and rejoices as we speak. I was blessed to have spent almost two years with him. He will forever be in my heart."

"That's what I meant, earlier when I offended you," clarified Anna.

"The worse mistake a primary caregiver makes is treating this like a job, a burden, and too often he or she becomes resentful. Lou, she's an angel and angels deserve respect and love. I rejoice and cherish my time with all my angels. One does this because you want to, and not because you have to. Once you understand this, the heart is in a better place. First things first, let's get Lou up and out of that chair. Walking is better than sitting. A woman with my foundation needs her exercise and Lou's just the person to help me regain my girlish figure."

Lou laughed out loud and clapped her hands. Wade and Anna burst into joyful tears. Liz was a miracle worker, thought Wade, the word miracle uplifting his heart. Just maybe, Liz could turn this thing around; bring Lou back from the brink. She was indeed one of a kind. He'd be sure to tell the good doctor he appreciated her recommendation. She probably already knew it.

8

Over the next couple of weeks Lou continued to improve, at least taking baby steps back towards her former self. These weren't dramatic on the grand scale but just seeing her smile, hearing her laugh and her having the ability to communicate, meant the world to Wade. Liz had indeed been the miracle worker. She treated Lou like a friend, not a patient. Lou lit up when Liz walked into the room and had regained mobility. She was actually able to walk about without assistance. These jaunts had to be closely monitored because her balance wasn't the greatest and she often became easily disoriented.

Liz had Lou using a fork or spoon and feeding herself most days. Food would be prepared in bite size portions for her, making it easier for her to manage the morsels on her plate. She sipped all beverages from a straw in spill proof glasses, an adult version of a sippy cup. Loud talking or noises still weren't her friend. She would become noticeably agitated. Doctor Garner was very pleased with her progress, but still warned Wade to not build up too much hope for long term success. Lou was in advance stages of the disease. Garner advised to spend as much time as he could with her while she was having such marvelous days.

Leanne visited most every weekend and spent at least one night before heading back. Heath called a couple of times a week but his visits were limited, still having a tough time dealing with his mom's illness. Wade would have thought, being a vet, would have made it easier for him to cope with the situation, but while he was excellent with dogs and cats, his mother was a different story. Fabian Pressley, her favorite student had even visited her twice, now understanding the reasoning behind her behavior that day in class. Anna and Wyatt were always a presence, happy to do anything that they could. Lou's closest relatives visited, but were more cameo appearances, in and out, and no real help in caring for her.

All was not a bed of roses. Lou's personality could shift at the drop of a hat. She could react negatively to the simplest of events. In angry tones she could spew some of the most vulgar language, words she would have never spoken out loud previously. The audience at hand didn't always react so kindly to her outbursts; not comprehending this was driven by the disease. Liz never altered her demeanor in these incidences, treating Lou as if she had just read scripture from the bible. Wade had to work a little harder to overcome the shock factor. He was getting better at it. Liz was tutoring him.

Wade had started a contract in the Greenville-Spartanburg area. The job site was just over an hour away, which allowed him to commute back and forth, no overnight stays. Liz was a constant, a rock and she stayed with Lou through thick and thin. As professed, she wasn't a clock watcher. Anna offered to sub, but rarely did Liz ever take advantage of the offer. There were few bumps in the road. Liz had it under control and oozed confidence that spread infectiously to those around her.

One particular Saturday morning Wyatt and Anna came by unexpectedly. Most of the time they spent Sunday afternoons there, so Wade thought it was mighty unusual for them to be stopping by so early on Saturday.

"Hey Wade, how's things going this morning?"

"Lou's still in bed but Liz said she had a good day

yesterday. What brings you two here so early on a Saturday. Were you bored?"

"Actually I have someone out in the truck just itching to see you and Lou."

"Come in Wyatt, you know the drill. It's always better when you check ahead to see if she's in the right spirits for visitors."

"Those are your rules. Liz always says the opposite. There is no good or bad time for visitors."

"You're just too hard headed," added Anna. "Lou always loved visitors, anytime, any hour."

"I know. I guess I'm just a little over protective at times. Bring them on in. I'll see if Lou is awake yet."

Wade offered Anna a cup of coffee while Wyatt escorted the visitor to the door. Wade had his back to the door, but turned when he heard it opening.

"What the hell," blurted out Wade, almost dropping his coffee cup. Rushing him with reckless abandon was a familiar sight, Kramer. The long lost pooch almost knocked him to the floor, paws and tongue spreading their joy.

"Where did you find him," asked Wade, between the wet tongue lashings.

"You know I'm on the city board," explained Wyatt. "I was in a special meeting yesterday afternoon discussing finances. The pound was struggling to stay afloat. Recommendations were to cut funding at the city pound and euthanize 40% of the animals being held to make expenses. Conditions were supposed to be deteriorating. I decided to stop by there this morning and see for myself. I spotted your friend in one of the holding pen flagged for being put to sleep. Monday old Kramer would have been history."

"He's been there all this time. After finding Honey in the closet, I figured Lou had let him out and had forgotten to let him back in, and he had gotten struck by a car or something. Thanks Wyatt. You're a lifesaver, literally. If Lou was herself, she'd be up there trying save all the animals."

Honey showed up and began to rub along Kramer's legs. Kramer gave her a sloppy lick and she hissed back at him, but it was an affectionate comeback. Before leaving, Anna asked if Wade needed any help today, but he waved her off, saying everything was fine. He was looking forward to sharing some quality time with Lou. He had even given Liz the weekend off. She would report back to duty before he departed for work Monday morning.

Shortly after Wyatt and Anna had left, Wade gave Lou a wakeup call, assisted her with cleaning up and getting dressed. He then served her breakfast, scrambled eggs and sausage, tomato juice and store bought biscuits. Lou managed to eat her meal with minimal assistance from Wade. He chatted to her almost none stop throughout the meal. She replied with a yeah or no occasionally, or nodded and smiled. Wade decided the day was too pretty to remain inside, so he and Lou ventured into the great outdoors.

Lou paused at her garden spot and frowned. "Weeds," she said. "Bad weeds…bad weeds." She knelt down, as best she could, and grabbed a clump."

"We need to do something about that, don't we," replied Wade, kneeling down beside her and plucking weeds too."

Amazingly Lou suddenly spoke, sounding like Lou, "I've missed my garden. Can we plant some okra?"

Wade beamed in delight. "We certainly can. He reached over and placed his hand on top of hers and squeezed.

She smiled and patted his hand with her free one, and said, "Everything is going to be all right, Heath."

Wade's heart dropped, but he didn't attempt to correct her. "That's right. Everything is going to be just fine. What you say we plant a few tomato and pepper plants too?"

Lou nodded. "I like tomatoes."

"You stay here and pull weeds, okay, Lou? I'm going

inside and make a quick phone call and rustle up us some okra seed and plants." Lou smiled back.

Wade returned a few minutes later after phoning a friend at Jerry's Produce. After placing his order, his friend said he would bring it to them within the hour. Wade panicked. Lou was not where he had left her at the garden. How had he been so stupid, leaving her here alone? Some caregiver he had turned out to be. His panic was quickly replaced by a sigh of relief when he spotted Lou sitting in the cedar yard swing. Wade rushed to the old oak.

"Lou, you scared the crap out of me," he blurted out in an elevated tone before thinking.

Lou cowered in the swing, grimacing at him, and immediately Wade regretted his reaction. "I'm sorry, Lou. I was just worried."

Lou smiled and patted the swing, her way of inviting Wade to have a seat beside her. It was Wade's time to smile. He sat down in the swing placing his arm around her. It was almost like old times. For a few precious minutes Wade said nothing, just enjoyed swinging with his wife, embracing the moment. Lou seemed content too.

Finally, after some soul searching, Wade broke the silence. "Lou, can you tell me what you are feeling right now?"

Lou stared at him, a most puzzling look on her face. Wade wasn't sure if she didn't understand his question or just didn't know how to answer it so he asked again. "Lou, could you tell me what you are thinking right now? How do you really feel?"

"I like swinging with you. It's fun. We should come here and swing more often, Heath. Did you know your father built this swing with his own hands? He's a good builder. He works too hard though, but he does it for us. How was school today?"

Wade wiped a tear from his cheek and said, "School

was fine."

"Where's Leanne? Is she inside doing her homework?"

"She's around somewhere. You know how she is."

Wade struggled to retain his composure. He was on the verge of losing it, but a tearful outburst would serve no purpose and would most likely upset Lou. He sucked it up, deciding this was not a bad thing. Lou was thinking and carrying on a conversation, so what did it really matter that she didn't know who he was, but deep down it did matter. He had hoped to share a husband and wife moment on the swing. It was not to be, not his time. There would be others. He'd remain patient.

"I'm hungry. Are you hungry?"

Lou couldn't possibly be hungry after the bountiful breakfast she had just consumed. Reality hit. She didn't remember breakfast, just like she didn't remember him. "Then we should go inside and have a bite, shouldn't we?"

Lou slid out of the swing. "What would you like me to fix you, dear, hotdogs and fries, your favorite? "

"I would like that," responded Wade, as they walked hand in hand back towards the house.

"I can't wait until we begin harvesting fresh vegetables from the garden," remarked Lou, passing by the weed laden garden spot. Your father sure loves my fried okra."

"He does indeed."

Opening the door, they were greeted by Kramer. Hindsight, thought Wade, he should have let Kramer out while they were outside, but Kramer wasn't so eager to go outside since his little ordeal. He no longer voluntarily stood at the door and begged. Just the opposite, he would dash off into the back bedroom when Wade mentioned the words, *outside, boy.*

Lou shied away from Kramer's advances. His meet and greet session seemed to overwhelm her. Wade attempted to assure her that Kramer was just offering her a little friendly affection, but Lou would have none of it. Wade finally had to drag the overzealous dog away and enclose him on the sun porch. Lou had always been so fond of animals; not anymore. This might explain why she had refused to allow Kramer back in the house in the first place. Possibly it was more than just forgetfulness as originally suspected.

And just as quickly, Lou had forgotten about being hungry or preparing hotdogs and fries; just as well, thought Wade. Her mannerisms had changed too. She became more withdrawn and less talkative. Wade crinkled his nose, realizing she had soiled herself. New challenge, remove the Depends adult diaper and clean her up. Liz always handled these bodily situations flawlessly, but why shouldn't she, she was a professional and accustomed to doing it. Wade was a mere rookie. It wasn't that he minded doing it; he felt it had to impact Lou and her dignity, invading too much on her privacy, her personal space.

He led Lou to the bathroom, chatting with her along the way, attempting to ease the mood. Again, this was probably more for him than her. With Lou standing there, Wade first slipped off her loose fitting loungers, placing them on the counter. When he reached for her adult diaper, all hell broke loose. Lou became a raging animal, grabbing hold of his hands, and then slapping and clawing at him, pushing him away. She was whining loudly, saying, no. Wade stepped back, caught by surprise and wasn't sure how to address the latest development. He had no play book.

"Lou, I'm just trying to help. We need to clean you up and get you into some fresh clothes," said Wade, speaking to her a low soft spoken tone.

Lou pulled away, and then backed into a corner. Her eyes were wild and disturbed, looking about frantically. She kept both hands raised, poised to fend off any more intrusions. Wade wasn't sure what to do next. He contemplated phoning Liz, but thought better. He had to learn how to handle these situations and not depend on Liz at the drop of a hat. Wade approached Lou, talking to her, trying to ease her apprehension.

He placed his hand on her shoulder and said, "Lou, this is me, Wade, your husband. You remember me, don't you? We've been married forever. You've had a little accident, nothing to be ashamed of; it happens to all of us." With his other hand, he reached for the Depends.

Lou freaked out. She snatched the soap dispenser off the vanity and whacked Wade hard across his right cheek. The lick stunned Wade and he reacted instinctively by knocking it from her hand and forcibly pushing her against the wall. Lou came back at him like a hemmed up bull. Her strength shocked Wade. She was manhandling him and shouldn't have been able to, given her size and his. Wade didn't wish to harm her, so he freed her hands from his clothing and backed away. Lou slumped to the floor, wrapping her arms around her knees. She maintained eye contact with the floor. Wade decided to leave her alone for few minutes and hopefully she would snap out of it.

He walked back into the den and collapsed on the couch, fully understanding Doctor Garner's insistence on him seeking help for seeing to her needs. The thought crossed his mind; had she thought he had been Heath doing this to her. Either way, it has to be tough having a family member see to your hygiene needs. Wade wasn't sure how he would handle it, if he were in her shoes. Honey jumped on the couch beside him and began rubbing all over him, purring up a storm. He rubbed Honey's sleek body, finding her sounds soothing. Wade regrouped his single wagon, wagon train, lost in a world of worry, and no closer to solving his immediate problem.

9

Wade sat at the kitchen bar, exhausted from today's events. He had eventually managed to gain Lou's trust and get her cleaned up, but then she became distraught as the evening hour approached. He had struggled to convince her she was at home and not in someone else's house. Plus she was convinced people were stealing her personal items. He had managed to keep his cool throughout and agreed with her notions as much as possible. Somehow he had gotten her to agree to go to bed.

Liz had helped him set up a guest bedroom with a single bed for Lou, saying he needed his rest and it was better if they resided in separate rooms. The single bed made it easier for them to handle Lou and was much better when those little accidents happened that soiled the linen. This really disturbed Wade at first. He and Lou had never slept apart, but Liz, and even the doctor, had said it was in everyone's best interest.

Wade fought off drowsiness, sipping a cup of decaffeinated coffee. His body screamed at him to go to bed, but his mind wasn't so ready to turn in. He was flooded with emotions and what-ifs. He found it tough to comprehend how anyone could do this for a living. It was hard enough doing it for a loved one. Wade had found new respect for Liz and all caregivers. He'd not wish this on anyone. Then just as quickly he kicked himself in the butt, thinking how selfish; look a Lou, she didn't ask for this. When it's all over, at least I …then he choked on the thoughts.

Wade dragged Kramer outside one last time before retiring. He sure hoped Kramer eventually overcame his phobia. Even the animals required therapy now. Just before heading to bed he checked on Lou one last time. She appeared snug as a bug in a rug. Liz had set up a baby monitor in Lou's room so he could hear her from his. It was half past midnight by the time Wade's head hit the pillow. He braced himself for the long night ahead, just moments before the snoring began.

The scratching and whimpering woke Wade. Opening his eyes he saw Kramer with his paws on his bedside. Wade glanced at the digital display, 4:13 AM. "Unbelievable, now you want to go outside, thanks a lot, boy." Wade slid out of bed and slipped on his jeans and shoes. Kramer ran ahead, pausing only to make sure Wade was following him. Wade paused in the den long enough to stretch and yawn. Kramer barked his disapproval.

"You must really have to go. Good, then make it quick."

Reaching the backdoor, Wade came to a crashing halt. The door stood wide open. He quickly checked the storm door. It was unlocked. "What the …" and then the sheer terror of the moment shocked the last bits of sleepiness from his system. Wade sprinted through the den, down the hallway and to Lou's room. Her bed was empty. He pulled a one eighty and hurried back to the access door, flipping on the flood lights as he exited.

Wade checked the garden first and then the swing, no Lou. How had he allowed this to happen? He began screaming Lou's name. He ran to the front yard, empty as the back. They lived on a rural road, no neighbors within a half mile. The night was deathly quiet. Wade yelled again, no response. What was he thinking? Lou in her present condition wasn't apt to reply. Wade returned to the house and called 911, déjà vu. He then called Wyatt and Anna before rushing back outside.

In a creepy old secluded cemetery, through the woods, almost a mile away, stood Lou Stetson. The ancient burial site had grave markers dating back to the 1800's, and other head stones you could no longer read, too weathered. Lou walked from one and then to the other, rubbing her hand over the cool surfaces. She seemed fascinated by her new playground in the full moonlit night. Her thin nightgown flapped in the breeze from the intermediate wind.

One particular tombstone caught her eye. It had this odd shaped star and a rose on the front. Lou ran her hands over the etchings and then kneeled in front of it. The name, Margarett Levine Reznik was inscribed, with the dates May 17, 1869 and May 17, 1890. A covered bronze plate was centered below the name, the dates on either side. A Hebrew caption engraved in gold lettering was at the bottom. Lou followed each letter, tracing them with her finger tips, awe stricken by her discovery.

Her finger tips tingled. Lou dropped to her knees directly over the top of the grave, hands still resting on the inscription, a series of invigorating sensations electrifying her body. She stared at the headstone, mesmerized by its beauty, her soul undergoing an unexplainable cleansing of sorts. The world was so vivid, the clarity of her surroundings were taking on new shapes and sounds. Lou jerked, a wave of spasms overcoming her petite body. Her eyes sparkled with the fire of life, the essence of a life long forgotten. Lou focused on the name leaping at her from the marble stone, Margarett Levine Reznik. She blinked, somehow recognizing that name.

A series of shocks jolted her, painful, excruciating, yet, almost sensual, exciting, stimulating, reaching her inner core. Lou, aware she was undergoing a transformation, somehow subconsciously fought vigorously against the invasion. The intruder was persistent, demanding and determined to have what was Lou's. Something felt dreadfully wrong to Lou. She was Lou and yet she wasn't. A vicious battle for control had begun and Lou was losing, unable to ward of the persistence, Alzheimer's leaving her ill equipped for such an epic battle.

Lou screamed, "Nooooooooooooo!" A voice within her said, "***But yes, my dear.***"

Lou's mind was reeling with visions of unknown places and unfamiliar faces. Intrusive sensations bombarded her body, sending her senses spiraling out of control. Overwhelmed, Lou began to weep. Before the tears dripped from her chin, she began laughing loudly, her voice echoing in the darkness, the pure essence of insanity. Lou wondered is this what it feels like to lose one's mind. She had realized she was ill and had struggled with everyday activities, so could this be the final straw, the last hurrah, the beginning of the end? She hadn't remembered reading these signs on the Net. Possibly no one had ever known they existed, except those ravished with the dreaded disease. The dead tell no tales.

Her perception became cloudy. Lou attempted to stand but suffered from vertigo like symptoms. She fell back to her knees, her right hand resting on the headstone, the electricity still traveling up her arm, the mere touch to the cold surface maintaining a conduit to the beyond. Lou continued to experience what was best described as watching home movies at lightning speed. The odd videos were filled with strangers but yet they weren't strangers. From a child's existence to that of an adult, her life, somebody's life was revealed to her, was her, but wasn't.

The scenes slowed, building to a climax. Lou yearned to experience one of those *live happily ever after* moments. Then, the unexpected happened, something going terribly wrong. The end of the world came crashing down, shock, horror, pain, and then complete darkness.

10

Wyatt and Anna arrived just moments after the police. Wade stood in the kitchen answering their questions, becoming more frantic by the passing moments.

"Like I've already told you, she slipped out of the house sometime between around midnight and when I phoned 911. I saw the door open when I was taking Kramer outside. Actually, Kramer didn't want to go outside. He was alerting me about Lou. Possibly Lou had just exited, but if she had I could not find here anywhere nearby."

"And you don't expect foul play, Mister Stetson?"

"No, officer, but we're wasting time. We need to find her."

"Were you and your wife experiencing any marital problems; possibly had some sort of argument?"

"This is bull crap. If you're not going to help me find her then just get the hell out of my way. We'll search for her without you."

"Calm down, Mister Stetson. We're just following protocol to learn the facts."

"The fact is my wife is missing. We can follow your protocol crap after we find her."

"Wade, they're only doing their job," spoke up Anna.

"Yeah, Wade, remember, you called them. Try to be patient," added Wyatt.

"Lou's out there somewhere and Lord only knows what may have happened to her. I have no time to patient."

"You do understand we can't declare her a missing person until twenty four hours from the time the incident has been reported."

"Then what good are you to me. You don't understand. My wife is suffering from Alzheimer's. She's not herself. She could be in grave danger."

"Why didn't you say so in the first place, Mister Stetson? Under those circumstances we can waive the twenty four hour requirement."

"Sorry, I'm not exactly at the top of my game right now, officer."

Kramer was going crazy, whining and scratching at the door.

"Do you want me to take him for a walk or something, Wade," asked Wyatt.

"Damn it," exclaimed Wade. "He doesn't have to go to the bathroom. He wants to find Lou. He's not a bloodhound by any stretch but I think it's worth a chance. Let me get his leash."

Wade leashed Kramer and opened the door. The dog almost yanked Wade off his feet. "Anna, you stay put just in case she wonders back here."

With that, Wade, the two officers and Wyatt followed the frantic pooch; nose to the ground and in full throttle. Kramer was a mutt on a mission. It was good Wade had him restrained or they would never have been able to keep up with him. Kramer was digging into the ground like a Troy-built tiller. Entering the nearby woods the officers whipped out their flashlights, mimicking sweeping search beams from any prison movie. Wade let out several yells for Lou, not really expecting a response, but hoping she would hear them.

"What's that up ahead," asked one the officers, his beam reflecting off some shinny white objects.

"It's an old cemetery. I don't think it's used any more.

It's been overgrown for years," replied Wade. "There are no more than about eleven or twelve gravesites, from what I remember."

Kramer was pulling harder than ever, standing on his hind legs, resembling a wild stallion. Wade, attempting to readjust the leash, loosened his grip just enough for the dog to pull free. He was off to the races, vanishing on the fringes of the flashlight beams. The others hustled to gain ground, entering the old graveyard. Wade's shouts to Kramer were undaunted. The dog had vanished.

"Spread out," barked the older of the two officers. "Prepare to sweep the area. Put about ten yards between one another." The policemen anchored both ends of the four man search party, flashlights sweeping the terrain ahead. Various grave stones speckled the landscape ahead. It appeared they were approaching the backside of the graveyard. This side of the marble markers was empty of any etchings. By their condition, most were very old, some even leaning.

They had already passed two grave markers when one of the beams caught glimpse of something moving ahead wiggling along at ground level. It was indeed an eerie sight, thought Wyatt. He envisioned fingers breaking the grave's surface. Victim of watching too may zombie movies; his imagination got the best of him. Wyatt mustered up a high pitched warning, pointing to the movement.

Whatever it was, appeared to be blocked by the huge marble stone. The officers closed ranks, moving cautiously towards their objective. Wade eased alongside the policeman with a better view and angle on the grave. Gradually the phenomena came into sight. There Kramer sat directly on top of the grave facing the huge tombstone. His ears were laid back and tail barely wagging.

"Come here boy," whispered Wade, unsure why he was whispering. It must have something to do with standing in the middle of the graveyard. Kramer didn't waiver, kept his eyes on the stone.

The officer on the left positioned himself so that he could see around the other side of the headstone. His flashlight detected what had held the dog's undivided interest. He closed the few steps quickly and knelt down beside the stone. Wade and the other officer converged from the opposite side, the officer and the darkness concealed what he appeared to be examining. He turned to the others and said, "She's alive."

Wade practically forced the second officer to the ground pushing past him. Lou sat with her back propped to the tombstone; head slumped over, chin touching her chest. She appeared quite lifeless. Wade dropped to his knees, placing one hand on her shoulder and the other under her chin. He raised her chin until he could see her face. Her eyes remained closed but he could see her chest moving. Thank heavens she was breathing.

Is there any way to get an ambulance in here," asked the younger officer.

"There's an old dirt road on the opposite side," replied Wade. "It should come out near the bridge on twenty five, but wouldn't it be easier if we take her out the way we came in?"

"Let's not move her until we have the medics check her out," said the older officer.

"I agree Wade. There's no need taking any chances. We've found her. Let them check her out before she is moved," chimed in Wyatt. "I'll phone Anna and let her know."

"It's going to be okay," whispered Wade, rubbing his hand through Lou's hair.

"Try not to move her about," advised the older officer. "Worst thing you can do is move her before we receive a medical report."

Kramer nudged under Wade's arm. "Good boy. You found her for us. There's a t-bone in your future, I promise."

"What about us," chuckled the younger officer.

"Dozen donuts, on me," replied Wade.

"Very funny," said the older officer "but I'll hold you to that promise. Make it a dozen a piece for both of us, but only when the 'Hot Now' sign is on."

The ambulance arrived within thirty minutes, having had to negotiate a rutted and overgrown road to reach the secluded cemetery. One of the paramedics commented she didn't even know the old graveyard existed. After a preliminary examination Lou was loaded onto a stretcher and transported to Self Regional Healthcare, Greenwood's hospital. She had remained in shock and unresponsive. Wade couldn't imagine the impact this ordeal may have had on his wife. Time would tell.

Lou had been admitted for observation. Wade awaited the arrival of Doctor Kelly Garner. Lou had already been examined by Doctor Manfred Peavy and he had found nothing physically wrong with her. Wade had contacted his kids but he had told them there was no need for them to rush to Greenwood. The danger had passed. He would keep them posted on her condition. There was really nothing they could do at this point. Liz Donley, Lou's caregiver, had arrived, having it no other way than to be there. Wade had decided to keep the event close to the vest otherwise and had not contacted any other relatives, including Lou's distant ones. What was the point?

He sat by her bedside, keeping a vigil over her, wishing he could do something. Liz stood over her, holding Lou's hand and making conversation as if she was wide awake. Wade really admired this woman and her compassion for those in need. He watched her as she attempted to weave her magic, that special way she had with her patients. She must truly be one of a kind, thought Wade. The door opened and both Liz and Wade turned to see Doctor Garner entering the room.

"Wade, Liz, sorry to be here under these circumstances; has she responded to either of you?"

"No, she has remained as you see her since we found her in the old cemetery."

"Liz can back me up. It's not uncommon for Alzheimer's patients to wander off like she did. Often they are traumatized by their little adventure. There are no signs of physical injury, so she should eventually snap out of this."

"Will there be long term affects?"

"Unfortunately I cannot answer that until she is conscious. As we have previously discussed, I fear she is in the extreme advanced stages. Not to bash your spirits, Wade, but please don't get your hopes up. Our job is to make her as comfortable as we can and provide her with a normal environment."

"Until she dies, just say it, I know its coming."

"Doctor," alerted Liz, "look."

Lou's eyes were wide open. She was perusing the room, making visual contact with Wade, then Liz and then with the doctor. She remained speechless but very alert. Liz took note how she was wiggling her fingers by her side and her toes under the covers. It seemed strange. She had never seen this sort of behavior, almost as if she was testing her limbs. Lou turned her head one way and then the other, checking out the room.

"Hello, Lou. Remember me. I'm Doctor Garner. You gave us quite the scare."

Wade was standing by her side and instinctively grabbed her by the hand. "You sure did but you're safe and sound now. You're in the hospital, but as soon as the doctor says so, I'll take you back home."

"First things first," said Doctor Garner. "Would the two of you please step out of the room for a few minutes while Lou and I have a little girl time?"

In the hallway, Wade was bubbling with joy. "What do you think, Liz? She looks great otherwise, doesn't she?"

"She looked better than that. I don't know; she had this glow about her, something I haven't seen since I've known her."

"What do you mean?"

"I'm not sure. Her eyes were so bright, aware, possibly slightly confused about her surroundings but something else. There was a sparkle, a twinkle in those eyes."

"I hope you mean this as a positive sign."

"I hope so too."

Moments later, Doctor Garner stepped into the hallway with a puzzled look on her face.

Wade panicked. "Doctor, is something wrong?"

She half chuckled. "Oh no, she's fine. Actually she's better than fine."

"Can we go back inside," asked Wade.

"Of course, but I must warn you first. She is chatting up a storm."

"That's wonderful," said Liz.

"Yes it is, however, her demeanor is all wrong. Her dialogue is disturbing."

"I don't follow you," said Wade.

"She told me she is cured."

"She thinks she's all right then," replied Wade.

"No, she said she no longer has Alzheimer's. She was quite direct and to the point. She even challenged me to test her. I must admit, she was quite cocky about it too. Her dialogue was not one I would expect from a college professor though."

"Was she using foul language," asked Liz.

"No, not this time; it was more, how can I put this,

her articulation and her choice of words was not of this century, if that makes any sense. She almost had a slight accent too. Possibly it is just me. I didn't really know her before she fell ill."

"Could this be a result from the trauma?"

"Perhaps it is, but why don't you go inside and judge for yourself, Wade. I would like to run a few more tests before I release her."

"Do what you think is best. I'm just glad she's alert and talking." Wade entered the room and was greeted by a huge warm smile, the likes he had not seen in a long time. She did look quite bright eyed and invigorated. She looked remarkably well, come to think of it.

"Wade, come here. I must kiss your warm lips. I crave for you tender touch, my dear husband."

Wade, caught off guard by her comments and gesture, had to agree; this didn't sound like something his Lou would say, unless she was just horsing around. That had to be it. He sat on the bed beside her and leaned to give her a peck on the lips. Lou grabbed him by the shoulders and pulled him closer, thrusting her tongue into his mouth. She had obviously missed him. Wade, regaining his composure, red faced, sat back and took assessment of his wife's actions.

"How do you feel, Lou?"

"How do I feel to you, Hon?" She ran her hand along his arm.

"The doctor said you believe you are cured."

"I've never felt better. This thing, Alzheimer's, must be a passing thing. I forget what it is supposed to make me feel like. Yes, like a breaking fever, it is gone."

"Very funny, Lou; you forgot."

"New me, why not call me Emma. Lou sounds like an old man's name. Look at me. Do I resemble an old man to you?"

"But you've always gone by Lou."

"I've been resurrected so why not resurrect a new name. Emma is my name, correct? So why can't I use it if I wish?"

"Emma Lou Stetson, we can call you anything you want. I'm just glad you're feeling better."

"Spry as an ole alley cat catching my fill of mice," she laughed.

"Do you remember anything about last night?"

"Let's forget the past. It's no good except for making history. When do we go to our home, my husband?"

"Doctor Garner has a few tests she'd like to conduct first. I expect that means an overnight stay."

"I'm fine. I can pass any test she wants to toss my way. Look, I feel wonderfully liberated. I really want to go home, so I can show you just how badly I have missed you. Is that too much to ask?"

Leave him alone.

"Foolish gibberish," said Emma.

"The doctor isn't spouting foolish talk. She only has your best interest in mind."

You will not get away with this, whoever you are.

"But I have."

"But you have what, Lou, I mean Emma."

"I have made a complete recovery. I am fit as a fiddle. I'm quite famished too, hungry enough to eat a horse, saddle and all."

He'll never believe you are me. You talk and act nothing like me. Leave, just get out of me. This is my body, not yours.

"Tell you what, Hon. Round up my clothes and we'll get out of this morgue. You can wine me, dine me and poke me until your heart is content. I'm aching for a little ole fashion loving, what do you say?"

"Let me talk to Doctor Garner first and then we'll see."

Emma hiked up her hospital issue gown and flashed her nether regions. "Make it snappy, the kitty is getting mighty hungry, husband."

That's disgusting. I would never act like that. He'll never buy into such obscenities.

Emma waited until Wade had exited the room. "Skip to my Lou my darling; I'll have your little hubby eating out my hand in no time. Men are so easy. Smother them with what they want and they'll blindly follow. First, we're going to have to work on your manners. There's only room for one of us and guess what; you're butting in too much with your goody ways, trying to spoil all my fun. You took care of yourself. There are a lot of good times left in you, ole girl, and I plan to take full advantage of what you have to offer. "

Who are you and why are you doing this?

"Because I can, isn't that obvious? Besides, I've broken the damn curse that bound me to that hole. I'm free to live again. I've got some catching up to do, and itches to scratch, and I need to find those who did this to me, and make them pay dearly. Hush your mouth and stay where I put you, unless you want something dreadfully horrible to happen to the beloved and naïve Wade, our husband."

You won't get away with this.

"Who's steering the mule? Not you, my sweet Lou, boohoo; you're merely along for the ride. In given time, you won't even be a fleeting memory. I just hope this body can live up to my reputation. For now, be gone and just maybe I'll allow your sweetie to live a while longer. Surely you don't want his blood on your hands, do you?"

Liz knocked and then entered the room, "Hey there."

"Hey there yourself," replied Emma.

"I must say you're looking quite fit, Lou. This is indeed a miraculous turn around. How do you feel?"

"Simply delightful; I'm just ready to dust off the old cobwebs and get back to doing what I do best. What about you? You're unemployed now, right."

"Actually your husband has asked me stay around for

a while. Doctor Garner thinks it would be a good idea too, to assist with your recovery and rehab, so I suppose you're stuck with me for a bit longer."

"I don't need a nursemaid anymore, Sweetie. I'm fit, can't you tell? You did good, nursing me when I needed it and now it is time to be gone. I'm sure there are plenty of needy smucks out there that could use your motherly love. I can fend for myself. You'd just cramp my style. I've kicked this thing to the ditch. I do apologize for being so candid, but I'm not one for babying things along. From my head to my mouth, no detours, you get it straight from this horse's mouth every time."

"Well, just the same, I think it is best for you that I stay around. I promise I'll not invade your privacy and will be there for you at every turn."

"Have it your way, sister. The pay must really be good. Don't get use to it. Gold diggers tend to wear out their welcome sooner or later."

Doctor Garner returned, along with Wade. "Lou, considering the circumstances, we will be keeping you here at least one more day. I'd like to under my care. This way, we can compare the before and after picture; where you were and where you are today."

"It doesn't sound like I have any say in this. Fine, get it over with."

11

Doctor Garner sat down with Wade to review what she would be doing.

"Remember, as we previously discussed, when Doctor Peavy recommended I examine Lou; there is no single test that proves a person has Alzheimer's. A diagnosis is made through a complete assessment that considers all possible causes. This will include the full gambit once again, a physical exam and diagnostic tests, mental status tests, a neurological exam, and brain imaging. We already have an excellent template from the first time."

"Is it really possible that she is cured?"

"Very doubtful, I must sadly concede. I wish I could be more positive but I don't wish to build your expectations. Alzheimer's patients can drift in and out of it, those good days and bad days but ultimately the bad days win out."

"What about one of those miracles?"

"He does work in mysterious ways; but again, please don't read too much into these extraordinary circumstances. Let me complete the tests first, and then we'll see what the results tell us. Maybe she has reached a temporary reprieve. That wouldn't be so bad, would it, to buy you a little more time with her?"

"I'd rather her be cured, but I'll take what I can get. Do you have an explanation for her change in personality? She's not exactly talking and acting like Lou."

"Extreme personality shifts are trademark of the

disease. Personalities are often polarized. You have seen firsthand her abusive language. This could be yet another phase."

"So what do we do first?"

"We'll start with the usual, a medical exam. Have there been any changes in her diet, any new medication, even across the counter? Has she gotten her hands on any alcohol?"

"No changes and no booze," replied Wade.

"I've already checked her blood pressure, pulse and temperature, heart and lungs. All are fine, very normal. I'll have the nurse collect blood and urine samples. Next I'll verify her mental status, testing her memory, ability to solve simple problems and other thinking skills. It is important to see if she knows dates, time, and where she is. Can she remember a short list of words, follow instructions and do simple calculations."

"And if she aces these?"

"We'll move on to a neurological exam. I'll reexamine her for any signs of small or large strokes, Parkinson's disease, brain tumors, fluid accumulation on the brain, and other illnesses that may impair memory or thinking. I'll save the brain imagining until last. I'll want to do an MRI and a CT. These tests are primarily used to rule out other conditions that may cause symptoms similar to Alzheimer's but require different treatment. Structural imaging can reveal tumors, evidence of small or large strokes, and damage from severe head trauma or a buildup of fluid in the brain. These came up negative the first time."

"And you're sure I'll be able to take her home tomorrow?"

"I don't see why not. It will take me some time to review all the results. Unless I detect something odd that may prompt more testing, I think she will be in good hands at home with you and Liz."

"I promise you she will not give me the slip again."

"Don't beat yourself up, Wade. People with this disease can be quite resourceful and most unpredictable."

"I know it wasn't my fault but still."

"Consider asking Liz if she would move in for some period of time. It's much easier when you have a tag team partner on the premises. Professional instinct tells me we're not out of the woods yet."

"You really don't think it is possible that she has beaten this, do you?"

"If she has, we've just made medical history. I've never heard of a case of Alzheimer's that went into remission. I'm not trying to paint gloom and doom, but I do deal in facts. I just don't want you to get your hopes up, Wade. The fall is tougher the second time."

"Can I ask you something and please don't take this the wrong way. Lou was very promiscuous earlier. She indicated she wanted to go home and have sex. If she isn't cured, how does this disease impact the libido?"

"Clinical studies have shown that this is often a difficult subject for both the caregiver and their spouse. Situations vary. Some people with dementia become hypersexual and need medication to decrease their sex drive. Inappropriate overtures to a non-spouse, verbal obscenities and undressing in public are behaviors that cause concern. When the spouse is exhibiting these behaviors, caregivers can find themselves even less willing sexual partners. I'd just suggest taking it as it comes. If it feels right for both of you, then do what is natural. Please be cautious because this can have negative ramifications too. Lou could become confused; think you're attacking her, even if she made the first advances."

"I guess all bets are off if you find out she is no longer at risk."

"Be careful either way. It could impact both of you

emotionally and mentally if it doesn't work as you expected."

"This is amazing either way, don't you think?"

"We are indeed fortunate to see her alert and responsive to her surroundings. The fact that she recognizes everyone is always a positive sign. But please heed my warning and take what I say seriously. This could easily go the other way, just like flipping a switch. Please don't read too much into to this."

"I'll hold back the cartwheels, but still, her face, she was just beaming in a way I'm not sure I have ever seen. She seemed so alive and emboldened, or something. I can't quite put my hand on it."

"Let's complete the series of tests and then we'll know more. Go back inside and enjoy the time with your wife, Wade. Time is precious."

Wade nodded. "Believe me; I'll not squander a single moment. Thank you for everything you have done, Kelly."

"I wish I could take credit for this, but this rides on Lou and where her mind is willing to allow her to go or remain. Please talk to Liz though, just in case, all right?"

"Will do, and I'll keep my fingers crossed about those tests."

Wade reentered the room. Lou was sitting up, more alert than he had seen her in weeks. She broke into a wide smile, her eyes sparkling, and she motioned him to sit by her side. Her eyes, there was something about her eyes that were different. He wasn't sure why but there was definitely something un-Lou-like, deep, almost piercing. Just his imagination, he finally convinced himself.

Leave him alone. Don't you hurt him, I warn you.

Harm him; I have no intent in harming him, my dear Lou; at least not for now. Your dear husband, our husband, will feel the pleasures a woman has to offer, erotica he never knew possible. Sit back and enjoy.

You sound or act nothing like me. Wade will not buy in

to your lustful ways.

Ah, but there is where you are wrong, my dear Lou. I, Emma am adapting to your language, your tone, your mannerisms and your demeanor. Soon, very soon we shall blend as one. You will become but an annoying whisper. He will enjoy the vigor of a vibrant twenty one year old Margarett Levine Reznik. He will be captivated by what I can offer and a slave to my every whim.

You forget. You have Alzheimer's. We have Alzheimer's. This won't last forever. Like me, you will forget things. You will die along with me. You've chosen yourself a death sentence. My body can neither support you long term or save you from an early grave.

I have been dead before, remember and for much too long. I will not squander this opportunity I assure you. After all, I'm cured; sadly you're not. It is simple as mind over matter in my case. Your mind, so what does it matter. I will become a medical marvel in your world.

I will not allow you to do this Margarett Reznik. I will find a way to defeat you. That's my promise.

You talk brass and bold for someone who just a few short hours ago roamed aimlessly, a mere shell of a woman, dying and hopelessly lost. Count your blessings. This way, with me, you live on. You too have a second chance. The difference, I lead us down the path I choose, not you. Out with old Lou and in with the new Emma; it is just a matter of time when those around us will be whispering, Lou, who?

You will never win, not as long as I live and breathe.

We live and breathe, must I constantly remind you. As for you, you are but a mere burning candle, flickering and melting, shedding no real light on what happens. Ah yes, you will feel what I feel, but you will control nothing. Sleep for now; I'll wake you if I need you.

"Lou, are you okay. You seemed dazed."

"It's Emma, remember, and I'm fine, my sweetness. I was merely pondering our future and second chances. It s not often one is snatched from the jaws of hell. I apologize for my drama, but if ever there was a cause for such behavior, I have earned the right to snub my nose at the grim reaper, don't you think, Hon? I have danced on my grave and have pissed on my marker."

Hon, thought Wade, what's with all this Hun stuff? Pissed on your marker, now that sounds nothing like Lou dialogue. Maybe the doctor was right. This is merely temporary. "It indeed calls for a celebration once you're released from the hospital. You name it and we'll do it."

"Choices at my demand, I simply love you for offering me this, my sweetness. I promise to make this worth your while. We shall bask in the bliss as one."

Choices, indeed, I have not felt a man's touch and thrusts in over one hundred years. I do intend to take full advantage of the warmth and wetness you, Wade, have to offer to fulfill the wishes of a wife you thought you had lost forever. Your gratification will be most appreciated. Once you have tasted what Margarett has in store for you between her spread wings, you shall forever forget sweet Lou and her pathetic existence. You'll beg for more from your loveliness, the lustful and satisfying Emma.

"Lou, I mean Emma, I have asked Liz to move in, occupy the guess bedroom for awhile; at least until we make sure we're out of the woods. Kelly, Doctor Kelly Garner has recommended this as a mere precaution."

Kelly, sounds like the doctor may have unethical bedside manners to me. Did you know your hubby might just be poking your doctor, Lou? He may have already tossed you out with the bath water. I'm sorry, in your mental state you could never have figured out that one, could you?

Wade would never cheat on me under any circumstances.

You're out of line with your accusations.

A man has his needs, but not to worry, I will have him falling back in our arms soon enough. Afterwards, we, I'll take care of the doctor bitch, not to worry. This Liz must go too. Not to fret little darling, no one will ever suspect you, I promise. I can't have her jeopardizing my future, flitting about, worrying with matters that concern you and your health. She'll not be wiping my ass, I assure you that.

You can't be serious. These women have done nothing to harm you, harm me. I forbid you to harm them.

You forbid, so laughable. Your say means absolutely nothing. You're a bird in a cage, chirping and entertaining, but that's about the jest of it. I suppose I should not be so abrupt; after all, you did free me from that dreaded cemetery. Fools, they thought they had destroyed me. Revenge is never held captive by a time piece or the passing calendar. It merely festers and oozes puss from an eternity of misery, until the infestation, plague if you will, can be inflicted on those responsible; and in this case, the ancestors of those who dared do this to me, will pay the ultimate price.

This is insane. You're insane.

Precisely and unfortunately, so are you, Lou. So are you. Now, goodbye.

"Yes, she shared your wishes, the doctor's wishes with me, earlier. I assure you I require no petting and watchful eyes, but if this soothes yours and the dear doctor's conscious, then who am I to argue. I'm sure the physician is just doing what is in my best interest, as are you my love. I will humor you for a short period, until I prove to both of you that I am no longer afflicted with this dreadful disease." **Unleash your little watchdog. I will send her yelping, tail tucked between her ham hock legs.**

"I certainly hope that is a fact. We must keep all hope alive."

"Hope, you sound just a bit cynical to me, Hon. Amazing healing powers exist at one's finger tips. Few ever reach deep enough to find them. Do you not believe in nisim, nes?"

"Believe in what," questioned Wade.

Slip of the tongue, she had spoken in Yiddish, the word miracle, and now she scrambled to rectify her error. The bitch had allowed her to make this mistake, fully aware of the word she should have chosen; she was certain of this fact. Two sharing the same mind was going to be more difficult than she had first anticipated. This Lou possessed a strong will. Apparently by pushing her to the back burner, it had also relieved her of the mind altering disease that had all but transformed her into a turnip. She posed a formidable adversary for the time being, but Margarett would deal with her soon enough.

"Sorry Hon, I'm not sure what gibberish is leaping from my tongue. Perhaps I still have minor hurtles to navigate yet. Not to worry; I am undergoing the complete healing process. Please humor me as I battle this affliction. I'm sure I will stumble on my path to regain control of my life."

Wade still had reservations about Lou and her present state. Possibly Kelly had been frank with him, because she knew this was far from being over. He had allowed his hopes to override the diagnosis, the reality that Alzheimer's is indeed an incurable disease. Maybe he had seen what he had wanted to see. No, he had to stay positive and upbeat; if not for him, for Lou. This was but one day in the battle, but had been one on the upswing. Build on it, and move forward, he attempted to convince himself. What other choice did he really have, unless he tossed in the towel? He wasn't ready to cry uncle just yet.

"I'm sure we have a ways to go to lick this. For now, you should probably rest. The doctor has those tests she would like to perform tomorrow, so you have a busy day ahead. I'll stay with you tonight if you'd like."

"You should go home and rest your weary head too. I could be more than a handful for you, once the good doctor admits she no longer has a patient."

"I could ask Liz to stay with you tonight."

"Please don't bother to inconvenient the nursemaid. She has done enough for one day. I am surrounded by medical persons. I'm sure nothing I could possibly do will go without the most deliberate scrutiny. I must say, I so despise being a bug under a magnifying glass. It makes me feel as if I'm some sort of dangerous prisoner." ***No way do I want this bohemian watching my every move.***

"They have your, our best interest at heart, Lou."

"Emma, remember; Lou is a thing of the past. I'm not one for all this coddling. I'm out of diapers now and I no longer require feeding like a wee baby. Soon as these damn tests are over, I'm homeward bound, husband."

Too worrisome, thought Wade; she's still not yet herself. I'll take this over the alternative, but the jury is still out until Kelly confirms her final state. Perhaps I have allowed my heart to overrule my head. Alzheimer's is too unpredictable to hang my hopes on this turn of events. Wade kissed Emma, his Lou, on the cheek and reluctantly exited.

How in hell's name have I managed to pick this lot? Stop your bitching, Margarett, you're above dirt now and free to wreak havoc on those responsible for this Kloolye. Curse, the word is curse.

12

Wade caught everyone up to speed on Lou's current status, as best anyone could determine. He informed them to please humor her and call her Emma. While he attempted to put a positive spin on the situation, he cautioned them to take it all with a grain of salt, until Doctor Garner completed her updated prognosis. Sitting alone at the kitchen bar, sipping on a cup of coffee, the chiming of the doorbell nudged Wade from his deep pondering. He glanced at his watch. It wasn't as late as it seemed, only half past eight. He opened the door and was greeted by the smiling face from their minister, Elijah Blaine.

The pastor was a portly soul, his head mounted on no neck upon rounded shoulders, no more than five foot, eight inches in stature. He had wavy, black, sheepish textured hair, almost like a close knit afro. His skin was glow in the dark pale, almost anemic in appearance. He wore a green plaid button up shirt with kaki corduroy pants. Blaine looked like the average Joe, nothing priestly stood out, even in his dialogue. That's what his flock loved about him. He was down to earth, easy to listen and talk to, a people's person for a man of the clothe.

"Wade, I do apologize for dropping by unannounced at this hour, but I had just heard about the latest development concerning Lou. Your dear sister-in-law, Anna, called and asked me to keep Lou and your family in my prayers."

"Please come in Elijah. We can certainly use all the

prayers you can conjure, that's for sure." Another thing the congregation adored about their pastor, he didn't follow the path of formalities, preferring to drop the pastor, preacher, and reverend titles. He was simply, Elijah. He always jested that being named after a biblical figure held enough merit without the clerical titles.

"These are indeed trying times for all. I'm here if you require a friendlily shoulder."

"Can I pour you a cup of coffee; it's decaf."

"Thanks, but this shrine of a body of mine doesn't function so well on java at this hour of the night, decaffeinated or high octane. I fear it would result in gaseous consequences and my Bessie wouldn't appreciate the trumpeting results tonight, not under the bed sheets," chuckled Elijah, his belly jiggling like that of old Saint Nick.

"Can I offer you anything else, then?"

"I'm fine. Tell me how are you coping with the current situation, Wade."

"Mixed emotions, I must confess. Lou, for all practical purposes, is more alert and in tune than she has been in quite some time. That being said, Doctor Garner has warmed me this could be just one of the up cycles and that I shouldn't become too hopeful."

"Heeding her advice sounds like the smart thing to do, given the circumstances and her expertise in the field, don't you think?"

"I suppose. I'm really trying to convince myself. It's just difficult to fathom how she can be so out of it and then spring back like this. I'm trying to ride the wave before it comes crashing down on me."

"There's absolutely nothing wrong with your thought pattern. I'd probably do the same if in your shoes."

"There's something else though. Lou isn't quite acting herself. I mean, I know that this disease can play havoc on ones' personality, but there's something else."

"Would you care to elaborate? Feel free to bounce anything off me, Wade."

"Maybe I'm just overreacting, but her personality, even some of her dialogue just doesn't seem genuine to me."

"From my experience, and I am no expert, it's not uncommon for persons with Alzheimer's to display opposite traits of their normal personality. When one of our church members, the elder Mrs. Vickers, suffered from this last year, rest her soul, she cursed me for everything I was worth during one of my visits and tossed a bowl of soup at me. I had known her for nearly twenty years and had never heard a harsh word come from her mouth, and never ever any profanity. Don't let this sort of thing get to you. It isn't who Lou really is, I assure you."

"I've seen those outbursts but that's not exactly it. She used the word, nisim, nes. I've never heard of such a word before, have you?"

Elijah smiled and nodded. "It means miracle. I have a few Jewish friends in the community, so I've picked up a little Yiddish here and there. Perhaps she has come in contact with Yiddish words or terms in her teachings. Sometimes these can be buried in our subconscious. I wouldn't be over concerned."

"I guess that makes some sense. Thanks for helping me work through it."

"I understand she could be home as early as tomorrow."

"If the doctor is satisfied with her tests results, she could be released, yes."

"Mind if I drop by if she is?"

"I'll phone you when I know for sure."

"Text or tweet me. It's much quicker. You do text and tweet, don't you?"

"Text, yes, I'm not into that tweeting stuff."

"I find it necessary to maintain proper contact with the younger flock. They can run but they cannot hide, not with the phone or IPOD or any other countless contraptions welded to their hands. One has to be quite versatile to spread the gospel these days."

"You're quite innovative, Elijah."

"Don't let these old bones fool you. I'm a geek at heart."

"I'm impressed."

"Shall we have a quick prayer before I leave?"

"Certainly," smiled Wade.

After Elijah had departed, Wade tried to unwind, but his brain was still too wired, even with the decaffeinated coffee. Emma, aka Lou, might be released tomorrow if Kelly was satisfied with the test results. Liz was scheduled to be here by late afternoon. He needed to ready the guest bedroom for her. Wade's mind was spinning with possibilities. Would Lou be Lou or Emma or someone else with no memory of any of this, of him, of their life?

Emma lay wide awake in her hospital bed, Margarett plotting her next move. Mimicking a chess master, she calculated several moves ahead, planned on worst case scenarios, unexpected turns in events and how to rid herself of the extra baggage, those standing in her way; the nurse maid, the doctor, and possibly Wade, to mention a few. She pushed hard to keep Lou in the recesses of her mind. The host was persistent though, relentless in her quest to regain control of her former self. Fortunately she was weak; at least much weaker than Margarett.

First things first, thwart the doctor tomorrow and her asinine tests. She wasn't a loony like Lou, so this should be a piece of cake. She knew nothing of what this doctor had in store for her but as long as she remained calm and collective, pulled from Lou's memory when needed, she should be able to come out on top. The unknowns did concern her. The hospital and all these fancy machines were not familiar. She had been in that ground way too long. The world had zoomed past her. While exciting, it did put her at a disadvantage and on shaky ground. She would adapt and survive.

Not if I can help it.

Ah the little princess is awake once again. You're all piss and vinegar, aren't you?

You should be very afraid. Those tests tomorrow will expose you for what you are, not me by a long shot. You're not prepared for today's technological advances. This is no longer a world of potions and leeches.

Listen to you spouting off about my world like I'm from some midlevel time period. You'll be babbling about witches brew with eye of newt and hocus pocus horse manure next.

You are evil. Whoever cursed and laid you to rest in the old graveyard did it for a reason. You were dangerous and a threat to someone. You were never meant to be again.

You left out all so powerful and mighty, my dear Lou. You can't keep a bad girl down. But you are correct, they did have reason to fear me, and still do, or at least their offspring will soon feel my wrath, in the most humble revengeful way, of course. You, with your worldly resources will help me locate them and will watch while I delver their punishment. I'm all giddy just thinking about it.

That's where you are wrong. I'll never assist you and your insane revenge. Prepare for the battle of your life.

Our lives, you mean. You forget we are one in the same, bosom buddies, a duet, all for one and one for all. What I do, so do you, Lou. You're in the catbird's seat, able to watch the scene unfold before your very eyes. I'm the playwright and you're a mere performer, acting out the part as I so direct you to do. This is simply marvelous, don't you agree?

Kiss my ass.

Kiss our ass, you mean, don't you? Be nice. I can easily dismiss you. You are but a necessary evil until I

work through these difficulties.

And you are but pure evil and I want easily be taken for granted. You brought the fight to me. This vessel you're occupying belongs to Emma Lou Stetson and don't you forget it. I will expose you for who you are, even if it jeopardizes my existence.

I'm shaking in your boots, Emma Lou Stetson. How many times do I have to remind you; I rescued you from a life as a soon to be vegetable?

You don't know the half of it. What I have has no cure. If I die, so do you. You're not as wise as you give yourself credit. You picked the wrong gal to possess or occupy or whatever it is you're doing inside me.

And you are naïve, Hon. My powers have purged your illness. I am as healthy as a horse. You should thank your lucky stars you will have time with your beloved Wade; at least until I grow tired of him and move onto the many lovers that await my arrival. Your body will serve my purposes well until I have the means to occupy, as you call it, a younger vessel. Oh yes, there are ways for me to leapt frog out of here in due time.

I think you're just bluffing. You're trapped and you know it. I will be your undoing. I'm quite resourceful when I put my mind to it.

There are two of us, remember. Survival of the fittest, and you're the prey and I am the predator. Soon my dear, Lou, I will show you what I am capable of, and then you will be a broken woman. I don't see you as one who has a stomach for where I will take us. Once I set my plans in motion, you will gladly cower in the background, close your eyes to the despicable things the new Lou is capable of perpetrating. Emma is going to thoroughly relish putting you in your proper place. The nursemaid will be the first on our list; that is unless someone else dares screw up my agenda. Ta-ta, sleepy town awaits you, sleeping beauty.

13

Doctor Kelly Garner arrived early at the hospital, ready to tackle this most puzzling case. She didn't believe for a second that Lou Stetson had licked Alzheimer's. It was a medical impossibility. There had never been a recorded case where this disease had gone into remission. The disease progressed at different rates in individuals, but ultimately it ended in death. It was the cruelest of cruel debilitating diseases. Lou was much younger than most who had succumbed to it. For that she felt so sorry for Lou and her family. Typically Kelly allowed the technicians and nurses to perform the necessary test and then she would review the results. For some reason she felt compelled to be hands on throughout this case. Intuition alerted her that this was too much out of the ordinary to ignore.

There was just something different. She couldn't quite put her finger on it, but undeniably it existed. Kelly, Mary Tyler Moore in appearance, was in her mid thirties and at the top of her game, an expert in her field without question. Single, she had thrown herself in her practice, too dedicated and consumed by her patients to consider a serious relationship. She had set out to make a mark in the world and hadn't quite made a dent yet, not by her standards. This case could be her defining moment, if her suspicions panned out.

Emma Lou Stetson was fit as a fiddle on the surface, but then again, many Alzheimer's patients were physically fit in the beginning. The disease took its toll on the body in the latter stages, saving the worst for last. Kelly was more interested in the mental status tests, the neurological exam and brain imaging results. It was her professional opinion that this was where the rubber met the road. Her files and personal research papers supported this premise. Wade should be here any minute. She had informed him that she preferred discussing what lay ahead with him first before administering the tests to Lou. Her heart ached for the primary caregiver in these situations. They were truly the unsung heroes. As if on cue, a knock at her office alerted her that he had arrived.

"Good morning, Wade. Please have a seat."

"Have you checked in on her this morning, Kelly?"

"I thought we might do that together. Familiar faces can have a calming effect."

"You're assuming if she knows who I am."

"Today is a new beginning, so please don't become too disheartened if she has experienced a relapse. How are you this morning? Did you sleep?"

"Not much, but I feel okay. Is this going to be any different that the first time you tested her?"

"No, not really, but this time we have a benchmark, how she tested the first time. This will allow me to assess her progression or, hopefully, the de-acceleration of the disease."

Wade nodded, sighed and then rubbed his eyes with his fingers. "What's first?"

"I'll perform a physical exam to help me determine her neurological health. It's pretty routine, reflexes, muscle tone and strength, Lou's ability to get up from a chair and walk across the room, her sense of sight and hearing. I'll verify her coordination and balance. We've already drawn blood. I expect those lab tests back this morning. It can rule out thyroid disorders or vitamin deficiencies. She tested negative the first time."

"She didn't do so well on some of these other tests the first time, if memory serves me well."

"Yes, there were some compelling signs, especially in her coordination and balance. I'll spend maybe ten minutes or so conducting a brief mental status test. We'll verify how the think tank is working. I'll see how this goes before deciding my next course of actions. Most likely I will conduct a more extensive assessment. This could take a couple of hours. If you remember, this dives deeply into her ability to safely manage important activities, like financial or medical decision making. I'll pose various scenarios to determine her problem solving skills."

"She flunked here royally too last time, didn't she?"

"She struggled a bit, yes. We'll wrap it up with the more technical stuff, brain imaging. This will include computerized tomography, magnetic resonance imaging and positron emission tomography. Sorry, these are better known for their acronyms, CT, MRI and PET. We'll be looking again for such things as strokes, trauma and tumors. These were also negative the first time. The MRI will provide us with brain images. Specifically we'll be looking for any signs of shrinkage in brain tissue or volume. Of course the last one, PET, is where Lou will be injected with low-level radioactive tracer and it will provide us with a dimensional image of her functional bodily processes. This one is often the toughest, keeping the patient still."

"You're just looking for changes since last time then. What if she tests better, what does that tell you?"

"You mean will that convince me she is cured? I do wish the best for her and you, but medically speaking, this just doesn't go away. It doesn't work like that. Alzheimer's is not a curable disease. I apologize for being so frank, but this is simple fact. My intent is not to diminish your hopes, Wade, but my understanding of this simply will not allow me to paint a rosy outcome for you. If she is indeed in one of those peaks, just enjoy your time with her."

"She's just too young to go out this way. We were supposed to have much longer with one another. She's not even a grandmother yet."

Kelly gave Wade a business card. "Hold on to this. It's the name and number of a caregiver support group. You're not in this alone. Sometimes talking to others can work wonders. Let's go check in on Lou now."

"Emma, she has this obsession with being called Emma. It's her belief in second chances, a new life, so we should humor her, if you don't mind?"

"Absolutely, Emma it is."

It's morning already. Where is God's gift to medicine; the husband stalker, the NAFKA? That means whore by the way in Yiddish. Lou, old girl, for all we know, she was sacked up with you hubby last night. They've probably been plotting how they will reserve a padded room for you. Not to fret, Hon, I'm here to make sure that doesn't happen. I will razzle-dazzle the doctor bitch and have her screaming uncle before she knows what hit her. There's no place like home, right?

You give yourself too much credit for being sly as a fox. These tests will foil your plans. This isn't the 1800's. Technology is too advanced. You will not be able to bluff your way through them. You're not me. The truth will set me free.

Ouch, AY-YAY-YAY, so hurtful; it almost sounded like you were ready to cast me aside. Would you rather they give up all hope and us stay in this godforsaken prison chamber? I don't know about you gal, but time is wasting. I have so much to do, and I can't be slowed by this crazy sickness horse manure. Keep your thoughts to yourself and let me answer for both of us and we'll do just fine. Now, it's sleepy time for you. I'll wake you up if I need you. Until then, mum's the word, FERSHTAY?

A tap on the door indicated her rival had arrived. "DRECK," exclaimed Emma-Margarett, shit in Yiddish.

"Pardon me," asked Kelly.

"A dearly fare do well to you this morning, doctor," greeted Emma-Margarett.

"Good morning. How are you feeling, Emma?"

"Come greet me properly, my husband. I'm sure the doctor will not be insulted by your bedside manner."

Kelly smiled and stepped out of the way. Wade approached her bedside and bent over to kiss her, and again his wife oddly and out of character put him in an aggressive lip lock. His face reddened in Kelly's presence. This did not go unnoticed by his wife.

"Wade, there's nothing to be embarrassed about, now is there? I wouldn't advise the madam doctor to follow us home though; there it might be a different story." She winked to make her point.

She's quite promiscuous, thought Kelly, scrutinizing Emma Lou Stetson's morning behavior. Wade's reaction alerted her that this behavior also bewildered him. Obviously this was out of the normal, an indication that the disease was still having its way with her personality. Kelly was itching to get started, but would allow the two a brief visit before commencing with the tests. Interaction with people could often assist in the diagnosis process.

"I bet you're chomping at the bits to poke and prod me, aren't you?" She smiled, patting Wade on the hand, and then turned to the doctor and said, "Guess you are too, aren't you, Doc?"

Kelly noted the sarcastic wit as odd. Most Alzheimer's patients are in denial, withdrawn and bitter about being questioned or tested. They typically refuse to acknowledge they have a problem. Most hide it as long as possible, covering up their mistakes, avoiding certain conversations. Lou was not following the yellow brick road. She seemed too easily accepting her surroundings, her predicament and her precarious circumstances. She seemed too sure of herself, almost defiant, a challenger, and ready to engage in combat.

Something told Kelly this wasn't going to travel the same path as the first round of tests. She wasn't sure if this was a good thing or a bad. Either way, she was positive it was going to be anything but boring. Lou had fire in her eyes and an air of arrogance swirled in the air. Kelly had never witnessed a patient on the brink of collapse to spring back in this manner. Lou was going to make an intriguing case study, no doubt. Funny, she had never thought of any of her patients as cases, not until now. Kelly sensed a defining moment lay ahead. In reality, she had no clue what atrocities the one known as Margarett had in store for her and those not of her world. It would indeed be a case for the books, but only if documented for posterity. The jury was out as to whether this would ever see the light of day for colleagues to ponder.

"I'll step out for a couple of minutes and give you two some privacy."

I'm sure you've already had your hands all over his SHVANTZ, haven't you, you damn NAFKA. I can tell he's a worthless MOMZER too; a bastard for bonking you, while his BALABUSTA lays her like a helpless SHLEMIEL.

"Thank you, Kelly," replied Wade.

Kelly, oh Kelly, you're more than just a doctor aren't you? I bet you'd rather be examining him instead of me, wouldn't you. GAY A VEK. Get the hell out of here, I say.

"Wade, I just wish to return home with you. There's absolutely nothing wrong with me. I'm not crazy. I'm not sick. I'm as healthy as a plow mule furrowing the back forty. This doctor is on a mission to undermine our happiness. She makes her fortune by taking advantage of people she thinks she can control and ruin for her own profit. I will not be one of those mindless sheep, I promise you that."

"No, you have this all wrong. Kelly has only your, our best interest in mind. She is an expert on these matters and nothing would make her happier than to see you completely cured."

"How is it that you and she are on this cozy little first name basis? In my day, a doctor was always addressed as the doctor."

A wonderful slip of the tongue, Margarett, and don't think Wade didn't take notice.

"Lou," started Wade.

"Emma," corrected Margarett.

"Emma, I know doctors are not your thing, but Kelly is just one who strives to be more personable in these manners. She removes the doctor-patient formalities. I for one appreciate this. She's truly sincere and genuine in her convictions. In time I believe you will appreciate her for this."

"In time, we will no longer require her services. Let's just get this over with so we can live our lives normally. I'm ready to kick up my heels and smell the flowers. I know, that sounds silly and over the top, but I feel as if I have been suffocated for way too long." *And I have, in that godforsaken hole in the ground, put there in the prime of my life by those who feared me and proceeded in taking my life. They had the gall to place that miserable curse on the once hallowed ground, clearly having no idea the full extent of my powers. Revenge has been a long time in the making, but vengeance will be mine, and that is a promise.*

"I'm trying to remain optimistic, Emma. Do you fully understand what you have been battling?"

"Some sort of old age sickness, but as you can see, I'm not old and I certainly don't feel ill. It is a mere misunderstanding. Perhaps the lady doctor is better suited to peddle snake oil to those who know no better. She is no better than a GONIF."

"A what," retorted Wade

"Sorry, I heard that word somewhere. It means a tricky, clever person; one of those shady kind of scoundrels."

"I assure you, you have her pegged wrong. She is not like that at all."

She's probably pegged you a time or too, hasn't she, the little angel. You're a LUFTMENSH, my poor excuse for a husband, with your head in the clouds. Or maybe up your ass. "Suit yourself. The days ahead will prove her otherwise. I'll not flaunt *I told you so* in your face, but you will remember this conversation and you will thank me for my ability to see through her crap and greedy little hands."

Kelly stepped back into the room. "We should get started."

"Yes we should, the sooner, the better," replied Margarett.

"I will phone you when we have completed the battery of tests, Wade."

I bet you can hardly wait for your next little opportunity for a little rendezvous.

"Okay, Emma, shall we get started?"

"So we shall," mocked Margarett.

Kelly verified her reflexes, assessed her muscle tone and strength. She identified no issues or concerns. She now asked Emma to have a seat in one of the straight back visitor's chairs. Margarett did it without protest. Kelly asked her to stand and take a step to her right. Margarett rolled Emma's eyes and completed the task, commenting about the absurdity of this silliness.

"Have I passed your KLUTZ test?'

"This is not intended to be an insult. It is merely standard testing technique."

"Standard to peg me as FERDRAYT, you mean."

"I don't understand that term, Emma. Where did you learn it?"

"It's nothing. You wish me to fail these tests, appearing confused about such simple doings. I assure you, chairs pose me no problems." ***Stifle the Yiddish, Margarett. Lou is not Jewish.***

"Indeed, I agree. Your coordination and balance are excellent. This is much improved from the first time."

"Should I stand on one foot with my eyes close, now, or would you like me to juggle for you, if that fancies you better?"

"Let's move on to your memory. I'll pose various hypothetical scenarios and will ask you a series of related questions. Please answer them honestly."

"Did you think I would answer them dishonestly?"

"I was not implying you would deliberately alter the results, Emma. I was merely stating the tests as factual as I could."

"Okay, so let's play your pretend game. Where am I and what am I doing?"

"Wade had previously disclosed that you were the gate keeper for managing the monthly bills. He has recently assumed these duties with your declining health. First of all, do you remember performing these tasks?"

Wake up Lou. You have permission to jump in here. Keep in mind, your failure to cooperate will only jeopardize your future. I think this doctor would jump at a chance to straight jacket you and keep you away from her lover, Wade. How do you, we take care of these monthly bills?

Lou remained silent.

"Take your time, Emma. We have no time restraints on the response. I know you have been away from these responsibilities for a while so it is understandable that you may need extra time to focus."

Lou, failure to bail me out here will have dreadful

consequences, I warn you. You stand to lose as much as me, sweetheart. Don't make us look like the court jester fool. That will only play into her hands. Lou, you're starting to piss me off.

Lou's subconscious remained quiet. She had no intentions of making this easy, even if it cost her dearly. Her objective, render this parasite useless. She would not allow this invader to ruin the lives of others dear to her, or implement her spiteful revenge on strangers. Her body would not be used as a vessel to deliver these horrific plans.

It was now apparent that the little bitch was not going to cooperate with Margarett. She would have to wing an answer, unfamiliar with the types of monthly bills due, nor the payment method. She cautiously weighed her response and decided to keep her response simple.

"I pay the debts as they are received. I am quite good at it. No collectors knock at our door. We are in good standing with all of them."

"What method to you use for your transactions?"

"Method, method, I pay what we owe and they are happy."

"Do you pay by check, on site or by mail, or do you prefer handling these on line?" Kelley could read the panic in her eyes. Alzheimer's patients attempt to conceal what they can no longer do or understand. Emma was displaying this trait.

"What difference does it make as long as I pay what is due? I pay by check. I go to their place of work and pay them directly. That's how I do it, face to face. I look them in the eye to let them know I am not a moocher, nor is my husband."

"Okay, very well; I have one of my checks on my clipboard. Here is my pen. Let's say you owe me one hundred thirty seven dollars and forty nine cents for the tests I just performed. Please issue the check to me in that amount."

"That's ludicrous. You would be making payment to yourself."

"Let's pretend it is your check and you're paying me. Ignore my name and address at the top. Complete it to me in that amount, one hundred thirty seven dollars and forty one cent. I'm not trying to trick you, Emma. I'm just giving you the opportunity to demonstrate what have just told me."

Margarett stared at the rectangular piece of paper. She had never seen a so called check before. She could read the inscriptions adjacent to the blank lines. One said date. She had no clue of the actual date. Another stated *Pay to the Order of*. Still another had a dollar sign. Two others stated Memo, Dollars and then a blank line with nothing beside it. How could she ever pull this off without Lou's help?

She held the pen above the check, hovering, unsure what she should do. Finally she asked, "Today's date is what?"

Kelly replied, providing her with the day and month. Margarett recorded this in the space.

Pay to the Order of, she guessed at this one. "Should I list your name or your service?"

"My name will be fine, Doctor Kelly Garner."

Next to the dollar sign she scribbled 137.41 and she repeated the exact same thing next to Dollars. What to do with the last blank? Of course, no check is valid unless it is signed. She almost signed her given name, starting an M, but quickly altered it to an E, then completed Emma Stetson, like the western hat. She handed the check back to Kelly.

Other than a couple of miscues, excluding the year and not writing out *one hundred thirty seven and 41/100*, she had completed the other requirements. This still signaled all was not well with Emma.

"How did I do?"

"Very close to perfect," replied Kelly, not divulging her suspicions.

Kelly next gave Emma an assortment of coins and cash, the correct combinations for her to make change for a twenty dollar bill. "Let's say I just purchased that drink mug from your side table for the amount of six dollars and sixty three cents. I only have a twenty, so you will have to make change for me from the extra money I have given you. Pay me what I should receive back."

The assortment of coins was unfamiliar. The bills were clearly marked, One, Five and Ten. Margarett used the pen to write 20.00 on her hand and then 6.63. She completed the subtraction and came up with the figure 13.37. She withdrew two five dollar bills and three one dollar bills. Now came the hard part; decipher the remaining thirty seven cents from the coins in the palm of her hand. She had no idea how to make this work.

"I'll just give you fourteen dollars. There is need to squabble over the extra money."

"That's okay, Emma. You demonstrated to me that you could perform the math and derive the correct answer. I commend you for that."

Margarett flung the coins across the room and shouted, "This is FERCOCKT."

"Why Lou Stetson, I've never heard such language from you." Elijah Blaine stood in the doorway, a black Fedora in his hand. "Pardon my intrusion, Doctor, I was in the neighborhood and thought I would drop by and check on a member of my flock."

"Quiet all right, reverend; tell me what did she just say that so offended you?"

"Yiddish slang," Elijah replied. "How should I put this in mixed company; she implied that whatever had transpired, was let us say, was screwed up, is a milder interpretation. I am still puzzled where you became so affluent in Jewish dialogue, my dear Lou. I don't remember any of your family being descendents and there are few Jewish in our community."

"I might pose the same question to you; how do you come to speak Yiddish?"

"Ah yes. I have had this conversation with Wade. I know a rabbi. He is a close acquaintance of mine. We twitter one another. He often tweets me in his native tongue, so I picked it up by necessity. You still have not explained your indoctrination to the language."

"We are in the middle of tests. The doctor is trying to find out if the madness has been purged from my loins."

"I do again apologize for barging in. How are these tests progressing, if you don't mind an old preacher prying?"

"No offense, I'm not at liberty to say, patient-doctor confidentiality, you understand."

"No offence taken, I assure you. Lou, how are you feeling?"

"Call me Emma. Lou was the sick one. I'm the liberated version. I'm fine as a pig wallowing in the mud. The doctor here doesn't think so. She wants me to remain sick and under her care. I suppose she has her reasons for wishing this upon me."

"Emma, I have only your best interest in mind, I assure you. There is nothing to gain by me for you being diagnosed with any illness. I wish nothing but the best for you and Wade. You are entrusted in my care and I will conduct myself professionally where your health is concerned."

"Believe her, my dear. She is sincere. We all wish nothing except for you to be well."

Get her out of me, people. Can't you see; she's not me? This has nothing to do with the symptoms of Alzheimer's. She's trying to take over my body, my mind, my very soul. Help me be rid of her, please.

Now you rear your ugly head, but unfortunately on deaf ears. I control your tongue. They cannot hear you, unless I will you to speak for us. I don't think that would be very wise, given your irritated state, do you?

"Reverend, she is not walking the righteous path you describe. She has motives."

"Now Lou, since when have you called old Elijah, Reverend?"

"Not Lou, names' Emma. I know…he's a preacher. You people are all working against me, aren't you?"

"Please play along with her," whispered Kelly.

"Emma Lou, I'll be on my way, but you need to stop fighting the folks that are here to help you. Let's bow our heads and have prayer."

"Hell no, they'll be no praying here. I forbid it. Clergymen have done enough. Be gone. Leave me alone."

Well done, turn on Elijah; you're doing better than I could have ever hoped. You're not me and that's a fact. I guess I haven't been me in a while, so you're just building their case for them. They'll never trust you now. You're a broken person, like me.

Shut your pie hole, bitch. This is far from over. Sleeping lions are the most dangerous.

"Sorry Reverend Blaine, please don't hold this against her."

"Please call me Elijah. Not to worry child, I'll say a little prayer for her just the same after I leave. I'll toss one in for you too."

Kelly stepped into the hallway. "It's the disease ruling her thoughts. I fear she has tough days ahead, as do Wade and Liz Donley, who will be assisting him with her care. I am perplexed though about this Yiddish gibberish that she has been speaking. This is most odd. "

"Doesn't Alzheimer's impact a person's personality? They do and say some of the oddest things, uncharacteristic to their normal way. At least that is what I have experienced with church members who have contracted it."

"Yes, that is correct, but speaking in other languages is typically not prevalent, unless that person is bilingual. The mind cannot conger up what is not there. She has no history of Judaism in her family. Yiddish is not something that just roles off the tongue of an amateur. Perhaps she was exposed to it in her teachings, but she tends to be more averse to using slang terms, often vulgar and malicious in context. Why would she only be exposed to offensive phrases and words?"

"The Lord and his adversary work in mysterious ways, Kelly. Lucifer often plays his role in these matters, just to shake the apple tree. I'm sure you will get to the bottom of it in due time. If you see Wade before I do, please give him my best."

"I will see him after I complete my examination of Lou, I mean Emma" she smiled. "Just speaking out loud, Elijah, but that is odd too, that she prefers to be called Emma instead of Lou. I've researched case studies and this is ground breaking. While it is not uncommon for patients to be confused by those around them, forgetting their names or mistaking them for others, they just don't request to be called by a new name, even if that name is part of theirs. I'm treading on virgin territory, Elijah, and trying to keep an open mind."

"You'll do just fine, my dear. I can think of no one better to solve these mysteries."

"Take care and thanks for lending a shoulder."

"Open invitation, these old shoulders can carry a heavy load. Tweet me or text me; I'm always on call and a mere key stroke away."

"You have a firm hold on the technological world so I see."

"One cannot rely on delivering the message from the

bully pulpit only. Modern advances have paved the way for us to reach a far larger audience. I'm sneaky creative, my dear. They never see it coming until it's too late."

Kelly watched Elijah vigorously striding down the hallway, pep in his step beyond his years, until he disappeared around the corner. She hovered outside Lou's room, preparing for new scenarios pertaining to medical issues this time. Based on Lou's belligerent tone, this could be quite combative. Denial, suggestive of the disease, she was moving closer to her suspected conclusion, at least from this phase of the testing. The MRI, CT and PET would shed additional light, as would the blood tests. Kelly's experience told her Alzheimer's was still in play and remission a medical impossibility. She held firm to this diagnosis unless evidence convinced her otherwise.

14

Wade, assisted by Wyatt and Anna settled Lou into her home environment, having been released from the hospital, all tests completed. He watched Lou intently as she moved from room to room touching various objects. For the first few minutes she remained quiet, almost too quiet. Her motor skills seemed excellent, no stumbling or staggering, or even the shuffled walk he had observed during some of her more difficult days, before her complete collapse, when she had become incoherent.

Kelly had not completed her evaluation but had seen no reason to confine her to the hospital. Physically she appeared extremely fit. Mentally she was alert and not delusional. Her verbal assaults had continued as suspected, again not uncommon. Wade had been there before so he should be able to handle anything short term; even better so with Liz there to assist and offer him relief from any strenuous caregiver duties that might develop. Wade's brother and sister-in-law seemed more than eager to support him and Lou. Kelly would focus on the results of the tests and research the anomalies that plagued her about this case. She stood by her convictions; remission or a cure was not possible.

Kramer sat at the far end of the den watching Lou's every move. Even though the pooch had been responsible for leading everyone to her in that graveyard, Kramer still didn't trust her, not after the pound stay. Who says dogs can't hold a grudge? Kramer sensed something not quite right about her. The dog possessed keen senses. He didn't sense this woman was really his co-master. She looked the part, but somehow she wasn't. He avoided her like the plague, not that she really paid him much attention. Anytime she approached him, he quickly scampered off in another direction, emitting a cross between a whine and high pitched growl.

Honey avoided Lou also. She would bristle up and hiss if Lou managed to corner her unintentionally. Lou showed no affection for the cat of the house either. Wade had noticed these peculiarities. He shrugged it off as animals can sense when things are not quite right, figuring they could detect she was far from being well. Lou had completely her tour of the premises, full circle. She now stood in the kitchen, hands on her hips.

"What does it take for a girl to get a little grub around here? I thought the nursemaid was supposed to be at my beck and call, caring to my needs. Hell's bells, I'm hungry. You would think she would be leaping at a chance to take my order, keep me happy as a morning lark, now wouldn't you?"

"What would you like? I'll fix it for you," replied Anna.

"Let's see; since my arrival home it calls for a special occasion, what about something meaty, like a mutton chop, maybe some garlic potatoes and a healthy heaping of baked lima beans and roasted red peppers with anchovies, freshly baked loaf bread, sound good for starters. What do you think? Can you manage that, Sugar?"

Wade exchanged glances with his sister-in-law. Lou had never been much of a meat lover, and he couldn't ever remember her having a desire for lamb. Anchovies, she would never eat anchovies. While the vegetables would be no big deal; fresh bread might be a stretch. The local grocery store did have somewhat of a bakery and deli. Wyatt volunteered to do the bread run and while there, purchase lamb chops. Anna nodded, checking the can goods and freezer for the other items. The cupboard was mostly bare. She penciled in peppers and anchovies on Wyatt's grocery list. She did find a bag of dried butter beans she would substitute for the limas and instant potatoes and minced garlic.

"How long will this take? I'm famished."

"I could make you a lettuce and tomato sandwich to hold you," replied Wade, knowing how Lou loved tomatoes.

"Keep that for yourself. Do you have any corn beef or pastrami, maybe a little goat cheese?"

You've got to be kidding. You're not putting that stuff in me. Never mind, you're playing your hand just fine. Wade knows me like a book and how peculiar I am about certain things.

"On second thought, Sugar, that tomato sandwich sounds quite scrumptious. Could you add a slice of onion and whatever cheese you might have?" **Thanks for that little handy dandy tip, Lou, old girl. See, we can work as one. Now, go night-night until I need you, Yenta.**

Margarett contemplated her next move, assessing her surroundings and these people who were stifling her progress. Didn't they get it; she wasn't ill and didn't require them suffocating her with their existence. Give me some breathing room she wanted to scream at the top of her lungs. Just what she needed, the nurse bohemian now graced her presence. She's glaring at me; what now?

"Lou, while your husband prepares your meal, possibly I could assist you in a bath?"

"Emma, the name's Emma. Drop the Lou crap. I've liberated her from her dark existence. I'm perfectly capable of washing myself, but you can draw my bath if that fancies you. May as well earn your keep, right?"

Liz just smiled, offered no rebuttal, accustomed to going along with her patient's wishes, aware that any confrontations were counterproductive to their well being. She whisked past Lou and disappeared down the hallway. Liz had witnessed the frequent shifts in moods and physical capability swings in her patients before, but this turn of events in Lou had been most unexpected. Lou had shown all the signs of one plummeting into a pit, rarely any ever returned; at least not to the degree of clarity, awareness and physical fortitude as she had displayed thus far. While happy with the turnaround, she remained leery of the long term ramifications.

After preparing Lou's bath, she returned to escort her to the bathroom. Lou immediately rejected her offer to assist her with disrobing and bathing. Again, this was not uncommon; especially when patients were still clinging to some thread of dignity. Lou closed the door, Liz hearing the click of the lock. Allowing a patient to lock themselves in a room was considered taboo from the caregiver's standpoint. It had happened so fast, Liz had not had the opportunity to intervene. She could only hope that Lou could negotiate the lock and exit when finished. More importantly, she hoped Lou wouldn't fall or scald herself.

Liz took a deep breath knowing she had failed miserably in one of the cardinal rules. She waited outside, listening for any signs of distress. Instead, she could hear Lou humming inside and splashing about. She didn't recognize the tune, but to her, it sounded like some sort of odd lullaby. After a few minutes, the bathroom became deathly silent. Liz tapped on the door and whispered, inquiring if Lou was all right. No answer, she knocked again, this time jiggling the doorknob and asking louder.

The door suddenly swung inward. Lou stood there

naked, hands on her hips, and head cocked to one side. "Are you getting your eyes full, Lizzy? Did it not cross your mind to give me clean clothes or does that cost us extra for those services?"

Liz had been so preoccupied by the locked door and her concern for Lou; she had indeed failed in retrieving the change of clothing. "Please wrap yourself in a towel and follow me. You may pick what you would like to wear from your wardrobe."

"So kind of you to allow me to pick from my own things," *you 'tuches lecker', ass kisser*, said Margarett, traipsing off behind Liz, unconcerned about her temporary nudity.

Perusing through her undergarment drawer, Margarett turned up her nose to most of the selection at hand. These too much resembled a prudish old woman's clothes, none sexy enough for her liking. She finally opted for the lesser of the evils, a black panty and bra, probably for some sort of special occasion, given the remainder of the selection. Liz attempted to push her towards what she called jogging sweats. SHMATTA, these would never do, thought Margaret, viewing the clothing as unfashionable rags. She instead chose white jeans and red lacy sleeveless top. Liz tried to talk her out of the selection, but this only made Margarett more determined to wear them.

She stood in front of a full length mirror and admired the results. "BEI MIR BIST DU SHAYN," she whispered, translated 'to me you're beautiful.'

They returned to the kitchen where Margarett spun around and paraded provocatively in front of Wade, enough so to redden his face. Anna even blushed at the antics but admired Lou for expressing some bravado, even under these circumstances. Lou sat at the bar and starred at her doctored up tomato sandwich, mustering up the courage to eat taste it. She had always despised tomatoes, a staple in Jewish cuisine.

Gobble it down, you worthless bitch. I'm hungry.

FERCOCKT!

It might be screwed, but you made this bed, lye in it, Maggie.

Margarett managed the first bite and blurted out, "CHAZEREI!" *This is garbage.*

Liz, Anna and Wade exchanged looks, not following Lou's gibberish. Margarett bit her tongue, finding it more difficult than she had realized to refrain from spouting off in Yiddish terms. Hopefully these imbeciles would just think she was having some setbacks to the illness. There was no possible way they could guess she was Lou and she wasn't. She needed to rid herself of them as soon as possible. She struggled with being a twenty one year old trapped in the body of someone twice her age. Luck of the draw, but at least she was free and walking back among the living.

Those who did this to her would pay dearly, or at least their offspring, if they existed, would feel her wrath. She had yet to test her powers in this new skin, but soon, very soon, she would find an opportunity to unleash an eternity of fury on an unsuspecting guinea pig. The ass kisser, the nurse, could provide the perfect vessel for unleashing hell on this earth. So far she had experienced very little of her new surroundings, having been confined to the hospital and now this place.

The horseless machines were unbelievable in this new world. She was in awe of their power and swiftness. Life had certainly bypassed her while she had remained prisoner of the curse. She had much lost time to make up for; her mind running rampant with the endless possibilities. Margarett choked down another bite of this gosh awful tomato and bread concoction, smiling to those watching her like hungry hawks. In time, she would learn the game; draw the necessary knowledge from Emma Lou Stetson, to mimic a person of this century. She was growing stronger while Lou was growing weaker. Soon, very soon, Lou would not be able to resist her demands, and then eventually, she would simply be no more.

"I really don't need all of your fussing over me. I am fine, really. I'm practically my old self, better than ever, actually. This sickness, the Alzheimer's is gone. I'm cured. The good doctor would consider me a medical marvel. I'd just like a little time without you hovering about. It's quite suffocating, I must say. This is almost as bad as being in that room in the clinic."

She called the hospital a clinic, how odd, thought Wade. And to think she has been cured of Alzheimer's; this is not a common cold we're fighting. I'm witnessing that miracle; one can only hope. "Wyatt, Anna, thank you for what you've done. Perhaps we should allow Lou to rest a bit."

Margarett almost snapped, call me Emma, but stifled it, thinking, the sooner they departed the better; why stir the pot right now? There would be plenty of time for that later, when they least expected her being responsible. Now was the time to get the lay of the land, milk old Lou's brain for information that would meet her needs. She might even work in a little play time with her husband. After all, it had been a long time since she had been poked by a man.

She had been a wee young thing when her mother had first offered her up to the men folks, charging them for the privilege to sample her daughter. Yes, she had been broken early in life, her virginity plucked away, and for what, to put bread and wine on the table. Fortunately, she had taught her mother a valuable lesson about using what didn't belong to her. That's when she realized she was special, more so than just a vessel for men's pleasures. The

power came to her in a rush, a rage and her mother was
no more.

No one ever suspected an eleven year old of
something so bloody gruesome. For many years she
had the essence of innocence on her side. Then they
discovered her secret and abused her far worse than her
mother's men folk. If not for them and their demands, she
would never have been exposed for what she had become.
They had been greedy and vengeful, uncaring about her
well being. She made them pay the price too, but by then
it was too late. She became a marked woman, an evil
entity that had to be destroyed at all cost. How easily they
had drawn her in, coddled her, tricked her and had caught
her completely off guard, realizing it much too late to
thwart their plans.

Look at me now, she thought. I have a second chance
to right their wrong, seek my revenge and bring hell on
earth to those who betrayed me. This Lou, she will help
me find them. She has the knowledge to seek them out,
wherever they might be, those who have for generations
kept me entombed in that secluded grave. Yes, they
are here and yes, they have played a hand in the curse,
guarded it all this time. I can almost smell them, a vile
sickening stench. They have worked diligently to keep the
secret buried, keep me buried, but the cat is out of the bag
now. I must act before they realize their precious grave
has been deserted. They will find out, and the fear will
consume them like a blazing fire. Yes, they will panic and
leap at mere shadows. I shall cherish every moment.

15

Doctor Kelly Garner, perplexed, reviewed the results of the tests. She should be exuberant, marveling at them, but instead she struggled to wrap her brain around them. The existence of Alzheimer's had all but disappeared. She clung to facts, that this is not a disease easily diagnosed until an autopsy is performed, but still, there was nothing that pointed in that direction now; except, Lou's odd behavior. Her patient's dialogue and perception of the world around her seemed skewed. Possibly trauma had triggered it but she didn't think so.

Something had happened and Kelly was not ready to call it a miracle, not yet. No one, absolutely no one, overcame this curse and indeed, the disease was considered a curse by many. There had never been a documented case of remission, not until now, maybe. No, it was medically impossible and that is just a fact. This was something else, but what? She should be happy for Lou and her family, but she couldn't shake it, couldn't allow herself to be overjoyed or consumed by whatever had happened. Perhaps she should consult others in her field. A second opinion couldn't hurt.

But what if Lou's condition had actually gone into remission; this could be a medical breakthrough of astronomical proportions. It could be monumental if it had. Was she really willing to share the spotlight with others of her profession? Hell no, not until she had answers. No one was going to steal her thunder. This could be a game changer for her future, the Holy Grail, the Nobel Prize in the medical field and she wasn't willing to share it with her colleagues. Greedy yes, but an opportunity like this doesn't come along often, and it had been dropped in her lap. She had an obligation to herself to see this through, so the decision had been made.

Settled, Doctor Kelly Garden would be the soul beneficiary of the discovery, wherever it might take her. She would become world renown, if she could solve the mystery and possibly develop a cure. Possibly she was setting her sights a little too high, but goals had driven her, her entire career. Development of a cure would most likely require assistance, but she would at least be heir to the discovery. She had to learn more before she would be willing to share that, though. Baby steps, one must take it slow, she reminded herself. Hell no, full throttle is more my way, she surmised.

Kelly reviewed the results a second and then a third time. Her conclusion remained the same. This woman could not be suffering from Alzheimer's. Had she diagnosed her incorrectly? No, absolutely not, the first tests had supported the diagnosis. Even Doctor Manfred Peavy had agreed with her findings. It had been there. Clearly Lou Stetson had all the symptoms of Alzheimer's. Symptoms, they were just symptoms, no, don't second guess, not now. The tests are reliable; have always been reliable, and there is no reason to discount the results.

Kelly decided to call Liz Donley, to get her read on Lou. It had been almost a week since she had released her from the hospital. If the disease existed, the signs would have surely been detected by now. Liz would have seen them, surely. She was a seasoned caregiver. Yes, Liz's opinion could be valuable in moving forward. She was, after all, the watchdog. Who would know better than she? Wade would ignore the signs, too hopeful about her recovery. An ostrich always buried its head in the sand. It was the easier road to take. Ignore it and just maybe it will go away. Make excuses, and life will return to normal. That was always the way, so predictable. Spouse, relatives, primary caregivers typically suffered the worst, unwilling to accept the inevitable and too proud to ask for help.

"Hello. Liz, this is Kelly. Is this a good time for us to chat?"

"Hi Kelly. Sure, things are a little boring around here right now."

"How's our patient?"

"She's one feisty lady. I have to put on my armor and prepare to do battle before I dare risk invading her space."

"That's not so unusual in these cases. Resistance is quite common, denial is what you expect, isn't it?"

"Denials yes, but she absolutely believes she isn't sick, and she backs this up quite well. Kelly, I'm not so sure she is either."

"You can read my mind. I was about to ask you your spin on things, Liz."

"For sure, she doesn't like having me around and she has done an excellent job in discrediting me in front of Wade. She's one shrewd lady, let me tell you. She's quite the schemer. I've never experienced someone as diabolical as she, not even in a healthy person."

"Care to share?"

"I don't know. She seems to have convinced Wade that I'm untrustworthy, a thief, if I can be so blunt. I really think she has planted evidence a couple of times to incriminate me."

"It isn't uncommon for Alzheimer's patients to misplace things and blame others. I wouldn't worry about that."

"It's more to it than that. Wade's Visa Card ended up in

my purse, this morning."

"How did Wade handle that?"

"He doesn't know. I found it while he was at work."

"Good, then he can't accuse you of stealing it."

"I wish it was that cut and dried. I also discovered two receipts; one for a seven hundred dollar big screen television from a local appliance store. I've never been in that store. I'm not really a TV person. The other one was for a plane ticket to my hometown in Pittsburg."

"Do you really think she is capable of pulling off something like that?"

"Do you think I'm a thief?"

"That's not what I meant, Liz. You've been around people in Lou's condition; what makes you suspect her?"

"She has it in for me; has had it in for me from the start. I had all but decided I would inform Wade he really no longer required my assistance, but then this. If I do it now, it will surely appear I have stolen these items and was about to make a run for it, back to Pittsburg of all places. I'm not sure what to do, Kelly. This has never happened to me before; I'd be lying if I didn't say it frightens me."

"Stay calm. I would suggest you confront Wade when he returns. Show him the card and the receipts and tell him the honest truth. That will dismiss any suspicions he night have for you trying to perpetrate this. Why would you do it and then confess?"

"You're right. That makes sense. I'll do it."

"Do you think she is still ill?"

"Alzheimer's? I'm not sure. The typical signs just don't seem to be there. Before that little cemetery episode it was undeniable. She was going downhill at a rapid pace, just as you had diagnosed, but now; I don't know, things have changed. In ways she is more vibrant, more alert than ever, but..."

"But what, Liz?"

"She's not herself. How can I say this so that you're not ready to schedule me for a round of testing? She's taken on an almost evil persona. I really am not sure who Lou has become. She isn't the Lou I first met. She's different, and I don't trust her."

"Trust can be tough love when it comes to Alzheimer's. They're always trying to conceal their inability to function normally."

"No, I don't trust her, as one would mistrust someone who is trying to deliberately discredit them or inflict revengeful harm; that's what I'm saying."

"You've done nothing to make her feel revengeful towards you."

"I think just me being here has upset her little applecart. She doesn't want me invading her world. I think she believes that I am a threat to her lifestyle. I'm infringing on her and she wants me gone. She'll do what it takes to get rid of me. I'm sure of it."

"Liz, I've never heard you talk about one of your patients in this manner. Are you okay?"

"No, I'm not all right. That's what I'm trying to explain to you. This is not normal behavior, anything but. I'm going to do as you have suggested and talk to Wade. I'll show him the Visa and the receipts, and then once we've cleared this up, I'm going to deliver my notice, effective immediately. I've never taken such harsh steps before, Kelly, but I must. I do apologize. After all, you did recommend me."

"I must admit, Lou's case is quite bizarre. Her medical condition is puzzling. That's why I called you, Liz. I wanted to hear firsthand what you had witnessed in the past week. I got more than I had bargained for, that's for sure. You owe me no apologizes. You just make things right with Wade. I'll talk to you later."

"Thanks for hearing me out. I don't have a blemish on my record and certainly don't want to be accused of something I didn't do."

"You'll be fine. Wade's not the type to jump to conclusions. Have him call me if you'd like. I'll vouch for you."

"I hope it want come to that." Liz thought she heard an odd click on the line, just before she ended her call. She shrugged; she had been too paranoid already.

Interesting turn of events, thought Kelly, replaying the conversation in her mind, and concerned more than ever about the case. Liz had witnessed no sustainable causes pointing to the onslaught of Alzheimer's. How was this possible, given her condition not more than a week ago? Shifts and swings were common, but not this, not when Lou had been on the brink of no return. She had been in adult diapers and could not feed herself. No one springs back from that amount of degeneration. It had to be something else, but what?

Kelly stared at the tests, attempting to draw a different conclusion. Had she missed something? No, she hadn't. It was as if the self proclaimed Emma and Lou was two entirely different people. I am cured, she had said; not that I am feeling better. I am cured. She had uttered those words with the utmost confidence. I am cured. The most recent tests supported her convictions. She had somehow been cured. No, it had to have gone dormant for some unexplainable reason, mimicking a hibernating bear. It existed somewhere in her subconscious. It will awake sooner or later, but what if it doesn't? I am cured. If she could be cured, then others could be cured.

16

Wade arrived home late, a long day now behind him. All seemed quiet. He needed quiet right now. His current project had suffered some setbacks; problems that were going to require more of his personal time. He already felt guilty about being away too much and now this. He was hungry but almost too tired to bother rounding up something. He settled for a banana and glass of milk just to hush his growling stomach. Skipping meals was not uncommon for him. He would survive, could even use dropping an extra pound or two. Breathing in, breathing out, he attempted to relax and wind down. If he didn't, sleep wouldn't come easy, even though his body was screaming for the bed.

Honey had arrived in the kitchen, curling in and out through his legs, purring up a storm. Kramer sat patiently at the backdoor, hinting to go outside. Oh well, fresh air might do us both some good before bedtime, thought Wade. He opened the door but Kramer, as had become his standard practice lately, refused to go outside until is master crossed the threshold first. He hadn't gotten over his stay in the pound. The pooch just didn't quite trust anyone yet. Wade stepped through the doorway first, holding it open, and then Kramer followed. The dog wasted no time completing his business and returning to the door. Wade opened the door and Kramer quickly disappeared down the hallway. Wade assumed he headed to his and Lou's bedroom. That was where he was heading, exhaustion still tugging at him relentlessly.

Wade peeked in the bedroom, a bedside table lamp still on, and to his surprise, Lou was sitting up, leaning against the headboard. The covers were tucked about her and she was naked from the waist up. She smiled and pulled back the covers, inviting him underneath. She was completely nude, not customary for Lou. She had always worn a tee-shirt and panties; flannels in the winter. She didn't flaunt her nudity, never had, and not that she was ashamed of her body or anything like that. She came from a modest upbringing, preferring to keep it that way, behind closed doors and under a cloak of darkness, or at least between the bed sheets.

"I've been waiting up for you, husband. I hope you haven't had a tiring day and have saved some time and energy for me."

Wade stood there like a tongue tied teenager having seen his first naked body. He teetered between concerned and excited. The excited side won out. He closed the bedroom door, and then he sat on the bed by Lou, still not sure how far to take this, remembering the conversation he and the doctor had had about people with Alzheimer's. Lou placed her hand on his cheek and pulled him to her, planting her lips on his. She then began to unbutton his shirt and basically undress him with her eyes, reeling him in. Wade forgot about the conversation and gave in to his wife, willing to see how this would go for both of them, hoping for the best, expecting possibly the worst.

Twenty five minutes later, he lay there in her arms, feeling he had just made love to a stranger. It had been the most wonderful experience. Basking in what Lou often dubbed afterglow, he was somewhere between worried and concerned, wondering if this was a temporary reprieve from her sickness, or if she was really cured. Kelly had said there was no cure. Lou had said she was. Who was right? Did it really matter at the moment? He had his wife back, and in some ways, better than ever. Possibly it was a miracle after all. She now cuddled up next to him, breathing deeply. He drew comfort in their closeness. Soon, he too had drifted off.

Emma listened to Wade's breathing. The rhythm left little doubt that he had drifted off to sleep. She mentally thanked Lou for sharing the wonderful sexual coupling with her. It had indeed been a long time coming, she giggled. Ah, but the perks, of being back alive.

You shouldn't have done that. He's MY husband, not yours.

He's never had what I offered him. Couldn't you tell? He reached new heights, something he could have never done with someone as prudish as you, my dear Lou. You should be thankful. You can't deny you enjoyed it too. I felt your presence, your little sinful trembling. You've never had it that damn good from your man before, have you? Be honest.

What do you really want with me, with us, you worthless body snatcher?

I admire your feistiness, but you're such a bore, so predictable, and oh so common. Are you what women have become in this century? If so, what a pity? In my day, women knew no boundaries. Well, possibly the aristocrats held firm to their prudish, snobbish personas, but deep down they desired to be ravished by their men. That was another time, though; and we have now, don't we, my little DRECK? Oh sorry, I just called you a little shit.

You go to hell.

Been there, sweetheart and it's not all that scary; thinking of sending you there, eventually. You may not feel the same way, though.

Why can't you just go and leave us alone?

What do I keep telling you? Think about where you were before I arrived. You were a drooling and babbling gravestone hugger, on your way out. Remember, you picked me. Oops, sorry, memory wasn't your best asset back then, now was it? You seem to be doing just fine now, thanks to me. Like I said, you are indeed one ungrateful bitch. Now if you will excuse me, I have a few unfinished tasks I must take care of while our hubby catches a few zzzz's.

You can't go through this. I forbid it.

You...forbid...so laughable. I'm shaking in your boots. Hush, I'll summon you if I require your help. I wouldn't wait up though, nor keep your fingers crossed.

Wade woke to the smell of bacon. Turning, Lou was not by his side. He had slept like he hadn't slept in ages. Maybe the burden had been lifted off all their shoulders. He shaved, showered and dressed, and then headed to the kitchen. Lou greeted him, cooking up the last of the bacon and half dozen eggs over easy in the cast iron skillet. She turned and smiled, then drew up her nightie, flashing her bare bottom underneath.

"Good morning. You shouldn't be doing that. Where's Liz?"

"Ah, our hired nurse; I'm not sure. Was she not in her room?"

"I'll check. She should be up and in here, preparing breakfast, not you."

"Not to worry, handsome, I'm perfectly capable of cooking you a manly breakfast. You, after all, deserve it after last night."

Wade gave Lou a quick peck on the cheek before heading down to Liz's room. He knocked a couple f times before opening the door. The bed was made, so where was she? He yelled out to her in the bathroom, but he received no reply. The door was open and the bathroom unoccupied.

Where could she be now, wondered Wade. He returned to the kitchen after a quick tour of the rest of the house didn't uncover Liz.

"She's not there. When did you last see, her, Lou?"

"Emma, remember. I suppose it was last night, just before I retired. She was asking a bit oddly, now that I think about it."

"Oddly, what do you mean by that?"

"Nervous, anxious, maybe; I walked in her room to bid her a goodnight and she was quite startled and seemed to be trying to hide something she had in her hands. Thinking back on it, I remember seeing a piece of luggage open on the bed. I'm sorry, I suppose I should have asked why it was there, but I had you on my mind and still had to prep for your arrival."

"Luggage, now that does sound odd." Wade returned to her room and checked the closet and underneath the bed. There was no luggage. Curious, he rifled through the drawers and found none of her belongings. While doing so, he noticed some shredded papers in the wastebasket. He retrieved them and pieced them together. One was a receipt from the local appliance store and the other was an ATM transaction slip. He recognized the account number. It was his business account. Instinctively he reached for his wallet. The VISA he used for his business was missing. What had Liz done?

Wade returned to the kitchen, perplexed by what he had discovered. "Breakfast is served," said Emma. "You seem troubled dear husband."

"Not sure what to make of it just yet, but it appears Liz has vacated the premises."

"Dear me, I certainly hope it wasn't something I said or did. I have been a bit testy lately, with her hovering about me like a bee after nectar. Maybe it is just as well, paying for her services when we don't really need them seems like such a waste. I wish her well. She was just doing her job, after all."

Wade didn't tell Lou about the receipt and ATM slip he had rummaged from the wastebasket. There was no need to stress her out about that, not until he got to the bottom of it. After breakfast, he would check his account on line. If he detected anything suspicious, he would alert the bank. For now, he would enjoy breakfast with Lou. She appeared to beam with pride that she had prepared it for him. He certainly didn't want to disappoint her by not eating it.

"I wish you didn't have to go off to your place of work today. I feel like getting out. It's such a lovely day. It would be just perfect for a picnic, somewhere along the water. We do have that lake nearby."

"Lake Greenwood, yes, less than twenty minutes away. We have had some wonderful times there."

"And we could have a wonderful time there today, if you could take some time off to spend with your wife."

This really posed a serious dilemma. Wade couldn't afford to fall any further behind, not given the hiccups already encountered on this project. How could he say no to Lou? She needed him, still in a fragile state. Who knows when this could go the other way? Wade had already witnessed the uglier side of the disease. What if this was only a momentary rebound before it ravished her again? How could he not spend precious time with her?

"Let me take care of a couple of things first, make some phone calls and see what I can work out. It is a beautiful day indeed and a shame to waste it."

"That would please me, if we could spend the day together. Do what you must do. I'll clean these dirty dishes and make myself presentable for you."

Easing from the chair, she opened her legs just enough to allow him a peek. Men were all the same; a tease worked flawlessly. More important things awaited her at that lake, or rather the countryside nearby. She had utilized Lou last night to locate the information she required, using the computer device. What had she called it, oh yes, MapQuest; it had pointed her precisely to her desired location. The drive to this Lake Greenwood would allow her to observe the parcel of land and those who resided there. All was falling into place, and much quicker than she had originally anticipated. No one would stand in her way.

Wade checked his account on line and as feared, there had been two purchases, one from the appliance store and another for what appeared to be an airlines ticket. A significant amount of cash had been withdrawn from the ATM. The bank hadn't opened yet but he contacted a friend who worked there and requested her to cancel his VISA, explaining what had happened. He divulged the identity of the perpetrator. His contact recommended he should contact the Sheriff's department. If Liz Donley had used her plane ticket then this matter had reached more serious levels. For now, he decided to keep the law out of it. Even though it appeared he had caught her red handed, he wanted to give her an opportunity to explain her actions and possibly work things out.

Now came the moment, to make a phone call he dreaded even more. He called his contract contact and shamelessly used Lou as an excuse for not coming in today, saying she had taken a turn for the worse. He hated fibbing. His contact understood, saying family comes first. Wade had never felt so deceitful. He again attempted to justify his actions, thinking she could backslide any moment, so he must enjoy her why he could. That eased his conscious a tad.

Emma-Margarett had packed a picnic lunch already, complete with a bottle of wine, a blanket and she looked beautiful to boot. No denying it, he had made the correct decision. He accompanied Kramer outside to do his business one final time. Kramer ran to the edge of the yard and just stood there whimpering. He sniffed at the ground and looked back at Wade, barked a couple of times.

"Come on boy. I don't have time for this." Kramer stood his ground. Wade pretended to head back inside. It worked. The dog broke in his direction. Kramer wasn't going to be left outside alone. Wade replenished both his and Honey's food and water dishes, before he and Lou headed to the lake. It was indeed a glorious day for a drive. He had no regrets.

Lou quizzed him on the drive, asking him numerous questions about who lived here and there. Some she should have known and others, maybe not. Wade chalked it up to the after affects of Alzheimer's or it might just be a sign that she really wasn't cured. He never questioned her inquiries. He simply answered anything she asked, as if it were a normal conversation.

Lou recognized the address on the mailbox along the driveways' edge. The house was secluded, almost hidden in a large stand of pines and hardwoods. She continued her game of inquiries, having set up her intended inquiry, asking about all the other locations that didn't really interest her. Unfortunately, Wade didn't personally know the individual who lived there. The last name on the mail box confirmed the identity, though. Lou recognized it. It was one of several she would be paying a visit. Three of the others were in the general area. Another was in the Greenville area and two had not been located. Seven had been responsible for this travesty, or at least their blood kin had. Seven would pay with their lives. With it, she could break the curse for good and regain what once had been hers.

17

Doctor Kelly Garner had made several attempts to contact Liz Donley, but her calls had gone to Liz's cell phone voice messaging. She was curious as to how Liz and Wade's little discussion had gone, and if Liz required input from her. Kelly had considered phoning Wade but decided that might be overstepping. Liz would call her if she needed her help. She was more than capable of straightening out any misunderstandings. It did trouble Kelly than Lou Stetson might be capable of such diabolic moves against Liz. Perhaps she should plan on dropping by in the next few days, just a friendly cordial sort of visit. No, that might appear too suspicious, her making an unofficial house call.

Kelly decided to bide her time and allow Wade and Lou some time to breathe. Lou had another appointment scheduled in a couple of weeks. She'd allow things to run their course until then. Wade or Liz would contact her if they had any concerns about Lou's condition. Besides, she had a conference coming up and would be out of town for the better part of a week. Everyone had her cell number. She would only be three hours away in Charleston. The low country wasn't that far from Greenwood in an emergency situation.

Still, Lou's case did intrigue her. She planned on sharing her folders with a friend and colleague while at the conference. A review of Lou's files, her tests before and after, a second opinion couldn't hurt. There is no cure of

Alzheimer's. Perhaps Kelly was doing this more for herself than Lou; wishing to confirm the impossibility of such a miracle. She regretfully expected Lou to backslide at any given moment. While a miracle cure such as this would be earth shattering, she didn't in her heart believe it was a real phenomenon. The medical world typically won out over miracles. Enough time wasted, dwelling on this, she had some packing to do for her trip.

The day on the lake had been worth the price of playing hooky, thought Wade. While Lou wasn't quite herself, she was still a far cry from the invalid she had almost become. Lou had continued to persistently insist she didn't need a caregiver, a baby sitter, as she called Liz. Wade had to agree. She seemed perfectly capable of taking care of herself, but still, if or when the disease reared its ugly head, could he gamble on her being alone. Neither of them needed another cemetery incident, her wandering off like she had. Wade decided he would try the arrangement temporarily, but would have Anna stop by periodically and check on her. Too bad Heath and Leanne didn't live close by, or he might have encouraged them to spend more time with their mother. For now, he'd keep mum on the situation, no need to worry either of them.

Tomorrow would be the first test, him reporting back to work and leaving her unattended. She assured him she would be just fine. Wade made her promise to keep her cell phone with her at all times. Emma-Margarett had promised, but she would require Lou's assistance in using the little contraption. While ownership of her host's body was leaning more in her favor, Lou still fought her tooth and claw when it came to sharing her memories or knowledge of this new century of marvels. Margerett would tip the scales, tapping more power, as she completed her revenge on those responsible for her curse.

The occupants of the house, Floyd and Ruth Abrams,

those she had spied on today, would be first on her list. With Wade away tomorrow and no meddling nursemaid to interfere, she would have more than enough time to do what would be necessary. She had still had one obstacle to overcome, transportation. How difficult could it really be to harness one of these automobiles? She would enlist Lou's expertise. Severe consequences would be in store if Lou refused to help. Margarett would not fail in her attempt reconcile being wronged.

Utilizing Lou's knowledge of tracking ancestors on the computer machine, Floyd Abram had been confirmed as a descendant of A.B. Abram, one of the seven who conspired to send her to her grave. A.B. had been a lawyer, smitten by the young thing employed at his home. He had taken many liberties, acting more as a slave owner than an employer. When threatened to expose him to his wife, he had quickly dismissed her, paying her mother a meager pittance to be rid of the nuisance. Margarett's mother had forbid any retaliation for his actions, sighting contractual obligation paid in full. Abram would be the first, but not the last, to taste the forbidden fruit, offered by her mother. His had only been the beginning of a tragic ending.

Morning had not broken soon enough for the parasite occupying Lou Stetson's body. Wade had kissed her on the cheek, thinking she was in blissful slumber, before dressing and slipping from their bedroom. The fool was so easily deceived. As long as he had his beloved Lou back he was blind to everything else. Lou should be more than grateful too, but the bitch hadn't learned her lesson yet. Disobedience came with a price. Margarett could not jeopardize harming the vessel she now used, but there were other ways to make her point, if the time came.

Rise and shine, Lou; we have urgent business to tend.

What makes you think I sleep? One's subconscious is always just below the surface, bid ones times.

Should I be shaking in our bones, my dear? Think as you will but dare not cross me with your scheming ways. You have much to lose in this world; those dear to your heart for starters. We have those two darlings, a son and daughter, don't we? It would be simply shameful to outlive one's children, wouldn't it?

How dare you threaten my kids? They've done nothing to you.

Do you not find it odd that they are not nearby in their mother's time of need? For the mind sickness to shorten your days in this world, you would think they would cherish every waking hour to be spending precious time with their mother.

They have jobs, lives, commitments. They check on me, call their father. They would be here in a heartbeat if they thought my days were numbered. You forget, you're responsible for them not being here; your miracle, I'm cured, remember.

So like Lou, convincing yourself they actually care. But, we could make a phone call using your cell phone over there, one to tug on their heartstrings, a plea, beckoning them by your side, fearing your mind is drifting away. I'm sure we could babble nonsense talk to cause them to hurry here. A mother, inflicted with a disease where her memory is her enemy, could do terrible things and not be aware of doing such atrocities.

Stop. Don't you dare threaten to harm my children?

Me, I would not harm a hair on their heads; but you, God forbid what you might be capable of doing. Wade would never forgive you, even though the doctors may come to your defense. A sad ending, don't you think? Must I remind you what happened to the babysitter?

You shouldn't have done that. You're pure evil.

Me, I did nothing. I don't exist, but you, yes; you did some truly terrible things, unforgivable things. Poor Liz,

poor, poor Liz, and those precious children...

What do you want from me?

See, isn't this so much better, us working through our differences. We do not have to be enemies.

Screw you. Let's just get this over with.

I like that; no questions asked. A mother's love knows no boundaries. What do they say, oh yes, unconditional. My mother didn't know the meaning of this. Hers were always conditional, never in my best interest. But that is another time, another story. Perhaps I will share that with you if our days are long, but I would not be too hopeful, my special subconscious. Enough of this mindless chatter let us prepare for a little jaunt in the horseless carriage. We must finish our task before your hubby returns.

The day had been a long one, Wade having made up for lost time. Yesterday had costs him precious time on the project, but it had been worthwhile, spending quality time with Lou. Regrets were few. Two phone calls to Lou during the day had found all was well. She had sounded more like Lou, the one before the illness. She hadn't even scoffed at him accidentally calling her Lou. Maybe she was over the Emma notion. It was tough to remember to call her Emma. She had forever been just Lou. He pulled into the drive, half pass eight, later than he had planned to be, but he had called Lou one last time, just before leaving. All still seemed well. She had been very upbeat and positive, more cheerfulness in her tone than he had heard in ages. Had she really been cured or was the Alzheimer's laying in ambush, just below the surface, ready to emerge again?

Wade opened the door and Kramer rushed through, making Wade question whether Lou had taken him outside as he had instructed her. Lou stood in the doorway smiling a glorious smile. He could smell home cooking drifting from the kitchen. A second whiff, and Wade recognized his favorite, crusted, pan fried chicken. He returned a smile, thinking just maybe we do have this thing licked. Kramer quickly finished his business but again, as often he did lately, ran to the edge of the yard and sat there and whimpered. Faking him out and heading towards the door, suckered him to come back as always.

Nice touch, Lou, my dear, assisting me with cooking our husband's favorite meal. I was beginning to believe you were not going to so easily forgive and forget what we did today. Ah, but for the love and safety of those you cherish the most, you came through for me. It would have been so unfair if you would have punished dear Wade because you failed to agree with our earlier actions. In time these matters will no longer weigh heavy on our conscious, trust me. I appreciate your silence. I'm in no mood to deal with you at the moment. Let's just try to have a civil night with Wade. He has had a long day at his work.

"I have made your favorite."

"Indeed you have. I smelled and recognized it, but you shouldn't have."

"Nothing is too good for the one I love. Your day of labor went well."

Day of labor, what an odd way to say it. "Yes, I gained some ground on the project. What did you do to occupy yours, besides slaving in the kitchen?"

"Life is but a bore but I made the best of it. I surfed for a while on the computer. It can be most entertaining. One can learn the most interesting tidbits doing this surfing."

"Care to share?"

"There is nothing of note, just browsing like one would do if shopping; but I'll not bore you with womanly infatuations. Shall we have our meal before it cools?"

Other than additional quirky talk, the meal and remainder of the night was uneventful, observed Wade. That was, until bedtime, when the amorous side of his wife emerged again. It had almost become like clockwork, her desires and persistence in satisfying them. Wade was not complaining, but just noting the change. Libido shifts weren't uncommon, so had been confirmed by Kelly. Be cautious she had warned, because these could sometimes be awkward and guilt ridden. So far, they had been neither.

Wade quickly drifted off to sleep, spent from the session and exhausted from the day of laboring, as Lou had called it. Margarett waited patiently until Wade's breathing mixed with snores, alerted her that sleep had overtaken him. She slipped from bed, retrieved her nightgown from the floor and slipped it on, and then headed to the computer. It was time to Google the next name, print out the address and prepare for tomorrow's visit. With her host's assistance, she had set up a personal folder marked HEIRS, and had begun storing related information on the remaining six.

The next name on her list, Cam Bergmann, ancestor of Abe Bergmann, lived in Ninety Six, eastward, but inside the county of Greenwood. He owned and operated a local newspaper. Abraham, his long lost uncle, had been a most brutal retch. While tracing the family tree, she had located many relatives; Cam was the closest, location wise. Destroying every living relative, while it would be most entertaining, served no purpose. She needed only to stake her revenge on one living heir, of each who had spelled her doom to strengthen her current position and eventually break free of the curse forever.

At first daylight, after Wade had departed for work, she and Lou would make haste to locate Cam Bergmann's abode. For the time being Margarett still required Lou's assistance in driving and performing other modern day tasks. In due time, she would be able to discard Emma Lou Stetson as a snake sheds its skin. She did not have the advantage as she had for the last one, having eyed the property prior to paying a visit. Bergmann might not be home and she had no idea how many others occupied the dwelling. She dared not question Wade about any of the others. To do so might draw unwanted attention. Margarett certainly didn't need anyone connecting the dots so early in the game. She must be more creative this time. A house fire, while easily accomplished, could not serve her purpose. There would be limitations to mere coincidences.

I wish you would drop this. Why must you be so ruthless? These are innocent people. They had nothing to do with what happened to you.

Perhaps we should satisfy your curiosity, Lou. We'll ask Bergmann. If he doesn't know, then possibly I may reconsider.

You can't be serious? Asking him would just raise flags. He would want to know why he was being asked.

He would remember your face, not mine. Besides, I thought you were interested in championing the innocent, so what difference would it make?

If it will save his life, then ask him, by all means.

This gives us gooseflesh, now doesn't it? To think, we converse with him prior to taking actions. Pity, you didn't make this suggestion yesterday. The intrigue and the anticipation are quite exciting. Can't you feel it too? To stare in the face of the guilty before inflicting revenge, I like it.

Innocent until proven guilty, must I remind you?

Formalities, they are. What shall we wear today? I think if we are going to introduce ourselves, then we should wear something sexy, something captivating, eye catching, don't you think? Distractions can be beneficial for our cause.

Wear whatever the hell you want, just stay true to your promise, if he has no knowledge of your demise.

You're in no position to render behavioral demands or promises, my dear Lou. Save your preaching for the choir. Just take your seat on the back pew and pray to your Lord

that I allow you to exist. In time, I promise, you will be no more. Besides, you already had a death sentence with the mind sickness, and you have reaped the benefits of a longer life by me being here. I've wasted enough time on you this morning. It is now time for you to do what I wish; a hunting we will go. Heigh ho, the dairy-o, a hunting we will go; we'll catch a fox and put him in a box, but this time, we'll not let him go. Catchy, I like it.

You're one sick bitch.

Look in the mirror when you say that, my dear, Lou.

Margarett ended the mental conversation with her host, Lou. She had an agenda with a tight schedule and time was wasting. Bergmann must be destroyed, but she would invite a face to face encounter, if the opportunity arose. This intrigued her, anticipating the look on his face before she delivered long overdue justice for sins delivered by his ancestor. She perused the list of others on her printed sheet of paper, three males and two females. Her skin tingled, a chill rippled down her spine, and it felt wonderfully naughty, reminding her instantly of the olden days, a time when she was all so powerful. Her gift had been well worth the barter with Azazel. Luckily it had no expiration date, no time limits, and even after all these years of lying dormant, she could again possess it in the fullest, once she had shed the blood of the seven; one down and six to go.

Less than one hour later, they, she and Lou, had located the Bergmann homestead. This was going to pose a greater challenge than expected. The house was nestled in a tightly woven neighborhood with much hustle and bustle along the roadway in front. It was still early morning and lights were burning inside. Margarett could detect shadows moving about from one room to another. Suddenly the porch light illuminated the front lawn. Margarett stepped behind an old red oak while watching as the door open. Two young chaps, both girls, emerged, while a woman stood in the doorway. The lady waved a goodbye and after they rounded the corner, she closed the door. Lou sensed they were heading to a bus stop and pleaded with Margarett not to harm them.

Margarett had no interest in the offspring. Her target remained Cam Bergmann, although, if he could not be reached, and if the children were of his true bloodline, options were open. An eye for an eye, spilled blood was spilled blood; any Bergmann would satisfy her needs. Lou, again, begged her to spare them. She offered no assurance. The question, was he still inside, or was the female alone? The female was of no use, unless used as bait to lure her intended prey. This was so primal and invigorating for Margerett, but not Lou.

A dog barked, not nearby, somewhere down the street. Margarett crept closer to the house, drawn to what appeared to be a lighted kitchen window. Blinds were open. She could peer inside. The woman she had seen on the porch now leaned against an island counter, sipping a cup of coffee. The lady was quite attractive, even without makeup. Her build was slim, with heavy breasts but narrow at the hips. She turned and glanced in the opposite direction, saying something. A man had entered the kitchen. This must be Cam Bergman. He was still here, perfect.

Margarett could detect no resemblance to Abraham Berman but that didn't really matter. Like the woman, he was not heavy, but of medium build, no more than six feet tall. He wasn't what she would consider handsome, but he was pleasant to look upon. Abraham had not been. He was pot bellied with thinning hair, and had a huge ghastly mole on his left cheek. Looks didn't matter if one was rich and old Abe had been quite wealthy. Riches could buy anything back then, even respect, and certainly companionship, as she was well aware. Cam was wearing a dress shirt and tie, coat tossed over his arm. He carried a leather brief case.

Obviously he was about to exit, most likely to leave for his place of employment, the newspaper.

Margarett would have to take him quickly, before he reached his transportation. Two such vehicles were parked in the driveway, one much smaller than the other. She returned to the old red oak conveniently located near them. From there she could easily pounce undetected, when his back was to her, while entering either vehicle. Doing so would not allow for the face to face encounter. She could not jeopardize that encounter, less he get the upper hand. Maybe, on his dying breath she could make full disclosure, the purpose for taking his life.

The porch door opened once again. Cam Bergmann stepped through the threshold and then turned to kiss his wife goodbye. Margarett gripped the long knife in her right hand, the largest blade she had been able to find in the Stetson kitchen. Her senses were on high alert. She could almost smell his scent, one oozing of cologne and death. He stepped from the porch, but instead of walking in her direction, he set out in the opposite direction, whistling a little unfamiliar tune. She realized he was not taking either of the vehicles, but instead walking to his workplace. With only open lawn between them she would not be able to close the distance undetected. Think, she told herself, I cannot allow him to reach his final destination.

The vehicle that they had arrived here in was parked half block in the opposite direction. She wasn't sure of the distance he had to travel to reach his workplace. It must not be far or he would not be going there on foot. People of this century loved their mobile transportation. She removed her shoes, having chosen heels to wear for the occasion. Hindsight, she should have worn a pair of those softer laced shoes from the closet, but had been too consumed by accessorizing. The shoes matched the dress she was wearing. She hesitated until he vanished from view and then she sprinted in his direction.

The approaching dawn gave way to few shadowy hiding places remaining. Margarett panicked, having lost sight of him. Looking about she detected movement. Cam had crossed the street. A vehicle approached from behind. She shifted her face away from the street to conceal her identity best she could. She quickened her pace, paralleling him. A cluster of buildings were ahead on her side of the street.

She hurried to reach them and gained ground, passing him. Luckily he never looked her way, preoccupied by the phone device held in his hands. She came to an alleyway between buildings. It was now or never. She positioned herself down the alley just out of sight from any traffic. Replacing her shoes, Margarett sprawled on the asphalt and then screamed. She heard approaching footfalls, the bait had been taken. Seconds later Cam Bergmann stood above her.

"What happened? Are you hurt?"

"There was a man. He stole my purse. He knocked me to the ground."

"I'll call 911."

"Please help me to my feet, first."

He half knelt and assisted her. She smiled and asked, "Aren't you the Bergmann gentleman from the newspaper?"

"I am one in the same. Have we met?"

"Aren't you a descendent of a gentleman named Abraham Bergmann? His friends called him Abe, I believe."

"Yes. How would you know his name? He's one of my long lost relatives. We really need to get you some help."

"I'm fine now, no worse for the wear. I knew Abe personally. He was a very naughty man."

"My dear, he has been deceased nearly one hundred years. You must have him confused with another Abe Bergmann."

"Afraid not, that's the one I knew."

"I fear you've taken a severe knock to the old noggin. I really do need to call 911 and get you some help. You know my name. Might I inquire yours? "

"Margarett Levine Reznik, born May 17, 1872, died May 17, 1880, and your relative played part in my murder."

"I've heard that name. What sort of scam are you pulling?" Cam took one step backwards.

"This is no ruse. Dishonest Abe is one of the bastards who slay me and then laid curse to my soul. Not to be concerned, I am here to right the injustice."

"Mrs. Reznik, or whoever the hell you are, I think you require more medical assistance than you might realize."

"Do you remember anything about me besides my name?"

"This conversation is over. I'll place that call now."

"You do, you are a bastard, apples don't fall far from the tree. Secrets are indeed passed along, aren't they?"

"You're insane and I'll not be part of your twisted little game."

"That's where you are wrong, Cam Bergmann. You are an intricate part of the so called game. Abe never atoned for his sins. He, shall we say, got away with murder and then some. It's time for redemption, an eye for an eye."

"You're on your own, lady. I can't help you." Cam turned to walk away.

Margarett planted the blade in his left shoulder, burying it to its handle, nine inches precisely. Cam whirled, made direct eye contact, and then he sucked in one last breath before collapsing. Margarett withdrew the knife, wiped in on his pants leg and then removed his wallet. She collected his briefcase, his phone and keys, and then she calmly walked away leaving Cam sprawled in the alley in her place. Almost immediately she sensed a surge of energy rush through her body. She drew strength from his death.

No automobiles passed. She successfully returned to her vehicle and allowed Lou to drive them home, arriving back there, just half pass eight.

This had gone much easier than expected. With a pencil, she scratched through the second name on her printed list, eyeing a third, Judith Grumman, descendent of Joseph Herzberg. It was simply amazing the wealth of information that could be obtained from the computer device and the genealogy program, as Lou had called it. The family tree could be traced to every limb, every a leaf, and every root.

Are you satisfied? I met him head on and it was obvious he recognized my name, the sins of their fathers, so to speak, or in this case, ancestors.

You're going to murder all of them, aren't you, no mercy, no benefit of the doubt?

Why wouldn't I? They murdered me.

They never knew you. They were born long after your death. How can they be held accountable? Those others are dead. Isn't that good enough for you?

The curse is not so simple. To lift it, blood must be spilled from the seven by my hands. In this case, blood relatives will suffice.

You're no longer in that cemetery. Can't you just leave it at that?

Are you saying you would prefer I share this body with you? I don't think so. Once I complete my mission I will have free rein to ride anyone's body I see fit. With you, my years are limited. Once the curse has been lifted, I live on for eternity. The risks are worth the reward, don't you see? The bloodletting will set me free.

Does that mean you will leave me and my family alone after you get what you want?

That is most troubling, you see. You know too much, all my dirty little secrets.

Who would ever believe me? Besides, how would I know where you had gone? You could be with anyone.

You do have a point. If you ranted about what I have done, it would only point to you. You did these things for all practical purposes. The knife was in your hands. Only your fingerprints are on it. Burning those people alive was done by you. You know too many details and given your mental state, I rest my case. Come to think of it, how are you going to live with that guilt once I'm gone? Must I remind you about what happened to your caregiver? Her blood is on your hands as well. How careless, us leaving that incriminating evidence. Plus she had called the good doctor, telling her she feared you were setting her up. The trails are clear, guilty or even a member of the jury. The possibilities are endless. Perhaps I might even be Doctor Garner. Can you visualize a straightjacket in your future?

18

Margarett had only been home no more than an hour when the doorbell rang. Peeping out a window she recognized the intruder, Lou's sister-in-law, Anna Stetson. What now she wondered. Was it not enough to be confined to this house with the stupid cat and dreadful hound? Now she had to be subjected to another meddler. Was there no end to it? Okay, time to put on a happy face and play nice, then maybe she will just go away. She sighed; I can't eliminate every little inconvenience without drawing too much unwanted attention.

You harm a hair on her head…

And what, you get blamed for it, Lou. Get serious. Your threats are meaningless and you know it. Help me get rid of her and you'll not have to fret over it. Believe me; my priorities do not include being bothered by your in-laws. That being said, and you should know me by now, I won't hesitate deposing of a nuisance. She goes of her own accord, or she simply goes, my way.

I'll help you. I don't want her harmed.

Good girl; see we really can get along and work through these situations.

There is no WE in this. You've done enough damage already. I just don't want any more people hurt.

Selfishly you don't want any more of your people hurt, admit it. You'll sacrifice others to keep them safe, right?

You did that to those others, not me. If I could have

stopped you, I would have.

Sadly, you're no longer in charge, now are you? I suppose it was destiny that we crossed paths now that I think about it. Your mind was already mush. That made you pretty much powerless. You were easy pickings, low hanging fruit, just a blink away from being a mere truffle. I saved the day, rescuing you from the world of the lost, a vegetable among people. Sorry, I just so enjoy digging my heels in every chance I have. Buried and dead for so long has that effect on a person.

My mind is sharp enough to know what you are doing is pure evil. You are Satan incarnate.

A mere disciple I assure you; but thank you for placing me on a pedestal. I am honored. Now, enough of this chit-chat, we do have your in-law to dispense with, and I only mean that with the utmost sincerity.

"Knock, knock, Lou, its Anna; may I come in?"

"You need not knock my dear sister-in-law. You are always welcome. Our home is your home. Please do come in. Remember though, please address me as Emma."

"How are you feeling, Emma?"

"Splendid, simply splendid, I am still on this side of the dirt, above ground and distancing myself from that horrid experience. The world is in for a rude awakening, I have returned from the dead. Reckoning day is here. Sorry my dear for the theatrics but I do feel so invigorated and blessed to be the product of a modern day miracle. I can hardly contain myself, as you can obviously bear testimony."

"I'm pleased you are doing and feeling well, Lou; sorry, I mean, Emma."

"You are family. You may call me Lou if that is more comfortable. Emma is symbolic of my new found freedom and second chance at life. That is all. I know it may seem petty and probably silly, but I do absolutely feel like a new person, revitalized and looking at the world for the very first time, or at least with a new set of peepers. How does it go, jeepers-creepers, take a gander at my new set of peepers, or something silly like that? Look at me. I'm so sorry. I must have runs of the mouth this morning, babbling nothingness. Might I offer you a cup of hot tea or coffee, my dear sister-in-law?"

"Thanks, but I've had my limit of the brew this morning. You're no longer requiring Liz's assistance, I understand. Wade mentioned she was no longer here."

"Did Wade mention why?"

"Not really; he just said you and she had parted ways. I assumed it was because you were doing much better."

"Leave it to my husband not to air the dirty laundry. He caught her with her hand in the cookie jar. She was a mere thief in nurse's clothing. I fear we weren't her first victims. She may have been a scam artist all along."

"But she came so highly recommended. What on earth did she do?"

"Embezzling and stealing, she skipped out, high tailed it to whence she came, her homeland, her birth place, so it seems. She is staying low and in hiding from what we understand. The collectors and constables have not located her."

Odd dialogue, thought Anna, but Lou had gone through a lot and had seemingly rebounded. With it, there must be some repercussions for her sudden recovery. At least she appeared to know everyone and was aware of her surroundings, even though, she questioned the allegations concerning Liz Donley. The woman just didn't seem to be the deceitful type, and she had done this sort of work for years. She would try to remember to ask Wade about it.

"How did you find out?"

"She had made some purchases with the plastic card and bought a one way airbus ticket to aid her hasty escape. Who knows what else she may have done before she left us high and dry? I was not at myself much of her time here, so she could have taken advantage of me and the situation. Think of all the other poor indefensible souls she may have preyed upon; so dishonorable, don't you think?"

"Indeed, it is terrible to fathom. Is there anything I can help you with while I am here?"

"If you would be so kind as to see to the dog's needs, I would much appreciate it. He has taken a sudden disliking to me since my little ordeal. Maybe I unknowingly mistreated her while I was not at myself. I so regret those times of which I have no memory. The feline isn't much better, avoiding me like the black plague."

"Gladly," and with that, Anna called for Kramer. After several attempts and a quick search, she located him in the back bedroom, the one that had been occupied by Liz Donley. Commencing a tug and war, by Kramer's collar, she managed to drag him outside. She had never witnessed him behave in this manner. Perhaps there had been an incident as suspected by Lou. It made sense given the circumstances.

Once outside Kramer ran to the backyard, began a whimpering growl, accompanied by what almost seemed to be pleading barks. His antics reminded Anna of one of those Lassie movies, when the collie was trying to alert Timmy about some pending danger or had something to share with his master. Anna approached the pooch, Kramer standing his ground, becoming quite animated and almost pleased that she was coming to his aid. Margarett, watching from the kitchen window, caught on to the mutt's game.

"Anna," she yelled from the backdoor. "I fear the cat has escaped and is outside. Please help me find it."

Anna again clutched Kramer by the collar and escorted him back inside. "When do you think Honey might have gotten out?"

"I think she may have taken advantage of the open

door while your attention was focused on the dog."

"I didn't she her, but I guess it is possible."

"I'm sure of it. I think I saw here skedaddle through the open door."

A quick search turned up no cat. Standing at the doorway Anna smiled and pointed behind Lou. Honey was inside, just sitting there staring at them. "She must think we're cheap entertainment."

"Thank you for your help. All of this has tired me out though. I do believe I need a nap."

"You sure I can't do anything while I'm here; fix you lunch or help in any the household chores?"

"You're too kind, but no, I think I have everything under control." ***Right, Lou? It's time for her to be off.***

"You have my number. I can be there in a jiffy. I so hate that about Liz. She certainly just didn't seem to be the type to do something like that."

"You never know what little dark secrets rest inside a person's soul. Go enjoy this lively day and fret not about me. I'm doing just fine."

Anna gave Lou a hug and then departed. She gave the backyard one last glance, wondering just why Kramer had been so agitated. Poor Wade and Lou, their world had turned topsy-turvy. At least Lou showed signs of recovery. Miracle or not, Anna hoped this was an omen of good things ahead. Even if it was a short term reprieve, it was good to have Lou back. Sure, she was a little quirkier than before, but who wouldn't be, given what she had already endured.

There would be no nap in the future. Margarett was already plotting her next revengeful scheme, the demise of Judith Grumman, descendent of Joseph Herzberg. Her elder, Herzberg had been one of the first to become suspicious about her growing powers. He had alerted the others, rallying them as one to take her threats seriously.

Yes, he had been the instigator, but not the ultimate perpetrator. He hadn't the means to do what had been necessary, but he made first contact with the one who did have the knowledge. They made an unholy alliance with but one purpose, destroy her and make sure she could not be resurrected. They had underestimated her pact with someone more powerful than them. The blood of thy kin shall heal thee and this new world will be at thy mercy.

Wade arrived home earlier than had been expected. The good husband had called ahead to announce he was on his way. That provided Margarett sufficient time to prepare for more role play. Deceitfulness came easily for her. Playing on their sympathy, she could do most anything she willed. As the day before, and with the assistance of Lou, she had prepared their husband a fabulous meal. He was most appreciative and pleasantly surprised. What she didn't sooth through his stomach; she would conquer in the bedroom. He was such child's play and she must admit, worth the effort so far.

"I caught the news on my drive home and you probably don't remember it, but one of the houses we passed on our drive to the lake burned to the ground day before yesterday. It was occupied by Floyd and Ruth Abrams. They perished in the fire along with two dogs. The cause has not been determined but it doesn't sound like they have ruled out arson. I hope it wasn't intentional. That would make it murder. I'd hate to know there was someone that ruthless in the area, someone actually capable of doing something so heinous."

"That is so sad. Death by fire must be one of the worse ways to go."

"Most times the smoke inhalation gets to the occupants before the blaze does. But I agree being burned alive would be a terrible way to die."

"Do you know them?"

"Not very well, but I did have some dealings with an associate of his a year ago. I submitted a quote for a job, but I didn't get the bid. I met Floyd Abram briefly. He seemed to be a nice enough guy."

"And now, in a puff of smoke, he is no more; how tragic. Do you have a busy day ahead tomorrow?"

"Afraid so, it could be midnight by the time I get home. Why don't I ask Anna to stay over for the night and keep you company?"

"You mean baby sit me. I don't require a diaper changer anymore. That time is no more. I am my old self, feisty and bullheaded as ever. Not to worry, I'm not going ca-ca on you again, I promise."

"This disease doesn't give you choices, darling."

"I am no longer sick, unless you count how I'm sick and tired of being told I might still be."

"I love you and just worry about you. Kelly says this is so out of the ordinary, we can't discount anything. I'm not trying to jinks us but I must keep an open mind, and so should you."

"My eyes are wide open and I am on top of it. Trust me, husband, I'll not hesitate to tell you if I detect any signs that it has reared its ugly head once again."

"Sadly, you might not know it if it happens. It impacts your memory and you may not even realize it if something goes wrong."

"I'll know and I'll not conceal it from you, if that is what worries you."

"Kelly is away on some sort of medical conference. To play it safe, I think we should schedule another visit when she returns."

"It is a waste of good money, but if it is important to you, then it is important to me."

"Thanks for humoring me."

Humor you, right. I have no intention of going back

to the female doctor. She is too suspicious and a threat. I have no time to deal with more interference. She knows the caregiver's version of what happened. I need no doubt casts on her disappearance.

"I will do what is necessary to prove to you that I am healed. I'm tired, sort of; might we retire to the bedroom?"

"Wonderful idea but let me to see to Kramer's needs first. I'll join you after I let him out."

Wade walked about the yard, illuminated by the floodlights, while Kramer sniffed and marked his territory. Something caught his eye; something that just seemed out of place. He walked over to the shed after spotting the leaner. The round nosed shovel was propped up against the shed near the back side. He picked it up and examined it. Residue from fresh dirt was caked on its blade. Had Lou been doing some gardening, he wondered. It was so unlike her to not wash it clean and replace it in its designated spot inside the shed. She had always been so meticulous with the gardening equipment, very anile. She wasn't quite herself though. He shrugged and leaned it back where he had found it. There was no need confusing her by moving it from where she had left it.

Preoccupied, Wade had forgotten about Kramer. He turned to check where he may be and there he sat at the edge of the yard, staring into the woods. The last time he had been acting this way was when he had trailed Lou in that old cemetery. Lou was inside and not lost this time, so why was he so enthralled with the wooded area? He called out and Kramer briefly glanced his way before returning his attention back to the same spot.

"Come on boy, it's time to go back inside." Kramer didn't budge. Wade walked over and patted him on the head. "What is it boy?"

Kramer managed a gruff half bark, ears back and no tail wagging. His hairs were hackled on his back. He let out a low whine and moved about nervously on his haunches. Something out there just didn't set right with the canine, but it was dark and too late to investigate. Wade clutched him by the collar and turned to escort the pooch back to the house. Kramer dug in, holding his ground. The only other time Wade had witnessed him act this way was when he refused to exit the car while at the vet. His behavior never wavered when it came to vet visits.

"I'm in no mood for this tonight. I'm going inside with or without you. You do remember the last time you were left out here, don't you? You ended up in the pound; not exactly a doggie all inclusive, if you catch my drift."

A breach in the bedroom blinds exposed watchful eyes. Margarett didn't like what she was seeing. She had made a grave mistake, leaving that shovel there. Then it hit her like a ton of bricks. ***It was you, wasn't it? You had me leave it there. You knew it wasn't the normal thing to do, didn't you? Damn you, I have warned you not to interfere.***

So much for little ole me being powerless, you think? Watch your back HON; I'm not down for the count just yet. You might think you run the show and have it all under control, but I'm still in here too.

My little skip to my Lou, my little darling, don't you know that good deeds never go unpunished. Goodnight for now. Three is a crowd and there will be no threesome in the bedroom tonight.

What are you going to do?

Anything I want to, haven't you learned that by now? Sleep well and think long and hard about the consequences of your actions. You are to blame and to be held accountable.

19

Margarett sat in front of the computer, sipping a cup of coffee. She hadn't quite acquired a taste for that herbal tea, but in the company of others, she drank the nasty brew to conform to their way and not cast suspicion on Lou. She was getting the hang of this computer and becoming quite obsessed with it, almost addicted. She clicked on the Favorites list and then the Index, the local newspaper. Smiling, she read the headlines out loud, the lead feature: **Owner of Index Murdered.** *Well what do you know, Lou? It says here that Cam Bergmann has been found in an alley, just a few blocks from his home. As had been his routine, he walked the few short blocks to the Index every morning. They suspect he was a victim of a brutal robbery. Presently they have no suspects. Poor baby, he left behind two daughters and a grieving wife, blah, blah, blah. He paid for the sins of others. Blame his hereditary genes, his cruel relative, and not Lou Stetson, right? She is as innocent as the day is long, unless they find that butcher knife and wallet she has stashed away for safe keeping. We won't let that happen, now will we, Hon? Not just yet.*

You're a cold blooded killer. You will not get away with this.

Idle threats my dear...I have more urgent matters to attend to, thanks to you. I hate distractions, but given your lack of loyalty and that shovel stunt, I must issue proper punishment for those crimes perpetrated by you, my dear Lou. You'll think twice for undermining me, I promise you.

Don't you dare harm anyone because of what I did?

Observe and learn the brutality of one's actions, my dear. By your hands, remember.

Please don't do this, whatever you have it mind.

Killing two birds with one shovel, so to speak, one must stay in practice.

Lou couldn't stand to watch but she had no choice. Her life was going to hell in a hand basket. There were worse things than Alzheimer's. This parasite that had latched onto her was destroying her life and the lives of those around her, and thus far she had been unable to prevent her from unleashing what she deemed justified revenge. Somehow, someway, she had to be stopped. Lou thought about that old television commercial, *a mind is a terrible thing to waste.* She still possessed some control over her mind, as had been evident in her strategic placement of the shovel without Margarett realizing the significance.

It was obvious, too, that this intrusive invader couldn't hone in on all of her thoughts, nor access every bit of memory, not without her assistance. She would play this to her advantage as long as she could, but time was not on her side. With each murder Margarett was definitely growing stronger, more powerful. With five remaining on her hit list and her sense of urgency to murder them, Lou would have to act quickly if she had any hope of reclaiming her life. She despised being along for the ride and manipulated like a marionette by an insane puppeteer. Lou almost wished the disease that had ravished her previously would take her life and put an end to this madness; almost.

Doctor Kelly Garner's conference was coming to an end. She had shared Lou's case with some of her closest colleagues. They had been as puzzled and intrigued as she, offering no explanations for what had transpired. None of them believed Emma Lou Stetson had been cured; each expecting a relapse sooner or later. Kelly had assured them that she would keep them in the loop. Even more troubling, she had been shocked by this morning's news, after reading about Cam's death on the Index's website. The newspaper mogul had been one of her closest friends. Her heart ached for his wife and children. Apparently he had been in the wrong place at the wrong time; such a senseless lost of life.

Kelly had made several unsuccessful attempts to contact Liz Donley. It wasn't like her to not check her messages or return any calls. Several times she had been tempted to phone Wade Stetson to see how Lou was doing, but she figured that could wait until she returned. If Wade had needed her, he would have called her. Still, she yearned desperately to know how her patient was faring, good or bad. She would make that a priority Monday, when she was back in the office. Kelly had skimmed over the article about the recent fire in Greenwood. Fires were so horrible, especially when lives were lost. She didn't personally know the victims.

She perused Lou's file, as had become common practice. Each time she reviewed the tests she hoped to discover an explanation, but each time, as the time before, she learned nothing new. Kelly realized her obsession with the case was unhealthy and nonproductive, but she couldn't help it. There was just something about it, something beyond the alleged miracle cure that haunted her. Like the tests, she just couldn't pinpoint the origin and why it dogged her so. Lou's demeanor and even her dialogue was no longer that of the woman she had originally met. It was as if the old Lou and this Lou were two entirely different women. Kelly caught herself leaning towards DID, Dissociative Identity Disorder. Most knew it by its original name, multiple personality disorder, made famous by the book and movie,

The Three Faces of Eve.

Could she have totally misdiagnosed it as Alzheimer's? Might Lou instead suffer from DID? Could this be the presence of two or more distinct identities alternating control? It might explain her behavior and her inability to recall personal information, beyond what is expected through normal forgetfulness. Some of the signs and symptoms did align with this theory. Studies have indicated that in each individual the clinical presentation varies and the level of functioning can change from severely impaired to adequate. In such cases the primary identity, which often has the patient's given name, tends to be passive, dependent, guilty and depressed with other personalities being more active, aggressive or hostile, and often containing more complete memories.

Lou had requested that we call her Emma, not Lou. She had explained that it signified a new beginning, life after the miracle. Could Emma be the other personality? Emma was cruder, more vocal, more demanding, wasn't she? Emma was the liberated version. Identities may be unaware of each other and compartmentalize knowledge and memories, resulting in chaotic personal lives. Kelly was both excited and disappointed by the revelation. If this was indeed a case of DID, then there was no miracle or potential cure for Alzheimer's. Name your poison, doc, she told herself. This is not all about me. It's about helping Lou Stetson. In order to treat it properly, I must successfully diagnose her condition.

If this is DID, there has to be a trigger. Kelley would have to dig deeper during the next examination. If Emma showed reluctance in discussing this, it might be symptomatic to situations associated with abuse, shame and fear, something unearthed from her past, or possibly a recent earth shattering event in her life. She had been dismissed from her teaching post. Could that have pushed her over the edge? Problem with that theory, she had already been showing signs of a life going awry. Had Emma already manifested and had her vulgar behavior gotten Lou in trouble at work? More of this was falling into place. The evidence was compelling, once Kelley stepped away from her original diagnosis. Wade had indicated Emma's being more aggressive sexually; the opposite of Lou. Kelley could hardly wait to get home and pursue this avenue.

Margarett had not been able to formulate a plan to visit relative number three on her list. Judith Grumman, descendent of Joseph Herzberg, would have to wait her turn. Tomorrow, she would pay Judith a little visit, have no doubt. She would pony up for Joseph's actions. She relished the thought of confronting her before she killed her. Lou had certainly been right on that aspect. It drew more pleasure than mere ambushes. Cam's look had been priceless. The up close and personal encounter had unleashed a more powerful result, the life forces of Cam surging through her body like a lightning bolt. Fire, a blade and now what could she use to end the Herzberg legacy? Keeping it fresh and different would make it more difficult for anyone to ever connect the dots. And so what, if they did, they would have only Emma Lou Stetson to blame for the string of murders; the icing on the cake that would be.

"Where has this day gone?" ***Lou, don't you think it would be nice if our husband took us out tonight to an exquisite restaurant? Think about one of your favorite places to dine, one that calls for a special occasion. We'll spring it on him when he arrives home. He'll do anything for me you know. I have him wrapped around your little finger.***

Lou remained silent. She had no interest in exchanging useless mind dialogue with this creature.

Kitty, kitty, where's the little kitty? Talk to me Lou.

Fine, we'll go out, somewhere special. Are you happy?

Famished and quite ecstatic, we will have a marvelous time. I'll change into something that does you justice. Dessert will be on me, or should I say, it will be me.

Have your way then.

Wade Stetson sat across from Lou in the booth, reaching across the table to caress her hands. "Don't take this the wrong way, sweetheart, because you look quite stunning, but I think you're a tad overdressed for McDonalds."

"There's nothing fancy about this place. It's like being at a carnival, all these screaming children and outcasts from humanity."

"Must I remind you, dear, you asked me to bring you here? I just obliged. I thought you were ready for a burger or something, but I must admit, I don't remember you ever being fond of fast food joints."

You bitch. You did this.

"So, how's your Big Mac and fries?"

"Take me home, please. I'm not hungry."

"Whatever you say, but don't worry about it, Lou, I have those impulse moments too. With me, it's fried chicken livers. You know how I love liver."

You think this is funny, don't you. I'll teach you to never cross me again.

Come on, where's your sense of humor? Love in the golden arches so fits you perfectly.

Same place as yours; we'll see who has the last laugh.

"Maybe by the time we get back, Kramer will be sitting at the back door. I still can't believe he wouldn't come when you called him, and you say he just ran off down the highway. That's so odd. He's never been one to wander off in that direction. He's not a car chaser and typically sticks close to the house."

"He could have been chasing something, I suppose. He was doing a lot of barking. He seemed distracted. I noticed him looking off in that direction, sort of growling and whining. What do you suppose would make him act like that?"

"Now that you mention it, he was acting a little like that when I took him outside just before bedtime last night. He'll probably be there when we get back. He doesn't want another stay in that pound."

"I hope so. You know how I love that mutt."

You lying bi...

Now, now, name calling is so un-Lou like. Besides, we can focus more on our task at hand, without the responsibility of that dog. Having pets sort of cramps our lifestyle, don't you agree? You have to feed and water them, let them outside or clean that nasty litter box. They're really such a bore and too needy. Aren't you glad we don't have children?

"Where were you, just now, Lou. What were you thinking about?"

"A night with you, where else would my thoughts be, Hun?"

20

Margarett read the note on the kitchen counter instructing her to phone Wade if Kramer showed up. He would have Wyatt check the pound this morning. She hummed a little tune as she carried the garbage bag outside and retrieved the shovel. She hadn't worked out an explanation yet, but she would come up with something by the time Wade arrived home tonight. Once she cleaned up, it would be time to pay Judith Grumman a little visit. She lived in a village named Iva, in the county of Anderson. MapQuest had provided directions to her home. Was there nothing that the computer didn't know? It was better than gazing into a crystal ball. If she would have had its power in her time, she would have been unstoppable. Come to think of it, who could stop her now?

Just before she had a chance to slip out, the house phone rang. She figured she better answer. Wyatt greeted her, saying Kramer was not at the pound this time. Her brother-in-law encouraged her not to worry; he'd probably show up sooner or later. What did he know? She cordially thanked him and was then on her way. A device in the car, one Lou had failed to tell her about, directed them along the way. It paid to ask questions and make threats. A woman's voice talked to them, telling them to turn here and there. Her initials were GPS, possibly Gertrude something or another. After comparing her selected route with those from MapQuest, Margarett soon discarded the paper version.

Within an hour she sat in the car parked out front of the Grumman residence. It was nearly 10 AM and no sign of activity was noted. Was she or wasn't she at home? This was the largest house she had ever seen. Lou, when asked, said it was a housing complex of many people. Judith lived in Apt 109, on the first floor. Margarett didn't bring any weapons this time, figuring she should be able to hold her own with another woman. She envisioned strangling this one to death, imaging how the woman's life force would tingle at her finger tips.

She located Apt 109 and nonchalantly knocked on the door, fearless of the consequences. No one responded, so she rapped again, harder; still no one opened the door. She had not anticipated not finding her here. Obviously her plan had its flaws. She almost accused Lou of allowing this to happen, but then heard a car door slam behind her. A robust lady waddled in her direction. She was ancient, no spring chicken. Margarett eased a couple of doors away, giving her some room to get where ever she was going. She paused in front of Apt 109, inserted a key and disappeared inside.

Strangling her was going to be difficult. Judith Grumman outweighed her by at least a hundred pounds and stood several inches taller. Setting a fire would be nearly impossible and she hadn't brought the butcher's knife. She glanced about; searching for anything she could utilize as a weapon, but saw nothing. People moved about, here and there, several giving her an inquiring look. She was becoming too conspicuous and had no choice but to return to automobile. What to do, what to do, she pondered. She didn't have all day and she certainly didn't want to leave without completing what she had come here to do. Apt 109 door opened and out came her prey, a white trash bag in each hand.

She quickly exited the vehicle and engaged in foot pursuit. Judith rounded the corner. Margarett was a few paces back. Arriving at the corner, she cautiously peeked around it. Judith was still ambling along. Margarret spotted them, two of those large green trash receptacles, just like the one at McDonalds last night. Just thinking about it enraged her once again.

She paused by a parked truck, a trailer in tow, concealing her for the moment. How was she going to take the behemoth down? With her hand resting on the trailer as she crept closer, she received her answer. An assortment of machinery and tools were affixed to the trailer. A sign on the side of the truck indicated that it was Ray's Lawn Maintenance Service. Surely this Ray fellow would not mind her borrowing the curved blade mounted on the stick, a bush ax. She would have gladly asked permission but no one was around. She clutched the wooden handle and it felt just perfect in her hands.

Judith had reached her destination, placing both bags on the ground while she attempted to push back a door on the big green receptacle. Margarett utilized Lou's quickness and sprang into action, not bothering to check for witnesses. She had but one thing on her mind, destroy Judith Grumman. As Judith leaned to pick up the second bag, Margarret called out, "Judith, Judith Grumman, heir of Joseph Herzberg, I'm here to take you home."

Judith turned and was greeted by the bush ax, razor sharp, and already in the air above the woman's shoulders, standing behind her. Her voice was cut-off in mid-scream, the ax hitting its mark. She fell conveniently between the two trash receptacles. The power surged through Margarret, taking yet another bite out of the curse. A scream, much louder, broke the silence. It wasn't emitting from the lifeless body of Judith Grumman. A second lady, black, fragile and elderly, stood by a picnic table, a leash in her hand, a tiny 0furry dog on the other end of the leash. Margarett had a witness; how unfortunate for the little old lady. She closed the distance quickly and a witness was no more. She tossed the ax aside, no longer needing it and sprinted to the vehicle, quickly speeding from the parking lot.

Crime scene investigators would appreciate the nice gesture, leaving the murder weapon behind, thought Lou. Just as quickly, she remembered; those were her finger prints on the handle, not Margarett's. Sometimes sacrifices must be made for the greater good. Evil had to be stopped at all costs. This time at least evil hadn't realized the error. Possibly Margarett didn't understand the miracle of modern day crime investigation, finger prints and DNA, things that never existed in her lifetime.

Problem at hand, Lou had no criminal record, so tracing anything back to her doorstep might be cumbersome. She doubted that a connection would be made to the deaths in Greenwood because Margarett had committed the murders differently, fire, knife and now ax. Lou's finger prints were on the knife. She had to find a way to point someone to the butcher knife. That could seal the deal and put a halt to these senseless killings.

The gas hand warning light signaled low on fuel. Lou decided not to share that valuable little tidbit with her co-pilot. Running out of gas and becoming stranded on a back road could play in her favor. It would be tough to explain the blood splattered on her blouse and pants to anyone who would stop to offer assistance; especially if that person was a state trooper. Yes, Margaret thought she was in charge, but ole Lou still had a few tricks up her sleeve, and had more say so then even the parasite realized. Her subconscious swam below the surface, undetected and scheming. Less than ten miles out of town, the car chugalugged to a stop.

What the hell's going on; why did we stop? Do something.

It appears we could be of gas.

Out of fuel? How is that possible?

See that fuel gage on the dash. It's that one to the left. It indicates we're on empty. You were so preoccupied with your little murder mission that you failed to makes sure the tank was filled.

How was that my fault? You're supposed to be watchful of these matters.

You're running the show, not me. How many times have you reminded me of that? There is just so much I can do from the backseat. You're much too strong now. I can't break through unless you allow me to intervene. You must choose just how much you allow me to interact. Otherwise, you're on your own, HON.

You have experience in these matters, so I am asking; what do we need to do to obtain more fuel?

We have options. We can sit here until someone comes along and offers us assistance. We could walk back in that direction. I think there is a minute mart five or six miles back, or we could walk to the nearest house. There's one other option and probably our quickest; use the cell phone and key in Star HP and ask for roadside assistance. Once you connect, just tell them who you are, where you are and that you are stranded, out of gas.

This was just too perfect, thought Lou. Let's bring the Calvary to our doorstep. A woman, in the middle of nowhere, out of gas, with blood splattered on her clothing, now if that doesn't raise an eyebrow on an officer, I don't know what will.

We have little time to dilly dally so phoning for help is the best option. I press the little Star button and then the letters HP, is that correct?

Press the call button first and then proceed. Use your charm and sound like a damsel in distress.

I did but nothing is happening. Assist me, please.

Crap, we have no signal. We're apparently in one of those dead spots.

Dead spots, what does this mean, dead spots?

No phone service, it's rare, but some rural areas don't receive the phone signals too well, and we're in one of the areas that apparently doesn't. We could walk back in the direction we just came from until the signal strengthens.

You're trying to trick me, aren't you?

Trick you, what do you mean? I'm trying to get us out of this mess.

We walk back towards where we have just departed and constables find us and arrest us. That is your wish, isn't it?

We're miles away from the crime scene. No one will be searching for the murderer here, I assure you. Look, we need help or we're not going anywhere. You decide. I'm just along for the ride.

We will walk, but not back in that direction. We go the other way and we locate a farmhouse and ask for assistance.

Suit yourself, you're calling the shots. Possibly the signal will improve and we can still make that phone call. Perfect, explain the blood when you get there.

Walking in the heeled shoes on a rural road posed its challenges, but a mile and half later they spotted the first mailbox. A white two story house was nestled on a hillside, maybe a hundred and fifty yards up a gravel driveway. It was half pass noon when they, the one that was and the one that wasn't, knocked on the door. No one answered. Lou suggested they check in back and doing so, they spotted a figure in a garden, hoeing and doing some weeding. That brought back a rush of memories, Lou thinking about how she missed her little garden spot. There was nothing better than getting dirt on your hands. She wasn't sure if she would ever experience that joy again, not with this hanging over her head.

"Excuse me, might I bother you, Miss?" The elderly woman, maybe in her seventies, looked up from her gardening task.

"My, what happened to you young lady, are you hurt? Were you in some sort of accident?"

Margerett, for the first time, noticed the blood, or maybe she had just forgotten about it, but explaining it away was going to be difficult.

"Please allow me to call someone and get help for you."

"Oh, this is not my blood. My cat was struck by a careless motor vehicle operator. I was rushing her to the animal doctor when my vehicle used its allotted amount of fuel. I need more so that I can reach my destination."

"You're out of gas."

"Yes, and if you would be so kind as to lend us more, I could see about my wounded kitty."

"Us, was someone with you?"

"Us, sorry, me and my kitty, I'm still quite shaken by the ordeal."

"I think there might be a gas can in the shed. Let's check and then I can drive you to your car."

"That won't be necessary. I can walk back there, no sweat, don't fret."

"But what about your wounded cat, is that wise, taking the time to walk back to your car?"

"Just get me the fuel, lady, okay?"

"There's no need to take that sort of attitude with me. I'm only trying to help."

"Can't you help a little faster, and dispense with the chattiness."

"You really should practice your manners."

"Look, I have a dying cat back up the roadway and I'm sorry, but patience is not tops on my list right now. Can we just find this fuel?"

The lady opened the shed door and pointed to the red five gallon container in the corner. Margarett gave her a frustrated look and then walked over, picked it up, shook it a couple of times. "Lady, this damn thing is empty. Do you take me for the village idiot?"

"I'm sorry, but my husband takes care of the yard work. I could take you to Mack's service station, just a few miles down the road."

*Check the cell phone; see if we have a signal. Good, two bars, we can call *HP, it might be quicker.*

What does the HP stand for, my dear little Lou-Lou?

Oh, that just means Help Person, the help person for roadside assistance. Be sure to tell them you are out of gas and you are in a hurry. Use the injured animal story. They may get here quicker.

"Hello, this is the State Highway Patrol, how may I assist you?"

Highway Patrol, I thought you said it stood for Help Person?

It's just another name they use for people patrolling the highways, looking for stranded motorist. Just give them my name and address, the location, and why you need their help. They'll send someone out here. Margarett did just that and then ended the call.

"There was no need to bother the police. I'm sure they have more important things to do. I told you I would gladly help."

"Police, I thought this was the number to call for the help people, those who patrol the roadways."

The elderly woman chuckled. "Star HP is for the state police, silly; but they are always eager to help."

You did it again, tricked me. You want us to get

apprehended by the constables, don't you?

"Lady, do you have some clean clothes? I don't want the fine policeman to see me in this bloody mess."

"Call me Rosalie, I'm Rosalie Martin. Please come inside, I should be able to find you something to slip over the top of your clothing. You can wash up and I'll be right back."

Don't you dare do what you are thinking about doing?

More lessons, you never learn, Lou. Her blood will be on your hands for crossing me, but I'll make sure we do her before we change. No need to bloody up a second set of clothing.

Why do you have this urge to kill? Murdering innocent people doesn't bring you any closer to the long lost power you are seeking. Please, I beg you.

You're correct. It doesn't. Let's just call it practice. One can become rusty if one doesn't practice, no matter what the topic might be. Practice makes perfect; isn't that what they say? You must remember you are not accustomed to such brutality. I have to ensure you will not breakdown in the middle of one of our little forays, and you do have a tendency to interfere. I promise I will make this swift for the old lady; no suffering, no confrontations, she's probably seen her better days anyway. Next we must decide how we are going to handle this lawman when he arrives. It is so unfortunate that you again misled me.

The trooper, blue light flashing, pulled behind the stranded vehicle. He sat behind the wheel of his cruiser, eyeing the approaching woman walking down the road towards a vehicle parked just ahead. As trained, he cautiously exited his car, keeping the stranded vehicle between him and the woman.

"Miss, are you the one who called for assistance?"

"Yes, officer, it was little old me."

"I'm Lieutenant Conroy and you are Mrs. Stetson,

correct? Why did you abandon it then?"

"I walked until I received a phone signal. I was just up the road a ways."

"I understand you are out of gas. I did bring a gallon. It should get you to the station a few miles eastward from here. You must learn to pay more attention to your fuel gauge."

"You're right and I will, trust me. This will never happen again."

"Where are you heading?"

"Greenwood."

"Visiting there?"

"No, I live there. I was on my way back from…a friend's house."

"Why didn't you phone your friend?"

"She's sick. She wouldn't have been able to assist me, I'm afraid."

"Let's get this gas in your tank and make sure it will start. I could follow you as far as the county line."

A call blared over his radio. Margarett overheard the conversation, asking him to report to an address, the one she recognized as being Rosalie Martin's. Someone, probably her husband, had apparently found her body. "I'm sorry, I have an emergency. Please make sure your automobile will start." It did and the trooper sped off towards what would become a crime scene.

I suggest we make a hasty retreat towards Greenwood. There are too many cadavers being discovered in the general vicinity, and we need not cast any reasons for them to consider Lou Stetson a suspect; at least not for now. Others require our attention. I've never slain a police officer before. I bet it would have been a satisfying experience; maybe, another day.

Later that afternoon…

"This is Lieutenant Conroy. Please send the coroner

and forensics. It appears we may have a murder; a possible strangulation from the looks of it. The victim's husband discovered his wife's body stuffed in a closet, after finding discarded bloody clothes in a bathroom. The intruder may have sustained an injury. By the looks of the clothing, I would say the perp was a woman. She may not have been acting alone. Send backup and the tracking dogs, just in case the intruder has fled on foot."

21

Lou, aka Margarett, as had been the theme, waited for the arrival home of Wade, dinner prepared, the happy wife playing her designated role. Cured, healthy and able, she continued to defy medicine, no longer ravished by the mind thief, Alzheimer's. This had been quite an adjustment for Wade, typically Lou putting in long hours at the college and never having been the homebody. It wasn't that she couldn't cook; she usually never had the time. Combined with his travel and hectic schedules, they rarely found themselves at a sit down meal at home together. He had to admit, the change had been rather pleasant.

Wade was still saddened that Kramer hadn't shown back up. He feared the worse, a possible dog-automobile encounter. More troubling news had greeted him. Lou reported that she thought Honey had slipped out the door when she had propped it open to take out the trash. Two animals in as many days had gone missing. This seemed a bit too coincidental, but Wade refused to blame his wife for any carelessness. He was so glad to have her back, he overlooked the possibility she could have been indirectly responsible. If they were okay, they'd show back up when their appetites got the best of them.

It was nearing ten o'clock when Lou suggested they should retire for the evening. Wade had caught himself almost saying he had to take Kramer outside. She went ahead, saying she would freshen up and be waiting. Wade began switching off the lights when the doorbell rang. Flipping on the front porch light, he opened the door. A gentleman in a tie and jacket was flanked by two state troopers.

"Hi, I'm Detective Jack Yates and this is Lieutenant Conroy and Sergeant Horne. I believe this is the residence of Emma Lou Stetson, is that correct?"

"Yes, I'm her husband, Wade, is there something wrong? Have you found our dog or cat?"

"May we step inside Mister Stetson?"

"Certainly, by all means; you haven't stated your business with my wife."

"We'd like to question your wife, if that is all right."

"Question Lou, about what?"

"Lieutenant Conroy assisted a woman earlier today, stranded on the roadway West of Lowndesville; said she was heading back to Greenwood when she ran out of gas. She identified herself as Lou Stetson."

"I assure you there must be some mistake. Lou has been ill and would have no business driving in that direction. She told me earlier she had been here all day. Even if she had been there, is it a crime to run out of gas?"

"Do you mind if we talk with her just the same. Conroy met her. We can easily dismiss this if she is not the one he assisted."

"Dismiss this, what do you think she did, rob a bank or something?"

"Or something, can we just speak with your wife?"

"Just a moment, I'll get her. She was preparing for bed."

Wade entered the bedroom. Lou was already under the covers, but she slid them back to reveal she was naked as a jaybird, wearing nothing but a naughty little smile. She patted the bed and motioned him to join her.

"You better slip on some clothes. We have company and they'd like to speak to you. Lou, you did say you were here all day, didn't you?"

"Where else would I be?'

"There's a state trooper in the den. Actually there are three policemen in the den, another trooper and a detective. He thinks he assisted a woman using your name, stranded on the side of the road, no gas."

"Tell them I'm already in bed and not descent for company."

"Lou, were you stranded on the side of the road today?"

"I don't remember leaving the house. I believe I was here all day, just like I said." Margarett decided to use the mind sickness card. A lapse in memory would explain everything. Wade wasn't going to take no for an answer so she slipped on her robe and followed him to the den.

Conroy whispered to Yates, "That's her."

After the preliminary introductions, Yates began the questioning. "Why were you in Anderson County today, Mrs. Stetson?"

"Please, call me Emma. I don't remember going anywhere today. What would make you ask such a silly question?"

"Ma'am, I responded to the call. You were out of gas. I brought you some. You told me who you were and where you lived. You said you had been visiting a sick friend."

"Who was this sick friend I was supposed to be visiting? I don't think I know anyone in Anderson County. Do we, Wade, do we have friends in Anderson County?"

"Not that I am aware of, care to explain why this is so important, Detective Yates?"

"Do either of you know Byron and Rosalie Martin?"

"Never heard the names," replied Wade.

"Are we supposed to know these people," asked Emma.

"Mister Martin found his wife dead. Bloody clothes were found at the scene. We think she was strangled and whoever did it may have been wounded, changed into some of Mrs. Martin's clothing, leaving the bloody ones behind."

"What has this got to do with us?" asked Wade

"Blood hounds picked up a trail, using the discarding clothing as the signature scent. They lead us about a mile and half up the road," explained Yates.

"Directly to where your car was parked, Mrs. Stetson," added Conroy.

"Is your car in the garage?" asked Yates

"Yes, both of our vehicles are in the garage," replied Wade.

"Do you mind if the Lieutenant takes a look, just to confirm if it is the car he saw earlier?"

"Don't you need a search warrant or something for doing this?" asked Wade

"Not if you give us permission; you don't have any issues with him looking, do you?"

"Certainly not, detective; we have nothing to hide."

Conroy was gone briefly and retuned. "That's the car."

"This is unbelievable. My wife is no murderer."

"We didn't say she was. We're just investigating all leads. Please be honest with us, Mrs. Stetson. You were there this afternoon. Maybe you were meeting someone, possibly someone you didn't want your husband to know about."

"Do you think my wife was having an affair? Is that what you are insinuating? I'd like to ask you to leave."

"We can't do that Mister Stetson. You see, we have a search warrant and we'd like to take your wife in for further questioning."

"I don't remember leaving the house."

"Detective Yates, my wife was diagnosed with Alzheimer's awhile back. Possibly she doesn't remember."

"I'm sorry to hear that. Please bear with us. I'm sure all of this will wash out and everything will be fine. We do have an investigation to complete and your wife was in the general area. This is maybe a gruesome thing to share with you, but we have the bloody clothes in a bag in the car. Would you mind looking at them?"

"I don't know if I want to look at bloody clothes. What is your purpose behind this?"

"Sir, just take a look and you tell us if you recognize them or not."

"Very well, whatever, if it will just get this over with; show me this clothing, but I assure you it isn't hers."

Yates had one of the officers retrieve the bag. It was see through, clear plastic, sealed. Wade flipped it a couple of times and swallowed hard. It did look remarkably like clothes he had seen Lou wear, but it was just mere coincidence. "It sort of looks like something I have seen her wear but it's so bloody. Impossible, though, she hasn't been to that location. I'm sure of it."

"We have ourselves a bit of a problem then, don't we Mister Stetson. Lieutenant Conroy has identified your wife and the automobile. It has put her in the general proximity of where the crime was committed."

"Let's say for argument, Lou was where your officer said he assisted her. Why does that make her a suspect in the Martin murder?"

"Again, we're not accusing your wife. We hoped she may have seen something. Conroy said she was walking towards her car from the general direction of the Martin farm. Mrs. Stetson, do you remember going to the Martin residence?"

"Sugar, I don't even remember meeting the Lieutenant or running out of gas."

"Could these be your clothes?"

She just shrugged and rolled her eyes.

"I found these in the hamper," said Sergeant Horne, holding up an assortment of clothing."

"Do these belong to you, Mrs. Stetson?"

"If you found them in the dirty clothes, Detective, I would say so."

"Do you recognize these," asked Yates to Wade.

"I can't say I remember everything Lou has in her closet. I'm just not that observant, I guess." Wade didn't remember ever seeing them. He didn't tell the detective that these didn't look like her style of apparel.

"Most men aren't," added Margarett. "They remember us without clothes, though."

"Do you mind if I take them with us?"

"Why would you want her clothes, Detective?"

"I'd like to see if Mister Martin has a better memory."

"Are you going to arrest my wife?"

"We have no grounds to make an arrest, Mister Stetson. We are merely following all the leads and hopefully we can determine what happened."

"What if this Martin guy thinks the clothes belong to his wife, then what?"

"Then we'll be back for more questioning. We'll have the blood analyzed on the other clothing to make sure it matches the victim and then we'll see what develops. Thank you for your time. I'm indeed right sorry for your illness, Mrs. Stetson."

Outside, Conroy pulled Yates aside. "Something is fishy about this. The nose knows."

"I agree, but she doesn't look the type to commit murder. Why would she if she didn't know Mrs. Martin."

"What if she did know her and maybe her husband was involved with the other woman," added Horne.

Yates shook his head. "Get real; she was an old lady for heaven's sake. I don't think this was a love triangle. Possibly she did it and doesn't remember. Alzheimer's is a cruel disease. My uncle suffered from it. I saw him go nuts a few times, raising hell, cursing like a wild man; and he was a retired minister. The mind sometimes goes and takes the body along for the ride."

"I'm still a little befuddled about this," spoke up Conroy. "The Martin lady was strangled. There was no blood on her clothing or at the crime scene, other than the discarded clothing. With so much blood, could we have another victim?"

"We'll leave that to forensics."

Conroy scratched his head. "What can they really tell us? If Mrs. Martin had no wounds and Mrs. Stetson had no injuries, then the blood will match neither. Where does that leave us?"

"Back to your theory, that it belongs to another victim or another perpetrator. We just need to locate that person and get our match."

"Someone sustained some serious injuries from the looks of it. There's too much blood," said Horne.

"Have the Greenwood police keep close tabs on the Stetson's just in case."

"Lou, those clothes they got from the hamper, they don't look like something you'd wear. I don't remember ever seeing them."

"Well, they were there and you certainly didn't wear them. Maybe I bought them and I don't remember buying them. Maybe I'm not cured after all, if I can't remember driving to another county today. Why would I have driven in that direction if we don't know anyone there?"

"I'm just as baffled as you, dear. Let's allow them to do their job and get this behind us."

Got yourself in a bind haven't you, Hon?

If I go down, you go down, just remember that, Little Lou-Lou.

But if we're behind bars, you can't harm anyone else; and you certainly can't regain all this power you're craving. If it stops you then it's worth it.

Point taken, so that means I need to speed up my plans

before the constables put two and two together. Tomorrow we take care of business, my little partner in crime.

What are you planning to do?

We'll put in a full day's work and complete a clean sweep; cross all the naughties off our list. After that, I ditch you and let you fend for yourself, while I hitch a ride with someone else. Guess now we need our beauty rest. I'll let Wade slide for tonight. He was becoming too boring anyway. He's not really enough man to handle or satisfy me. He suits you just fine. You're the perfect little pathetic pair.

"What if it is true, my husband? What if I actually did drive to this place in Anderson County and have no memory of doing so? That is a scary thing to envision. If I did, I'm not healed. My cure is meaningless. Does that mean I am going to die?"

You're laying the drama on a little thick, aren't you, Margarett?

Looking to our pleading and pitifully confused eyes, your hubby is putty in your hands with me running the show. He would do anything for you, my dear. I think he would confess he killed those women before he would allow you to take the fall.

No, you're wrong. He wouldn't lie to the police, not even to protect me. No, it's just a matter of time before they piece this together and they will be back. I'd rather be behind bars if it will keep you from murdering more innocent people. There you'll be trapped just like me.

You have to be so negative, don't you? You bring me down. Go away. I'll summon you if I need you.

"Lou, and I'm calling you Lou, not Emma; if you did what they say, it isn't your fault. It's the Alzheimer's. They can't possibly hold you accountable."

"Do you think it is possible that I killed that woman?"

"No, you would never harm a flea, not knowingly."

"I sense you have some doubt."

"The state trooper seemed so sure he recognized you and our car. They're trained to observe. He said you, or the person, gave him this address and your name. It isn't stacked in our favor. But if you were there, stranded on the side of the road, that doesn't mean you killed anyone. Why would you?"

"Maybe the woman refused to help me or would not lend or sell me some petro. I could have gotten angry and who knows?" *I've got to paint my defense, just in case. Surely they wouldn't arrest a sickly woman with a dreaded disease that steals one's mind. I must use the computer to find out more of this sickness. It knows all. Playing the part is my only hope, I fear. I must be prepared to stall for time, until my mission is complete and they're all dead.*

"Let's not think that way, Lou, but just in case, I'll call Ron Pearson, our lawyer. We should be prepared for the worst, I suppose. I don't think there is any denying that you were probably in the vicinity. I just don't think you committed the crime."

"Thank you for believing in me. Your faith, love and support are very important."

"Never doubt it. You know how much I love you. We will get through this together. We always do. This time will be no different."

Blah, blah, blah, I couldn't care less about your beloved little bitch. I just require the luxury of time and then you and she can pay the pied piper as far as I'm concerned. You need your rest and I need that computer. I might just have to deliver a knockout punch after all, just to put you to beddy-bye my husband. Sex is the cure all and perfect tranquilizer for the male species. Hump, grind and then snore. You're all the same.

22

Doctor Kelly Garner had still been unable to reach Liz Donley. All of her calls had gone directly to voice mail, at home and via her cell phone. She feared something had happened because it was not like Liz to fail to return a call. After some soul searching and deliberating, Kelly decided to take the intrusive approach and phone the Stetson residence. After all, Lou was her patient and she had recommended Liz. Her last conversation with Liz had been disturbing, the bogus charges and such she had discovered on Wade Stetson's charge card. Possibly this had ended badly when she had confronted Wade. Maybe she was too embarrassed right now to talk about it. That could explain her failure to return the calls. No, Liz wasn't the type. She would have met this head on, until she cleared herself of any wrong doings.

Kelly fiddled with the numbers on her cell, calling up the Stetson's residence. Glancing at the clock, it was half pass eight in the morning. She took a deep breath and pressed the send button. On the third ring someone picked up.

"Hello, this is Doctor Graham. I was just checking in on Lou. To whom am I speaking?"

"You're in luck, Doctor. Emma Lou Stetson is talking back at you."

"Great, how have you being doing?"

"Depends on who you ask, I suppose."

"Have there been any problems; I mean…have you experienced any setbacks?"

"Depends on what you call setbacks, but who am I to say? I'm the one with the bad memory, right?"

"I take it there have been some issues, then. Would you like to share them with me, or would it be better if I discuss them with Wade or Liz?"

"Wade is at work and Liz, well, she doesn't work here anymore."

"You're there alone."

"Is that a problem, Doc?"

"You indicated there may be some concerns."

"Only if you talk to the police, I suppose."

"Police, that doesn't sound very good. Does this have anything to do with Liz Donley?"

"Why would you ask that?"

"I talked with Liz before I left for my conference. She did share with me that there was some sort of mix-up about a credit card or something."

"Mix up, I don't think so. She was caught with her hand in the cookie jar. Good ole Lizzy was stealing from us; using our credit cards, buying stuff, taking our money."

"Oh my, did you have her arrested? Is that why the police are involved? I assure you, Liz wouldn't do anything like that."

"I guess we'll never know. She skipped out on us. The heat was getting too hot in the kitchen. Police haven't found her."

"That's very difficult for me to believe."

"So you're taking her side over ours, Doc? You weren't in cahoots with her, were you? You did have Wade hire her, didn't you? Could be a nice little side scam."

"I'm offended by those accusations. I would never be involved in anything like that."

"That's good to know. Doctors are supposed to be ethical, aren't they?"

"Have you been staying alone?"

"Yep, and everything had been just peaches until yesterday when those constables showed up at our doorstep."

"I thought you said they hadn't found Liz."

"I did and they haven't. They think I drove off to a place called Iva and strangled a stranger, an old woman out in the middle of nowhere. Can you believe that?"

"Are you driving now?"

"Funny thing, I don't remember going there. I'm not sure if I'm driving or not. I suppose that shoots all sorts of holes in my cured assumptions, doesn't it, Doc?"

"I think we should schedule a visit, sooner, the better, Lou."

"I'm sort of busy right now, but you're probably right. If I'm still sick, you might be able to help me."

Busy, thought Kelly. "I have an opening tomorrow at 9 AM. Do you think you could have someone drive you here?"

"How should I know? If this sickness is what it's cracked up to be, I might not even remember talking to you, right?"

"Perhaps I should contact Wade and have him make the arrangements. Do you mind if I call him?"

Like you need an excuse to call him; Sugar, I know you must have the hots for ole Lou's hubby. "Yeah, you better set this up. I can't be trusted to follow through with anything. I might have more people to maim and murder. The sooner you stop my killing spree, the better, right, Doc?"

"First of all, I don't think you've committed anything as heinous as murder. I'm sure there's a logical explanation for the police's concern."

"There is, they think I killed that Martin woman. Who

knows, maybe I did and this sick brain of mine is hiding it from me. Have you ever had one of your Alzheimer's patients kill anybody, Doc?"

"I can't say that I have and cases are extremely rare for the afflicted to take it to those extremes. Sadly it is usually the caregiver who reaches a breaking point."

"So you're saying I should watch my back; Wade might do me in?"

"No, I don't think you have anything to fear from Wade."

"But Liz, I'm not so sure. Getting caught red handed didn't set well with her. I think she would have bumped us off if she thought she could have gotten away with it."

"Again, I think you're wrong about Liz, but that is none of my business. I'll call Wade and schedule your appointment. I don't think you should be there alone."

"You're probably right. It's too easy for me to sneak out and go on a rampage, isn't it?"

"I didn't mean it like that. For your safety, you should have someone there. What about your sister-in-law, could she come and stay with you until Wade's arrives home?"

"Good idea, I'll call her." ***Fat chance that is going to happen; I can always say I don't remember talking to you, Doc. I have my agenda laid out for today and it includes no meddling sister-in-law.***

Kelly sat at her desk after ending the call, totally flabbergasted; a woman murdered and Lou, a possible suspect. This wasn't the act of a person afflicted with Alzheimer's, but it could point strongly to her DID theory. Had another personality been involved and could this other personality have committed murder? The possibilities were even more intriguing than the path towards an Alzheimer's cure. She, being involved in a case such as this, especially if a crime had been committed, could launch her career into the limelight just as easily. This could be indeed groundbreaking, not that she was wishing that it had actually happened.

She phoned Wade and shared with him, her conversation with Lou. She disclosed the schedule opening to see Lou and he confirmed the appointment, saying he agreed and would bring her. She informed him that Lou had said she would contact her sister-in-law to come by and stay with her, if available. Wade added that he would call Anna Stetson also. Kelley opted not to pursue the Liz Donley debacle. It really wasn't any of her business, unless Wade drew her into the conversation. He didn't. She figured he must be uncomfortable discussing it with her. She didn't really blame him. Although curious, she wasn't really that keen on the idea either.

Margarett had used that Google thing and had asked the computer to tell all it knew about Alzheimer's. Several of the places that came up offered symptoms and signs. After reading over them she soon realized she could pull this off flawlessly if need be. It really wouldn't be that difficult. Forgetfulness was the key and she had already played the denial card, saying she was cured. Acting unlike Lou would be easy enough. She wasn't Lou and had no desire to remain Lou. Granted, Lou's petite little body had offered the perfect cover to surprise her unsuspecting prey, but the next host she would choose would be a better fit, younger, stronger and a head turner; a woman that could have her way.

Time was wasting. A busy day lay ahead. She had mapped out the route that would take her to a great, great grandson of Horatio Thomas. Horatio had not accosted her like the others, but because of monetary reasons, had allowed the others to sway his opinion. Just being present when they delivered their verdict and death sentence made him guilty as sin, just like those other worthless bastards. He had been at the wrong place at the wrong time. Margarett would never forget the expression on his face. He appeared to enjoy what the others were doing, even though he had first tried to talk them out of it. A few extra coins in his greasy little palm had persuaded him to look the other way and ease his conscious.

Derrick Thomas would now pay for Horatio's involvement, a tie to the bloodline so said the computer machine. He resided in the township of Due West. He was some sort of professor at an Erskine College. From photos she had uncovered, the man was older than dirt and had spent too much time above ground already. He appeared frail and thin, no match for her. She had grown giddy, anticipating doing him. Her weapon of choice, a claw hammer, should do nicely. She so enjoyed the brutality of her devilish deeds. Those bastards, drugging and hanging her, the last curse would be on them or their kin in this case.

Road trip, so Lou named it, Margarett pulled out of the drive, rather enjoying the feel of this motor coach at her fingertips now. Rounding the corner her mind consumed with Derrick Thomas, Margarett had failed to notice in her rearview mirror, Lou's faithful sister-in-law pulling into the driveway. Anna had seen what she thought was Lou's vehicle heading up the street. When she accessed the side garage door her suspicions were confirmed. The car was gone. She immediately phoned her brother-in-law. Wade, upon receiving the heads up call from Anna, keyed in Lou's cell phone number. On the second ring Lou answered.

"Lou, what are you doing?"

"Just sitting here bored as usual; and what is my beloved husband doing? I hope your day of labor is going as you might wish."

Wade hesitated, not sure if he should call her on this or not. He wasn't sure how she might react, if she even knew what she was doing or where she was going. If he informed her that he knew she was in the car, could that pose more problems? He finally told her that he had another call and would phone her right back. He skimmed his contact names and pressed Doctor Kelly Garner's number.

"Kelly, this is Wade Stetson. I think I have a problem and I need your advice."

"Yes, Wade, how can I assist?" Kelly listened to the unfolding event. Wade even recapped the visit from the officers, figuring she should be privy to the full story, from his perspective. She weighed her response carefully. If this was Alzheimer's, of which she now had her doubts, then confronting her could confuse her even more, or she would just simply deny it. If they were dealing with a second personality and if this other personality had been involved in the incident being investigated by the police, it could be tipping their hand. There would be no telling how the second personality might react, not knowing the traits of the new personality. She took a deep breath. Wade required an answer, but she hadn't shared her DID suspicions with him. There wasn't enough time to go into now.

"Wade, given what you have told me, and to possibly avoid any negative reactions while she is behind the wheel, I think there is but one alternative. You should contact the police and have them pull her over. Let them know she has Alzheimer's and that you are worried about her safety and others on the roadway. Tell them she is no threat and you or I will come get her and bring her back home."

"I don't know; the police might scare her more if she isn't sure what she is doing. What if she doesn't even recognize their authority and doesn't stop; they might take more evasive measures. I don't want them to hurt her."

"And you have no clue where she might be headed? She hasn't mentioned wanting to go anywhere?"

"No, Anna is trying to catch up with her. Maybe we should hold off on the police intervention."

"I really think you should make that phone call before someone else is harmed."

"You think she did it; killed that woman, don't you."

"I'm not insinuating she had anything to do with that. I'm simply stating that it might be dangerous, her being behind the wheel."

"All right, I'll call them, and I'm heading back that way so I can be home with her."

"I'll meet you there. Keep me posted when they catch up to her."

Anna Stetson had stuck to the main road but had yet to catch another glimpse of Lou's vehicle. It was as if she had vanished, but if she had no idea where she was headed, how could she even be sure she was looking in the right direction. Wade had called to say he had alerted the sheriff's department. What neither of them knew, an unmarked state trooper cruiser was shadowing Lou. She remained a person of interest in the Martin murder and they had kept her under surveillance. The young lawman paced her, keeping his distance as ordered. He had not been instructed to intervene, even after Wade had phoned in his request. The intent was to observe and see what she was up to, do not detain or apprehend. Wade didn't know they had a different agenda.

Just turn around. Let's go back home. You don't have to kill again.

But I do, my dear Lou. I must complete the circle before I will be empowered to restore what is rightfully mine. Blood must be spilled from those responsible.

They didn't harm you. They don't even know you. They're guilty of nothing, don't you get it? There must be a different way to get what you want. Just be satisfied. Use my body and don't harm anyone else. You can live through me; just don't commit anymore murders.

Do you really think you can live with that on your

conscious, the blood on your hands of those already dead?

I thought you were controlling the show. Can't you will me not to think about it?

You're not that naïve, Lou-Lou. I'm on to you. You're just stalling, trying to throw me off my game. This won't be over until I've made all of them pay, and then you're rid of me for good. I hop a new ride and you can go back to your pathetic little existence. Well, so long as the constables don't sniff you out. I'm not real, remember, but you are flesh and blood, present at the scene of all the crimes. I'd suggest you do my bidding or I let that little cat out of the bag after I depart for greener pastures.

You're going to do it anyway. You're going to make sure they come after me. I have access to you too. Your thoughts and feelings are mine. I know what you're planning.

And that buys you exactly what? You can't stop it. You can't change it and you certainly can't rat me out. You're sick and capable of doing this. I've already planted the seed in the doctor's head. She gets rid of you and Wade is all hers. Even a sightless dimwit could see it; she's using you and your pathetic illness to stick her claws into your husband. You're no more than a bag of garbage, needing to be taken out one last time. She had an agenda. They've been doing this behind your back. I've tried to help you, reeling him back in, but even me through you is not enough to quench his thirst.

Stop it. You're lying. You're just playing deceitful games. Wade is not like that.

It didn't seem to bother him, poking you in your fragile state. Wave it under his nose and he does what they all do. He'd rather have a half witted wife who can still screw his brains out, instead of going without; or maybe have the best of both worlds, you and a mistress. Double dipping, men like that sort of compromise, but that's just over the short haul, until you're gone and forgotten, in the crazy

house or the graveyard. I don't think the doc really cares which one. Now, be gone. I have serious matters requiring my attention, with no distractions needed. I have this hammer and hankering to do some nailing. I just need to hit it on the head, first time and we're done.

"New orders, Hampton, pull her over and bring her in," broadcast the voice of the speaker.

"But I thought you just wanted me to follow her."

"Anderson County forensics has turned up something new. Orders just came through requesting that we pick her up."

"Does that mean I am supposed to arrest her?"

"No, tell her that her husband contacted us and was concerned about her safety. You're taking her to the station where he will meet you and take her home."

"What if she refuses to abide by the request?"

"Try to remain cordial but insistent. We can't make any sort of arrest until we know what they have. They also want to compound her vehicle."

"This sounds serious."

"They sounded quite serious but would not elaborate."

"All right then, I'm closing the distance as we speak. She has exited hwy 25 and is now heading towards Donalds."

The little town of Donalds was just a stone's toss from this Due West and Erskine College, her intended destination. She fondled the claw hammer, resting beside her on the seat. Lou's skin tingled as Margarett anticipated her little rendezvous with the old codger Derrick Thomas, decedent of that old fart Horatio. The flash of blue light in the mirror disrupted her fantasies. She wasn't sure what to make of it, until Lou prompted her she better pull to the side of the road. Why did the constable wish her to stop? She certainly wasn't in distress, and she wasn't out of petro as before.

Regretfully, she pulled the vehicle off the roadway and

into the grass. Lou gave her no further instructions as what to expect, so she opened the door and stepped outside, the hammer held behind her back. State trooper Hampton was trained to approach with extreme caution if the driver or a passenger exited the stopped vehicle. His hand instinctively touched his holster, proving easy access to his revolver. Over the speaker, he advised her to return to her vehicle. She eased back into her seat, but still facing the door, her feet rested on the grass.

Hampton didn't like this either and he stepped out of his cruiser, and then approached from her the passenger side. Margarett seeing this stood back up and peered over the top of the car.

"I'm over here, not that side, silly."

"Please sit back down and place both hands on the wheel."

"You're behaving quite oddly. Why do you wish me to do that? You hailed me. I thought you wanted something."

"Just do it, please." Hampton was becoming edgy, his hand clutching the revolver in a death grip. He continued following protocol, but prepared to react if he had to.

Margarett sighed and did what he asked, slipping the hammer beneath her legs on the floor board, just before placing her hands on the steering wheel. She didn't appreciate the delay. Hampton noticed the maneuver, the dipping of her shoulder, as if attempting to conceal something or retrieve it. All the warning signs were there. Sweat dripped from his brow. His back felt soaked as well. While training had prepared him for this sort of scenario, he still found it difficult to go through the necessary motions and remain calm.

Hampton, instead of approaching the open driver's side door, he eased up to the passenger's side back door panel first and then peered though the widow to assess the situation. The Stetson lady stayed in place, hands on the wheel. He couldn't see what she might have on the floor from his angle. He barked a new set of instructions, asking her to step from the vehicle and place both hands on the top of the door frame where he could see them. She did what he had asked. Hampton then peeked inside the front seat passenger window. He spotted the hammer on the floor.

"Ma'am, please place both hands behind your head and step five paces away from your vehicle."

"Are you serious?" She turned, dropping her right hand from the wheel and resting it on the seat, just inches from the hammer.

Hampton removed his weapon and tapped the barrel on the window, repeating the instructions loudly. Margarret startled by the appearance of the gun, did what he asked, but in her attempt to exit, she accidentally griped the horn. As it blared, the window shattered from the discharge of his revolver.

23

Odd sounds and voices hovered somewhere in the background. A blinding light shattered the darkness. Blinking, Lou opened her eyes. The doctor griped her eyelid, a flash light aimed at her pupil. The doctor was talking. She could make out his lips moving but not what he was actually saying.

"She's coming around. Can you hear me, Mrs. Stetson?"

Margarett mentally elbowed Lou out of the way. "Yeah, I can hear you just fine. Now get that damn thing out of my face. Are you trying to blind me?"

"Do you remember what happened?"

Got it, this is my moment to shine. "What happened, where am I? Who are you? What do you want?"

Overplayed, Drama Queen, you think?

Be gone, you're crowding me, Lou.

Fine by me, you're flying solo, crash and burn for all I care, whatever it takes to stop your murderous ways.

Playing the sympathy card, this sickness you have and how to know what you do and not to do, just like the computer has told me how this sickness works; we'll be just fine. AND I WILL COMPLETE WHAT I STARTED.

"Mrs. Stetson, I'm Doctor Altman and you are in the emergency room at Self Regional. You have no recollection of what happened prior to being admitted?"

"Who's this Stetson woman you're babbling about, Doc? Is that the lady in white standing beside you?"

The emergency room doctor glanced over at the nurse and whispered, "Could be a possible concussion when the bullet skimmed her temple. Has any of her family been contacted?"

"Officer Hampton has reached her husband. He is on his way here. Her husband suggested we contact her physician, Doctor Kelly Garner. I received her voice mail and I filled her in as best I could on the message."

"You're going to be just fine, Mrs. Stetson. You're one lucky lady. Your wound is only superficial. I don't even expect any scarring at all."

"Wound, I'm wounded?"

"Please relax; your husband is on the way."

"I have a husband?" ***I am quite the convincing little actress, missed my calling for the theater.***

Detective Jack Yates from Anderson County arrived, accompanied by Sergeant Horne. Hampton brought them up to speed, explaining how he had seen her going for something underneath the seat. He excluded the one little fact, the horn as the triggering factor; too embarrassed to admit to being so jumpy. He showed them the evidence, the hammer secured inside a Ziploc. He'd had no choice but to react and ask questions later, unsure if she might have been going for a concealed gun. He stressed he had done nothing wrong, had followed protocol. Even so, he would be placed on administrative duty until a preliminary investigation of the incident was completed.

"What was the urgency to pick her up?"

"Clothes confiscated at her residence were identified by the husband of the slain woman, and we have discarded clothes found at the other woman's home that have been determined to contain two additional person's blood, neither belonging to the slain woman who had been strangled."

"Are you saying Stetson may have strangled the one

lady and attacked two others?"

"Forensics suspects the other blood types and amount indicate that other people had been assaulted, yes."

"Have you identified these other two people?"

"Under investigation, but we do have two murdered women in the general vicinity, attacked savagely, and no witnesses. Blood samples are being taken and will be compared to those on the clothing. All is circumstantial for now, but puzzle pieces are beginning to fall in place. If the blood from the slain ladies matches the blood on the clothing, and we can validate that the clothing belongs to Mrs. Stetson, then we have a multiple homicide on our hands, a virtual trifecta."

"Do we have motive?"

"Not presently, but Mrs. Stetson has not been well lately. Her husband says she has been diagnosed with Alzheimer's."

"That doesn't make people go psycho, does it?"

"I'm not an expert on the illness. That would be something left up to the DA and input from physicians who do understand the boundaries of the disease. Dead is dead, just the same, whether she knew or didn't know what she was doing at the time. It would only impact jail or possible commitment to a hospital."

Hampton nodded. "I had an uncle that had it. It's pretty much a death sentence, no cure and he didn't live too many years and basically became a vegetable before he died. I remember his language getting a little salty but nothing that would make me think him capable of killing anyone."

"We'll have to rely on the doctors to determine her mental state and capabilities. The courts will decide her fate if indeed she committed these murders. First, the blood matches must be confirmed and then we'll go from there. I must admit, Hampton, you discharging your weapon may have muddied the waters up for us."

"I told you she was going for something under the seat. I had no option but to react."

"Settle down, son. I'm not accusing you of anything. I'm just saying it could complicate the situation, that's all; shooting a woman with Alzheimer's who only had a hammer. It makes for PR nightmares when the press gets wind of it. We'll look like the bad guys; just fact and we know it."

"For the record, I'm not the shoot first and ask questions later type. I've never discharged my gun in the line of duty. I don't have a blemish on my record, Detective."

"I'm sure that will weigh heavily in your favor. Life isn't fair when it comes to something like this. Most of the time is just has to do with perception by those folks we are paid to protect and just how much the media wants to make of it. Then you have those ambulance chasers and rights wacko's. One can never anticipate how these matters will eventually play out; just be prepared for the worst and keep your fingers crossed, I'm just saying. Excuse us now. I'm going to see if the doctor will allow us to talk to her."

"The doctor might, but I'm not going to allow you a word with her until you talk to me first," said Wade, now standing directly behind them, accompanied by Wyatt and Anna.

"Mister Stetson, we do regret the circumstances by which your wife was detained," spoke up Yates.

"Detained, she's in the damn emergency room, or haven't you noticed? What were you people thinking, shoot first and ask questions later? What possessed you to do this to my wife?"

Hampton started to respond but Yates cut him off. "I assure you it was a misunderstanding and the officer just followed protocol when he surmised his life might be in jeopardy. We only wished to detain your wife for additional questioning. The officer had been merely asked to bring her in but your wife acted irrationally. He had to protect himself on the pretension that she was armed and attempting to use a weapon concealed underneath the driver's side seat."

"Lou would harm no one. She wasn't capable, even before she became ill."

"Again, please accept our most sincere apologies for what has transpired. It is my understanding that she sustained no life threatening injuries."

"Excuse me. She was shot in the head; just what do you consider life threatening, Detective Yates?"

"Merely grazed, and if the officer would have wanted her killed, she would have been, but it was just a reaction to a most unfortunate action. Please, do you have any idea where your wife may have been going? It was my understanding she wasn't supposed to be behind the wheel."

"She has a valid driver's license and I'm sure she had some destination in mind. Actually my sister-in-law saw her when she left and was attempting to stop her. You forgot an even more important detail, Detective; I'm the one who phoned the police and asked them to stop her. I regret that decision now. Her doctor advised me to contact them. She should be here shortly. I phoned her back after I received word of her being here."

"Sorry, I didn't realize you had done that. Why hadn't someone told me this?" snapped Yates

"You said you were simply trying to detain her, didn't you?"

"I did. I must confess. We had your wife under surveillance. I made the request to bring her in for additional questioning."

"On what grounds, Detective, if you don't mind my asking?"

"We have additional evidence in the case; the one we asked her about during our visit. The clothing we confiscated in your hamper was identified by Byron Martin as belonging to the deceased, his wife, Rosalie. That would place your wife at their home and now that casts suspicion on the bloody clothing we found at the Martin residence. You did say you did not recognize them, correct?"

"Not that I can remember ever seeing them but like I said, I'm no fashion expert."

"I recall you saying you weren't very observant."

"You said the Martin woman had been strangled and my wife had no injuries. Bloody clothes, what does that have to do with your case?"

"I'm not at liberty to say, not until forensics has completed their analysis."

"Perhaps I should contact my lawyer and have him present before I allow you to proceed with your questions and accusations."

"I don't recall accusing your wife of any crime, Mister Stetson. Possibly she is a mere witness. One thing for sure; there is no denying that clothes from the Martin residence ended up in your hamper. It's to be determined whether the bloody clothes are your wife's or not, and even if they aren't, she somehow brought Rosalie's Martin's back to your home, the identical clothing she had been wearing that very day, according to her husband. We must be able to pencil in the rest before we can draw any conclusions."

"I am calling our lawyer and I forbid you to talk to my wife until he arrives."

"Do you have something to hide?"

"I'm just protecting my wife in her ill state. She's innocent unless proven guilty, right; isn't that the way this is supposed to work, Detective Yates?"

"Very well, please by all means, contact your lawyer. In the meantime Sergeant Horne will remain posted here for her protection. I'll return shortly."

"Posted, you mean so she won't flee like some common

thug, don't you?"

"Your words not mine; make your call. Hampton, you come with me." Yates couldn't afford the young officer contracting diarrhea of the mouth, especially if the news hounds caught whiff of this and they surely would, sooner or later. He wasn't prepared to go into accelerated damage control just yet."

As they exited the hospital, Hampton nudged him in the ribs. "Index Journal, that's Chris Trainer. The cat's out of the bag now. This will be front page news, I guarantee it."

Doctor Kelly Garner also passed them in the hallway. Neither knew her, nor did she know them. Reverend Elijah Blaine followed her by a few steps. Wade had asked Anna to contact him, uncertain of Lou's condition at the time, figuring a few prayers couldn't hurt. Margarett held firm to her little ruse, portraying Lou as confused and disoriented, remembering absolutely nothing about the altercation nor where she had been headed. So far it was working; however, her patience was wearing thin. This ordeal had mucked up her plans. The sooner she could clear these pesky people from her hospital prison room, the quicker she could make haste her escape. This little scratch on the head meant absolutely nothing.

Kelly spotted Wade in the hallway ahead talking to a doctor and a gentleman she didn't recognize. His brother and sister-in-law were standing nearby. She feared Lou's situation might be grave and quickened her stride. Wade saw her, nodded and smiled, and then motioned her to join them. The good reverend mimicked her pace and sped up too, thinking Wade's gestures had been meant for him. Sergeant Horn gave them some breathing room but stayed within visual distance of the room.

"Hi Kelly, I appreciate your coming."

"How is she, Wade?"

"I haven't been in yet but the doctor did tell me she

would be fine. The wound is not serious. By the way, this is Chris Trainor, journalist for Greenwood's Index Journal. Chris, this is Doctor Kelly Garner. Chris is a close family friend. We grew up together. I was just catching him up to speed." Wade noticed the expression on Kelly's face. "Not to worry, you can speak candidly in front of Chris. Hello Elijah, thanks for coming too." Elijah placed his hand on Wade's shoulder and nodded.

Kelly took in a deep breath before speaking. "All right then, do we know why the officer shot her?"

"She was reaching for a hammer underneath the seat but the police claim they didn't know that and say the shot was fired to thwart what they perceived as aggressive behavior. The doctor also told me she has no recollection of the incident or where she was going. I guess the Alzheimer's has returned with vengeance."

"I don't think so."

"How can you say that given the circumstances?"

"I fear I misdiagnosed her condition. I don't think she is suffering from Alzheimer's."

"Is this good news or bad?"

"Good in the fact that we may be able to treat her if I am right, and I am reasonably sure I am."

"Our prayers have been answered, Glory be to God," said Elijah.

"So where do we go from here?"

"I'll know more after I talk to her. But first, you should go inside and see how she is doing. She needs your loving support."

"Curious," spoke up Chris, "What prompted you to alter your original diagnosis? You can be frank, Doctor. Consider our conversation off the record. Wade and Lou are my friends and I care about what happens to them. I'd not print anything without his consent."

"Chris can be trusted," added Wade.

"Very well, I performed a second examination and compared it to the first and something was out of kilter. Gut instinct kicked in then, doctor intuition so to speak and I researched other possibilities. Signs lean more towards DID, Dissociative Identity Disorder."

Both Chris and Elijah had that puzzled look on their faces so Kelly explained in depth the disorder and her theory, skimming over the medical mumbo jumbo. Chris jotted down some notes, assuring her it was just for his own reference and research. Both Wyatt and Anna listened in on the explanation.

Anna spoke up first, "Sounds to me like she's possessed."

Kelly smiled. "I suppose you could say that. DID is very comparable to being possessed in the sense that other personalities fight for control. These personalities can be very independent and bring out abnormal characteristics, cause the person to act and do things differently, often an element of evil verses good. "

Wyatt spoke next. "If what you suspect is true, do you think Lou or her alter ego is capable of murder?"

"Highly improbable but I suppose I can't rule it out completely. If she did, she can't be held accountable for her actions."

"Can that be defended in a court of law?" asked Chris

"I can't answer that. I'm not a lawyer."

"What can be done for our dear, Lou, besides keeping her in our prayers?" asked Elijah

"Let's wait and further this discussion when Wade returns. Where I take this rests on his shoulders. I caution you that what I have shared with you stays among us."

"I gave you my word," replied Chris, "but this will become news. Others will not be so discreet. Even I will have to post the incident in the index but I will base mine on police reports only."

"Don't look at me, Doctor. I'm a man of God. I'm not

a gossip."

"She's family and we'll do what is best to protect her and my brother," chimed in Wyatt.

A staff orderly mopped the floor just a few paces away, diligently eavesdropping on the conversation. He had previously overheard the exchanges between the Stetson man and the officers. He mumbled to himself, thinking how this was like one of those thriller type movies he always rented from Netflix. He was tingly all over, unbelievable, something like this unfolding in his hometown and him being a part of it. He hated his shift was about to end. Oh how he would love to stick around and hear more.

Wade stood over Lou's bed, an all too familiar spot lately. She looked up at him a managed a smile before speaking. "Is there something I can do for you?"

"I was just wondering how you were feeling."

"What damn business is it of yours? Should you even be in here?"

"The doctor said it was okay for me to come in."

"Does the doctor know you? I certainly don't know who the hell you are." ***Got to lay this on thick and send him packing.***

"Lou, it's me, Wade, your husband."

"Jabbering nonsense, who is this Lou person? I really think you should leave." She rose up in bed and began beating on the side rail while screaming at the top of her lungs.

Horne burst into the room, his hand on his revolver, just instinct. A nurse quickly entered and attempted to calm her down, asking Wade to please step outside. Reluctantly he abided her wishes. He was met by the others gathered outside. Anna asked, "What's happening with her?"

"I don't know. She acted like I was a stranger. She didn't even recognize her name."

"She's nuttier than a fruitcake," commented Horne.

Wade turned and gave him a *go to hell* look. Horne stood down.

"Excuse me," said Kelly, "I'll step inside, see what I can do."

The orderly froze in motion, watching and listening to the unfolding scene. He propped the mop in the bucket, and then licked his lips and rubbed his hand through his hair. This was getting too good to just simply walk away. He inched closer so he could hear every little tidbit. He sloshed the mop back onto the floor to keep it real.

Trainer excused himself, saying the family needed some alone time to deal with their emergency. Elijah offered up a quick prayer. Lou's screams and rants continued. Wyatt attempted to fill Wade in on what Kelly had shared with them, more in his terms instead of her technical version. Kelly had asked Horne to leave. He now stood outside with the others. She suggested that Wade wait outside too.

"It's like she's possessed," added Anna. "Other entities are acting on her behalf. She's not really responsible for her actions while they are in control. One of them may have killed that lady."

"Lou hasn't killed anyone," shouted Wade, elevating his voice to compensate for Lou's yelling.

"You're absolutely right, my son. The Lou we know is incapable of doing something so terrible."

"It's not Lou who is doing these things," added Wyatt, "but perhaps we should allow Kelly to determine if her suspicions are valid. Maybe Lou is suffering that DID crap."

Wade backed against the wall and slid to the floor, his hands resting on his head, and tears rolling down his face. Anna squatted beside him, attempting to comfort him. Elijah placed his hand on Wade's head and continued to pray. Wyatt pounded his hand against the wall, feeling helpless watching his brother in such distress and hurt.

24

Margarett had overplayed her theatrical performance prompting the emergency room doctor to administer a sedative. The parasite living within Lou wasn't accustomed to being sedated and struggled to maintain her composure. Lou realized this and decided it was now or never. Mustering a counter, she had but one chance possibly to do what needed to be done. She weighed her actions carefully; intent on optimizing what might be her only chance.

Kelly held Lou by the hand, talking softly, "Lou, this is Doctor Garner, you remember me, Kelly. We're going to lick this thing. It's my firm belief you do not have Alzheimer's, but instead an identity disorder. You rest now and I'll be back once you're up to it. Hang in there kiddo."

Lou opened her eyes and starred directly into Kelly's. "Margarett Levine Reznik…May 17, 1872…May 17, 1893, please…" **You bitch!** Lou went silent, closing her eyes once again.

Kelly grabbed the clipboard at the foot of her bed and scribbled down the information. "Lou, what are you trying to tell me? Who is this Reznik person?"

Sorry, she's unavailable for further comment…as I am. Darkness closed in around both of them. The sedative had done its job, but not before Lou had launched a counter. It would be up to Kelly now to decipher the mystery. She could only wait and hope.

Kelly reread what she had just written. The dates

represented a twenty one year span. Just who was this Margarett Levine Reznik? Could she be the other personality? The dates, they were 1800's, what did they mean and just why were they so significant to Lou? Maybe it was all gibberish brought on by her drugged state. She'd ask Wade did the name mean anything to him. She patted Lou on the hand and exited. She collaborated with the emergency room doctor and recommended admitting her for observation. Outside, the others gathered around her, waiting for her verdict.

"Have any of you heard her mention a female named Margarett Levine Reznik?" All acknowledged they hadn't.

Wade inquired, "Why do you ask?"

"She said her name and then quoted a couple of dates; both were from the 1800's."

"Did she say anything else," asked Anna.

"Only the word, *please*, and then the medication kicked in. It almost sounded like a plea for help. She's resting now. I've instructed them to admit her at least overnight for further observation. I'll examine her in the morning. I'll have Doctor Peavey take a look at her also."

"Thanks, Kelly, for everything," said Wade. "Why don't the rest of you go home? I'm staying tonight."

"I'll be right back," she said and disappeared around the corner.

"Are you sure, brother? We don't mind staying here and keeping you company?"

"I'd really don't prefer any company right now. I need to think."

"Tell that to the cop. It looks like you'll have company whether you want it or not. They're treating her like some common criminal, a flight risk or something," fumed Anna.

"Don't fault them, Anna, they're just doing their job," stated Elijah.

"Oh, I can blame them all right," she said, placing

both hands on her hips and giving the policeman a look of displeasure. "They shot her and caused this mess." She said it loudly enough for Horne to hear. He just turned and looked the other way.

"Guilt if I ever witnessed it," said Anna. "He can't even look me in the eyes. Just watch; it'll be a huge cover-up when all is said and done. Wade, you should have Chris post an article about their corrupt behavior."

"Calm down, honey," said Wyatt. "You're just allowing your emotions to cloud your judgment."

"Yeah, right; you just wait and see."

"Wade, can we bring you anything from home?" He almost told Wyatt to check on the pets but caught himself.

"I'm fine. Try to get some rest. I'll probably need you later." After exchanging hugs, the two of them left.

"You'll both be in our prayers, son."

"Thank you for coming." Elijah patted him on the back and ambled down the hallway.

Wade was finally alone except for Horne leaning against the emergency room waiting room door and a staff person across the hall, finishing up his mopping chores. He attempted to muster up a smile for the orderly and he simply nodded, and then wheeled the mop bucket down the corridor and out of sight. Hearing footsteps, Wade turned to see Kelly approaching.

"Wade, why don't you go home too," she told him. "She'll be out for the night. She needs the rest as do you. Have you contacted your children?"

"Damn, no I haven't. I should probably do that, shouldn't I?"

She smiled and nodded. "Can I get you a cup of coffee?"

"That would be great and while you do I'll call Leanne and Heath. Thank you again, Kelly."

"Not to worry, we'll get her back to normal."

"But what if she killed that Martin woman; then what?"

"Like I said earlier, I'm no lawyer, but I will do everything I can medically to profess her innocence. If it is DID, this should offer some exceptions to her behavior."

Detective Yates said at his desk viewing the findings on his computer screen. This was beyond unbelievable. Still he'd need more to make it all fit nice and tidy. The forensics said they had a third set of hair follicles that hadn't been identified. It matched none of the others. He crossed his fingers that identifying them would break the case and link the murders. The trifecta was falling into place.

As predicted, Lou remained sedated though the night. Wade sat by her side, wide awake and vigilant. He worried that the woman he had known forever may have committed the most horrific act. He didn't yet believe it but he couldn't dismiss it either. So far no one had presented concrete evidence to prove her involvement. Still, why had she been in Anderson County, close proximity to the crime scene? The clothes swap puzzled him. Even though he was reasonably sure now that those bloody ones found at the scene, if not Lou's clothing, looked all too similar, he wasn't quite ready to admit that in a court of law just yet. Still there remained the origin of all that blood. His heart hung low, contemplating this story was only going to worsen. His hopes hung on Kelly and if she could reach a proper diagnosis and cure.

Lou stirred, just a few arm and shoulder twitches and eye flutter but more than he had witnessed. He reached over placing her hand inside his, gently stroking it. Her fingers flexed. She was coming around. Wade didn't know what to expect so he buzzed the nurse's station. When someone came over the speaker he informed the female voice that he thought she was waking up. A minute later Kelly stepped through the door.

"I was at the nurse's station when you buzzed them. I arrived early, making my rounds with a couple of other patients and was about to head here. She rested well, then?"

"Never moved," replied Wade.

"And what about you, did you catch a nap?"

"Squirmed like a snake all night, but I'm doing fine. It doesn't take that much sleep for me."

"I see you still have company outside. I saw that same policeman there. Looks to me he pulled an all nighter too."

"I'm going to ask you what I asked you last night. Could she have committed murder?"

"Let's step outside."

"Okay, I could use a cup of high octane."

Out of earshot of the guard they continued their conversation. "Could she have done this, tough to say if she has no recollection, but possibly hypnosis could reveal the answer?"

"Wouldn't that be admissible evidence to convict her?"

"It could if the police were on board, but remember I have doctor patient confidentiality. I can do this without them being privy to it."

"What if she admits to it while hypnotized, then what?"

"Sadly I'm in virgin territory. Her case is not like anything I've ever encountered, and there's hardly any documentation to support what we are dealing with I'm afraid."

"You're still ruling out Alzheimer's then?"

"I was so sure in the beginning and now this transformation has totally botched that. It's almost as if she is and she isn't if that makes any sense."

"It doesn't but not much does to me right now."

Wade's cell phone rang. It was his son, Heath. "Dad, I think we have a serious problem. Can you access YouTube from your phone?"

"I can I guess but it's not something I normally do."

"I'm going to text you a link. Please take time to look at it and then call me back."

"Of all things, Heath wants me to watch something on YouTube. Do you know anything about viewing stuff on it? If you do, then by all means use my phone after I receive his text."

"No problem, glad to help; got it, here goes."

Ninety seconds later they both stood speechless and replayed it a second time to make sure they had seen and heard what they thought they had. The number of hits indicated it had become a viral phenomenon. This possibly changed everything. If for no other reason this would no longer be a low profile case.

Kelly finally spoke up. "I think I've seen that guy."

"Me too, right here, last night, mopping the damn floors, he had to be listening in on some of the conversations."

"Maybe so but he has put his spin on it now and people are eating it up. This is going to be a circus, Wade. Don't look now but it appears our Detective Yates is back and by the expression on his face I'd say he has seen it too."

"Is your wife up to answering a few questions this morning?"

"No, she isn't," replied Kelly. "I'm her physician and she is still heavily sedated."

"What do you want to ask, Lou?'

"Mister Stetson, it saddens me to tell you this but we have identified the blood on the discarded garments and it belongs to two females who were murdered at an apartment complex. They were attacked brutally with a stolen bush ax."

"I don't see what that has to do with anything concerning Lou."

"Maybe, maybe not, but we have finger prints from the bush ax. We'll like to, with your permission, check those against your wife's. The bloody discarded clothes at the Benson residence and then Mrs. Benson's clothing found in your hamper are not painting a good picture for your wife. Do you know a Judith Grumman?"

"No, should I?"

"She's one of the victims. The other is Adele Stills."

"Never heard that name before either," replied Wade.

"Might we take your wife's finger prints, Mister Stetson?"

"Not until I contact our lawyer."

"By all means, please do but we will do this eventually so your cooperation would be greatly appreciated."

"I'm not in a cooperating mood, Detective. You're standing here and have been accusing my wife of murdering three people, tell me why should I make this easy for you?"

"It's the right thing to do for one. We have three homicides and unfortunately your wife appears to be entangled in the mystery. She's sick. I get that and you have my sympathy, but think about the families of these three women. They're hurting too. They deserve answers."

"Lou is not a murderer."

"Under normal circumstances I honestly believe you are right. I fear this is anything but normal circumstances. Three people are dead, all killed in a very short time span and we can rule out robbery as a motive. Either there is some tie to them or this was purely a random act. I'm sorry, but we're just doing our job. "

"I appreciate your honesty," Kelly butted in, "but please allow me some time with my patient before you start grilling her. Possibly I can shed some light on this once I've had an opportunity to thoroughly examine her."

"Tell you what, if Mister Stetson will agree to the fingerprinting, I'll give you some breathing room, at least until we can verify and compare the results."

"Or I could wait until you acquire some sort of court order," added Wade.

"There's no need for the attitude, Mister Stetson."

"Sorry, but I don't appreciate the implications." His

phone rang. Yates listened to the caller and then cursed under his breath. "This is a damn mess. Have either of you seen a recently released YouTube video?"

"We saw it just before you arrived," answered Kelly.

"This just became high profile. Prepare yourselves for the media blitz."

25

"Lou, this is Doctor Garner. Can you hear me?" Kelly leaned over the bed, easing her eyelid open shinning a flash light.

"I'm not deaf or dumb. I can hear you perfectly. How about you aiming that damn light wand someplace else."

Light wand, another curious phrase thought Kelly. "How do you feel?"

"Feel like getting the hell out of this bed, how do you think I feel?"

"You've been shot. We're just taking every precaution."

Margarret felt Lou's head. "Hardly a crease; guess I'm one hard headed gal."

"Do you recall anything about the accident now?"

"Accident, someone shot me by accident? Most people get shot for a reason. Did I piss someone off or something?" *Laying on the charm, I am.*

"Let's try something different. Do you know who you are? Can you tell me your name?"

"Trick question, Hon, I'm Lou."

"Very good, so you do remember."

"Remember…hell didn't you just called me Lou. That's an odd name for a broad."

"Emma Lou Stetson, you go by Lou."

"When do I get out of here?"

"It's not that cut and dried. Your memory loss concerns me."

"So if I remember who I am I can leave? Fine, I'm Emma Lou Stetson. There you have it, satisfied? "

Kelly smiled, "I appreciate your humor even under these conditions."

"You have a strange sense of humor. I find nothing funny about this." ***I've got to get rid of her; should have done it a long time ago.***

This was tougher than Kelly had anticipated and time was of the essence. Fingerprints had been taken before Lou had regained consciousness. Those results could impede her progress if the worst possible scenario developed. Hypnosis appeared the methodology to obtain the quickest results. Wade was on board after a bit of persuasion but just how agreeable Lou would be might be a different story. Kelly stood by her second diagnosis that this was more than just mere Alzheimer's, even though there was an element of it mingled. Lou was too sharp and had rebounded significantly to have been in the advanced stages as previously suspected. The personality shifts were troubling. This seemly other identity had a darker more sinister side; one Kelly could almost envision doing something quite callous, even murder.

The other troubling factor, the YouTube video, it would bring the world in on the ever evolving case. The hospital orderly had obviously overheard several private discussions, weaving a tale worthy of a horror movie. He had claimed demonic possession had driven Lou to go on a serial crime spree. The public ate this sort of thing up. This would most certainly doom them for unwanted publicity and an onslaught of curiosity seekers. Good old tabloid television thrived on this sort of crap. Unbeknown to her, the feeding frenzy had already begun.

Spencer Misenheimer, parapsychologist, had just booked his flight from Boston to Charlotte, where a rental car awaited his arrival. Spencer specialized in a number of ostensibly paranormal phenomena, including the full gambit, telepathy, precognition, clairvoyance, psychokinesis, near-death experiences, reincarnation and apparitional experiences. He had recently signed a reality television deal with R. W. Saunders, the famed Ghost Stalker. Spencer had committed to provide expert feedback for this season's eight episodes. Saunders had contacted him from Atlanta, Georgia after seeing the YouTube posting. The show was a little cheesy for his taste but the eight episode package paid big dividends, with an option for a second year if it proved successful. Reality series were the going thing right now so why fight it.

Spencer pegged Saunders as a redneck hick from the Peach state but he couldn't deny his success. This would be the beginning of season three and his ghost stalking weekly one hour show had been a ratings hit on the Myths and Monsters Channel. Saunders was looking to expand his investigations beyond just mere haunting events. That's where his expertise would come into play. A film crew would be accompanying the ghost stalker from Atlanta. What troubled Spencer, they had no permission or signed release forms to conduct this investigation. Nothing guaranteed they would be allowed to speak with this Stetson woman or any of her family members. The orderly had already agreed to spill his guts for a fee but what could he say that he hadn't already said on the YouTube posting.

Spencer didn't expect doctors to cooperate with them due to doctor-patient confidentiality. Saunders was banking on a mole within the police department. Greasing a cops hand for information was common practice. Even he had gone that route a time or two, citing information from undisclosed sources. Another angle they could play, utilizing his experience and success as a parapsychologist to assist them with their investigation. If all else fails, so said Saunders, you can always flush out a cop from the underbrush who is a sucker for the television camera. Small towns were notorious for the type. Spencer figured he should be settled in at this Greenwood location by nightfall, providing he encountered no hitches in his flight. Saunders had them booked at the Inn on the Square, how quaint it sounded. He had moved quickly, wishing to capitalize on the story before others caught wind of it. In his redneck slang he had likened it to pissing on the shrubs and marking his territory first.

This was by no means a marriage made in heaven but Spencer was willing to do the needful to make this a successful venture. Saunders after all, had done his marketing and had found a viewing audience, so why muck that up. Spencer could fall back on his theatrical background for the camera. He was no stranger to the stage, performing in numerous plays at Boston's Huntington Theater as well as Boston's Center for the Arts. Acting had been his passion since college, an excellent stress relief and he was quite the performer, a favorite of the local critics. He had already done his homework, discovering that Emma Lou Stetson also shared a love of the arts, a professor at Newberry College in South Carolina. Perhaps their mutual interest would be the key to opening the door. He folded his final garment in his bag, zipped it up and glanced at his watch, time to hail a cab and head to Logan International.

R.W. Saunders sat in the terminal at Hartsfield–Jackson Atlanta International Airport. Glancing at the monitor, his flight was on schedule, no delays posted. The production crew had left earlier in the van, shouldn't be more than a three or so hour drive for them. It was too costly flying with all the equipment unless doing so was the only option. Frugal, he cut corners where he could always opting to pocket allowed expenses when he could. This deal had been a honey hole thus far, the ratings holding steady, and he aimed to keep it that way. He had done his homework on the parapsychologist, having even noticed he had acting credentials. Every crime crusader required a sidekick. That being said, the sidekick's job was to support the head honcho, and speak only when input was required. As long as Spencer knew his place in the pecking order, all would be fine.

Kelly was in a virtual battle of wits with her adversary, her patient, Emma Lou Stetson; yet to be determined the origin of the potential other identity, if indeed this was DID as she suspected. The storm clouds were blowing in quicker than had been anticipated and not from where expected, the media. The reality show duo would make their presence known soon enough; a game changer loomed on the horizon. That name, Margarett Levine Reznik, loomed large, could she be the other woman? Personalities were typically manifested from within, and not quite so elaborate. If this was indeed another personality then Lou's subconscious had been very creative. It stirred her curiosity. Kelly still intended to Google that name, just to verify if an actual person existed. Possibly this name had been filed away and had surfaced for a reason.

"Okay, straight talk, Doc, when can I fly this coop? I'm as healthy as a horse; fit as a fiddle, just damn peachy and I see no reason I shouldn't just spring from this bed and out that door."

"First of all, you have been placed here due to your wounds and to ensure there are no existing conditions associated with the gunshot. Secondly, and regretfully there is a police officer posted in that hallway. I don't think he's going to grant you permission to just leave."

"Am I under lawful arrest?"

"No, to my knowledge you have not been charged with a crime."

"There you have it. I'm free to go when and wherever I please, with or without the constable's permission. I say

I test this and see what happens. Do I have other clothing besides this pitiful excuse I'm wearing? It isn't properly sewn, has a split completely up the back."

"Please. I think you should calm down, Lou and do nothing irrational."

"I'm both calm and rational and I am tiring of this conversation."

"Please, wait here while I retrieve your husband. Perhaps he should weigh in on this decision."

"Perhaps you should do just that." **Leave now or feel my fury.**

What are you planning on doing?

No more hid and seek, Lou; to what do I owe the honor this time?

I have more at stake in this than you. You've already gotten me shot. What's next, my death?

Please, give me more credit than that. You die, I die along with you. I've already been dead. Trust me it is highly overrated. You should know more than anyone; I'm more the killing than the dying type. I must complete what I have begun to rid myself of you and possess the flexibility to pick and choose my destiny. I can't achieve my goals from this hospital room. The doctor is gone and so are we.

Where can you possibly go? You have no car, no money and I'm not even sure you have clothes. Trust me, in this gown; being inconspicuous is not going to happen.

To save the lives of those near and dear to you I suggest you contribute instead of hinder. You know this world, think of something. Time is of the essence.

The door swung open. Kelly entered, accompanied by Wade. Lou had accomplished what she had intended, distracting the parasite to stall. The escape plan had been removed as an option, at least for now.

"Lou, Kelly would like to try something different. It might help get to the root of your illness," said Wade.

What do you and your little girl friend have planned?
"Why do you all insist that I'm sick? I feel fine. If people would stop shooting me in the head, I think I'd feel even better."

"The shooting was a misunderstanding," added Kelly.

"So I heard; a gun beats a hammer every time. Why would I have a hammer hidden under the vehicle seat? That makes absolutely no sense."

"Lou, you're absolutely correct. I'd like to try something that could jog your memory; possibly explain things as simple as how the hammer came to be placed under the seat."

"You think I put it there, don't you? Do I look like a carpenter to you?"

"Lou, Kelly is only trying to help. She's on your side."

"We're picking sides now? So if the constables are on one side then that would mean you've chosen the side of the bad people. I'm guilty of something apparently or at least they think so enough to come out with their guns blasting. Do I look like a threat to you?"

"Lou, she would like to try hypnosis."

"What are you going to make me do, quack like a duck? I've seen these little sideshow con jobs before, people pretending to do stuff and not remembering they did it, just for cheap entertainment. I'm nobody's duck and will not be made a mockery of for cheap theatrics."

"I assure you, this is nothing like that. Possibly the key to what has been happening is buried deeply in your subconscious. This is similar to having the key to the lock."

"You think I'm crazy, don't you? Key, right, you want me locked up and the key tossed away. You have your reasons, don't you, Doc."

"I'm not sure what you mean by that. I have no hidden agenda."

"Woman to woman, Doc, you're a damn liar."

"Lou, that's uncalled-for. Kelly is just trying to help."

"I get her bedside manner loud and clear. You'll be using no hocus pocus, mumbo jumbo, horse hockey on me. Go use your witchcraft on someone else. This little chit chat session is over. When can I leave?"

"Yes, I'd like to hear that answer too."

Turning, Wade and Kelly eyed Detective Jake Yates standing in the doorway. His expression said it all. He was not a happy camper by a long shot. Yates, short, wide and rather robust, with his black hair combed straight back, slick and greasy looking, and bushy eyebrows and matching mustache, could easily pass for one of Tony Soprano's wise guys, if not for his thick southern accent. His voice certainly didn't match his demeanor. It had a Strother Martin twang to it. You almost expected him to say 'What we've got here is…failure to communicate', depicting the prison captain from the 1967 film, *Cool Hand Luke*.

"How is the patient, Doctor?"

"Why don't you ask the patient, Constable" snapped Margarett, "I'm here in the room too."

"This wasn't a cordial request, Mrs. Stetson, more professional, wondering how long your doctor intended keeping you hospitalized."

"And why would you ask that?" Wade asked but he thought he already knew the answer and he wasn't really sure he was ready to hear it.

"Doctor Garner, could you please respond to my question first, before we open up a round of twenty questions?"

"Ironically, we were just having that discussion. My opinion varies wildly from my patience's assessment. Given the circumstances and the trigger happiness of the police department, I'd still prefer keeping Lou Stetson here for a bit longer for observation and additional analysis."

"Define a bit longer, if you would be more precise."

"Minimum, a couple of more days, but it could be longer."

"A couple of more days, that is entirely out of the question," voiced Margarett.

"Lou, I think Kelly knows what is best under the circumstances," said Wade.

"And just what do you hope to ascertain, Doctor," inquired Yates.

"Might we step into the hallway, Detective?"

"Lies and secrets, both of you have personal little agendas, don't you? One wants to commit me to the crazy house and the other one wants to lock me up for a crime I never committed and toss away the key. Come to think of it, it washes out about the same way, doesn't it? I'm the loser either way."

"Lou, please try to calm down and allow them to do their jobs," said Wade.

"Right, I'm out of your hair either way and you and the white coat can take it from there." I hope I'm not spreading this a little too thick but they have to think dear Lou has crashed and gone to hell in flames.

Not to worry, you had it right. They're either going to commit us to a hospital or arrest us. Either way you'll not finish what you started and you'll be stuck with me. It saddens me to admit that but it puts a stop to your murderous ways, so I'll make that sacrifice for the greater good.

You underestimate me dear Lou-Lou. They think they are dealing with you. They have no idea they're really dealing with me. I can inflict a world of hurt even without my full powers restored. Should I recap for you; dead dog, dead cat, dead caregiver, and four others if my math serves me. You've been a busy little beaver if truth be known, and your little killing spree is far from over. I'm just lulling them into thinking they have you confined and reeled in, and then when they least expect it, we'll make

steady our escape and make you out to be quite notorious and famous. We do make the perfect Jekyll and Hyde, if I do say so myself.

Great analogy, Stevenson's character ends up dead.

And eventually you might just be, but I will be long gone before that happens.

"Okay, Doctor, we're out of earshot of your patient; fire away."

"Detective Yates, I sense there is some urgency to your seeking her release from the hospital. Do you intend to arrest my patient?"

"Like you, Doctor, and your doctor-patient confidentiality, I can't divulge the particulars of this case, even with you."

"You are going to arrest her, then. You must have new evidence, something to tie her directly to the lady's strangulation. For the record, it is my medical opinion that Lou Stetson murdered no one."

"Live by the sword; die by the sword, Doctor. I deal in facts, not assumptions. Now answer my question, how long do you really plan to keep her here?"

"Like I said, until I complete my evaluation and make sure she is out of harm's way."

"You're just delaying the inevitable."

"Maybe I can prove she didn't do what you think her capable of doing."

"You're playing a bad hand, I promise you. Off the record and to be frank, the little lady is capable of more than you can possibly imagine."

"And I'll be frank and off the record with you, Detective. I believe she suffers from DID."

"Dispense the acronyms, what does that mean?"

"Dissociative Identity Disorder, a form of multiple personality," she explained.

"Ah, so I get it now. She didn't commit these crimes.

You think some imaginary person inside her head did."

"And you just articulated crimes, plural, so what other atrocities do you accuse her of committing?"

"Touché, but no cigar, you're quite perceptive."

"Like you, Detective, my profession hinges on observations and details. Screening through the clutter to get to the truth goes unsaid."

"I do like you, Doctor Garner. I think we have similar objectives in mind."

"Not so sure about that; mine is to help my patient, and I fear yours is to convict her at all cost."

"Harsh words, remember, innocent until proven guilty in a court of law; I just allow the evidence to make the case."

"I'm tiring of the charades and rhymes. Please, just allow me to do my job."

"Same here, I'm just trying to do mine. Finish your little evaluation. I'll give you your couple of days and no more and an officer will be posted 24/7."

"Innocent until proven guilty, Detective?"

"Protecting the innocent from stumbling into something unlawful is my civil duty."

"I don't recall that being part of your serve and protect protocol."

"Wiggle room, when necessary, I wouldn't want any harm to come to our person of interest. You'll let me know if you find other persons playing hide and go seek inside her head won't you? Sorry, that's confidential isn't it? Let's put it this way then; it would make an excellent defense for her lawyer if you prove your DID theory. Tell both of them good day for me, Doc"

Kelly bit her tongue. She could hardly wait to converse with the good cop. She had certainly had her fill of the bad cop. Obviously Yates had some sort of new evidence that would lead to Lou's arrest. The clock ticked against her; two days he had said and Lou or possibly this other personality wasn't exactly cooperating. Margarett Levine Reznik surfaced in her head. This person just didn't sound like a fictitious entity; too out of the normal for Dissociative Identity Disorder.

"Lou, please work with Kelly on this. She's just trying to help."

"Why should I believe you; just because you and she say you're my husband? You could both be liars. You two do seem a bit too cozy for my taste."

"Lou, you're ill. You've been ill for quite some time, even though selfishly I have been trying to convince myself you were doing much better. Please allow Kelly to do her job. Perhaps everything can then be sorted out and maybe we can have you back on the road to recovery."

"Do you really want that? I'm not so sure. I believe you wish this person you call your wife would just go away and never return."

"Don't say things like that. I love you."

"Love, I'm not so sure I'm feeling it. If you really loved me, you would help me skip out of this place."

"I wish it were that easy. Our life has become quite complicated I'm afraid."

"I'm sure it has. I stand in the way of your happiness, a life with that slut."

"There's nothing further from the truth. She's your doctor, nothing more."

"How come she's Kelly and not Doctor then? I got her pegged don't I, and what about you my allegedly trustworthily husband?"

"Stop this nonsense. I only love one woman, you. I'm damned determined to see that you get well."

"Let's see. If that miracle happens, then the constable is chomping at the bits to run me in. Either way, I come out on the bottom or in this case being on the bottom comes with no fringe benefits, my so called husband. I prefer to choose the way I get screwed."

"Lou, this is not you talking. It's this other person, one who has invaded your head."

"Oh, you're the expert now. You think I'm crazy do you? Leave, just get out of my sight."

"Sorry, I can't do that."

"Sure you can. It's not that hard." ***I'm out of here either way.***

26

The nurse entered the room, syringe on a tray, prepared to administer the sedative as prescribed for the patient under the covers. She stood beside the bed, setting the tray on the side table, before retrieving the medication.

"Mrs. Stetson, I have something that should make you rest, doctor's orders."

Peripheral movement caught her attention, but the metallic bed pan struck its mark before she could react. Dazed, the nurse slumped over the bed, falling onto an assortment of pillows and blankets arranged underneath the sheets. Blinking and attempting to clear the cobwebs, the second blow rendered her almost unconscious. The needle from the syringe finished the job, plunging into her neck.

Kelly sat in her study, sipping a glass of wine, still pondering her path moving forward, one of uncertainty. Given the circumstances and the references by Yates that multiple crimes were intertwined, Lou was a person of interest, so he had called her. This obsession, the Margarett identity had displayed, accusing her and Wade of having some sort of relationship, while not unusual for such cases, she just wasn't buying it. She had it pegged as a smoke screen. This other person who had invaded Lou Stetson's mind was just too cunning, devious, had an agenda. Nope, this was no typical DID case. It went deeper. Kelly couldn't quite put her finger on it yet, but, a piece of the puzzle was indeed missing.

Just for the hell of it, she decided to Google Margarett Levine Reznik. To her surprise, a person of that name appeared, only once, but there it was up close and personal. She clicked on the link. Margarett Levine Reznik was born May 17, 1879, her death listed as May 17, 1890. She had lived and died in the Greenwood area. The cause of her death wasn't listed, nor was the actual burial site. It did mention one parent, her mother. One thing did catch her eye. In the brief paragraph it referenced she had been suspected of witchcraft and possibly prominent elders of the era had played a part in her demise. There were no actual names listed of those who may have persecuted her. If she had been accused and placed on trial for witchcraft, then there should be court records, surmised Kelly. She perused several more internet pages but came up empty. This was the only article. The source of the posting wasn't listed.

Was it mere coincidence that the other identity shared the same name? What were the odds that an alternate personality would manifest utilizing the entire name, Margarett Levine Reznik? Possibly Lou had also seen this name on the internet and filed it away in her memory, it only surfacing when she needed a strong willed person to step forth and help her through her dilemma and illness. Margarett acted too much like a person from the 1800's now that Kelly replayed in her mind the dialogue, references and so forth. Could this be a case of possession? Margarett was after all allegedly accused of witchcraft. Stick with the program, Kelly reminded herself, you're a medical doctor. This is not in your wheelhouse or remotely possible.

Her cell phone tucked in her pocket, still on vibrate mode, almost made her jump out of her skin. Retrieving it, she recognized the hospital number.

"Hello, this is Doctor Garner."

Kelly remained speechless, listening to the caller. Sighing, she said, "Are you sure? I'm on my way."

Arriving in less than thirty minutes she spotted Detective Yates and several uniformed officers in the hallway outside Lou Stetson's room. Someone clutched her arm from behind. It was Wade Stetson. He pulled her down a side hallway, saying nothing until he had steered her into a waiting room. Several other people occupied the room so Wade kept his voice barely above a whisper.

"She's gone. She attacked a nurse and now she's disappeared."

"I'm sorry. I ordered the sedative that she used on the nurse."

"Did you not hear me? She attacked the nurse, walloped her good with a bed pan, and then afterwards they believe she used the needle on her. Is this normal for multiple personalities?"

"No, it is a little extreme for DID. That's why I'm reconsidering my diagnosis still yet again."

"Pardon my attitude, but you can't seem to settle on one, can you? You were convinced she was in the advanced stages of Alzheimer's and then you say she has this DID. Now what, you're wrong again? Police think she's a deranged killer or something and now she's attacking nurses. My Lou would never do any of these things. Please help me understand just exactly what's going on and what we're going to do about it."

"First things first, do the police know where she is or where she may have gone?"

"They're scratching their heads too."

"Do you know where she may have gone?"

"I wouldn't be here if I did. I fear the police are geared to shoot first, ask question later. They've already attempted shooting her once. That's why I wanted to talk to you first and keep them out of it."

"I can't say Yates is on my top favorite's list either. He thinks she is responsible for more than one murder. He all but said it to me earlier."

"This is crazy. Lou absolutely would never kill anyone."

"Well, who would have thought she would attack a nurse with a bedpan. Lou is no longer in control, not for the most part. I think there is a struggle for control of her mind and body and she's losing that battle right now. Remember how she screamed out earlier, proclaiming she killed them. That was your Lou, attempting to do the right thing. Margarett isn't so willing to relinquish her control. I think she has an agenda."

"Listen to what you're saying, Kelly, You're talking like they are two entirely different people, different lives and now agendas?"

"Margarett Levine Reznik was a real person, not a fake personality. She died in 1890, a mere twenty one year old. She lived in this area, died here, under what could be suspicious circumstances."

"Now I do question your medical credentials, Kelly. Sounds like you're saying this Margarett person has possessed my Lou."

"I'm not convinced possession really exists, no more than I believe in witches and witchcraft, but something extraordinary is happening here."

"Witches, are you now telling me that this other woman was a witch?"

"Alleged, but the question remains, how did Lou come up with Margarett's name? Haven't you found it queer that her dialogue often changes, a language of a different time?"

"I might be better off siding with Yates and his bunch of crime investigators. Yours are teetering on something out of a Tales from the Crypt episode."

"I understand your frustration and your concern, Wade."

"I don't think you do. I want to find my wife before she harms herself or someone else, or before the trigger happy police force guns her down like some diabolical criminal."

"Too late, Yates is here."

"What sort of little sidebar do we have here?"

"Mr. Stetson is concerned about his wife, Detective. I am her physician, thus we have common ground."

"Dare I ask what you've being advising your patient's hubby to do? Never mind, I'm sure it would be confidential. For the record, your patient has balls. Whacking the nurse with that bedpan and juicing her, and then dressing in her nurse outfit, got her past the posted guard."

"Perhaps your elite security force isn't so proficient in guarding the only door of a hospital room. They're more accustomed to shooting first, aren't they?"

"You best keep your nose into doctoring and out of policing, Doctor. I don't take too kindly to your condescending attitude; doesn't say much for your bedside matter, does it?"

"Enough, both of you, we need to find Lou before…"

"Before what, Mr. Stetson, before she strikes again?"

"Before she hurts herself, and I don't take kindly to your condescending bravado, Detective Yates."

"APB has been issued. She can't get far on foot and dressed like a nurse."

"She got passed your posted guard with no problem, didn't she? I'm going to toss you a little bone, Detective. Heaven knows why, except we all wish for the same thing, her safe return, right?"

"Absolutely, so what little tidbit do you have for me?"

"Use your resources and find out what you can about a woman named Margarett Levine Reznik."

"Victim," asked Yates.

"Possible accomplice," replied Kelley. "Promise me you will share what you find and I'll do the same, my suspicions."

"Do you have a tad of sleuth blood running in those veins, Doc?"

"Find out what you can and we'll compare notes."

"Please promise me you will not harm my wife."

"We will do everything within our means to bring her in safe and sound. Do either of you have any idea where she may be headed or holed up?"

"The key lies in anything we can learn about Reznik, or that is my humble opinion."

"All right, Nancy Drew, let's see what we can drum up on this female. Where might I find you two?"

"You have our cell phone numbers. Isn't modern technology grand?"

Yates cursed to himself as he walked away. He didn't like being jerked around, especially by a smartass head doctor, female one at that. She was hiding something; best he play along for now. As for this Lou Stetson, her welfare rested in her hands. He would not chance losing an officer to this psycho; that you could take to the bank.

Parapsychologist Spencer Misenheimer sat at the Inn on the Square's bar sipping on a glass of Johnny Walker Red, awaiting the arrival of self proclaimed ghost stalker R. W. Saunders. His cohort had just checked in and required time to freshen up. No amount of time would improve on the hick's freshness, thought Spencer. He motioned for the bartender to hit him again. He was going to need several to tolerate Saunder's redneck demeanor. Apparently the viewing audience ate up this country bumpkin persona, all down to earth and laid back. Now, here he was, lodging in the Deep South, Greenwood, South Carolina. He almost felt like a rebel without a cause, himself. He tossed back the last of his glass, thinking how Saunders had referred to him as a Yankee, saying how it should work wonderful for the camera, the good ole boy and the Damn Yankee teaming up together.

"Damn Yankee, indeed, you remnant of the Confederacy," mumbled Spencer.

"Spencer, see you started without me." Saunders slapped him on the back, quite hard, another southern tradition; these people had to touch you when they made conversation for some godforsaken reason. Spencer didn't like being touched by anyone.

"Hey boy, hit me with a Jack and coke, how about it and keep them coming until me and ole Spence here need a designated elevator driver." The young black barkeep didn't take too kindly to being called boy but he kept it to himself; he needed this gig because it did pay well.

"I presume your flight went well."

"Hell yeah, smooth as a baby's butt, and the drive from Greenville-Spartanburg Airport was a straight shot after I got on hwy 25. The camera crew should be here most anytime. How was yorn?"

"Uneventful, the way I prefer them," replied Spencer, badly requiring that refill.

The bartender delivered the drinks. "If you're waiting on us, you're backing up, boy; might as well pour us another one while you got the hang of it because there won't be no dust settling under these puppies."

Spencer rolled his eyes and almost downed his in one gulp. This was going to be more difficult that he had first surmised. He had to remind himself that this was a mere stepping stone; take advantage of the cash cow and bide his time.

"Any new information on the Stetson woman?"

"I hadn't had a chance to strike up any talk with the hospital yet or with local cops, but be patient, Spence, they have her under lock and key over at the hospital, a person of interest she is."

"Perhaps we should consider venturing to the hospital and scoping out the surroundings."

"Might not be such a bad idea at that, sniffing around and digging a little. What you say we have one more round for the road and then head over there. I think its pretty close by. Do you really believe the gal is possessed by that dead witch, Reznik?"

"To be honest, possession is not my field of expertise."

"Man, I thought that's why I contracted you because you knew about all this crap."

"Apparently you didn't scrutinize my resume. I specialize in a gambit of unexplainable phenomena but that isn't one of them."

"What the hell, we'll wing it for our loyal fans. They'll never know the difference. By the way, I did get the skinny on the whereabouts of the graveyard where the witch is supposed to be buried. We'll get some footage there tomorrow. She was snuffed out at a ripe age, twenty one. Sources tell me several of the uppity folks had it in for her back then. Could be that she was trying to work spells on them or maybe blackmail them; either would make for good TV. I've got a pal of mine trying to track down any living relatives of the witch or those she might have been messing with back then. He's an internet geek and works dirt cheap."

"It appears you are doing your homework."

"It pays to if you're going to stay atop the ratings. Plenty folks out there just hankering to take your spot if you give them half the chance. Down the hatch, here's looking at you." Spencer downed his drink as well, growing weary of this conversation.

Greenwood's Self Regional Healthcare was just a few blocks away. Luckily for both, this could head off a potential DUI, not that either acted the least bit intoxicated, but consumption told another tale. Saunders strolled into the lobby like it owned it. Spencer took a lesser low profile, maintained his distance from the ghost chaser. He seemed too unpredictable, a redneck loose cannon. He asked if Doctor Garner was in the building and as luck would have it, she was. Surprisingly so, Saunders applied actual protocol to their visit, at least for the moment. The desk attendant paged Doctor Garner. In less than two minutes she arrived.

"Hey Doc, I'm R. W. Saunders, host of the number one rated Ghost Stalkers and this here is my new sidekick, Spencer Misenheimer, parapsychologist extraordinaire. We're here, willing and able, ready to help you solve your witch possession case. Just where is the lady in question."

Kelly crossed her arms over her chest and eyed the two of them before speaking. "I don't recall requesting your assistance, Mister Saunders."

"R.W., I'm not big on that mister stuff. Surely you've seen my show and how we investigate so called hauntings and such. We're very objective and strive to get to the bottom of them, fact or fiction."

"I assure you I have never watched your show."

"Little lady, do you live under a rock. Neilson is all over us. We're one hell of a popular reality show, let me tell you."

"I appreciate your interest in this case but I'm not about to transform this into a circus for the sake of television ratings. If you will excuse me, I have urgent matters to attend to. I have no time for this nonsense."

"Oh, you've plunged a dagger through my heart with that one. I assure you we're legit. We're the Real McCoy. Hell, I've even located where the witch was buried. We're going there tomorrow to film some footage. Did your patient, Mrs. Stetson by some chance visit the cemetery? I'd bet money on it. That's how the witch got her claws into her and body snatched her."

"You know where the graveside is located?

"Got your attention, didn't I? We're serious. We don't play around when we're involved in an investigation. I even have my team of researchers digging up any connections to folks that may have wanted her out of the picture. Yeah, you heard me right, Sugar; I believe she met an untimely and premeditated death. What else would explain her being such a restless spirit and a young pup to boot?"

Spencer remained quiet, utterly amazed at the detail Saunders had already lent to this incident. Perhaps he had misjudged and underestimated the stealth and sincerity of his new partner. If one could push aside the good old boy charm and redneck mannerisms, maybe there was something to this gentleman after all. In his words, he had the ratings and hit show on his hands, possibly enough said.

"Listen little lady, let's just say for the sake of conversation that she crossed the wrong people back in her day, or maybe her powers and practices just scared the crap out of the wrong people; either way, they did her. Twenty one years old is just a tad too young to be under dirt, don't you think? I got my team researching what they can find on her medical history just in case."

"For the sake of conversation, I'm going to play along with your hypothesis for just a bit. You think my patient has been bewitched so to speak by the malevolent spirit of Margarett Levine Reznik."

"Possessed, to use the right terminology; she's using the Stetson woman for evil intent is my guess."

"You've pieced this together and you have never met or interviewed Lou. Aren't you reaching a bit for mere entertainment purposes?"

"I'm a professional. It's my job to sort through the evidence at hand, Little Lady. This isn't mumbo jumbo, sleight of hand, ole medicine show conning. My credentials speak for themselves. I'm in high demand and I promise results and deliver the goods. We get to the bottom of every single paranormal phenomenon."

"And where do you figure in on this, Mister Misenheimer?"

"I delve into the additional aspects, those not covered via R.W.'s conventional equipment and means." Spencer was getting into the flow of this.

"Gentlemen, I do appreciate your candidness and enthusiasm, but my profession doesn't allow me to entertain such absurd assumptions."

"Right, you can believe in multiple personalities invading one person's head but you can't be open-minded about a spirit doing the same thing, a witch to say the least. The Catholic Church believes in possession and many documented cases support it too. Hell, some priests are trained in performing an exorcism. You can't sweep that under the rug. Possession is the real deal and it's reared its ugly head right here in the fine state of South Carolina. We're here to prove or disprove it."

"Can we at least meet Mrs. Stetson, "asked Spencer.

"Impossible," answered Kelly.

"What do you have to hide from us," spoke up R.W.

Kelly took a deep breath. "Nothing, she's not here."

"Ah, so she has been released. I have her home address and phone number already. We can meet her there."

"You won't find her at home I'm afraid."

"Don't tell me you have her stashed away somewhere or might she have been incarcerated?"

"To be honest, I have no idea where she is. She attacked a nurse and has vanished."

"Vengeful little witch, this spirit is. You sure you don't need our help, Doc."

"This is a police matter. Perhaps you should take it up with them."

"Have it your way, girlie. I just thought you had more compassion towards your patience's health and welfare. Correct me if I'm wrong but haven't the police already shot the gal once."

Wade approached the gathered threesome. "Kelly, did I hear this gentleman speaking about Lou?"

"You must be the Mister to the Missy. I'm R. W. Saunders and this here is Spencer Misenheimer. We were just offering up a helping hand in locating your wife. You may have caught my show, The Ghost Stalker, prime time every Tuesday night on…"

"They were just leaving," interrupted Kelly.

"Whoa, I have seen your show a couple of times. Why are you interested in my Lou?"

R. W. rolled his eyes and exhaled loudly. "I reckon I got to go through this a second time." He did and after the dust settled, Wade welcomed their assistance to the protests from Kelly. Wade played the angle R.W. had laid out so well; the police were too trigger-happy. They needed to find her before they did and before she dug herself a deeper hole, so explained R.W. Like it or not, they were in with Wade's blessing.

27

Lou had convinced Margarett to go home for a change of clothing. Prancing around in the nurse's outfit was only going to draw unwanted attention. She had hoped Wade would be there. He wasn't. Then she figured here would be the first place the police would look and she had been right. An unmarked cruiser had been parked two houses away, but Margarett was nobody's fool. She had spotted the policeman too, saying she could smell and feel constables, second nature. Margarett was quite resourceful. She stayed out of view of the watchful officer and eventually smashed in a back window with a yard Gnome. In the house she was free to take her time. She accessed the computer, jotting down names, addresses and directions to her remaining victims' heirs.

Lou tried to come up with a plan. Somehow she needed to plant information that would foil Margarett's murderous intentions and she had to do it without her knowing it. For now she was barely holding her own with the parasite, but if Margarett was speaking the truth, and then she would become stronger with the death of every new victim. This wasn't going to be an easy task. There were no secrets between them. She had to outsmart her, convince her to do the wrong thing for the right reason. She saw one chance but pulling it off carried high stakes and probably every ounce of willpower Lou still occupied by the invader. She concentrated, centering her focus ob but one subconscious thought. By golly, it appeared to have worked. Question now, would Wade notice it before it was too late?

Time to fly the coup, sweet Lou, but we're going to need us some transportation. Where do you suppose we can scrounge us up a ride?

You don't really think I'm going to assist you in your little murderous crime spree, do you?

You're always the disappointment, my little wild flower, aren't you? Not to worry, you have a front row seat to my unfolding drama and you can neither run nor hide. Might I remind you, I can snuff out your dear Wade on a mere whim, so please reconsider being so snooty.

I warn you.

Threaten me, certainly you must know better by now, Lou-Lou. I'm not one to be taken lightly. Slaying those who stand in my way is of no consequences. It means no more to me than swatting a mosquito on my thigh. The blood is a mere splatter, nothing more. I'll ask one last time. Where might we commandeer a motorized carriage, any old one will do.

My car has been compounded and Wade has the other one. I have nothing else I can offer. You could call a cab but I don't think it would go unnoticed by the policeman parked outside.

Ah yes, constable; thanks for reminding me. See you can be quite resourceful.

Detective Yates had found nothing significant about this Reznik woman. She was deceased, had been for nearly 120 years; died young, a mere twenty one year old. What did she have to do with this case? So what, maybe Stetson imagined she was Reznik or something; wasn't that why they called it multiple personality disorder? Doctor Garner seemed to think it held some sort of key. Yates wasn't connecting any dots. Worst still, no one had located Stetson.

One thing he knew for sure, she was extremely dangerous, whether the doctor or her husband agreed or not. Multiple murders had been committed and the bread crumbs let to Stetson.

Proof in the pudding, she had assaulted the nurse. That alone demonstrated the extent of her capabilities. He regretted how it reflected poorly on the local police, thankful he resided in another county. He had only been allowed to lead the investigation because the crimes were committed in Anderson and not Greenwood County. She muddied up the water though when she attacked the Self Regional Healthcare nurse. Now the locals could stake a claim in the case. His phone rang.

"What do you mean you've lost contact with the officer staking out the Stetson house? Send over back-up and see what the hell is going on. Yeah, go ahead, get the other line, I'll hold."

After a slight pause, the officer came back on the line and began explaining. Yates listened briefly and then responded. "Neither he nor his vehicle are at the scene. What's that supposed to mean? Did he pull out on his own or did he take on a pursuit? Neither…so where the hell is he? I suggest you search the premises and call out an APB on the missing officer. I'm on my way." *First the incident at the hospital and now this; come on folks, we're looking like a bunch of idiots.*

That was almost too easy. The constable wasn't expecting an ambush, was he Lou-Lou? I hope he is comfy and cozy in that back seat. How convenient that they place this cage between the front and back seats. Those mandibles should hold him quite nicely if he so happens to awaken from his slumber.

You hit him quite hard. He might be dead. You shouldn't have done that.

He's still breathing. You fret too much over things that are of no consequences. We must locate Bo Hanson in a quaint little village named Six Mile. The MapQuest instructs us we should arrive there within an hour, forty one minutes if we follow the path it has provided. This firearm should provide us with the means to quickly dispose of the Hanson gentleman. Of course, I will announce my intent if given the opportunity. These fools deserve to know the penalty bestowed on them as a result of their ancestors' treachery. See, I do have a heart after all.

Heart, I don't think so. You enjoy this. I fully understand why you were stopped and served the fate you obviously deserved. Pity you aren't still where they planted you.

Ah but we are together now aren't we, two peas in a pod, my partner and unwillingly participant. You'll feel the wrath of those seeking to serve justice when I am elsewhere. You'll never talk your way out of it with all the evidence mounting against you. I'll so cherish observing your demise from a safe distance.

That radio chatter indicates the jig is up. They're looking for the officer and this patrol car. They've issued an all points bulletin seeking him. A police car will stand out like a sore thumb, especially one with Greenwood County markings. You'll never reach your destination now.

Perhaps we should hedge our wager. There is no advantage in making the journey quietly, now is there? Show me how to engage the bright lights and that gosh awful screaming siren. Never mind, you just did. You think. I do. We're such the perfect pair. With all this noise it will guarantee other motorized carriages will offer us clear passage. I have to quicken our speed and we'll be there in a no time at all. Bo Hanson, here we come, ready or not.

Wade Stetson arrived home just as Detective Yates

pulled into the driveway ahead of him. Yates rolled out the driver's side looking none too happy about the mounting circumstances. He had hoped the detective had arrived to tell him they had found Lou but his demeanor indicated otherwise. Wade didn't particular like Yates. The man was obviously obsessed with bringing Lou in, possibly not caring if she was dead or alive. Wade perceived Yates as a man on a mission and one who thrived in the spotlight. He was usually a good read on character.

"Detective, any news on Lou?"

"I was hoping she had contacted you."

"No, not a peep and I'm certain she fears the consequences surrounding the latest events. You and your fellow officers with your guns blazing and take her anyway you can attitude has caused her to go into hiding."

"That was an unfair assessment, Mr. Stetson. We're only doing our duly sworn job. By the way, one of our gun happy officers is missing along with his patrol car. My gut tells me your wife had something to do with this since we haven't been able to hail him on his radio."

"You're just out to blame every crime in the surrounding counties on her, aren't you?"

"The officer was on stake out here at your home. Now he's not. Yes, your wife no doubt had something to do with his disappearance. For her sake and yours I hope she has done him no harm. I fear the worst case scenario given her pattern thus far."

"Pattern, how dare you? You have no concrete evidence my wife has perpetrated any of these crimes."

"She assaulted a nurse, must I remind you?"

"The nurse is okay. She just sedated her. She didn't kill her. You drove her do that with all these accusations."

"My, my so now we're to blame for her actions. Get a life, Stetson. We've fabricated none of this. Visit the morgue if you require proof. Now, with your permission of course, I'd like to search the premises."

"We'll do it together. I'm weary of your trigger happy agenda."

Yates rolled his eyes. "I'll go in first and I assure you it is simply protocol that I stand on ready just in case." He smiled just to get a rise from Stetson.

A quick search and the evidence left little doubt; Lou Stetson had been here. The discarded nurse uniform was found on the bedroom floor. Yates, weapon drawn, did a room to room search, enjoying every second of it at Stetson's expense. He found the broken window. It appeared his wife had exited the premises and it became more evident that she had hijacked the police car. Yates called it in, stating to approach Lou Stetson with extreme caution, she was most likely armed now and to be considered dangerous. Wade objected to those remarks but Yates just shrugged, stating fact was fact, and he would not jeopardize losing another officer, given the unknown fate of the missing one.

Yates questioned whether Wade could identify any missing apparel that may help render a better description. Wade couldn't be certain. Yates sarcastically replied she shouldn't be hard to find commandeering a stolen police car. While Yates didn't expect her to return to the home, he informed Wade that he would have an officer stationed inside just in case, and then bode him farewell. Wade displayed his poker face; not willing to show any emotion that he was certain would float the detective's boat.

Wade paced the kitchen, sipping on a glass of sweet tea, racking his brain, trying to figure just where Lou might have gone. He was drawing blanks. Wade began recapping events, attempting to unravel the mystery since Lou had been diagnosed with Alzheimer's and then this DID crap. Stepping back and breathing it in, he could see more clearly the odd patterns. Both pets had gone missing. This didn't seem to be so coincidental now. Could Lou have done something to these animals she so loved?

Then there was the encounter with caregiver, Liz Donley. Liz had not seemed to be the type that would steal from those requiring her services. She had sort of dropped off the radar too. Could Lou have had something to do with her disappearance? No, impossible, Lou didn't have it in her to harm animal or person. Unfortunately the Lou he had witnessed lately, while she looked the same, she didn't act or talk the same. No, he mumbled; Lou could not have been responsible for any of these atrocities. It just didn't make sense.

Wade walked from room to room, not looking for anything in particular but hoping to uncover some clue of her whereabouts. Nothing jumped out at him. The doorbell ringing almost prompted him to drop his glass. As promised by Yates, a uniformed officer greeted him as the door. Wade granted him access and offered him a glass of tea. The policemen declined and stated he was going to sweep the premises before settling in. Wade nodded and then told him he would stay out of the way and would be in the other room if he needed him. Lost, Wade flopped down in front of Lou's computer, placing the glass on the desk and his face in his hands.

Rubbing his eyes, he took a deep breath and stared at the screen. It was blank. He unintentionally placed his hand on the keyboard and the scream burst brightly in his face. He chuckled to himself, almost embarrassed he had allowed it to startle him. Then it struck him like a lightning bolt. This computer had been turned off; he was certain of that. Lou was a stickler for always logging off and shutting down the computer when finished with it. That had been enforced by the IT department at Newberry College. Lou had forced this routine on Wade.

Almost hyperventilating, Wade realized Lou had taken time to access the computer while she was here. Impossible, she would have shut it down before leaving, creature of habit, right mind or not. He was sure of that fact. He moved the mouse and noticed she was still signed on. Respecting one another's privacy, each had their own passwords to access their personal settings. He didn't know hers so she had definitely taken the time to use the computer but why.

28

"Spence, old buddy, this has more quills than a porcupine. We're onto something huge, I'm telling you. We got ourselves a little homicidal witch spirit using this Stetson woman to do no good. Police think she might have snuffed out at least three women already and she cold cocked that nurse. My sources said she might have carjacked a policeman and his patrol car. Man, it don't get no better than this. We have a rating's sensation bursting at the seams. We got to stay on top of it while the trail is red hot."

"I must admit this case is quite intriguing."

"Take it from ole R.W., this is a little honey hole for sure. So much so it calls for immediate action. I'm going to round up the crew and visit that graveyard tonight. This stuff always works better filming it in the dark; adds that spooky affect the viewers just eat up like Candy Korn."

"Can you find this graveyard in the dark?"

"We'll find it in the daylight but we're not going to film until after dark. I know this is your first rodeo but have no fear, that's why I'm here. We'll do us a dress rehearsal or two and I've got one hell of an editor so not to worry if you screw up on camera, Spence."

"I have no concerns performing for the camera, I assure you."

"Forgot, you're Mister Broadway Joe, aren't you?"

"Yes, I'm a seasoned theatrical professional if that is your insinuation."

"Half the reason I hired you, for your acting skills, and you'll wow them with your in depth analyzing, I'm betting the bank on that. We'll feed off one another and keep the audience on the edge of their Lazy Boys."

"Are we going to risk inviting the doctor again?"

"She had her chance. She snubbed us, her loss, even though her pretty face and credentials wouldn't hurt our cause. Why don't you toss her an invite this time? She might warm up to your charismatic stage presence. She isn't too fond of my Bubba charm."

"Do you have a phone number by which I can reach her?"

"Up close and personal, that's the way to handle it; just drop by her office and lay it on thick."

Spencer obtained the address and drove his rental to her office. He was in luck. The receptionist said she was in and asked him to have a seat. Three other individuals occupied the waiting room, two women and a man. He wasn't summoned until after each took their turn. The receptionist granted him permission to enter. Doctor Kelly Garner leaned against a counter, coffee mug in hand, wearing her poker face, looking unimpressed by his arrival.

"Under the weather, Mr. Misenheimer, are just on another witch hunt?"

"Bedside humor, without the bed, how refreshing, Doctor."

"Where's the ghost buster, out chasing our local Casper?"

"You're not going to make this easy, are you?"

"Easy come, easy go, what can I do for you, Mr. Misenheimer?"

"We're proceeding to the gravesite this afternoon, just thought you might be interested in accompanying us. Tonight we're filming the segment there."

"Curious, just why are you offering me an olive

branch?"

"You appeared sincerely interested in your patient's well being. If the deceased woman can shed any light on her treatment it could be beneficial, would you not agree?"

"If I do agree to go to the site, I will not participate in an appearance on your little side show circus."

"That is your choice, not mine. If you are interested, we'll stop by and pick you up within the hour. Wear something a little more outdoorsy. By the way, the same invitation goes for Mr. Stetson. You have our permission to have him meet us here also, if you'd be so kind as to contact him. Until then…"

Conflicted, Kelly was undecided if she should attend this staged event or not. A part of her wanted to know the truth about Margarett Levine Reznik, but what could really be learned by visiting her resting place? One thing for sure, she'd not be made a fool of by these two reality show shysters. Against her better judgment she phoned Wade. He picked up on the first ring.

"You won't believe this but I was just about to key in your number. I think I'm on to something. Can you come by?"

Discounting the invite from Misenheimer, she responded, "I'm on my way."

"Be forewarned that I have company. An officer is stationed here so let's keep this between just you and me for now. Pretend you're just stopping by concerned about your patient and I'll act surprised by your visit."

"You don't trust Yates either, do you?'

"Not in the least when it comes to Lou's safety."

"Ditto on that, I should be there in twenty minutes."

Margarett zoomed up highway 25, a four lane roadway towards Greenville. MapQuest instructed them to remain on 25 for 35.7 miles then turn left on Pelzer HWY/SC8 for another 12.5 miles. Short spurts on this road and then that would prompt a decrease in the current speed. Operating the emergency lights and siren prompted unwanted attention from those speckling the rural landscape.

Neither Joe nor L.J., the television crewmen, questioned his request. They dropped to the first mound of dirt and began digging like a pair of hounds. Within minutes Joe withdrew his hand and stood up, pinching his nose and fanning the air. The others quickly got a whiff of the stench. The scent of death burned their nostrils. With a little encouragement, but not before covering their mouths and noses with their tee-shirts, the crew dug until they caught sight of the stench's origin.

"What you fellers got there?" asked R.W.

Before Joe could answer, he turned away and heaved, unleashing the bile that had built up in his throat. L.J. stood up and turned away from Joe now puking his guts. Stepping away from the hole, he pulled down his shirt from his face.

"It's some sort of animal carcass. If I had to guess, it looks to be maybe a dog. I guess somebody uses this place to get rid of their pets, a final resting spot for old Rover."

"Well, what'cher waiting for boys, there's two more; let's see what we have behind door number two."

"Is this really necessary, digging up animal remains?"

"Spence, settle down, we didn't even have the cameras rolling so your reputation is intact. You know what, that's not a bad idea. Joe, you're not cut out for this digging so how about manning the camera. This might make some good footage."

Joe nodded, happy to oblige. He wiped his mouth with his shirt tail and retrieved the camera as instructed while L.J. went to work on the second mound. The foul stench still permeated the breathing air so it was difficult to tell if what rested in grave number two added to the suffocating odor. Quicker than before, L.J. rested on his knees and fanned the air.

"Dead cat, been her longer than the dog it appears."

"Enough is enough, we're wasting our time here," grumbled an irate Spencer Misenheimer.

"Keep the camera rolling," ordered R.W. "Go for it L.J. No need stopping now. It adds to the suspense. We might just have to cover up that dog and re-film the dig too. The viewers love sitting on the edge of their seats."

While the camera remained rolling, the trusty light and sound guy dug handful after handful from the mound. R.W. stood, arms crossed, growing impatient. Spencer shook his head and turned his back to the scene, mouthing *unbelievable*. He stared at the gravestone, the one signifying the last resting place for Margarett Levine Reznik, thinking what a waste of time. He second guessed his intentions, regretting getting hooked up with this redneck sideshow freak.

Suddenly L.J. sprung to his feet, wiping his mouth with the back of his hand and stumbling backwards. His eyes were wild and his facial features were distorted, a man gripped in terror. He mumbled incoherently before finally making eye contact with his boss.

"Holly mother, it's a body, a real person's body, not an animal. We have a dead person here."

29

"I got here as quickly as I could," said Doctor Kelly Garner, standing in the kitchen doorway.

"I think I may have stumbled into something here, something that might help us close some loops, but if I'm right…"

"Calm down and take a deep breath, Wade. Can I get you a glass of water?"

"I need something stronger than water to get my nerves in check."

"Then perhaps you just need to sit down and compose your thoughts."

"You don't get it. I really don't want to be thinking what I'm thinking right now."

"Okay, start from the beginning. What have you found that has upset you so?"

"Her computer, Lou's computer, it was still up and she was signed on. She never does either of those things. She always logs out and shuts it down when she is finished."

"So you're telling me she was here."

"It appears so."

"This is a stressful situation and given the terrible circumstances, I'm sure she is not thinking clearly."

"There's more. Come with me. I think I can better explain by showing you what I found on the computer."

Kelly looked over Wade's shoulder as he clicked on

the dropdown box that listed the most recent computer searches. MapQuest appeared numerous times but so what. As Wade carefully perused the listings, a series of names appeared, still meaning nothing to Kelly. There were even website searches for Alzheimer's, a logical search for someone with her possible condition.

"You don't get it, do you?"

"Honestly, no, so how about explaining what this means to you."

"Note, specifically, after each inquiry about a person's name, it is followed by MapQuest. Lou was searching for these particular people and then she Googled MapQuest to locate their addresses and possibly map out how to get there."

He read the list of names; Floyd Abrams, Cam Bergmann, Judith Grumman, Derrick Thomas, Bo Hanson…

"Okay, but I still am not following why this is significant."

"Understandable, I didn't at first until one name clicked with me. You do recognize this person, don't you?"

"Yes, he was the owner of the Index. Wasn't he robbed and killed a while back?"

"Yes he was. There are other names here. I have verified that all of them are deceased for one reason or another, some still under investigation, one acquaintance of ours died in a fire. The kicker, one of the females killed in Anderson is right there."

"Oh my God, are you telling me that you think Lou researched these people, found out where they lived and then…"

"It's there, Kelly, no denying it. I truly hope I'm wrong. Lou is no murderer; I'd swear my life on that."

"If she did commit these crimes, then why? Clinically it

makes absolutely no sense. No one with Alzheimer's could or would plot something this devious. I find it difficult to fathom a person with DID would do this either."

"Then what? You tell me. It's there in black and white. Those people are dead and appear on our computer."

"Margarett Levine Reznik…"

"What is that supposed to mean?"

"I'm not exactly sure. If my suspicions are point on, then we're dealing with something beyond my expertise and, to be perfectly honest with you, purely supernatural and unfounded; just my opinion."

"You think this Reznik woman has possessed Lou, don't you, just like those ghost investigators said."

"Please don't put words in my mouth, Wade. I'm not professing to believe any such thing but I'm open to bringing in someone who is more knowledgeable in these matters, if you are."

"Do we really have a choice? I'm more concerned about the police and what they might do to Lou and what she might do if confronted. Plus, those last names on her search are alive, at least as far as I can tell. Does this mean we contact Saunders and Misenheimer?"

"I'm not going that far because I'm not sold on their credibility or their sincerity but Misenheimer did tell me they had located the Resnik woman's grave. He asked if I'd like to accompany them. I didn't turn them down but I came here instead. I had hoped Yates would follow that lead but I guess our reality show hosts are better at this than he."

"Or the detective just has this hard on about nailing Lou…"

"Your call, Wade, what do you want to do?"

"I just want to do whatever it takes to make sure no harm comes to my wife, regardless of the implications."

"You do realize that this could be perceived as obstructing the judicial system, don't you, withholding evidence in a crime investigation?"

"Only if we let the cat out of the bag; and for the record, I really don't want you to jeopardize your career and break any laws for the sake of helping me."

"Lou is my patient. I only want what is best for her. I'll go along with this a far as I feel comfortable. If we do find her before the police do, then I'll back off and allow you to do what is necessary to protect her."

"I'd suggest you back off now. Once you cross the line I think you're in it by default. The legal system won't allow you to wiggle off the hook on a mere technicality."

"I'd not be able to live with myself if I walked away from this now. To be honest, this case has intrigued me from the start. For pure selfish reasons I'm going to stick this out, not that I don't care for Lou's safety."

"Thanks for being honest, Kelly. For the record, I know you do care for Lou beyond mere patient loyalty."

"Okay then, I'd suggest we phone those ghost busters and see what they've uncovered. I sure hope we're not stepping into a pile of dung." Kelly made the call.

"Doc, to what do I owe the honor?"

"I've been thinking. I'd like to take you up on your offer, accompanying you to the alleged Margarett Levine Reznik gravesite."

"Sorry, we're way past that invite now. Snooze you lose. Possibly I can interview you later for a segment."

"You don't understand. I've uncovered evidence that might imply Reznik did indeed possess my client."

"And I've uncovered a whole lot more that might not set so well with you and the lady. My crew is at the gravesite as we speak. More is buried here than just our witch and I have the exclusive, even before the cops get their filthy little grubby hands on the crime scene and yes, I do believe we're sitting on one hell of a powder keg right now. I do appreciate your offer but now is not a good time."

"What if I told you I have a list of names of potential victims, possible murders and this Reznik woman may have used Lou as a vehicle to perpetrate these heinous crimes."

"Then I'd say you and I do need to talk about your little discovery. I'll give you directions to our locale and have one of my crew members meet you by the roadside. It's sort of tough to find. I warn you though, this is not for the squeamish, and please don't tip off the police just yet or all bets are off."

"Trust me, Mister Saunders; I have no intention of involving the law right now."

"A woman after my heart, you are."

"Wade Stetson will be accompanying me."

"Wonderful idea, having the hubby present for this."

Kelly made no comment. Once Saunders had provided her with directions she promptly ended the call. She then shared the information with Wade and to her surprise he reacted quite oddly. A perplexed yet concerned look shadowed his expression.

"This secluded cemetery is not so secluded by way the crow flies. It's practically in my backyard. I never knew it existed, not until we found Lou crumpled by that grave marker. There's a marsh back there behind our property and one hell of an overgrown thicket. I never explored beyond the marsh because it is so desolate and near impassable due to all the briars and swampy land. We're no more than ten minutes from the old road he mentioned."

"It sounded as if they had stumbled upon something quite significant, something more than just her gravesite. I could sense it in Saunders's voice. The policeman in the kitchen, do you think he will be a problem?"

"Hope not; he's supposed to be on watch here for Lou."

"But, it might raise an eyebrow if we leave together."

"Good point; you go first. I'll give it about ten minutes before I join you. I'll tell him I'm heading to see my brother or something like that. I'll print out the info from her searches."

"Good luck, see you in about twenty then."

30

Lou-Lou, it appears we're getting close or so says these MapQuest directions; just a couple more turns, four miles and we will arrive at the humble home of Mister Bo Hanson, carrying the torch for his long departed ancestor, Zachariah Hanson.

Lou remained silent, refusing to allow Margarett to get to her. She focused all her energy on blocking the invader from reading her thoughts. The witch had to be stopped before another innocent unsuspecting person fell to her revenge. Lou could not believe police had not intercepted the stolen cruiser yet. They had passed at least one highway patrolman but he had been preoccupied writing a traffic violation ticket; never bothered to even look up from his diligent actions.

I can almost feel the energy surge, the rush I will receive from ending yet one more of my tormentor's lives. Don't even think about starting that pathetic argument that Bo Hanson never harmed a hair on my pretty little head. His bloodline was responsible and an eye for an eye is justification enough. What are you up too, Lou-Lou? I sense you are deliberately shutting me out. Don't be foolish. You can't delay or stop the inevitable."

Lou used every inch of her remaining willpower to fend off the bombarding inquiries. With the effort it took, she had little energy left to formulate and conceal a counter plan to Margarett's murderous intentions. She could only hope that Bo Hanson was nowhere to be found and that possibly Wade might stumble into the clues she had planted for him. Either way the options were slim. She couldn't bear the thoughts of more blood on her hands and indeed these murders were being perpetrated by her very own hands. Little relief came from the fact that she had no control over her actions.

Margarett accelerated, the police cruiser serving only to bolster her confidence that she would succeed in her mission. Lou could detect the tingling sensations, her parasite becoming exited, anticipating the pending encounter. The witch sensed her quarry was nearby. Lou hoped she was wrong. Wheeling around the next curve, Margarett eased on the brake, pulling to a driveway and eyeing the mailbox. Hanson in bold white letters adorned the side of the black mailbox. They had reached their destination with fate.

Wade Stetson had tap danced his way around the officer guarding his house. He had concocted a frivolous lie stating his kids were meeting him at his brother's house. He asked the officer to please notify him if his wife had been located. So far, so good, the scheme appeared to be working. Just in case it wasn't, Wade had backtracked a couple of times to ensure he was not being tailed. He now pulled off the roadway just behind Kelly's SUV, a rental car and a white cargo van with Saunders's reality television show painted on the sides. Kelly was standing next to a man Wade perceived to be a crew member.

The gent, flashlight in hand, led them through the thicket. When asked what they had found, he just responded he wasn't at liberty to say. He was a loyal subject to the core but there was no hiding it; he appeared visibly shaken by the ordeal. A few minutes into their trek, bright lights could be seen through the trees ahead. Their guide pointed saying they were set up for filming purposes. Wade could make out shadows, silhouettes moving about and could barely hear some chatter. Kelly nodded, confirming she saw and heard it too. Within twenty yards of the site the stench of death overpowered their senses. Wade gagged. Kelly appeared unaffected. The crew member pulled up his tee shirt over his mouth and nose. Obviously he had played this game.

"Greetings, have I got a ditty to share with you here. Doc maybe you can lend your expertise and examine the decomposition and hang a timeframe on the cadavers. By the way, hope you don't mind, we're filming. You can sign waivers later."

"You said cadavers, plural," verified Kelly.

"I did indeed. We have three. Go figure, all nestled right close to our witch's final resting place. Something tells me this is no coincidence."

"Are the remains human," asked Kelly.

"Yes and no; it appears we have a variety pack, all freshly planted I must add."

Spencer remained silent, embarrassed by his partner's antics and insensitivity. Sure, anyone could bury animals, no big deal, but that third grave contained the body of a person and obviously this had been no normal burial. The intent had been to conceal its presence. Spencer wasn't sure how the two animals played into the scenario unless they were merely sacrificial; possibly paying homage to the witch. This was a crime scene for heaven sakes and R.W. was still referring to it as an excavation site. He was certain that the police would have a different view; most likely they'd be incarcerated for disturbing and potentially destroying evidence. If they were arrested, his cohort would simply view this as free publicity and would most likely capitalize on it to boost the premiere of the segment. He had to hand it R.W., he had this routine down pat.

"Have you contacted the police," spoke up Wade.

"Way too early for that; they'd just chase us away. No, this is primetime footage, priceless, and will be a blockbuster segment. Hell, I envision this being a multi-segment extravaganza. Consider it our version of Shark Week on Discovery. I've never done that before but there's always a first time."

"We really should call the police," Wade added a second time.

"In due time, Stetson, in due time, but right now we must learn what we can, and just how it links to your wife; you do want our help, don't you?"

"Please just tell us what you have found and cut out the theatrics," stated Kelly.

"A cat, a dog and a female, is that direct and to the point for you, Missy? It must be some sort of ritual if I had to guess. You care to take a gander?"

Kelly stepped forward. Wade held his ground, not so sure about this. A cat, a dog and a female played over and over his head. What sort of psycho would perpetrate something like this, and practically in his own backyard? Kelly peered into the first grave, the one with the cat and then the hole containing the dog, but it was the final hole that took her breath.

"Oh no, please no."

"What," spoke up Spencer, "Do you recognize her?"

"Wade, its Liz Donley."

"You must be mistaken."

"Look for yourself, but I'm telling you it is Liz."

R. W. peered in as if to confirm what she had just said and then asked, "Who is this Donley woman?"

"She was my wife's caregiver before I caught her embezzling money from us." Wade took a quick peek and indeed the body inside the grave was Liz.

"Is this the way you serve justice in Greenwood," chuckled R. W.

"This is no laughing matter," snapped Kelly.

"I agree with Doctor Garner, Saunders, stifle your sarcasm and perhaps we should now contact the authorities."

"Not so fast, Spence; we still have some file footage to shoot yet. What's her connection to the pooch and feline?"

"That's Honey and Kramer, our pets. Both disappeared a while back. Liz Donley dropped off the face of the earth too, shortly after I accused her of stealing from us."

"I don't think our killer was too fond of any of them unless they were part of a sacrifice."

"Don't you get it? All three were connected to my household." Wade suddenly went pale, his legs shaky, barely supporting his weight. "Lou had issues with all three; not my Lou but the one suffering from the illness. She supposedly accidentally allowed both animals to escape from the house. She liked Liz at first but then turned on her. We thought it was the Alzheimer's. Kelly, Lou couldn't have done this, could she?"

"Let's not jump to conclusions, Wade."

"Man oh man is this getting good. Keep that camera rolling."

"She did it. She had to be the one to do it. And those others, the ones I showed you. Kelly, those names, the other names, those still alive; she's going after them too."

"Hold on there, partner. You better do a little sharing. It goes both ways. I showed you mine, now show me yours."

"May as well tell him," sighed Kelly. "We might just need his help when all is said and done."

Wade explained what he had found on the computer, the names, the searches, those deceased and those still apparently alive. R. W. quickly phoned his geek squad to have them research the names and any ties to Margarett Levine Resin.

"Now we phone the authorities," advised Spencer.

"Hold on to your horses, not just yet. They'd just root

us off the hind tit. Nope, we got to sit on this a tad longer and see what we can come up with. What you two say?"

"I agree with your cohort, we need to call the police," said Kelly.

"Hear me out, little lady. What if Stetson's wife is truly possessed by Margarett Levine Resin; you bring in the police now and you'll never be able to prove her innocence and exercise the demons so to speak. We're the only chance she has for getting a fair shake; if we find her before the cops do."

Bullshit and you know it, thought Spencer. The man had a nose for sensationalism and this plot reeked of it. Against his better judgment he remained on the sidelines, content to allow it to run its course. Spencer hated himself for thinking like this but he had committed to the contract, end of the story, and possibly the line once the police caught a whiff of what they had done.

"Kelly, Saunders is right. Yates couldn't care less about what happens to Lou, as long as he solves the case. This thing has grown too many tentacles. It's going to take an asserted effort by all of us the clear Lou of any wrong doings."

"Wade, if she committed these acts it is going to be tough to prove her innocence. Possession by a dead witch isn't going to cut it. I'm not even sure DID is going to be a valid defense. We're on thin ice but I do agree with you about Yates. He's as much of a showman as these two."

"Ouch, that one hurt, little lady; I wish no harm to the Stetson woman. Face the facts. If the witch has somehow taken ownership of her then we're not dealing with a wholesome happy housewife. She's a ruthless killer and capable of anything. Sorry Stetson, not your wife but this thing now controlling her, and who knows what sorts of supernatural powers she possesses."

"Boss, should I keep filming?"

"Keep her rolling and make sure you have plenty of video and battery. This could make the big screen, the reality movie of the century."

"You're disgusting," snapped Kelly.

"It's a natural born gift, darling" rebutted R. W. "Let's take the rental vehicle just in case there is an APB out for your SUV or Stetson's car. Park them up that old right of way entrance road. Joe you and the camera ride with us. L.J. you follow us in the van."

"I think we should check out the addresses and names on Lou's last Google and Map Quest searches," added Wade.

"Good idea; she probably has them in her crosshairs," responded R.W. "Let's rock and roll, spooks wait for nobody."

31

"Well, well, we're in luck, Lou-Lou, there stands Mister Bo Hanson, not a care in the world," whispered Margarett, standing just outside Hanson's kitchen window and peering inside. "I could shoot him right now but the fun is in the confrontation. Plus, absorbing his life force is only effective when I'm eye to eye with one of these worthless scoundrels."

Lou had to derail this before another fell victim to her evil ways, but how? Even she could feel the parasite's power had grown much stronger. It was all she could muster, just keeping Margarett at bay, preventing her from invading her thoughts. There must be something I can do, she fretted over the pending consequences.

Margarett headed towards Bo Hanson's front door, swagger in her steps. She moistened her lips, a predator licking its chops just before the final kill. Lou experienced her anticipation, along for the ride, preferring to be elsewhere. The witch now stood at the threshold, fingers on her left hand wiggling with excitement while her right hand clutched the police officer's sidearm. Lou felt the finger twitching on the trigger, her finger. She was about to commit murder again, another stranger and distant relative to those who persecuted Margarett in a time long forgotten. Those killing her had obviously been justified in their actions. They recognized her for what she was and thought they had stopped her. Unfortunately they had underestimated her powers and now Lou paid for that grave error.

Instead of pressing the door bell, Margarett knocked aggressively. Lou's knuckles throbbed, the witch now sensing blood in the water. Her veins pulsated from the increased heart rate. This was it. There would be no stopping her. The door opened. A child, a girl no more than six or seven greeted them with a smile. The mere sight sent a ripple of chills through Lou's body.

"Run," screamed Lou, the gun rising at her side.

Detective Yates was still troubled by the officer's disappearance. There was no doubt that the Stetson woman had been responsible. The question remained, had the officer been physically harmed. He had been disturbed by the other officer's remarks stationed at the Stetson home; that something seemed amiss between the doctor and Wade Stetson. The officer had failed to act on his instincts; had allowed both of them to depart the premises. Neither had been tailed and Stetson had not shown up at his brother's home. It had been a bogus lie. They better not be aiding and abetting or he would have their asses.

Why had no one located the missing cruiser? Pity the vehicle had been an older version lacking the tracking chip for newer models. Eye witness surveillance was so old school. The incoming call jolted him from his deep thought. Doctor Gardner's SUV had been located, abandoned on a rural road. Two notions came to mind. Either she had rendezvoused with Wade Stetson or she had fallen victim to his wife. Before he had an opportunity to ponder further, the patrolmen informed him that they had also found a vehicle registered to Wade Stetson nearby, locked and abandoned too. What the…, were they on foot or had they both fell victim to the ruthless killer.

Yates called in more officers to the scene to comb the area and treat it like a crime scene. He engaged his siren and lights and then sped in that direction. He'd tolerate no mishandling of the site. This case was becoming screwier by the minute. There would be no more careless mistakes on his watch. He'd be exclusively hands on from this point forward, not that he hadn't already been thus far.

"Map Quest has us heading up highway twenty five," stated Wade.

"Google matches general location as the residence of a Bo Hanson. Hopefully we've picked the correct one from her inquiries," added Kelly.

"Working in reverse order, choosing her first inquiry would be an adequate assumption," stated Spencer.

"It is the closest address to ours," said Wade.

"Kill them as I come to them. That's exactly what I'd do if I were in her shoes," announced R.W., nodding to the others.

"How long before we arrive, asked Spencer.

"Less than hour," replied Wade.

"Less than that," responded R.W., applying his lead foot to the accelerator. The van kept pace behind them, darkness enveloping both vehicles.

"Getting caught speeding; you think that's going to help our cause?"

"You worry too much, Doc."

"Yeah I do and your employee videoing this is the incriminating exclamation point for the prosecution."

R.W. ignored her comment, too focused on the mission. He could only hope that they actually caught the Stetson woman in the act and if not; bloody carnage left in her wake would be just as good. Blood and gore, a recipe for the squeamish and perfect for the ratings, all equated to viewer ownership. He'd own his time slot if the pot tipped in his favor. R.W. didn't believe in blind luck. Luck was for the foolish, the reckless gamblers. He made his luck, by hook or by crook. The audience really didn't care providing the storyline captivated them and kept them entertained.

This one would be off the charts.

The little girl screamed at the sight of the gun in the strange lady's hand. Frozen, she couldn't run, fearing the woman would shoot her if she tried. Lou seized the opportunity, Margarett surprised by the child answering the door; she forced the witch's reflexes to go limp and drop the gun. The little girl seeing this swirled and sprinted out of sight.

"I underestimated you my dear Lou. Not too worry, there comes the Calvary, daddy to the rescue." She bent down and retrieved the gun just as Bo Hanson closed to within three feet. He came to a screeching halt, the gun now waving towards his face.

"Greetings Bo, I'm an avenging angel here to settle the score, one inflicted on me by your great, great and not so great uncle. Does the name Margarett Levine Resin strike your fancy?"

"Lady I don't know who you are or what your connection is to my family but please don't do something foolish, something you may regret later."

"Regrets, nope, I don't think so; but I will spare the child, one family member satisfies my needs and rectifies the wrong doings in full. Your uncle played a role in my untimely murder. You can clear your family's indiscretions and make the world a safer place for your darling daughter."

"You're making absolutely no sense, your talk of murder. It's quite obvious you're alive and well. Please just leave and I promise you I will press no charges."

"Sweet talker just like your dear uncle, aren't you. The roly-poly bumble bee tasted my nectar more times than I care to count and still it didn't satisfy his lust. I enjoy the pleasures of pain just as well as the next person but he took his liberties a bit too far, even for my taste. Then, when I refused his bidding and conjured up a little payback for his wife, he convinced the others to deal with me swiftly.

They eagerly joined him, fearing I would inflict equal pain and punishment on them and theirs. Justifiably so, I would have in due time. My mother used me to provide her with the finer things in life, living comfortably off my talents, perceiving me as young and too afraid to resist or rebel. Live and learn."

"Again, I don't know what you think I or any of my family has to do with your hardships but I assure you, we've never done you or yours any harm."

"But you have and you will compensate me by forfeiting your mortal soul. Chit chat is over." The thunder of the gunshot rattled the windows. Lou could do nothing but bear witness to another tragic ending by her hands. Margarett leaned over, kissing Bo Hanson on the cheek before shoving the gun against his crotch and empting the round. She then laid the gun on his chest and walked away. The power surge jolted Lou, shock waves rippling through every inch of her body. Margarett was yet one step closer to becoming unstoppable; even Lou realized it.

Detective Yates and a handful of officers stood mesmerized by the unearthed gravesites in the shadow of a stone marker with Margarett Levine Resin's name etched on its face. Someone had obviously disturbed these shallow graves and he had dibs on the doctor and Stetson, but if so, where were they now? Both their vehicles had been abandoned. Had they become victims of Lou Stetson or was someone else involved in these murders?

This wasn't going the direction Yates had envisioned. The water was becoming way too muddy for his liking. The news folks would only make it worse if they caught wind of the latest so he instructed the officers to keep this low profile for now, explaining the best way to catch Lou Stetson was not to play their hand just yet. He called in forensics and hoped they'd be able to ID the female in the unmarked grave. Even more troublesome, there was no word on the missing cruiser.

"That's it. That's the address we're looking for," announced R. W. Saunders.

"By all accounts, a Mister Bo Hanson should reside here," added Wade Stetson.

"Let's saddle up and call on Mister Hanson and see if he had crossed paths with your wife."

If he has, it probably spells bad news, thought Spencer Wisenheimer. These encounters had not gone well thus far. An open door wasn't a good sign either. Spencer as had the others, had noticed the large wood frame door was half open. No one would do that knowingly, especially since there was no outer screen or storm door. With R.W. leading the way and Joe filming, the rag tag bunch approached the front door.

"Holy crap," exclaimed R. W., motioning for Joe to close in with the camera. "I think the little lady has already left her calling card."

Spencer, as did the others, took turns taking a peek inside. A man sprawled in his own blood lay in the foyer; a revolver resting on his chest. It didn't take a crime scene investigator to note he had been shot multiple times. Wade dropped to his haunches, hands over his face and wept openly. L.T, with no stomach for this, began puking again. R. W. motioned for Joe to get a shot of the bloodied husband. Kelly placed her hand over the lens and pushed the camera away, daring anyone to challenge her resistance.

R. W. took center stage and hammed it up, describing the scene and his suspicions concerning Lou Stetson and her suspected possession by Margarett Levine Resin. To CYA he added that the police must be contacted immediately. He winked at Spencer at an angle the camera could not catch him doing so.

"That's the most intelligent thing I've heard you utter," said Kelly. "I'll call 911."

Before she could key in the numbers, and before R. W. could derail the call, they were distracted by a whimpering sound somewhere within the confines of the house. R. W. nudged Spencer in the general direction, giving Joe the keep filming sign. If Lou Stetson was still here, R. W. had no intention of being her next victim. It was time for Spence to be in the limelight, just in case the worst case scenario awaited them. Cautiously they proceeded, almost moving as one.

The whimpering grew louder just ahead and then abruptly stopped. The person had evidently sensed their presence. R. W. placed his hand on Spencer and gave him a slight push. Spencer didn't appreciate the encouragement, but inched further down a darkened hallway. They heard it again, someone attempting to stifle a cry. The sound was coming from behind a door just to their left. The hallway suddenly lit up in a burst of light. L. J. gave them an excuse me shrug, his hand resting on a wall switch.

Spencer clutched the door knob, took a deep breath and quickly yanked the door open as he strategically positioned himself behind the door. Joe had no such luxury as R. W. made sure he had a clear shot of whoever was hiding inside. At first they saw no one, but then something shifted just out of sight below the hanging garments. Kelly pushed past them and knelt down.

"It's okay honey, we're not here to do you any harm."

"Is that mean lady gone?"

"Your name is…"

"Candice…"

"I'm Kelly. Did she harm you?"

"She had a gun but she dropped it and yelled at me to run."

"Wade, please call 911. Saunders, switch off that camera, now."

R. W. started to protest but the look on the doc's face

made him rethink that decision. He nodded and Joe halted the filming. "Stetson, you wouldn't happen to have a photo of your wife, would you?"

"Why," Wade asked.

"He wants to confirm the identity of the mean woman," stated Spencer.

"You do want to know don't you, Stetson?" asked R. W.

Before keying in 911 he fumbled in his wallet until he found a photo of the two of them on vacation in Daytona Beach. He handed it to Saunders, but not before folding his picture behind. There was no sense traumatizing the little girl by him being in the picture with the possible mean woman.

"Is this the mean lady," asked Kelly.

"That's her. Where's my daddy?"

Wade pressed 9…then 1 but his finger wavered over the top of the *one* button. He took a deep breath and then pressed the end call button and placed the phone to his ear pretending to make the call. He repeated the address and described the scene and then ended the alleged call. He felt dirty for doing this but he was no longer a rational man. He had to find Lou before something terrible happened to her. His decision had been based on Candice's comment; *the lady dropped the gun and yelled for her to run.* Now convinced more than ever, Lou was fighting back. First the computer and now this, she was in a battle for control of herself, he had no doubt now. He needed to confirm this with Kelly but the circumstances offered little opportunity.

"Guess the jig is up then," announced R. W. "We find ourselves at a second crime scene and in a most uncomfortable situation when the police do arrive."

Against his better judgment, he pulled the two ghost hunters off to the side. "Do either of you have any experience in ridding spirits from those possessed?"

"What's your angle, Stetson," asked R. W.

"Simple, I want to locate my wife and cast this witch from her body. She's battling for her life, I just know it. She made sure I knew where she was going and then she did what she could do to save Candice."

"Too bad she couldn't save her dad," added Spencer.

"You're pushing for an exorcism, aren't you?"

"And I didn't make the 911 call," confirmed Wade.

"Yeah, this is Yates. What…shots were reported…the cruiser was spotted…where? Close off that general area but don't do anything until I arrive."

Lou-Lou, our first stop was quite successful, don't you think, despite that lamebrain attempt to derail my efforts? I had no intention of shooting that child; at least not if her father was at home. Then again, blood lines are blood lines.

You're a murderous insane bitch.

Nasty thoughts you're having my dear. Must I remind you that you pulled the trigger? Your finger prints will be found on that weapon. Your modern advantages will ultimately convict you of the crimes. Your computer is a resourceful tool for understanding the best ways to stage a crime scene. Your world is rather advanced from the one I occupied. I look forward to my life here.

My world has no place for the likes of you.

Snippy tonight, aren't we, Lou-Lou. Okay, let's check the remaining crime scene candidates on our little list. Ah yes, Erma Kravis, a grand old niece of Martin Kravis, never married, a spinster after my own heart. She resides in Central Pacolet in the Spartanburg Community and we are one hour and sixteen minutes away. A hunting we will go and using these lights and noisy sirens seem to make haste so we should improve on that time. Off to Grandma's house we go said the big bad wolf bitch.

"This is beyond risky taking Candice with us," objected Kelly. "It equates to kidnapping, not to mention disturbing our second crime scene."

"You had the choice little lady. You could have remained with the child, hailed 911 and explained the situation to the police. No one twisted your arm," rebutted R. W. "So tell me, Doc, what prompted you to accompany us?"

Kelly simply bit her lip and clutched Candice to her side. The little girl didn't question their motives; relieved to be away from the house and the evil woman who might return. The two car caravan continued; this time heading toward the next address on the list, one belonging to Erma Kravis.

"Spence, if you'd be so kind, how about reading the information we've received from my elite geek excavators."

"It appears all suspicions about the alleged witch, have been confirmed." Spencer read the report and names of those accused for being responsible for the twenty one year old Reznik's death. Attempts had been made to bury the ties but the computer experts had deep mined and located the dirt. He read off a list of names and each correlated with either a recently murdered ancestor or others names from the Google list Wade Stetson had retrieved from Lou's computer.

"So the gal has revenge as a motive," commented R. W.

"I'm still not convinced the dead can seek revenge," added Spencer before reading on. Twenty years after Margarett Levine Reznik's murder, one of the gents stepped forward, unable to cope with what the lynch mob had done. He confessed and identified all that were involved, and gave the authorities the location of Reznik's unmarked grave. All were brought up on charges and Resnik was laid to rest properly. The only catch, because the community was gun shy about the witch rhetoric, she was reburied in a secluded graveyard reserved for the criminally insane.

Kelly ran a hand through her hair. "She never knew her killers had been brought to justice then, did she?"

"Twenty years later, not hardly, and that's not all." Spencer summarized what had become of those arrested and convicted. One had fallen ill and died of natural causes before he could be sentenced. Another had hanged himself in jail. Two served out their terms but never regained their standings in the community. Another was murdered while incarcerated. His murderer was never identified. The snitch received immunity but was eventually committed to an asylum. Only one walked scott-free, Erma Kravis's relative. He had the funds to buy his way out apparently.

The snitch testified that Margarett Levine Reznik had placed a curse on the lot of them, swearing if not them, their offspring would pay dearly for their crimes if they harmed a hair on her head. This didn't prevent the aristocratic society from hanging her. It also states that Resnik had previously been arrested for prostitution and for attacking one of their wives. Her mother had been accused by a neighbor on more than one occasion of being involved in witchcraft. These charges were never proven.

"I still say the key take away from this is she never knew those responsible for her death had been charged and convicted for her murder," repeated Kelly.

"What's that have to do with anything," asked Wade.

"If she had, and I'm not saying any of this possession mumbo jumbo is real, she would have had no reason to seek revenge on their ancestors. Justice had already been served."

"Partially correct, but what we have here is a witch that wants to walk the earth again and I think she's drawing her powers from these deaths," added R. W. "For all we know she might be capable of most anything once her powers have been restored. She could be the damn antichrist or something worse. Remember that dog and cat being killed. That has sacrificial ritual written all over it."

"Spell it out," demanded Wade. "Can an exorcism

restore Lou to normal?"

"She wasn't Catholic, she was Jewish, says this report."

"That explains the Yiddish dialogue she often used," added Kelly.

Wade tossed his hands in the air. "So does that mean we need the assistance of a Rabbi?"

"You know that does make perfectly good sense, Stetson. You're falling in line quite nicely."

"Then I'm going to make a phone call to our preacher, Elijah Blaine and see if he knows a Rabbi that might help us."

"Do you really want to get your pastor involved in this," asked Kelly.

"Lou and I are part of his flock and, if I know Elijah, he'd do anything to help her."

"Make the call then. We might just need us a good Rabbi if and when we confront the witch. I'll have my researchers find out if there is any such thing as a Jewish exorcism ritual."

"I still think we should call the authorities. They could have officers report to the Kravis residence before it is too late," urged Kelly.

"If the police get to her before we do then all bets are off about performing an exorcism. They'd never allow us to do it," warned R. W.

Ratings, you bastard, thought Spencer. This is nothing more to you than a career jump; another ticket to fame and fortune. We're digging a hole we'll never got out of and I'm just going along with it like I think it will not impact my credentials. There's no safety in numbers. We'll all take the fall on this one. I can visualize Saunders throwing all of us under the bus tires to save his worthless hide. Regretfully, I agree with Doctor Garner; we should call the police; then what am I waiting for? How pathetic, I'm feeding off this too. Sadly my curse is to see how this ends.

32

Yates assessed the crime scene, a bloody mess it was to say the least. The Stetson woman, if indeed she had committed this murder, was a fruit cake for sure. The revolver had been identified as police issued. Yates suspected it belonged to the missing officer. He now feared the worse, had visions that the policeman lay dead somewhere. Murder was murder but he'd not tolerate a cop killer on his watch, assuming the officer had been killed. The crime spree skipping about from one county to the next posed jurisdiction issues and he'd abide where he could, but his main objective was to stop the killings. If he bent a few rules along the way, so be it. This case was his and would end in his hands.

One of the officers reported that a neighbor said there should have been a young girl in the home, Candice was her name. A sweep of the house had not located her. This spelled additional woes; especially if she was now a hostage. Stetson's behavior simply made no sense; no rhyme or reason to these senseless killings. People snapped. Sometimes the signs were there all along. What were they missing? Had being dismissed from her college teaching position sent her over the edge, he wondered. Stranger things have triggered these sorts of incidents.

He wondered if the identity of the lady in the shallow grave would lend any clues. What was the explanation for the dog and cat buried there? Yates had entirely too many puzzle pieces and none were fitting cleanly together. Complicating his efforts, he had just received word that SLED would be taking over the investigation. That's all he needed right now was the meddling South Carolina Law Division screwing up his case. They'd certainly stifle his vested interest. He'd have to take his orders from them. Luckily they hadn't arrived yet so until then he'd do what he needed to do; including avoiding contact with them until he had no other options.

Lou-Lou, we're less than fifteen tick-tocks of the clock from healing those seeking repentance for their sins.

Justify it as you will but it still remains cold blooded murder.

Not to worry, you will pay dearly for your crimes, Princess. Erma Kravis pays the piper first. Her kin did me the worst of all harm and led the charge to have me silenced. The mere thought of her demise titillates my senses to a near orgasmic outburst. To be blunt, it sends my nature to my head in furious waves of heat; well possibly not my head. You must really learn to laugh on the inside and take all in stride.

"How close are we to the next destination," asked Spencer Misenheimer, appearing quite flustered by their chosen course of action.

"Twenty five minutes, my best guess," responded Wade Stetson.

"I just hope we're not too late," spoke up Doctor Kelly Garner. "I really think we should reconsider contacting the police. Perhaps they could intervene and prevent another senseless tragedy."

R.W. rolled his eyes. "Explained that already, Little Lady, or haven't you been grasping our dilemma. Once the cops have their fingers in this, we're out; and if we're out, we can't help your patient and Stetson's wife. There will be no need for a Rabbi and exorcism. By the way, how's that going, Stetson, no word yet from your preacher?"

"He texted me stating he had gotten my voice mail and would call me once he completed a visit with eighty nine year old Eva Sweeney, recovering from surgery in the hospital."

"Must tend to the flock first, got it."

"I want my daddy," whined Candice Hanson. Kelly did her best to console the little girl, fully realizing the ramifications of them bringing her along. This little escapade could ruin her practice; possibly cause her to lose her license, if it didn't land the lot of them behind bars.

"Yes this is Yates. Please tell me some good news for a change. Wonderful, keep her under surveillance but do nothing to raise her suspicions. Engage only if she exits the vehicle." Things might just be looking up after all thought Yates. A highway patrolman had spotted the officer's missing cruiser and had confirmed its only occupant, a female behind the wheel, not wearing a uniform. The patrolman had taken note when the cruiser passed an intersection, siren and lights fully engaged, traveling at an unsafe speed, even given emergency circumstances. Presently the female had disengaged the emergency systems and she was traveling just above the posted speed limit.

Yates was nearly an hour from that particular vicinity but was speeding there ASAP. He remained in constant contact with the officer via cell phone, just in case Lou Stetson was monitoring radio chatter. He had purposely decided not to report this to SLED, understanding the ramifications if this backfired on him. Still, this was his case to solve and he would not be denied the opportunity to apprehend Stetson. He would receive ceremonious reconnection from the department and the news media, especially if she was the cop killer he suspected her as being. Not to worry, if she hadn't killed the policeman, she had certainly murdered a slew of others; possibly even her husband and the doctor. She seemed to think they were having an affair and maybe they were. That might explain why she had snapped, motive, a woman scorned by an adulterous husband and her personal doctor.

Wade Stetson's cell phone rang to the Clemson Tiger's Tiger Rag. Answering it, he recognized Elijah Blaine's voice. Over the next couple of minutes he recapped as best he could the unfolding events. R.W., Spencer and Kelly eavesdropped on the conversation, at least one side of it. Would the preacher help remained in limbo and if he would, did he know a Rabbi, one readily available in the immediate area, and if so, would the Rabbi assist them to the extent of performing an exorcism? R.W. had already assigned his cracker-jack geek team the task of researching Jewish exorcisms, fact or fiction.

R. W. could hardly wait until he ended the call. "So what did your leader of the flock have to say about that little story? Is he with us?"

"He'll be praying that we do the right thing."

"That's it," fumed R. W. Saunders.

"That and a phone number for Rabbi Raul Torres, who just so happens to live in Spartanburg," replied Wade. "He's going to give him a call and fill him in on what we are up against. No promises but he said give him about ten minutes before I called the rabbi. He mentioned the rabbi owed him one so we'll see."

Flashing lights in the distance in the darkest reaches behind them was closing fast. Kelly sighed thinking this is about to be over. R.W. phoned the van instructing his crewman to pull up close and provide cover for the rental car. At the next intersecting roadway on the left he planned to veer in that direction and advised the van to stay the course. As luck would shine in his favor, the next curve offered a blind spot for the maneuver. He pulled down the road; hit the brakes, coming to a sudden stop. He then shut off his lights. Seconds later the screaming siren and flashing lights zoomed past them. A minute later the van announced false alarm, the speeding cop car had passed him too. R.W. prompted Spencer to rejoin the van and throw caution to the wind. They needed to make up time lost.

Yates had zoomed past them, unaware of the ghost hunter alliance with Wade Stetson and Doctor Kelly Garner. He had but one focus, one mission; apprehend Lou Stetson. The game changed abruptly, the trailing state trooper phoning to say she had pulled to a stop in front of a residence. The officer had already verified the home owner. The address was listed as belonging to an Erma Kravis. Lou Stetson remained in the cruiser, lights off. The patrolman was no more than one hundred yards back, parked at the corner of a four way stop, lights also off. Yates was thankful that Lou Stetson had left the missing officer's revolver at the scene of last crime.

The patrolman whispered, "She's on the move, just exited the patrol car. What do you want me to do, Detective?"

"I guess we have no choice, pursue and apprehend but take no chances. This woman is dangerous. She's killed more than once thus far."

The patrolman eased from his vehicle, the interior lights exposing his exit. The light temporarily obstructed his view. He was a rather large man, both in size and girth so gracefulness wasn't an attribute. He sort of rolled from the seat and out the door, one knee hitting the pavement. In that blink of an eye he had lost sight of her. She had blended into the yard's landscape and shadows. He instinctively removed his gun from its holster and then wiped sweat from his brow. Ritchie Hagen had never pulled his gun on a suspect before; his heart was racing. He was only twenty three, less than a year of duty under his belt. He swallowed almost too loudly and advanced slowly, attempting to close the ground as cautiously as possible.

Ritchie was confident she hadn't seen him, not from the angle of her parked vehicle and his. Unfortunately he no longer saw her either. Shouldn't he be radioing for backup now? No, he couldn't, like Yates had said, she could be monitoring any radio communication. Ritchie located a hedgerow two houses down and clung to it as he approached. When he ran out of that cover he sprinted quickly behind a Ford Bronco and then to a cluster of Leland Cypress trees bordering the next yard. Slowly but surely he made his way to a detached garage, apparently belonging to the Kravis woman. He took a few deep breaths, his back to the garage, opposite the house.

Opting to slink around the back of the garage and avoid the street lights, he had to veer wide to avoid a couple of trash receptacles near a side entrance. This placed him momentarily out of the shadows. The flash and thunderous sound was instantaneous, as was the force that knocked him on his back. His hands were numb, his breathing labored. Blinking he attempted to sit up but couldn't. He must have the wind knocked from him was his only thought before he died from the shotgun blast that had ripped open his chest cavity.

You didn't have to do that screamed Lou from her subconscious prison, while staring at her very own hands gripping the shotgun that had been retrieved from the police vehicle. Dogs were barking nearby. A porch light came on across the street. She could see someone peeping through an opening in the blinds just before she turned and ran towards the side entrance to Erma Kravis's home. She was going to finish what she had set out to do, eliminate the ancestor of Martin Kravis. There was no stopping her now. Blood was in the water.

The street was swarming with vehicles, flashing lights

and policemen hungering down, not sure what to expect at the scene. The patrolman's vehicle was parked and located as previously reported to Yates. Lieutenant Ritchie Hagan was nowhere in sight. The stolen police cruiser was parked out front of the residence. Lights were on in the house but no movement or activity had been viewed thus far. All exit roadways had been blocked and police had secured the perimeter within several blocks in every direction. Yates was confident that they now had Lou Stetson surrounded and boxed in. Soon this ordeal would be over.

A uniformed city cop approached Yates and advised the detective to follow him. Near the back of the adjacent garage they had found Lieutenant Ritchie Hagan's lifeless body. Cop killer, the game had changed for all who now stood down awaiting orders. Yates realized that this would be his last opportunity to handle the case himself. He had already gotten word that SLED was on their way. If he was going to act, time was not on his side. The original case from Anderson still slated him as sort of the commanding officer, working with locals of course; but it gave him a little leeway temporarily. He had to act quickly though and take advantage of his current status. Local SWAT had arrived, awaiting instructions. Yates collaborated with the ranking officer on site, offering his opinion of course, and painting a bleak picture that swayed the balance in his favor.

Designated driver and parapsychologist, Spencer Misenheimer, pointed out the blue light specials, as R.W. pegged them, blocking the roadway ahead. This spelled nothing but more gloom and doom in his mind. Something tragic had either occurred or they had Lou Stetson in their sights. Either way, this most likely meant the end of the road for them. No exorcist would be required after all. He glanced over at R. W. and could read the concern on his face. The doctor, Stetson and little girl remained quiet in back seat. The crew continued filming the unfolding saga.

Spencer had no other choice than to pull to a stop at the road block. The policeman advised them to turn around, offering no initial explanation. R. W. Saunders wasn't going to be blown off so easily. The showman kicked into gear. Spencer cringed, fearful of where this might take them. The snake oil peddler took center ring.

"My good man, perhaps you don't recognize me in this environment but I am R. W. Saunders, producer and star of the acclaimed Ghost Hunter television series. We are currently filming an episode and you're on camera. Might I inquire why we are being prompted to exit the area?"

"Oh yeah, I do recognize you now that you mention it. I love that show" replied the young policeman. "What brings you to our neck of the woods?"

"We've been following a woman, a complicated case of spiritual possession. It reeks of witchcraft and the occult. It most assuredly will put South Carolina and its rural communities on the map."

Spencer couldn't believe he had laid that on the line. What was he thinking? Did he want to get them arrested?

"A female professor for Newberry College has been implicated in a series of gruesome murders in the area. We have reason to believe that she may be possessed by a one hundred year old witch. It is our understanding that Anderson County detectives are involved and are running the show here in your county, and they have pursued her to this location. You must excuse us; we have been monitoring radio chatter. It goes with the territory. Hopefully you're not allowing detectives from another county the opportunity to steal this case from your hands."

"You must mean the Stetson woman," boasted the officer, now posing for his moment in the spotlight. "Yeah, we have her cornered ahead. This should be over any minute. Spartanburg law enforcement has it well under control but now I must ask you to turn around, please."

"So this is about to be over then."

"That you can carry to the bank. She ventured into the wrong county. Am I still on camera?"

"Yes son, footage is being filmed as we speak from the van behind us. For the record, has she killed anyone else?"

Wade could hardly bear this line of questioning. He wanted to leap from the car and run to her rescue.

"I shouldn't be the one to say this but reports are we have a least one of our officers down and have located a stolen cruiser from Greenwood County. That's about all I'm at liberty to say."

An announcement blared over the officer's radio. "Suspect is not in the house; repeat suspect is not in the house."

"It has been a pleasure to make your acquaintance Mister Saunders but really you should clear the area. By the way, I'm Corporal Randolph Pinson. "

"Here's my card, son. If you wish to be involved further in our segment about Mrs. Stetson, please don't hesitate to contact me."

Spencer wheeled the car around and they backtracked to a convenience store they had passed. "They didn't nab her," grinned R.W. "We're still in the hunt."

Yates with the cooperation of the locals had closed in on the house after receiving no communication or resistance. The house had been searched and no one, including the owner of the home had been located. It had been determined that a white Nissan belonging to Erma Kravis was missing, but that didn't mean that it had been stolen. Kravis may have been away when Stetson arrived. An all points bulletin had been issued just the same. Yates was no longer running the show. SLED had arrived and had taken over the investigation. Detective Yates had had his one shot. Now he had no choice but to play it by the book.

He was betting that Stetson had stolen the Nissan Maxima. Question, did she now have a hostage? Sadly, the missing police officer's body had been found handcuffed in the trunk of the stolen cruiser. There were no obvious wounds on the body. The coroner would later identify heart attack as the cause of death. For now though, it was simply two officers down and the cops' killer was still on the loose. They wanted justice for two of their very own.

"There's only one last name on Lou's Google list," answered Wade Stetson to R. W.'s inquiry. He read the address and Spencer keyed it into the GPS. One chance remained.

"What makes you think they haven't already arrested Lou," asked Wade.

"The witch is not going down that easily. I'd wager she's done her bidding and off to finish what she started. She has one more score to settle. We'll head her off at the pass."

"And what makes you think we can beat her to her next destination, if that is where she is heading" asked Kelly Garner.

"She's heading there all right and she's on the run. We're not. She shrewd but she must be careful if she's going to complete her mission. And she thinks she's thwarted the police. She doesn't know about us yet."

"Just gets better all the time, doesn't it?"

"Didn't you hear what that policeman said? My Lou may have killed a police officer. You insensitive bastard," yelled Wade, reaching over the seat for him.

R.W. slapped his hands away. "You want to help your damn wife or not? The witch is in charge, not her and she's probably becoming more powerful with every kill. At least that's my best guess."

Wade stopped in mid action.

"That's better. Call that Rabbi and see if he's in or not, and if he is in, find out where we can pick him up. I'll have my boys go fetch him. Once we catch up to her, my gut tells me this thing is going to unravel at a break neck speed so we better be ready to kick our asses into exorcism mode. She's not going down without one hell of a fight."

"Promise you want harm her," begged Wade.

"Hell, man, it's us you better worry about. We have no idea what she might have up her sleeve or just what she may be capable of conjuring up."

"Really, R. W. you are giving her a bit too much credit, aren't you? These are mere assumptions. We have no facts to support supernatural or superhuman powers. No one has died in any manner to indicate otherwise. Plain and simple, we are pursuing a murderer, and whether Mrs. Stetson is aware of what she is doing or not remains the question. I say stifle the theatrics. This is life and death. If you weren't so into your ratings, you'd hand over that last bit of information to the authorities."

"Not you too, Spence, you're going soft on me. I might just have to rethink your contract."

"Rip it apart as far as I'm concerned. I couldn't care less. This has gotten out of hand."

"You damned turn coat. I ought to boot you out right now. Never trust a Yankee."

"I beg to differ," spoke up Wade. "It's two against one."

"Three," added Kelly, still consoling the little girl by her side.

"Fine, have it your way, but the cameras keep rolling to the very end. Do something useful; call that Rabbi, how about it?"

Your world can be quite complicated, Lou-Lou. Too many meddlers exist, each trying to stick their nose in my business. I must admit, I'm growing tired of it too. I liked the other vehicle better, the one with the sirens and lights. It had that fenced in back seat too. It would have come in handy about now. I wouldn't have had to load Erma

Kravis in that trunk. Didn't have much of choice though; too many meddlers were messing in my business, didn't have time to do her right. Oh well, I'll just have to double up. Might be fitting, the one last power surge I'm going to receive when this is finished.

They're going to catch you, you know.

Catch you, not me, remember. By the time they do, it will be history. I will have leap-frogged from you, leaving you to pay the piper. I hope I can stick close by just to bear witness to the end of Lou as we know her. I'm going to enjoy taking my time with Kravis. Her ole ancient uncle was the worst of the worst. I'll so cherish filling her in on just how corrupt her genes are. Soon I will be free. Resurrection has such a nice sound to it.

They're on to you. You have not a chance in hell in completing this. They're looking for this Nissan and you've murdered a policeman. They take care of their own and will be driven by what you have done. You'll never make it to your final target. If you resist, then we'll both die, and I'm okay with that.

Gloom and doom, gloom and doom, you're just no fun, Lou-Lou. The sooner we part ways, the better. I require a strong female body to do my bidding. Once I have her, the world will be at my finger tips. Your world has never dealt with the likes of someone with my powers, once I am whole again that is. I'll be the puppeteer, controlling who I want, when I want and doing exactly what I desire them to do. Waiting in that grave all these years has allowed me time to simmer, to grow, to realize just who I am and just how powerful I can be.

Thinking and wishing is not doing. Perhaps your visions are just that, make believe. I've not witnessed you having any special powers. You're no more than a common criminal, a murderer, killing people with tools from my world as you call it. Sure, I'll hand it to you; you've managed to escape that *cold dirty resting place but where are these almighty powers you boast of? Show me something magical. Make a believer out of ME.*

I have not the time or patience to toy with you right now. Besides, I know you, all too well, Lou-Lou. You only wish to distract and deceive me. I have nothing that needs proving to you. The fact I own you is proof enough. Victor Cranston is our next stop and final call; just a hop and skip according to MapQuest directions. Our destination is Cowpens. Kravis and Cranston, poetic justice is about to be served. Shame on me, I have no tool by which to serve the final verdict. That will never do. What must we do to reconcile this oversight, Lou-Lou?

"Cowpens, Victor Cranston, we can be no more than fifteen minutes from there so says our little intuitive Garmin GPS," announced R. W. "The boys have to pick up the Rabbi and I'd estimate it taking them about thirty minutes to get him and return, and I suppose it depends on where we corral our little witch to work out the particulars. You're the designated camera man until then Spence."

"Why did you not just send one of them, instead of both?"

"Oversight on my part, Spence; I'm near perfect but do have my flaws. I tend to allow myself to look too far down the road and not what's around the next curve. You'll do just fine. These cameras are pert near dummy proof."

Turn right at the next intersection prompted the electronic voice.

"These things are a hoot, aren't' they. Don't piss them off and go off route though; they'll badger you with legal u-turns."

"What are you going to do if we find her," asked Wade.

"I figure we got her outnumbered so we should be able to handle her. Might let you sweet talk her for a little distraction."

"I'm going to say this but one more time," warned Wade Stetson. "You had better not harm a hair on her head or it's me that you're going to be dealing with, and heed my warning, it wouldn't be pretty for the camera."

"It's not my policy or good television to harm any of the participants and I don't plan to start doing anything differently now. I tend to shy away from potential lawsuits."

Take a right and then the next left; you have reached your final destination.

"Showtime, we're here. Park this puppy and fire up that video camera, Spence. Honey, you might want to wait here in the car with the little girl. The men folk will take it from here."

Kelly fought back the urge to give Saunders the finger, thinking better of it with Candice by her side. He was probably right; no need to expose her to any more violence that they had to.

"Stetson, let's do this right and march up to the front door. If she's here, she needs to see your concerned face first. We'll stay out of sight and off to the side, back-up when you need it."

For once Wade agreed. He wanted to handle this to make sure it was done correctly. Lou, even in this state, had not attempted to harm him. He felt he somehow grounded her. Possibly with his help Lou could overpower the witch, if this witch bullcrap was even real in the first place. He had witnessed no evidence to support possession by an evil entity. Sure, she was suffering from some sort of disorder but nothing pointed towards anything supernatural, other than all the gibberish they had been digging up on the other woman. Saunders just wanted this to be real for his viewing audience; that was all; just good old fashioned staged reality TV.

Wade took a deep breath and then rapped on the front door, a wooden one with no screen or storm door. He waited, listened, but heard no one approaching. He rang the door bell. Still, no one answered. Three possibilities, no one was at home, they had beat Lou here or the worst case scenario; Lou was inside with a hostage or had already murdered the Cranston man. Wade fingered the doorknob before finally allowing himself to grip it. It tuned. The door was not locked. He looked over at Saunders and he motioned for him to open it. Spencer steadied the camera nervously.

Wade shoved the door open, instinctively stepping back, partially hiding behind the door facing just in case a hostile environment awaited them. No such thing, all was quiet. His estranged wife was not lurking in attack mode. Spencer peered over the camera to confirm the coast appeared clear. R.W. cursed under his breath, really hoping for something spectacular. The trio cautiously entered the Cranston residence, Wade still leading the way, Spencer just behind with the camera and R.W. bringing up the rear, still yearning for a surprise attack or a mangled body or something camera worthy.

Flicking lights on, they conducted their version of a room to room search, uncovered nothing out of place. There were no signs of a struggle, or any evidence of a violent attack, no blood nor body. This wasn't going well, thought R.W. but he kept his disappointment to himself. The sweep completed, the trio paused to strategize their next move. Wade Stetson was on the verge of tears. This roller coaster ride was taking its toll on him. He just wanted to find Lou and for this to be over.

The tap on the window startled Doctor Kelly Garner. The face staring back at her terrified her even more, a face she didn't recognize. The man's expression depicted sheer terror, his face pressed against the glass and he was mouthing something. She shifted to the opposite side of the backseat, clutching Candice. The stranger opened the door, an almost pleading look on his face. A second face emerged from behind the man. Kelly recognized this one, Lou Stetson. Twelve year old Candice did too and began to scream and flail at the door, looking for an escape route.

"My, my, the adulterous doctor, to what do I owe the pleasure?"

"Help me," pleaded the stranger.

"Hush now, Cranston, I'm conversing with the pretty doctor. I see you've been to the Hanson residence."

Kelly noticed that Lou had a tire iron raised over the man's head. What she couldn't see was the butcher knife pressed to his spine. So they had finally found Lou, now what? And where were the others? Candice was still fumbling with the door, whining and desperately attempting to escape. She held her tight and whispered in her ears trying to calm her.

"I see the key dangling there. You'll be doing the driving so tell you what pretty lady, you and the little chap slip into the front seat and try on these handcuffs for size, one to that wheel and the other on your wrist. Get her under control too or we can just leave her, makes no mine to me. I certainly don't need another Hanson now. Try anything funny and I'll run this knife through Cranston's back. One more thing, I have another member of our party to retrieve so sit tight until me and ole Cranston here get our other guest. Again, remember, try anything and their deaths will be on your head."

After Kelly handcuffed herself to the wheel, she tried desperately to calm Candice. The little girl looked at her wild eyed and then bolted from the car, vanishing into the darkness. She didn't blame her for her actions and actually sighed, glad she had. A moment later Lou prompted Kelly to press the button that opened the trunk. Erma Kravis and Victor Cranston were loaded in the rental car's trunk, both with hands secured behind them, Kravis with a second pair of cuffs and Cranston with a wire cloths hanger. Both were gagged.

Lou slipped into the front passenger side door. "Little bitch couldn't take it, huh? Just as well, don't have time to be a babysitter. We have more urgent matters to attend to." We," blurted out Kelly. "So it's true. You are really Margarett Levine Reznik and Lou is in essence being held hostage by you too."

"Not just pretty, you have more than just medicine smarts, don't you doc? That won't buy you a hot cup of tea right now. You see, Lou-Lou has to take the fall by her lonesome. I don't really exist. Who really believes in ghosts and witches anyway. I'd like to keep it that way, just between you and me. Given your current situation, I don't think you're in a position to dispute my wishes, now are you? Well looky there. It appears we have company, your lover, my husband."

"That's where you're wrong. Nothing could be further from the truth."

"Lou may not see it that way when all is said and done. Women don't take too kindly to being betrayed, not by a lover, and especially not by a hubby. It's that woman scorned thing that does them in every time. It makes them react dreadfully. It's so degrading. Kravis's jealous wife pushed her husband into doing what they did to me. Possibly I should add her kin to my list, just to settle the score. Right now, engage this vehicle and let's make our hasty retreat."

As they pulled away the trio got a good look at the rental car's driver and passenger. Wade screamed at the top of his lungs, his wife's name. Kelly gave them a quick look, desperation on her face.

"Now what," asked Spencer, filming their departure

"Not to worry, our chariot has just arrived," he replied, pointing to the Ghost Hunter van pulling into the driveway, earlier than had been expected.

Keeping the rental car's taillights in sight, they climbed aboard and R.W. gave the *follow that car* order, and then prompted Spencer to hand over the camera to all the professionals, and for goodness sake keep it rolling.

"Rabbi Raul Torres, I assume," spoke up Spencer, offering his hand as he introduced everyone.

"So this is what they refer to as being in hot pursuit, how exciting. The alleged witch must be in that sedan then."

"My wife is in that car. As for the witch, we really can't say for sure."

"I understand your grief my son. I do apologize. One can so easily become caught up in the hype."

"Rabbi, one question, have you ever performed an actual exorcism before," asked R. W.

"I can't say you would see that on my current resume but I am astute in the proceedings."

"Just great, like saying you just stayed in a Holiday Inn Express" said R.W. throwing up his hands in disbelief. "Just how old are you?"

"I'm twenty seven but my age is not relevant. I chose my calling even before I reached puberty. Now days, many don't pursue becoming a Rabbi until they are well into their forties or fifties, even older; often as a second vocation. There are really no age restrictions, as anyone interested in becoming a priest, or reverend or clergyman in general. When I received the call from Reverend Elijah Blaine, I was immediately intrigued by the case. Does this cause you concern?"

"This may require your performing an exorcism. Does this cause you ANY concern?"

"Let us take this journey together and decide what is best for Mrs. Stetson. There are alternatives to exorcism. We must only use this path in the most extreme case. After we have assessed her situation, we may determine much simpler causes are in play. Tayvl cannot be blamed for all man's woes. Ah yes, sorry, tayvl is the devil, Satan, Lucifer, or whatever one prefers to call the evil of the day. Choose your flavor I always say."

"You sound like us. You don't talk in that Yiddish gibberish, Rabbi."

"Not to be perplexed, I assure you I can speak Yiddish with the best of them but what purpose would it serve here? It would merely be a theatrical overture for your viewing audience. Why so surprised, I am an avid fan of your series."

"Tell you what; when we hook up with the Stetson woman, it would be kind of cool if you tossed some of the ancient tongue around. It would make it appear creepier."

"Very well, playing to the audience, I will wow your viewers with old school pizzazz, if that floats your boat. I can lay it on thickly when I have to. "

"I still say you don't act like any Rabbi I have ever met," added R.W.

"Boss, I still have your rental vehicle in sight," announced L.J., the wheel man for the Ghost Hunter van.

"I wonder if the little girl is still with them," commented Joe. "I'd hate to see her get hurt."

"I didn't see her but she could have been hunkered down in the back seat," responded Spencer.

"They have a child with them; no one said a child was involved."

"Not to worry, Rabbi, I don't think the witch is a kid killer. She had her chance back at the Hanson house and passed on it. The little gal is his daughter and my guess is that the good doctor would protect the little chap with her own life."

"Lou would never harm a child," confirmed Wade.

"Maybe not," replied R.W. "But that witch has been on one hell of a killing spree, using your wife to deliver the deadly deeds."

"Sotn," whispered Rabbi Raul Torres. "Sorry, just another name for this demon we pursue."

"Car is slowing," chimed in Joe, now manning the camera.

"VUS MACHA DA?"

"What," asked R.W.

"Sorry, you said keep it real for the camera; Yiddish for *what's up*."

"OY VEY!"

"Well put Mister Saunders. I especially liked the southern twang you interjected into it. "

"I do like you, Rabbi; you're going to be good for this segment."

"Please, call me Paul."

"No can do; Paul is a take away and not good for what we're doing. I'll stick with Rabbi if you don't mind. Once this is behind us, I'll buy ole Paul a drink though. First comes first, we defang the witch."

"MAZEL TOV, that would be good luck my friend."

L. J. updated the status. "She's pulled into what looks like a cemetery ahead. Do we follow?"

"Damn right we follow," said Wade.

"Not so fast. This requires the element of surprise," cautioned R.W. "The witch didn't get this far by not being on top of her game. Kill the headlights and ease forward."

Headlights from the Sedan continued to illuminate the inner regions of the secluded little cemetery as it moved slowly, deeper into the graveyard. The van stopped just sort of the entrance and killed the engine. The occupants watched and waited; for what, Wade didn't understand. Suddenly the headlights shut off and the cemetery went dark.

"Joe, you go with us. Make sure we have plenty of video and juice to film this. L.J., take the van and make sure there is no other way out of this graveyard. If there is, block it.

Okay gang, its show time. We hoof it from here. Rabbi, are you prepared to perform this exorcism at the drop of a hat."

"As mentioned, there may be other options. I must examine the woman; have time to digest the situation. If we do proceed, it is no simple task; not as easy as waving an exorcism wand. There is much preparation involved."

"Just answer me, Paul; are you prepared to do it if we have to?"

"Yes, I have what I need, mostly any way. This is quite a rebellious move for me and my faith, but I am willing to do what must be done. I confirmed this with Elijah when he asked for my assistance. He cares for this Lou Stetson and her family and agonizes over the evil that has fallen upon them. Tokhis oyfin tish, *put up or shut up*, it is said."

"Mostly…mostly sounds like we're in dire straits here, Rabbi," commented R. W.

"The actual exorcism requires a minyan."

"For this part, speak English, please."

"Okay so we have a few minor technicalities. A minyan is a group of ten adult males who gather in a circle around the possessed individual. The group recites Psalm 91 three times and then the rabbi blows a shofar, *a ram's horn*, which I do have in my bag, and if it all goes well, we deliver a knockout punch. The shofar is blown in a certain way, with various notes and tones, in effect to "shatter the body" so that the possessing force will be shaken loose."

"Minor technicality; are you kidding me? We're just a tad shy of ten adult males, don't you think? I believe it's a little late to bus them in. Are you sure you know how to blow this sheep horn?"

"We'll improvise and yes, I have practiced the art of replicating the necessary notes to drive the entity from the possessed, if indeed Lou Stetson is bewitched as you suspect."

"What else are you not telling me?"

"A mastered practicing Kabbalah performs this ritual but I have been present for one."

"You were in the viewing audience for an exorcism? This is so much crap."

"No, I participated as one of the ten reciting Psalm 91, but I am very familiar with the Kabbalah's role, not to worry. After it has been shaken loose, the rabbi, that would be me, begins to communicate with it and ask it questions such as why it possesses the body of the possessed. The minyan may pray for it and perform a ceremony for it in order to enable it to feel safe, and so that it can leave the person's body"

"More frigging minor details…I can see this is going to require a lot of editing before I can air it."

"Cut him a break," spoke up Spencer. "Everything is subjective right now anyway. What's really at stake here is that we stop this woman from committing more murders."

"The WOMAN is my wife and I'll warn you one last time that she better come to no harm. Not to allow it to slip your grimy, greedy, little minds, but must I remind you, as far as we know, the so called witch has hostages, Kelly and Candice."

"It is not our intent to harm you wife," spoke up Spencer. "I'll personally see to that. This is no longer about television ratings, I assure you, not as far as I'm concerned."

"You have absolutely no say-so in what's best for the series, Spence."

"Stop your bickering and focus," snapped Wade.

Rabbi Raul Torres intervened. "I concur; we must focus on what's most important; providing the help needed for Lou Stetson."

"Camera rolling, we're entering the graveyard, where the witch possessing Lou Stetson has disappeared with her potential hostages. I am accompanied by her husband, Wade, parapsychologist, Spencer Misenheimer, and Rabbi

Paul Torres. Our intent is to put a stop to these systematic murders and possibly utilize Rabbi Torres's skills to exorcise the she-demon from her hiding place, that of the body of Lou Stetson. If not for the poor cell phone coverage, we would have already contacted local police to assist us with this matter. Unfortunately, due to the urgency and complexity, we must proceed without them."

"Covering your ass," whispered Spencer.

34

Kelly pulled the Sedan to a stop in the back portion of the small cemetery as instructed, while Margarett was thinking this was only too fitting. It had begun in such a setting, may as well end the same way.

You should feel right at home.

See, Lou-Lou, you do have a sense of humor, even when the end is so near.

Doctor Kelly Garner observed Lou curiously. She seemed to be in deep thought, preoccupied and unconcerned about her presence in the driver's seat. Why should she be? After all, she was cuffed to the wheel and going nowhere.

"Lou, tell me what you're feeling right now. What are your thoughts?"

"Really, you think this sort of bedside manner works with me. Lou is tucked away and unavailable to chat with you. You know, Doc, you're a smart gal and quite the looker and I'll bet you have it made, cash wise. I could do worse."

"And your point…"

"I could hitch a ride with you once I dispose of those two in the back. Think about it. I, as you, could seal old Lou-Lou's fate, hands down. I'd be her doctor after all. Even her hubby would hang on my every word, right? Yes, I do like the thought, me being you. The pleasure I could introduce to that body of yours would boggle your mind. It's settled then. You and I will have a lasting friendship;

well, until I tire of you."

"You're totally insane."

"Perfect, keep saying that about me as Lou. It was quite sincere and believable. You're getting the hang of it."

Lou did the best to conceal her thoughts. Her chance might be the very moment Margarett leapt from her body to the doctor's. Hopefully she could catch her off guard. Question, would she be as powerful as she lays claim. If so, it might be a moot point. Sadly, the ability for her to make the transformation would spell death for those two in the trunk. The doctor didn't deserve this fate either. Lou wondered if she could muster the strength and somehow plunge the butcher knife into her own heart, and would Margarett die along with her or at least be helplessly trapped. It was certainly worth a try, but could she pull this off without interference from the blood sucking parasite?

"It's a travesty what you are doing with this woman's body and soul?"

"If not for me she would be a drooling mindless idiot suffering from the Alzheimer's sickness. I have saved her from that fate."

"And you have portrayed her as a mindless killer, some trade."

"It's a give and take world, Doc. You'll experience it soon enough, I promise. We're wasting valuable time with this girlie talk." With that, she retrieved the butcher knife and popped the trunk. Just as she opened the door to step outside, the knife she clutched in her right hand plunged towards her chest.

"Has anyone spotted the sedan yet?" inquired R.W.

"I think I have it in view," replied L.J peering through the lens of his camera. "It's parked just ahead."

"Can you see Doctor Garner," asked Wade.

"There is movement, but too dark to tell who is who or what," reported L.J.

"VUS MACHS DA?"

"In character early or just practicing," R.W. asked the rabbi.

"Sorry, it means what is happening."

"Gentleman I strongly recommend we call 911," insisted Spencer. "This is beyond reality television drama now. People's lives are at stake"

"Pipe down or we'll lose our element of surprise, Mister Voice of Reason," warned R.W. "Hell, they've been at stake; where have you been? Nothing has changed since we started this, except we're closer to solving it. Let's move in that direction, where the action is. Keep her rolling. This might get good."

The knife had penetrated Lou's rib cage but had been thwarted before striking any vital organs. Blood trickled from the puncture wound. Margarett now held the knife in front of her host's face and then rubbed a finger over the red stain. She rubbed the blood between finger and thumb before suckling the warmth from the finger tips. She smiled and looked over at the doctor.

"Momentary lapse on my part, I assure you. Lou is one sneaky little bitch. She lays in wait for any opportunity still. Time's a wasting; let's be done with the suspense. Those two meet their maker and then you and me get quite chummy, Doctor Garner. We then leave old Lou here for the scavengers. The constables can pick up the pieces and do as they will. We'll help guide them of course."

She yanked first her lady captive then the gent from the trunk, plopping both unceremoniously on the ground. She toed her male sacrifice in the crotch before hauling back and kicking him firmly. Kneeling down, she then pushed the hair from Erma's Kravis's face and rubbed her fingers across her captive's lips before thumping her nose. Margarett drew pleasure from toying with her last two links to the past. She now straddled Victor Cranston and with both hands, raised the tire iron above her head, set to deliver the final blow. A deranged smile of utter satisfaction adorned Lou Stetson's face.

"Oy Gevalt," yelled Rabbi Torres witnessing the scene as it unfolded before his very eyes.

Lou stopped in mid swing, glancing over to her assembled viewing audience and Margarett repeated, "Oy Gevalt indeed, oh how terrible this must seem." She then delivered the deadly blow to Cranston's skull, blood splattering her clothing. She quickly turned her attention to Erma Kravis, but not before smiling triumphantly to the Rabbi and others. Raising her weapon a second time, she swung downward to finish what she had started.

A deafening sound interrupted the graveyard silence. Lou dropped to the ground in mid swing, the tire iron landing a blow just an inch from Erma Kravis's head. The smell of a discharged fire arm permeated from the bushes nearest the fallen woman. Out stepped Detective Yates, pistol still grasped in both hands.

"What have you done," screamed Wade, now running to his wife.

Yates followed him with the gun, still pointing it towards the woman lying on the ground.

"You get all of this, L.J?"

"I think so. Is she dead?"

"Never mind, just keep shooting," ordered R.W. "Not you detective," he said, slightly raising his hands as a gesture.

"She's still breathing," announced Wade, just as Lou grabbed him by the throat with one hand, while scrambling for the butcher knife shoved in her belt with the other.

Yates quickly advanced and crushed her knife welding hand with the heel of his shoe, and then bent down and retrieved it, tossed it aside. Stand back, all of you; this crime scene must be secured."

"Screw you," snapped Wade, sitting on his butt just out

of reach of his wounded deranged wife.

"Untie the lady," ordered Yates to the onlookers.

"What about me," yelled Kelly Garner still handcuffed to the steering wheel. .

Yates handed Spencer a key and instructed him to free the doctor. Footfalls and the rustle of bushes made everyone flinch. Joe came crashing into view, having heard the shot from the van. R.W. quickly confirmed to Yates that he was part of his crew.

"How did you know where to find her," asked Wade.

"Gut, followed my nose after SLED secured the house and took over the investigation. Saw your van acting suspiciously and just followed it. The billboard on wheels isn't easily ignored. I figured you might be on to something for your television series. A couple of policeman had told me earlier that you had offered them, should I say, a bribe for information."

"I would never bribe an officer of the law."

"Even with a chance to appear on your show, get real Saunders, seen your type too many times."

"What about some medical help for my wife," interrupted Wade

"Screw you and your medical help," spewed Margarett, still in control and regaining her composure and strength, even with blood oozing from the fresh wound to her forearm.

"Hold on before you make that call for help," insisted R.W.

"Why should I listen to you?"

"Please hear him out," added Rabbi Torres. "She is still in grave danger, all of us are."

"Rabbi, what's in this for you? Why are you hanging with these scoundrels?"

"I'm here to save her soul. We fear; I fear Mrs. Stetson is possessed by evil, a restless and vengeful spirit by the name of Margarett Levine Reznik, allegedly a witch from a hundred years past."

"Rabbi, don't tell me you have bought into this?"

"Trust me Detective; merely incarcerating this ill woman will end nothing. She will murder and will find her way back to complete what she has begun. She could then be a powerful, an unstoppable force, delivering her evil to our world."

"Baloney, they've brainwashed you or have either paid you dearly to go along with their little charade for the sake of good TV, haven't they?"

"I assure you that Rabbi Torres is here on his own accord, and he speaks the truth. An exorcism in the only way we can end this. Bear with us, please. Let him perform the exorcism, and then afterwards you can run her in as planned."

"This is so much bull, Stetson. Your wife is a psychopathic murderer, nothing more."

"Please," begged Wade "Allow them to perform the exorcism and then do what you must to confine her within the legal system."

"Exorcism," protested Lou. "I'm as sane as the next person and I am not possessed. I take full responsibility for my actions, constable." Lou sat on the ground, handcuffed. Margarett had but to buy some time and indeed she would take one last relative from those who had done the unspeakable to her years gone by. Once she had accomplished that, no one could stop her rein.

R.W. clapped his hands in response. "You're fooling no one, witch. You fear the exorcism, don't you and you're powerless to stop it?"

Fury inflamed Lou's expression. Margarett could not allow this exorcism. The constable could be her only salvation. Bide her time and finish what she had started, indeed. Lou had experienced the power surge from

Cranston's untimely demise. The witch was an eyelash from possibly becoming too powerful to stop. It was now or never. She had covertly slowly but surely wiggled her way into the subconscious of Margarett Levine Reznik. They were one and now it was show time.

Yates gun was suddenly snatched from his hands and tossed to the ground, ten yards away. He glanced at his empty hands and then to where the gun had landed. Looking at the others, he searched for answers. R.W. only shrugged but wore a wiry smile. Everyone else appeared as perplexed as the detective.

R.W. broke the deathly silence. "Proof detective, she is a powerful witch and will only become more powerful if we don't stop her now, right here, with that exorcism. Of course, that is assuming you didn't just throw your gun over yonder. "

"Tricks, what are you and your stage roadies trying to pull?"

"Get real, detective, how could any of us have plucked your weapon from you? You're a professional and if I were you, I would be hesitant about reporting how easily you were just disarmed; especially when none of us were close enough to actually pull this off."

"Don't believe the snake oil peddler, he spews untruths, constable" shouted Lou. *You'll not get away with this crap. Lou-Lou, I assure you.*

"For the record, Detective Yates, my Lou would never address you as constable. That's old school dialect, something a one hundred year old witch might say, wouldn't you agree?"

Yates scrambled to retrieve his gun and then pointed it wildly, aiming at one then another of the wackos assembled about him. He flexed the fingers on his free hand and then wiped the sweat from his brow. He ran his fingers around his shirt collar, loosening his tie, attempting to process what had just happened. He could muster no sound explanation. His revolver had been forcefully snatched from his two handed grip and as bad as he hated admitting it, none of these people had been close enough to have done this. He remembered now how his hands had felt as if burning from hot embers. Could this Stetson woman actually be possessed as they insisted she was? He dealt in facts, not fairy tales, but he had no facts to back up what had just happened, and he didn't like being placed in a corner.

"Rabbi, do you honestly think this woman is being controlled by a one hundred year old witch?" Yates choked on those words, struggling to even believe he had seriously asked the question. Worse still, he had to hear the answer and dreaded the confirmation.

"One cannot say for sure. I have only just met her. I should not say that because I have not been formally introduced. However, what I can say is that I witnessed what just happened and I have no explanation, do you?"

"What if I go along with this farce, what's involved in performing this exorcism and how would you know if it worked?"

"There is a Jewish ceremony that would be performed to drive away this spirit. If successful, we would return the alleged witch to her resting place. Mrs. Stetson would then be in full control of her faculties."

"I deal in specifics, Rabbi. What's involved and how would we know it worked?"

"Detective, to deep dive into the theology of my faith would take quite some time and I fear we do not have the luxury of such an extensive discussion. Perhaps afterwards, we could chat. As for proof that we have dislodged the unwanted one, there is a method to the madness I assure you. Again, leave the driving to the experts, I always say. You're a detective. I'm a Rabbi. We do what we do. We have both been trained to deal with the situations that fall into our wheelhouses. This is my wheelhouse, catch my drift?"

"You don't sound or look like the Rabbi's I am accustomed to."

"Amen," chimed in R.W., motioning to L.J. to keep the camera rolling.

"I thought it was unlawful to profile, Detective Yates."

"Touché."

"All of you, cease this nonsense. You're on a literal witch hunt. I'm no witch. I have no idea why I have been doing these despicable things. Ask her. She's supposed to be my doctor. I am not well. Shouldn't she have already treated me for my sickness?"

Kelly, now free from the cuffs, rubbed her wrists, before taking a step towards her accuser. "My patient, if you will, has confessed to me that she is Margarett Levine Reznik, and she has laid out in much detail what she planned to do after executing her two captives, relatives of those who she says wrongfully murdered her."

"You are sworn to not discuss patient-doctor conversations. ESS DRECK Tokhis leker."

Rabbi Torres whispered, "She just told the good doctor to eat shit, ass-kisser."

"My Lou would never say that in Yiddish or any other language."

"Lou Stetson is my patient. Margarett Levine Reznik is not."

"NAFKA…whore…"

"Calm down. There is no need for such vulgarism," warned the Rabbi.

"Ikh hob dir in drerd, MOYL."

Torres chuckled. "She told the man who circumcises baby boys to go to hell. I'd say we have our proof that the female known as Reznik is indeed possessing our Mrs. Stetson. She is out of the wood pile so to speak."

Spencer stood frozen, thinking this was beyond

anything he could have ever fathomed. He owed Saunders an apology. The redneck's suspicions had been dead on about this possession. Joe, meanwhile, thought back on the graves and what they had found in them. He was fighting back nausea once again and an urge to piss his pants. Wade just wanted his wife back, safe and sound.

"MOMZER," shouted Lou, as an invisible hand slapped Torres on his face, the rabbi flinching from the harsh blow.

"Okay, so now she's crossed a line and struck me, and called me a bastard to boot. Detective, we really do need to proceed with this exorcism before she inflicts serious harm to one of us."

Yates suddenly aimed his weapon at Erma Kravis, his finger pressuring the trigger. He grabbed the gun with his free hand as if fighting for control and he was. Yates looked about, pleading for assistance. Erma flinched as the gun fired. Lou laughed, "SCHMUCK, AY-YAY-YAY."

35

R. W. Saunders couldn't be happier. This had gone much better than had been expected. Heck, it was over the top and would be a ratings blockbuster; that is, if everyone signed release forms, including the detective. Sure, he had obviously been skirting on the edge of the law, specifically not reporting the graveyard and what they had found at the other crime scenes, but reality television colors outside the lines. That's what makes it so successful and marketable. He had a hunch about this little ditty from day one, beginning when he had received that first phone call from the hospital custodian.

He played hunches well, was quite intuitive when it came to selecting the next greatest unsolved spooktacular occurrence. Once this puppy had been properly edited, the network would be drooling to make this a miniseries, or at least a multiple week event. Hell, he might just take this one to the big screen. Moviegoers ate this sort of crap up lately. Dollar signs twinkled in his eyes. L.J. continued filming the unfolding tragedy in its entirety. He'd have to consider replacing Joe though. That boy just didn't have the stomach for it when the gruesome side showed its ugly head. There he was again, in the bushes, puking out his guts at the mere sight of more bloodshed; good for the camera, not so good for Joe.

Wade kneeled down over Erma Kravis while Spencer struggled with Yates to assist the detective in disarming himself. The gun waved around wildly and had discharged a second time. Fortunately that bullet had only lodged in a nearby tree. Kelly grabbed the tire iron and against her better judgment, whacked Yates across his forearm. He screamed in agony as the gun fell to the ground, his arm now fractured from the blow. Rabbi Torres removed a handkerchief from his trouser pocket and promptly blindfolded Lou, suggesting if she couldn't see her surroundings, perhaps she couldn't manipulate them.

"She's still alive," announced Wade, applying pressure to the gunshot wound in Erma Kravis's thigh. Erma lay on her back, eyes glazed over and apparently in shock.

"I'd advise strongly that we dispense with the drama, secure the witch and push forward with the exorcism," spoke up R.W.

Rabbi Torres mouthed a head count. "We're two shy of the number we require performing the exorcism; that is, providing the wounded lady is up to it. The minyan requires ten adult males and that gender number is a little skewed too."

"Damn, we could have sure used Cranston," remarked R.W. "Yates, could you make a call and recruit a couple of officers to round out this thing?"

"I haven't committed to this nonsense. If I call for backup, I'm taking the lot of you in for questioning, along with this crazy bitch."

"Did you not witness and experience what just happened," asked R.W. "Either you just shot an innocent woman or the witch did. Which is it? I'd suggest you think about those ramifications before you attempt to run us all in."

Yates, clutching his broken limb, sighed and then responded, "Point taken but if I call this in, there is no way I can allow the exorcism."

"I suggest we wing it, ladies and gentleman," stated

Torres. "It will either work or it won't, but I'll have to concur with Mister Saunders, we must attempt to rid Mrs. Stetson of this evil entity. What I have witnessed is proof enough for me that she is indeed possessed."

"I saw a mailbox not too far from where I parked the van," said Joe, still very pale and puny looking from his heaving episode. "Maybe I can round up volunteers there."

"You can't be serious," said Spencer. "We can't pull in strangers at this juncture and expect them to comprehend this, or agree to an exorcism."

"I'll call Wyatt, my brother. He'd make nine."

"I may have a solution," said Torres, keying in a number on his cell phone. After ending the call, he suggested they go to his church, where Elijah Blaine would meet them to round out the ten number.

"You forget, we have a murder scene here," Yates reminded them. "And the woman I...she shot needs medical attention."

"Whether we stay or leave this sight doesn't really change that, does it?" asked R.W. "Besides, we have Doctor Garner here with us to administer temporary medical attention, do we not?"

"I'm sorry, but this is getting totally out of hand," added Kelly.

"Precisely," said R.W. "And we must put an end to it immediately before this witch has a chance to do more damage."

"This is...FERCOCKT!"

"Please gag her," advised Rabbi Torres "She has one filthy mouth. I suggest we make haste and do what must be done. I for one am prepared to face the consequences for my actions if the church disagrees with my decision."

R. W. folded his arms and patted his right foot. "In or out, time to put up or shut up, kiddies."

Wade raised his hand. "We must help Lou. Please, I

beg all of you."

"Crap or go blind," spewed Yates. "They'll have my ass and my badge for this, but I do have the smoking gun. Do I really have another choice right now? Hells bells, let's do it."

"She's coming around," advised Kelly. "Hope she has no objections."

Erma Kravis, in a weakened voice, spoke up, "I've overheard most of what you have been saying about the one who kidnapped me. If she's responsible for all of this and can harm others, then I feel it is my obligation to finish what my kin started. It appears he had good reason to do what he did a hundred years ago. Evil needs to be buried and that poor woman set free from this terrible haunting."

"To my MISHPOCHA then, my extended family, let's do this as one."

36
The Exorcism

Ten, count them, thought R. W., drooling over the prospects of what was to come. Rabbi Alex Torres would preside over the exorcism. Rounding out the ten would be Spencer Misenheimer, his television crewmen, Joe and L.J., Wade Stetson and his brother, Wyatt, Detective Yates, Doctor Kelly Garner, Erma Kravis, Elijah Blaine and Robert Wilson Saunders, television personality extraordinaire.

Lou remained cuffed, blind folded and gagged. It tore at Wade's heart to see her like this but he understood it had to be done to protect her and them. It still didn't make it any easier to swallow. He wanted to just hold her in his arms but it wouldn't be her he would be holding. He just hoped this worked.

Not going as you planned, is it? Soon I'll be rid of you and there will be no body hopping in your future, just dirt and your rotting bones.

This is far from over, Lou-Lou. This motley crowd grossly underestimates my powers. I have a few tricks up your sleeve yet. This farce of an exorcism by mere amateurs has no chance in hell at succeeding. The wantabe rabbi has never performed one, and just look at this cagily ten. They're pathetic at best. What do they think I'm going to be doing while they're blowing their silly ram's horn and chanting their nonsense? I'm shaking in your shoes.

If you're so sure, then why were you so insistent to avoid it? This will work and you know it. I can feel it. I can smell your fear and I like what I am sensing. Your end is evident.

You must think about what you wish on me, Lou-Lou. If I'm gone, what happens to you?

Stop your silly threats. They fall on deaf ears. You can't leap frog your way out of this now and these people are on to you. I am confident that I will be exonerated eventually of the crimes you committed. And if not, I'll still draw satisfaction in your demise.

So naïve, we are. A BI GEZUNT. Use your Google to seek the meaning but mark my thoughts, it will not apply to you. Now, GAY AVEK, GAY SHLAFEN, I have work to do.

"We should begin. Form your circle around Mrs. Stetson. You each have a copy of the Psalm 91. On my say you will begin reciting this, but not until I have beckoned you to do so. Whatever happens, do not break your rank, keep the circle in tack and continue to read the Psalm three times."

L.J. had set up three cameras at various angles. He had the ability to control them from a hand held remote. Microphones had been attached to the lapels of Rabbi Torres, Lou Stetson and R.W. A forth microphone was hanging from a jib above those encircling the possessed. On R.W.'s queue, the rabbi would begin the ceremony.

Kelly had been able to stop the bleeding from Erma Kravis's wound. Luckily she had lost a minimal amount of blood and the wound was not life threatening. She had managed to secure Yates fractured arm in a sling. Everything else was beyond the scope of her medical profession. As the detective had so eloquently pointed out, she too would probably have her ass served up on a silver platter and medical license yanked, and sued by the relatives of the deceased. She had witnessed the powers of this witch first hand so be it; as long as they put an end to her reign of terror. Counting her blessings, at least the witch could not possess her now as she had threatened to do.

"I am debating removing the blindfold and gag," added Rabbi Torres.

"Do you really think that's a smart move, given what happened last time," asked Yates. "I'm not removing the cuffs so don't even ask."

"Priceless, you do believe," hooted R.N, slapping the detective on the back.

Yates didn't respond. Instead he gave Saunders the go to hell look. He took a deep breath and said, "Let's get this over with; rabbi, please begin."

Neither Wyatt nor Elijah Blaine had witnessed what the others had seen, but Wyatt stood by his brother, as did the preacher. Erma Kravis shifted about nervously. This hadn't gone unnoticed by R.W.; the woman knew something; his gut told him so. He fought the urge to call her out. Right now, he had to make sure his crew got this on tape. He hoped for something spectacular, something that would shock his viewing audience and gain him fame and fortune the likes of which reality television had never seen. Just for a nanosecond he remembered that empty Capone vault opened for the live television by Geraldo Rivera and his stomach flip flopped.

"It's going to be okay," whispered Doctor Kelly Garner to Wade Stetson.

Overhearing this, Margarett mouthed a series of profanities through Lou's gagged mouth. She squirmed to free herself, all in vain. Her powers fell shy on that little feat, but if she could somehow finish off Kravis, she could deal this assembled lynch mob a deadly blow. These people were no different than the ones who had murdered her. They snuffed out what they didn't understand. This absolutely would not happen to her a second time. This was her time, not theirs. Margarrett gathered all her powers and channeled her command to the weakest link.

Joe stepped forward from his position in the circle that surrounded Lou Stetson. He pulled the gag free from her mouth and reached for the blindfold. Yates shouldered him with such force that Joe tumbled to the ground. Blinking wild eyed, he looked about as he was trying to sponge in his surroundings.

"You little dick, what in the hell do you think you're doing," yelled Yates.

Joe just shook his head, perplexed at the question.

"Don't blame the crewman, detective; it was not his doing. She manipulated him," clarified Rabbi Torres.

"Blame game, how pathetic, Rabbi; games, all of this is mere games and show for the church and this television nonsense. LUFTMENSH, MAZEL TOV, MEESA MASHEENA, a messa mashee af deer. MOMZER."

Torres repositioned the gag. Everyone hung on the edge of their seats, awaiting the translation of the witch's latest rants. R.W. spoke up first. "Okay, let's have it. Just what the hell did she yell at you?"

"She fears what is to come. She realizes her defeat is imminent. This exorcism will soon lead a pathway in her journey to leave the body she now possesses."

"I get that but what did she just say?"

"Nonsense mostly, unfounded threats; she called me a dreamer, hailing good luck to me before wishing me a horrible death, possibly her version of a warning shot over the bow. It has been suggested that Masheena is the origin for the insulting name for Jews of Sheeny. She is desperate and merely took advantage of her freedom to speak, nothing more. She did refer to me as a bastard, untrustworthy I am in her opinion. Mere words, like the nursery rhyme, sticks and stones may break my bones but words can never hurt me. Let us prepare our hearts to see this through and not be swayed by her antics. To do so would only embolden her."

Rabbi Torres mustered a smile. R.W. wasn't buying it. His gut told him the rabbi's cage had been rattled by her rant. The young rabbi was on shaky ground and his inexperience was more than evident now. This could signal troubled waters ahead, thought R.W. and then he too smiled interpreting sensational television in his future. People love to pull for the underdog and he viewed Torres as just that, going up against the hundred and twenty something year old witch. Good versus evil, it didn't get any better than this. He glanced one last time around at the equipment to ensure he had it covered at every possible angle. All he was missing was Michael Buffer from fight night announcing *'Let's get ready to rumble'*. Possibly he could acquire permission or pay for the rights to use that as a sound bite when this was aired. Hell, he might even be able to get Buffer to deliver it live for his show, just before airing the segment.

"We should start. Please, in unison, begin reading verse one of Psalm 91 from your handouts. No matter what happens, if anything does happen, do not stop reading until you have completed all sixteen verses. Then, from the beginning, you will read the verses a second and then a third time. It is crucial that you follow my instructions to the letter, understood?"

The ten chosen ones nodded and/or articulated they understood and so they began.

1. Whoever dwells in the shelter of the Most High
will rest in the shadow of the Almighty.

2. I will say of the LORD, "He is my refuge and my
fortress, my God, in whom I trust."

3. Surely he will save youfrom the fowler's snare
and from the deadly pestilence.

4 He will cover you with his feathers, and under his
wings you will find refuge; his faithfulness will be

your shield and rampart.

⁵ You will not fear the terror of night, nor the arrow that flies by day,

₆. nor the pestilence that stalks in the darkness,
nor the plague that destroys at midday.

⁷ A thousand may fall at your side, ten thousand at your right hand, but it will not come near you.

⁸ You will only observe with your eyes and see the punishment of the wicked.

⁹ If you say, "The LORD is my refuge," and you make the Most High your dwelling,

¹⁰ no harm will overtake you, no disaster will come near your tent.

¹¹ For he will command his angels concerning you to guard you in all your ways;

¹² they will lift you up in their hands, so that you will not strike your foot against a stone.

¹³ You will tread on the lion and the cobra; you will trample the great lion and the serpent.

¹⁴ "Because he loves me," says the LORD, "I will rescue him; I will protect him, for he acknowledges my name.

¹⁵ He will call on me, and I will answer him; I will be with him in trouble, I will deliver him and honor him.

¹⁶ With long life I will satisfy him

Lou squirmed through the first reciting, Margarett attempting to free herself from her bondage. She mumbled vigorously through the gag, muffled protests and curses, having no impact on the proceedings. She struggled to channel another assault, mind searching for one of the ten she could recruit to do her bidding. Not ready to admit or claim defeat, but the Psalm recitation was disrupting her ability to focus, that and the insider now attacking her. Lou had sensed her weakness and had gained a slight foothold, nothing significant yet, but still a slight crack in the door. Both she and her parasite were operating blindly, unable to witness the proceedings through the blindfold. Lou persisted at being an annoying presence, an onslaught to reclaim what was once hers. .

The ten minyan wantabes recited Psalm 91 a second time. Rabbi Torres spoke along with them, remaining focused on Lou Stetson, restrained to the chair within the circle of ten. He hoped the deviation from a typical exorcism would prove effective, but this was his first solo rodeo; one could not know for sure. Fact, between the restraints and the chanting, the alleged witch possessing Lou Stetson was not a happy camper by a long shot. Her disgruntled facial expressions, as evident through the blindfold and gag, were animated and extremely discontent. Torres surely hoped this meant the exorcism was working.

R.W. focused on their captive too, searching for any signs that the witch might be succumbing to the incantation. He had mixed emotions. Part of him wanted to see this through successfully, but another part of him selfishly wanted to see this thing blow up, actual supernatural evidence caught on camera would be one of hell of a gig. So far, however, it had been boring. Ten adults surrounding a woman secured in a chair while chanting scripture for the Bible wasn't spectacular enough to suit him. It had no wow factor. Nothing presented itself as this being a real phenomenon. He needed to do something to change this, up the ante, but what. One more recitation of the Psalm remained; might as well ride it out and see what happens, he figured. Where was *Linda Blair* when you needed her? Some good ole fashioned levitation, slimy, green, puke spewing or speaking in deep, raspy, demonic voices could go a long way about now.

The third recitation completed, Rabbi Paul Torres let go a mighty series of blows on the shofar. Torres did his best to mimic the various notes and tones he had heard in a previous exorcism. The premise was to shatter the body so that the possessing force would be shaken loose. He removed the shofar from his lips, unsure if he had successfully shattered Lou Stetson's body enough to loosen the witch's hold. Judgment time had arrived. Torres would have to remove the gag and begin communicating directly with Margarett Levine Reznik to determine why she had chosen to possess the Stetson woman. Taking a deep breath, he removed the gag, leaving the blindfold in place for the time being. The minyan held their ground as instructed. He may still require their involvement yet.

"This is Rabbi Alex Torres speaking to you, can you respond?"

"Yes."

"Can you tell me to whom I am speaking?"

"Yes, I am Emma Lou Stetson."

A tear ran down Wade's cheek. He fought the impulse to break the circle and rush to his wife, hold and hug her. It was difficult for him to man his position, hearing the tone in her voice, his wife's voice. The exorcism had miraculously worked. R.W. rubbed his chin, smelled a rat; wasn't convinced.

"How can I be absolutely sure they I am conversing with Emma Lou Stetson and not Margarett Levine Reznik?" The exorcism to this point was only supposed to shake the spirit loose, not chase it from the body. He too sensed a ruse taking place.

"I am who I am. I don't understand your question. Why can I not see you or move my hands?"

"It is for your own protection, my dear."

And ours, thought R.W.

"Protection, I don't understand. Why would I harm anyone?"

"It's my wife, can't you see," spoke up Wade. "Please, set her free. She's frightened."

Kelly placed her hand on Wade's arm and whispered, "Be patient. We must be sure this isn't a trick."

"Trick," an agitated Lou elevated her voice. "Is that you Doctor Garner?"

Kelly made eye contact with the rabbi, mouthed could she respond. Torres nodded she could.

"Yes, it is me, Lou. Do you remember the conversation you had with me earlier, while we were together in the automobile?" The witch had threatened to possess her once she had murdered her last victim.

"We were together but things are foggy," repeated Lou.

"Yes, I understand your confusion. You were explaining your plans to me."

"Plans, what sort of plans. I don't remember this."

"What is the last thing you do remember?"

"I'm not sure. It is so confusing to me. I was lost. I think I was in the forest but I don't know why. Is that sweet lady, Liz Donley here with you? She might know why I was lost. She is so kind to me. I really like her."

"See, it is my wife. She would never harm someone as dear as Liz. Please, Rabbi, take off that silly blindfold and handcuffs. My wife deserves better treatment than this. It is time to take her home, where she belongs."

Wyatt, Wade's brother rubbed the back of his neck, taking all this in. Something seemed out of place with this conversation but he couldn't put his finger on it. This entire mess was quite troublesome and confusing, all this junk about witches, possessions and now a damn Jewish exorcism. Surely this scene was being orchestrated by the ghost hunters to just make for good TV. He didn't like this Saunders feller and his bunch of rating's hounds. He didn't trust any of them as far as he could toss them. They weren't here for family. They were here because they smelled dollar signs.

Erma Kravis, her gunshot wound now throbbing, had her reasons for being here; beyond just being one of ten and bringing closure to her ordeal. The Kravis name was at stake, dirty little secrets tucked away for the past hundred years. She had recognized the witch's name immediately and totally believed in her existence and resurrection. She understood the ramifications and this was no mere possession as the others wished to believe. This was one hell of a serious matter and if not nipped here and now could balloon into something the others couldn't possibly comprehend. Secrets were secrets for a reason. She'd not share hers with these strangers, nor acknowledge them in front of the witch. The sins of our fathers had never rung so true.

Rabbi Torres contemplated Wade's request. Freeing the woman from her bondage without knowing for sure if the witch still possessed her or not, could result in terrible consequences, and he wasn't sure he could regain control of the situation if he did. No, he must be sure. This portion of the exorcism shouldn't so easily chase the spirit from the possessed.

Spencer just wanted this to be over so that he could officially severe the ties with Saunders, but only after cashing in on the fame and fortune first. He wasn't that stupid. He grasped the significance of this ever evolving episode. Played the right way, it would be a game changer for his career. Sadly, he and Saunders did agree on this. His only regret, allowing it to play out too long and costing innocent people their lives, and for that, he would never forgive himself. No, now was not the time, he decided.

"I understand you have your concerns, rightfully so, Mister Stetson, however, we must complete the exorcism as designed. Cutting corners could be detrimental to our goals."

"My wife does not deserve this harsh treatment. Isn't it obvious by now that she is innocent of these wrong doings? You didn't restrain the constable for using his weapon so why persecute my wife?"

"Please, everyone, refrain from the chatter. The effectiveness of the exorcism can only be effective if we focus on the task at hand."

"Rabbi, do what you need to do to purge the demon from her loins," spoke up R.W. "I don't have an endless supply of film to burn."

"Contrary to what you may believe, this isn't about you, my son," stated Elijah Blaine.

"I hesitate to say this, but I agree with Saunders, Rabbi; let's get this over with. Witch or no witch, I'm taking this woman in. You've got ten minutes to wrap this up."

"Detective, an exorcism cannot be restricted to a time table. It doesn't work like that."

"Ten minutes," Yates repeated, holding up his arm and displaying his wristwatch.

"Please, free my wife, detective; those cuffs are no longer necessary."

"Fat chance, she's in my custody and she stays cuffed to that chair, end of story."

"SCHMUCK," mouthed Wade.

"If you two gents are done; can we get this thing rolling; time is money," interrupted R.W.

"Please read the prayer at the bottom of your hand-outs while I continue my inquisition of the inflicted."

"Rabbi, I'm here, if you haven't noticed and my name is Emma Lou Stetson, not this other person you seem to have me confused with. For the record, I take exception to this little inquisition of yours. I'm no witch. I'm a college professor. My students might argue I'm one and the same though," she chuckled.

"She's lying," ranted Erma Kravis.

R.W. eyed her curiously and then spoke. "Humor us, Honey, just what do you really know about the witch? I think you're holding out on us. What did your elder do to her that has you fretting so now?"

"I have no idea what you're talking about."

"Sure you do," said R.W. "My researchers have mined the dirt on your ancestor and I say he was a key player in her untimely demise."

Lou, still blindfolded, cocked her head in the direction of the exchange. She gritted her teeth and again tried to free herself from the awful mandibles that restrained her.

"Martin Kravis, your long lost relative, he is the reason you are here and why you are so concerned about the witch and her revengeful motives; your hide for that of your Martin's indiscretions, and eye for an eye, so it goes. Let's face it, my dear; you're the last one standing. She has reconciled the debt she paid with her life. Just why did she really save the best for last?"

Erma Kravis clutched her ailing wound, becoming faint and fidgeting nervously.

Rabbi Torres attempted to regain control of the proceedings and baited the woman he still felt possessed by the entity. "I address this question to Margarett Levine Reznik. Is it true what Mister Saunders has stated; that this long forgotten ancestor orchestrated the tragedy that led to your death at such a tender young age?"

"What would I know of this woman? I cannot identify who I cannot see."

"Certainly you recognize the Kravis surname?"

"Ask her more questions. Perhaps it will jog my memory. I pride myself in researching and recalling history. Remove this dreaded blindfold and I can see her for myself. A picture is supposed to be worth a kettle full of words, right?"

Liar, you're such a liar and you know it.

You must dispense of such rude interruptions, Lou-Lou. We're breaking ground here. We're so very close to ending what we started.

We; I'm no part of this insanity.

There you go again; washing the blood from your miserable little hands. I forgive you though. You have served me well. Soon, very soon, you can have your pitiful, sickly, little life back to do with it as you wish. Do they still hang murderers? For now, stop interfering. I wish to hear the Kravis woman's confessions before I end her worthless life.

"Sweetheart, you either spill the beans or I will," threatened R.W. "It's time to lay the cards on the table. Confession is food for the soul."

"Please, Miss Kravis, if you have something beneficial to add, by all means please do so. If it could assist us in the exorcism and ending this madness, then by all means, speak your peace."

"Rabbi, do you believe she is still her; I mean, the witch, is she still inside that woman's body?"

"I cannot say for sure. Let us continue. Please, share with us what you hold inside. Possibly it will cleanse your soul and free you from your obvious torment."

Erma fumbled with her words, woozy headed and terrified of just what might happen once she shared the family's dirty little dark secrets, those passed along for generations. She was the sole heir to this information and hated knowing what she had known for too many years. Could airing the soiled laundry really set her free?

"Must I remind you again that I don't have time for this nonsense? There is an unreported crime scene back at that cemetery, including a murder victim. That's it. I'm halting this craziness now. It's over, done."

"Ah, but watch what you wish for Detective Yates," spoke up R.W. "You keep forgetting; you discharged your weapon. You shot Erma Kravis, an unarmed and quite defenseless woman, for no apparent reason. I'd think you had more at stake here than the rest of us combined. How else are you going to defend your actions? If we prove the witch exists and we, the witnesses, stick together to corroborate the story that she controlled your actions, you might just keep your badge, and stave off a prison sentence to boot. Do I have your attention now, son?"

"This better work is all I'm saying."

"Please, Miss Kravis, would you be so kind as to share your story with us; that is, if it won't disrupt the exorcism," said R.W.

Rabbi Torres nodded. "We're winging it anyway; we may as well see where this takes us, I suppose; any objections from you, Mrs. Stetson?"

"NARRISHKEIT."

"Foolishness, maybe, Miss Reznek," smiled Torres.

"PUTZ, zoist ligen in drerd."

"What did she say," asked Kelly.

"She called me a fool and said I should lie in the earth; her version of drop dead. Our Miss Reznek is still in charge so it seems. I think our little ritual has already had considerable impact. She no longer can hide behind Mrs. Stetson's skirt tails. She has been shaken loose, by design. Miss Kravis…please tell us what you know. It could save this woman's life, as well as your own."

Wyatt nudged the preacher, "Is this rabbi for real?"

"The real deal, I assure you," answered Elijah Blaine.

"What about this witch stuff?"

"Stay tuned, we'll complete this journey together."

37
May 17, 1872

"Miss Kravis, do you feel compelled to share with us what you know about this?"

"Rabbi, I shouldn't be held responsible for any actions taken by my ancestors. Certainly my death cannot reconcile anything that happened over a hundred years ago. I watched as this woman murdered another innocent descendent in cold blood. She planned to do me next. Doing so would have changed nothing."

"Not wishing to sound like a prosecutor, but could you stick to the story and just tell us what you know about the original incident," chimed in R.W., motioning to his crew to keep those cameras rolling.

"Very well, at this juncture, what harm can it do? Perhaps the burden will be lifted off my shoulders and this dreaded curse that has plagued my family can finally be broken. Understand that what I am about to describe is written in documents passed along from Martin Kravis. He confessed to his sins before he died; possibly out of guilt or maybe just to prepare his offspring for what might be if the resurrection of Margarett Levine Reznik ever occurred. Until now I thought it was the mere rants and gibberish of a troubled soul, a mad man and airing such dirty laundry served no practical purpose. Now, I am a believer. I've seen firsthand what this witch is capable of doing. If she would have succeeded in murdering me, just maybe no one could have stopped her. Martin Kravis warned of this very day."

Martin Kravis had perversions, lustful and demanding, and in his day, prominent folks could do most anything they wished, without fear of persecution or incrimination. Martin, a judge in the highest court of the local community, ruled the kingdom, so to speak, in this section of South Carolina. He possessed the powers to manipulate lives for good or bad, whichever he chose to forward his agenda. Shamefully he was quite ruthless; his lawless lawfulness knew no boundaries. Fail to do his bidding and you suffered the consequences. Refuse to do what he demanded and you were certain to spend the rest of your miserable life behind bars or worse.

Furthermore, he had connections to a higher hierarchy, a secret society, others with political aspirations, their tentacles originating in places even he would never admit or expose; unless a favor was needed or blackmail necessary. One should never eat their own. That rule never applied to Martin Kravis. His alliances were no coincidence, there to service his needs for as long as he needed it, and let there be no doubt, he was loyal to no one. Anyone was expendable. Martin always held the upper hand; a trump card, a piece of valuable information to use against an enemy or associate. The fine line remained blurred in his eyes.

"Excuse me, Miss Kravis, I do hate to interrupt, but did he actually state these facts in his writing," asked Rabbi Torres.

"He boasted of them, much the braggart, proud of everything he stood for and had accomplished. His confessions had nothing to do with his power and how he achieved his goals in life."

"Let the woman continue, how about it, Rabbi, so we can get to the witchcraft portion, hopefully," interrupted R.W.

"Sorry, but I do feel it necessary to paint the entire canvas, to educate everyone here as to why these circumstances we find ourselves in presented itself in the first place. Assuredly this is an example of evil versus evil. Sadly, good played no role in this scenario whatsoever or in my ancestor's motives. Possibly we might uncover a key to the door and the she-devil can be locked away forever this time."

"I say we allow her to tell this her way," advised Spencer.

"So you're calling the shots now, Spence?"

"Just making a logical observation," he replied to R.W.

"Please continue, my dear and I do apologize for the interruption."

"By all means, get all of this crap off your chest," chimed in detective Yates. "We're sitting on top of a powder keg and the fuse is lit and burning toward an ending that just plain pisses me off."

"I find this quite intriguing," whispered Kelly to Wade.

"This is BOBBEMYSEH," mumbled Wade, too low to be detected by those encircling Lou Stetson, still cuffed securely to the chair and remaining silent for the time being.

Martin Kravis was married with seven children, but much of his happy home life was just a front for political convenience and assuring that the community perceived him as the ultimate family man. His darker side influenced his true persona. You see, Martin had a fetish for the untouched and unblemished, those innocent and yet to be deflowered. In today's society he would have been considered the worst of the worst. He was a serial child predator and his molestations knew no boundaries. For whatever reason, he included the details of the sheer brutality of his affliction in his memoirs. These materials are quite graphic and shameful; and for the sake of furthering the story, I refuse to go into detail, as doing so only justifies his legacy. These horrific acts go beyond anything ever portrayed on the cinema or through the scribbling of any published work. My relative was a monster of the worst kind, preying on the innocence of those ill prepared to defend themselves or seek help from those willing to offer it. Power is everything and Martin Kravis oozed of it from every stinking pore.

He had a virtual network in his employment, those willing to furnish him an endless supply of young girls to satisfy his animalistic urges, in exchange for bountiful amounts of hush money. He paid these flesh pimps well to ensure blackmail never invaded their thoughts. When he was done with his toys, he discarded them, paying off any family members to keep his little secrets; that and threatening them with dire consequences if any ever crossed him. He eventually met others with similar traits and he demanded and accepted political favors in exchange for making their dreams come true. Martin Kravis was the all powerful OZ of the then Emerald City.

My ancestor enjoyed fishing, almost a much as he enjoyed his little secret pleasures. One particular spring afternoon while 'wetting his hook' as he called it, along the banks of the Saluda River, a little secluded spot he had stumbled upon in the northern boundaries of Greenwood, he met a woman living near the river's edge in a modest little shanty. Her name was Abaigael Devra Reznik. Martin would soon determine that she had been banished from society after becoming pregnant with a prominent Pelzer lawyer's bastard child and for the suspected use of witchcraft. Her hasty departure and choice to become a woodland recluse had saved her life on both counts. This filthy and pathetic derelict had meant no more to Martin than dog feces on the bottom of his shoe until he had spotted the timid little girl in the shadows of the dilapidated dwelling.

Martin, in awe of this little treasure he had unearthed, immediately began questioning Abaigael to determine if the lass were still virtuous and became hopelessly bewitched by the twelve year old's beauty. He decided then and there that he must have her and to his shock, the mother offered no resistance to his request. She only asked in return that he would keep her secret and tell no one of her and where she lived; that and living expenses to improve her modest lifestyle. Twelve year old Margarett Levine Reznik had been bought for a relatively cheap fee. Martin was quite ecstatic with his new found toy.

Unlike his other sexual molestations, he soon discovered that young Margarett was special, gifted, and thus, he ended up moving Abaigael and Margarett into an out of the way cottage, paid in full, the child there for his bidding and the mother utilized to work her magic where it benefited him the most. Margarett, as she reached puberty, developed powers of her own, and had an uncanny ability to forecast events. She could alter certain situations utilizing spells handed down by the mother. Abaigael, realizing the value of her daughter and her own powers, became more demanding of Martin, seeking the better things in life.

She eventually crossed a line that Martin could not tolerate. She had dug her nails too deeply into extortion, blackmailing being the seed that only Martin was allowed to sow; thus the mother of Margarett simply disappeared one night under the cloak of darkness. Martin did not detail the assumed murder in his scribbling, but he did state her demise did not go as well as envisioned. Dire consequences resulted; something too diabolical for him to put into words. The day she vanished, he did mourn the death of his oldest son, but provided no details of cause of death.

With Abaigael's demise came an uncanny strengthening of Margarett's powers. Martin could neither explain nor understand this transformation. He struggled to bridle it, the young girl somewhat taking on the persona of her mother, cashing in on her favors, becoming quite the force to be reckoned with. Martin gave into her, still taken by his little beauty. His fixation was soon replaced by fear. While at a price he could still encourage her to do his bidding, he no longer controlled the reins. At sweet sixteen she began calling many of the shots and demanded more of Martin's attention, shunning his family, the shoe on the other foot. Bewitched, Martin could not refuse her, dared not. He had witnessed too many unexplained events to deny her any of her quirky perks. The most diabolical and devious player of the land had met his match and he had paid dearly to remain ruler of his kingdom so to speak.

By age eighteen Margarett no longer had patience or tolerance for Martin's sexual advantages. Martin had actually grown tired of her as a play thing also; much too old for his likening, but he couldn't resist the pull, the magnetic draw of the gifted one. Shunning him only made him desire her even more, however, he allowed his bitterness to adversely impact his decision making, too often giving in to her whims, or possibly just fearful of what she might do if he refused. He had lost control of his child protégé. Others within his inner circle had encouraged Martin to reconcile the situation. They too had fallen prey to her numerous schemes. She was no longer their pawn. She had become the queen of the chessboard.

Just shy of her twenty first birthday she demanded that Martin's wife and children be banished from the household. Margarett had decided herself worthy of being the only mistress of the home. She threatened to disclose this fact to his wife and the rest of the world. Martin had gotten his fill. He and his cronies had decided to end the madness, but weren't sure how to outsmart the fox. Margarett had the uncanny ability of perception. It was as if she could read their thoughts. Many were convinced this was fact, not mere paranoia. Martin stalled; pushing back on her request, as he and his assembly of fellow henchmen contemplated their next move, one they hoped to conceal from the little witch. One could never be sure though, not until they succeeded on their actions.

Finally the day arrived. The ruse was placed into motion the day she turned twenty one. The most loyal of his inner clique, those so recognized by Margarett, assembled to pay tribute to the special occasion. Bearing extravagant gifts and in a private secluded setting, it was portrayed as a mini gala event. The sweet young thing straight from the bowels of hell, as Martin referred to her, seemed oblivious to what really lay in store for her. While he would sorely miss her and her powerful gift, this had to be done. This was his world to rule, not hers.

Several bottles of the most expensive wine from his cellar were served to those gathered around the blossoming adult. A gold goblet, with the initials MLR, a special gift from Martin Kravis was filled from the first uncorked bottle. A toast, commemorating the blessed occasion, advanced the agenda of those gathered to covertly pay their last respects. Margarett gulped the contents, droplets running from the corners of her mouth and landing on her bountiful breasts, exposed by the low cut scarlet red silk blouse. She dabbed the droplets and suckled them from her finger tips. The brief smile on her face transformed to pure rage when she realized the grave error she had committed, intrusting these greedy bastards. The horde quickly swarmed her, binding her hands and feet, and placing a hood over her head. Overlooking one critical aspect of their onslaught, they failed to gag her, thinking the laced wine would immediately silence any banner and put her under. Groggy, she managed to deliver her warning, her curse in an already slurred speech.

Fercockt, a khalerye. If you do this, I curse you, your children, and your children's children. All will live in fear of my return. Their tainted blood will pay for your sins, delivered by my hands. Your foolishness is but that. I cannot be destroyed by those more corrupt than I. You stole my virginity, my youth and dare rob me of my destiny. Martin Kravis, you and yours will pay the ultimate price, the path to my resurrection travels through your veins and your seed. And to the rest of you miserable mortals, *Zalts im in di oygenm feffer im in di noz. Shteyner af zayne beyner. Er zol kakn mit blit un mit ayter. Er zol hobn paroys makes bashotn mit oybes krets. Zol es im onkumn vos ikh vintsh im. Zol er krenken un gedenken. Meesa Masheena.*

"Just like that, they hanged the twenty one year old alleged witch, Margarett Levine Reznik. As promised, she had wreaked havoc on generations of our families, until fulfilling the curse, her resurrection quite evident now. She's back and I'm all that stands in the way of her legacy."

"What was all that last bit of gibberish," asked R.W.

"Allow me to attempt to translate," spoke up Rabbi Torres, having scribbled on his prayer notepad. "To each and every man she said all screwed up, a plague on you. Throw salt in his eyes, pepper his nose; stones on his bones. He should crap blood and pus. He should have the Pharaoh's plagues sprinkled with Job's scabies. Let him suffer and remember. Let what I wish on him come true, a horrible death."

"*Eyn imglik iz far im veynik, abrokh tsu dayn lebn,*" added Margarett. "I'll translate this one, Rabbi. One misfortune is too few for him; for them, all those who played a hand in my hanging, your life should be a disaster."

Wade Stetson grabbed Erma Kravis from behind, his right arm looped under her chin, his left pinning her good arm to her side, gripping Martin's ancestor in a choke hold. "*Heng dikh oyf a tsikershtrikl vestu hobn a zisn toyt.*"

"Hang yourself with sugar rope and you'll have a sweet death," repeated Rabbi Torres.

"Stop him…her…" yelled Spencer.

Wyatt grabbed his brother in a head lock as she shouted, "I knew that wasn't Wade earlier. He kept referring to Lou as his wife and not calling her by name. That's not how he talks."

"It's her," said Kelly. "She's somehow controlling Wade's action, his thoughts."

Erma had lost consciousness and was growing pale by the second. Wyatt could not break his brother's death grip on her.

"Shoot him," yelled Joe, looking over at Detective Yates.

Yates didn't bite. If he missed he might hit her. He had already shot this poor woman once. He wouldn't make the same mistake twice, especially when he was in full control of his faculties this time. He did join Wyatt in trying to pry Wade's arm from her throat. With all his strength he could not budge the vice like grip he had had on Erma.

"Hell, shoot her then," Joe repeated, looking over at Lou still cuffed to the chair. R.W. gave his crew the look, warning them to keep filming.

Rabbi Torres began chanting a prayer while Elijah clutched his bible and prayed too. The circle of ten had been broken and Torres feared the exorcism had failed royally.

Doctor Kelly Garner rushed over to Lou Stetson and leaned down, face to face, nose to nose. "This is all wrong, Lou…fight her. Don't let her do this. Margarret, listen to me. What you are doing isn't necessary. Justice has been served on those who perpetrated this heinous act a hundred years ago. One of their own snitched on them. They were all brought to justice for the crime committed against you. They paid for their part in murdering you. There is no need to punish their offspring for what they could not prevent. They played no part in your death."

"Lies, you speak lies, gornisht helfn, gonif."

"She tells the facts like they are written, little lady,"

yelled R.W., now squatting down beside Kelly. "Google never likes."

"Google said this," questioned Margarett. "You asked the machine…the computer?"

"My experts did and one of their very own did indeed turn on them, spilled the beans on the whole lot. He killed himself to boot after confessing. They even dug you up from an unmarked grave and gave you a proper burial in that cemetery, marked by a headstone. You don't have a dog in this here hunt, dear. Being pissed off at any of their kinfolks is pointless. Justice has already been served."

"It's true. Redemption, it has been paid in full. You can rest in peace," beckoned Kelly.

Wade relaxed his grip. Wyatt and Yates were able to pry his arm free. Yates eased Erma Kravis to the floor. He checked her vitals. She was still alive. Wyatt saw to Wade. He was looking about wildly, oblivious to his previous actions.

It's time for you to go, Margarett. You don't belong here. Your final resting place awaits you. May peace be with you and God forgive you for your sins.

Lou-Lou, for once you are right. I no longer need to seek revenge. Those who did this to me paid their debt to society. I am so sorry for what I have put you through. I only wish you the best, whatever happens from this day forward. I allowed myself to be consumed by hatred and bitterness, misusing my powers for evil. May all forgive me for what I have done and for what I am about to do.

"Evil attracts evil. The witch is deceitful and can not be trusted or believed," spoke the Rabbi.

The gunshot echoed through the building. Yates stood over Erma Kravis, holding the proverbial smoking gun, one bullet to her head, Martins offspring, no more.

"Now that's sensationalism if I ever witnessed it," clapped R.W. "That's a damn wrap, boys, money in the bank."

"Wade, go to Lou. She needs you," said Elijah.

"Lou, it's over," he said as he looked into her yes.

I love you and am so sorry for what has happened. I want to go home.

"It's my Lou. I can see it in her eyes, even if she can't speak."

Kelly stared at the couple, wishing the best, but thinking anything but…this part was over.

Epilogue

"Lou, your garden looks wonderful this year," remarked Anna Stetson.

"Best looking okra I've seen there, sister-in-law," added Wyatt to his wife's observation.

"Leanne and Heath helped," replied Wade. "The kids have been home more lately than when they lived here."

"That's what family does," smiled Wyatt. "How are you holding up?"

"Me, doing just fine; it's good to have Lou back where she belongs."

"Believers or not, the authorities got it right, Wade."

"Well, thanks to everyone present giving their sworn testimony, judge and jury had a tough time prosecuting her given the circumstances."

"Yeah, it was tough for the prosecution to discredit a rabbi, a preacher, a doctor and detective, not to mention the rest of us."

"One thing bothers me though; how Saunders video got ruined. Everything should have been captured on those recordings, the ultimate proof to support us."

"I guess nobody hated that any worse than him and his crew; a lost opportunity for his viewing audience. I heard he up and quit the network, just walked away from his highly rated show. Maybe this thing took a toll on him too."

"I won't lose any sleep over that bastard's misfortune. He used every one of us for the sake of his story. He got what he deserved."

"It's too bad Yates didn't get to keep his job but I guess considering he shot the Kravis woman twice, he's damn lucky to be released on probation. He can thank Rabbi

Torres for that, but his elders were none to happy with him performing that exorcism."

"I guess we're all lucky, Wade. If that witch would have pulled this off, we might all have paid the fiddler. Is there any doubt in your mind that the witch possessed Lou?"

"No doubt whatsoever; she couldn't have killed all those people. It's not in her."

"What is Doctor Garner saying about Lou, now?"

"Same as she's been saying; Lou is in the final stages but hanging in there." Wade adjusted Lou in her wheelchair and wiped drool from her chin.

"She seemed healthy as a horse…"

"No regrets, I'm glad to have my Lou back, and if that means that the Alzheimer's returns, then so be it. It was a far worse death sentence being controlled by Margarett Levine Reznik. I'll cherish what time I have left with her. This is the hand dealt us, the original one. We'll play it to the end."

I love you, Wade and always will. I agree this is the best thing for all of us. I just regret I was used as a tool to harm all those innocent people. I tried to stop her, I did. She was so powerful. I'll miss you my dear husband. How does it go; until death do us part.

The door bell rang a third time before he answered it. "A sight for sore eyes, what brings you here, Spencer Misenheimer? I haven't heard from you in over a year and you just show up on my door steps."

"Can I come in for a little chat, Saunders?"

"Sure thing, what's eating you?"

"You, I don't get it. Why did you do it?"

"Do what?"

"Why did you claim the video had been ruined? You lied and you know it. The footage was gold to you. I originally suspected you had horded it until after the trial;

figuring you didn't wish to waste it freely for the news media. But then, you quit the network and you still haven't pressed forward on a cinema production."

"What is this to you, Spencer? I paid you for your time; quite handsomely."

"More than generous, considering I wanted no more to do with this phenomenon, but there's more to this. What are your real motives?"

"My business is my business. I'd suggest you cut your loses and leave."

"I've been replaying the events, attempting to solve this little mystery, and finally I believe I have the answers. I'm only here to confirm them."

"Look around, Spencer, this isn't a confessional and you're not a priest. Hell boy, you're not even a rabbi, not that it will rate you any higher on the saint scale."

"The exorcism failed, didn't it? Detective Yates eliminated the last link. Margarett Levine Reznik's prophecy, the curse was fulfilled with Erma Kravis's death. Reznik didn't want the footage to ever be seen. It would legitimize her existence. You're just waiting and bidding your time, aren't' you? Giving it a little breathing room until everyone forgets the horrible story and forgets the popularity of the show."

"Pure fantasy, Spencer; you should have been a screenwriter. You're quite gifted. I underestimated your partnership. When you open a door, don't forget to close it. Treat your mouth accordingly."

"Factual, I assure you. Tell me. When do you wake the evil?"

"Loose tongues are worse than wicked hands Spencer."

"Priceless, you are good, but not perfect. Your flaws shine through sure as the light creeps underneath the closed door. With much wealth come many worries."

"Pray that you will never have to bear all that you are

able to endure. Not to have felt pain is not to have been human."

"Whoever does not try, does not learn."

"Prepare your proof before you argue."

"While this is entertaining, exchanging Jewish phrases has reached a climatic bore. I'll end our little volley with this, old mighty parapsychologist. He that can't endure the bad will not live to see the good. A pessimist, confronted with two bad choices, chooses both. For you Spencer, coming here was your first mistake. Confronting me was your final one. Every chess master utilizes her pawns. You'll make a fine edition to my board. Who knows, if you serve me well, perhaps I will knight you."

"Margarett Levine Reznik, truth is the safest lie. The righteous say little and do much."

"Let our journey begin together, Spencer. The world is at our finger tips. I still can't believe you and your pathetic bunch could really think your non-Jewish roots could send my spirit back to the grave. And with that little greenhorn rabbi, thinking he could actually perform an exorcism. You would have benefited much better by just simply ambushing me."

Thunder rattled the windows; lightening had struck its mark. R.W. Saunders lay dead in a pool of his own blood. Yates stepped into view, gazing through the window's broken glass, after empting his weapon. Spencer opened the door. "What took you so long? "

"Persistent and talkative rabbi," interrupted Rabbi Torres, stepping into view. "I had to complete the prayer before allowing the good detective to test his marksmanship. Margarett Levine Reznik should forever rest in peace now, ambushed as she suggested. What you give for the cause of charity in health is gold; what you give in sickness is silver; what you give after death is lead. Our good detective certainly gave an ample supply of lead, didn't he? Dead within the confines of

Saunder's body ensure she can not leap to another host."

"Let's bury this witch in wolf's clothing and be done with it," said Spencer. "But not before we retrieve that video to ensure it doesn't fall into greedy hands."

"Ding dong, the witch is dead," clapped Torres. "If at first you don't succeed, become ruthless. May the All Mighty both forgive and bless us for what we have done, what had to be done, as I have no regrets for my decision and my participation. Lucifer's pawn is no more."

Emma Lou Stetson looked into Wade's eyes and smiled, and then managed to whisper, *"She is leaving him, not all at once, which would be painful enough, but in a wrenching succession of separations. One moment she is here, and then she is gone again, and each journey takes her a little farther from his reach. He cannot follow her, and he wonders where she goes when she leaves."* And just like that, she died peacefully in her husband's loving arms.

Loss and possession, death and life are one,
There falls no shadow where there shines no sun.
– Hilaire Belloc

LOU WHO?

www.ingramcontent.com/pod-product-compliance
Lightning Source LLC
Chambersburg PA
CBHW061622210726

48287CB00001B/244